Rich Men, Single Women

By the same authors

FLING

Rich Men, Single Women

A NOVEL BY

Pamela Beck & Patti Massman

Delacorte Press

Published by
Delacorte Press
The Bantam Doubleday Dell Publishing Group, Inc.
666 Fifth Avenue
New York, New York 10103

Grateful acknowledgment is made for permission to reprint excerpts from *Breaking Free: 20 Ways to Leave Your
Lover* by William Fezler. Copyright © 1965. Reprinted
by permission of Acropolis Books Ltd., Washington,
D.C.

The trademark Delacorte Press® is registered in the U.S.
Patent and Trademark Office.

Library of Congress Cataloging in Publication Data
Beck, Pamela, 1954–
    Rich men, single women.
    I. Massman, Patti. II. Title.
PS3552.E2486R5   1988   813'.54   87-33042
ISBN 0-385-29667-3

Manufactured in the United States of America

August 1988

10 9 8 7 6 5 4 3 2 1

Once again, to the men in our lives who have by being themselves made our lives rich.

Dennis, Brandon, and Dustin Beck
Stephen, Michael, and Brent Massman

Acknowledgments

Ken Ballard, Andrea Bell, Patricia Mendes Caldeira, Alfredo and Shyval Dodds, Cathy Fine, Alex Glant, Elliot Gottfurcht, Lynn Hiller and Bob Hollman for their vivid accounts and insights which enabled us to paint with accuracy and detail the world in which you are about to meet our characters.

. . . And to Susie Nace, who taught us how to read our characters' minds.

To Marjorie Miller whose love, guidance, and inspiration will keep her forever in our hearts.

To our friends at Dell/Delacorte, Carole Baron, Jackie Farber, and Susan Moldow for their great enthusiasm and for the outstanding job we know they will once again perform for us.

To our very special and unique literary agent, Ed Victor, who was *always* available, *always* supportive, and whose understanding and sensitivity to a writer's fragile makeup never failed to keep us going.

To Dennis Beck, our third and silent partner (though not always so silent). We thank you for your editorial advice, your business advice, and for being our general encyclopedia.

And finally another special thank you to all our single friends (although some of you are no longer single) for your frank and valuable input. In fact, you imparted *such* intimate and revealing material in some instances, we've decided to keep your identity confidential. But you know who you are. . . .

Rich Men,
Single Women

Chapter 1 ~

From rags to riches—it was a modern-day Cinderella story. Only, she didn't slave by the hearth, she slaved over legal memorandums in a Century City law firm, and her rags were not really rags, but knockoffs of designer labels. And, finally, her prince was not really a prince, but a very rich client who fell madly in love with his lovely young female lawyer, a feisty brunette from Brooklyn. And the pair was to live happily ever after in Beverly Hills.

Paige Williams was positively green with envy at the fairy-talelike way things had turned out for her oldest and dearest friend, Kit Thorton.

Reveling in unaccustomed luxury, she looked around the all-white cloudlike bedroom, which seemed to be the perfect backdrop for all this elegant flurry, the age-old ritual of readying the bride. Across the hall in the master suite was the bride, being preened for that long-awaited march down the wedding aisle. Poised at its finish line would be the kind of prize prince Paige herself had nearly given up on finding. He was rich, nice-looking, divorced, *but* with no kids, and according to Kit, he was even a nice guy.

Lucky Kit, Paige thought with a keen awareness of the con-

trasts that had developed in their lives over the last decade or so
since Kit had moved with her family out to California. Their
shared childhood in New York felt like a lifetime ago. Paige and
Kit had kept up with one another faithfully over the years,
scratching out addresses and telephone numbers as they moved
through their respective courses: Kit going the route of law
school, then joining a prestigious firm in L.A. near her family;
Paige going the route of Broadway, pursuing a dream she had
never been able to relinquish. It wasn't until recently that she had
actually come to terms with the fact that her desire was bigger
than her talent. She had the calling all right—it was in her blood
—but she didn't have the acting ability to back it up. The truth
was, it had been her dancing that had kept food on her table all
these years—hamburgers instead of steak.

"I could definitely get used to this," Paige remarked wryly,
crossing over to the small antique table that had been laid out
with what the bride had casually referred to as snacks. *Some kind
of snack,* she thought, coating a light, intentionally bland French
cracker with a layer of sour cream, then adding a thick smear of
the pearl-gray beluga caviar they had been consuming in great
quantities all weekend. She took a bite of it, careful not to lose
any crumbs to the woven white carpet beneath her, then sighed,
exulting in the exquisite blend of texture, taste, and privilege. It
summed up the weekend beautifully.

"Why her and not me? That's what I keep asking myself!"
Paige was careful to make it sound like a joke as she addressed
Kit's other two bridesmaids. They were all three lounging around
in the silk robes Kit had given them as gifts for being part of the
wedding party, and Paige wondered if they didn't feel the envy as
acutely as she did. Kit's life looked like it was going to be ambro-
sia from here on in, while they were all struggling in one way or
another.

Tori Mitchell, Kit's long-legged raven-haired cousin from Atlanta, glanced up at Paige from behind a thick issue of *Town &
Country,* looking like she belonged on its glossy cover. "Poor Kit.
She's been as gracious and generous as a person can be, and here
we are all jealous as hell!" she exclaimed in her cute Georgia
drawl.

The truth was, Paige didn't think Tori had a jealous bone in her long willowy body. Tori's uptight and aggressive mother, on the other hand, who had come out for her niece's wedding, appeared to have enough jealousy to go around for a whole town, certainly for Buckhead, the elite suburb of Atlanta where Tori grew up.

Although Tori was putting on a commendable front, Paige and Kit's other bridesmaid, Susan Kendell Brown, both knew it was *only* a front. They had seen Tori's mother issuing digs all weekend. Her niece had achieved the ultimate, in her eyes, and so could her daughter. Typically Tori's mother passed over the fact that Tori was already in love. Not that Travis Walton didn't warrant being passed over. The object of Tori's love was a married man, separated, but in no great hurry to actually get himself a divorce. Paige couldn't imagine why the pretty brunette put up with him. Between her meddling mother and her married boyfriend, it was miraculous Tori managed to maintain her sanity.

"Well, here's to good old healthy green-as-can-be envy," Paige said, draining what was left of her Dom Perignon and then refilling her fluted glass. "And *please* don't ever say 'poor Kit,' " she insisted.

Susan Kendell Brown, who had been the bride's roommate at law school, chuckled without looking up. Susan was curled into a voluptuous sofa by the unlit delft-tiled fireplace, deep into the work she had brought out with her from her home in Stockton, California—or trying to be. Susan was exactly as Kit had described her: serious, but with a good dry sense of humor, hiding behind tortoise-rimmed glasses that were much too big for her face. "With a little work, she's Christie Brinkley undiscovered," Kit had said affectionately of her small-town friend. Kit had only great admiration for Susan, who had somehow managed to rise above her blue-collar farming-community roots to put herself through law school in spite of great opposition from her family. Now Susan's dishwater-blond hair, which could have done with some lightening, was pulled tight into a terry turban, making her tortoise-framed glasses stand out even more than they ordinarily did. But Kit was right, the potential for being a knockout was definitely there. Paige was eager to see what Susan would look like after being worked on by the "hot" Hollywood hairstylist and makeup team Kit had hired to beautify all of them for the ceremony.

"Would you sit down and relax? You're a nervous wreck," Susan said suddenly, peeling off her glasses as though in response to Paige's thoughts. "You'd think it was *you* getting married."

"Ah, but don't I wish!" Paige said honestly, wandering over to the large French windows that were like picture frames for the enchanting garden view. *Don't we all wish,* she was tempted to add but didn't. It was impossible not to be affected by all the stir and anticipation that was going on throughout every inch of the groom's sprawling eleven-thousand-square-foot Bel Air estate, and Paige gazed out over the expansive grounds below, taking in the bustle of activity where countless crews appeared to be working painstakingly on every last detail. There were caterers, rental crews, flower designers, and even video technicians, angling about, getting it all on tape for posterity.

The setting was so wondrous, with all the dazzling white freesias, the hibiscus, and the oleander. She could almost smell their rich perfume as she stared out, entranced, already envisioning the processional that was to take place on the elegant lower terrace. A white bridge constructed from scaffolding across the pool added a nice dramatic touch. There were plump white water lilies floating on either side of it.

What a production, Paige thought, watching the dozen or so florists who were still hard at work weaving thousands of orchids into an ivy-covered wall. She felt as though she were observing the building of an elaborate outdoor stage set. And, in a sense, she was. Given the staggering budget Kit had described, Paige probably could have come close to launching a Broadway show. She could have even bought herself a decent part in one. But then another thought occurred to her, which came more as a revelation. Given her choice between starring, so to speak, in this "wedding production," which offered only one grand appearance but then a wonderfully rich and easy life afterward, versus a lead role in a musical, something she had been dreaming about for nearly all her life, it struck Paige she would opt for the bride bit. What Kit was about to have—security on a grand scale and a man to share it all with—suddenly seemed like the greater coup. The longevity implied in that dream and the easy existence were tempting.

Paige's dream had lost its luster.

Susan put down her glasses, ready to call it quits. It was impossible to concentrate with Paige roaming back and forth and Tori nervously turning the pages of her magazine. They were all just passing time, closed off from the bustle of the rest of the house, waiting to be transformed into the kind of glamorous bridesmaids that would befit such a wedding. Hairstylists, makeup artists—this was all such a far cry from any wedding to which she had ever been. It was certainly light-years away from her own simple church wedding in Stockton. God, had she ever really been married? Susan felt a wave of sadness and a stab of regret as she looked back. At the time it had seemed like the most perfect union ever conceived. They were high school sweethearts, both voted the most likely to succeed, both voted the one with whom you'd most like to be stuck on a desert island. They thought they would have the most incredible kids. She remembered her mother that day. What a nervous Nellie. She had done all the cooking herself. Her father, naturally, had gotten rip-roaring drunk. He kept saying it was the happiest day of his life. And he kept crying. Susan's mother had been beside herself with happiness, embracing Susan with thick arms that wobbled like jelly beneath the print voile of the dress she had made for the occasion.

Maybe if she hadn't been accepted into law school a few years later her marriage might have stood a chance.

Now Susan looked down at the tiresome contracts in front of her. Why did she ever promise her boss that she would review these documents when she should have known that Kit would have them busy every waking hour of the day throughout the three-day stretch of prenuptial parties and activities? Their shared suite at the Beverly Hills Hotel, where they were being put up as guests of the bride and groom, had been like Grand Central Station. This had been Susan's first opportunity to even open her briefcase, and she couldn't have been less in the mood.

Not that she was complaining. These had been the best three days she'd had in ages.

So much for good intentions, she concluded, packing up the blue-backed legal briefs and calling it a day. It was just as well, because as she clicked her case closed the doorbell rang, and Susan presumed that this time the arriving staff was for them.

"Beauty crew," Paige confirmed after crossing over to the large bay window that looked out over the circular stone-paved entrance. Susan joined her there just in time to see an attendant speeding away with another Mercedes. It was a 560 SEC that had BLOW DRY on its personalized license plates.

"God, the cars!" Paige said, echoing Susan's thoughts exactly as they looked out over the lineup of flashy cars that had already formed. If all of the workers were arriving in Mercedeses, Ferraris, Porsches, Jaguars, and Rolls-Royces, what would the guests be showing up in? Susan wondered.

Tori tossed aside her magazine and joined them over at the window. "Obviously the caterer's Rolls," she commented, pointing toward a big black Rolls-Royce with EATS on *its* personalized license plates.

Paige had a funny little smile on her face as she moved across the room, back to where the caviar was laid out. "Probably bought it off the deposit from Kit's wedding," she quipped demurely.

"Come in," Susan called out in response to the knock at the door. She moved curiously out of the way, appraising the hip-looking group as they moved boisterously into the bedroom, carrying weighty-looking duffel bags and a big boxlike black case. There was one hairdresser, one makeup artist, and one assistant. The three of them decided to set up shop in the large adjoining bathroom, which was mirrored almost entirely and had great sunlight flooding into it through a domed skylight. The hairdresser's assistant arranged a series of three chairs, then directed each of the women to a particular seat, while the makeup artist heaved her cumbersome case up onto the white marble countertop and then opened it. The jammed case looked complete enough to fill an entire makeup counter in a department store.

Later, seated in front of the mirrored wardrobe in her bra and underwear, her hair and makeup done, stretching on panty hose, Susan sat marveling at her reflection. The makeup artist had succeeded in giving a dazzling, almost unfamiliar quality to her large wide-set eyes. She had even been talked into having her eyelashes dyed, and they fluttered now, dark and full, fringing her eyes and making them stand out like a couple of jewels. She felt almost giddy with the triumph of it all. Her pale skin glowed, and her ordinarily mousy hair gleamed with luster. No wonder all the women in this city seemed so superior-looking. They were being attended to by professionals who, for a steep fee and a large block of time, transformed ordinary looks into magazine-quality extraordinary looks. Susan cringed at the thought of having to do this routinely. She felt great *now,* but what a drain, both in terms of energy and cash. She imagined breezing into her staid Stockton law firm this way and grinned at the astonished reactions she would receive.

The reaction she was really toying with had to do with one man in particular. She wanted to knock the socks off Billy Donahue—William J. Donahue III, now a senior partner in his family's firm, where Susan also worked. He was reasonably bright and *unreasonably* good-looking. For the last couple of years he had been Susan's boyfriend. It was one of those on-again off-again relationships that was based more on convenience for both of them than on love. Susan had been crazy about Billy when they first met. He was charming, fun to be with, and unattached. *Unattached* being the operative word in a small town like Stockton, where most of the available men were ex-husbands of girls with whom she had gone to school. Billy's biggest problem was that he was an incurable player. Actually it wasn't Billy's problem at all. It was Susan's.

What am I doing with my life? she wondered, staring soberly at her now-glamorous reflection. There was no trace there of the anxiety she was beginning to feel. It was not just the rut she was in with Billy. That was symptomatic of everything else. But eventually Susan had to think about direction, to redefine her own. She had met her professional goals, but now where was she headed, besides straight into a brick wall? What about the rest? What about the part of her life that was hanging in the balance—

the part she had abandoned all those years ago and now needed badly in order to feel whole? She wanted it all. The career, a husband, children. Not necessarily on the kind of grand scale Kit was doing it. But that same package nevertheless. Her fingers felt icy against her skin as she touched the seed-pearl choker at her throat, which Billy had bought for her last Christmas. It had been part present, part peace offering after she had found out he was sleeping with her secretary. Her life was indeed a mess, she thought, blinking back tears, trying to hold on to her sense of humor.

"I didn't look this good at my own wedding," she remarked to Paige and Tori, who were also getting dressed.

"Maybe that's why your marriage didn't last." Paige's bright green eyes flashed as she flipped a silky cascade of russet-colored hair off her face and back over her shoulder. It was a fluid movement, as were all her movements. Paige was a professional dancer working now in the big Broadway musical *Cats.* Kit had said that she was an incredible dancer, and Susan imagined that she was. She had that kind of ease with her body, a smooth sensual awareness of her curvy shape, which was poured now into the sexiest-looking lace undergarment Susan had ever seen. Her body language was as sassy as her wit.

"Now, that's hitting below the belt," Susan responded, laughing, thinking about how much she liked Paige Williams, when she had been so certain that she would not. Paige, Susan, and Tori had been hearing about one another for years, but they had never actually met until this weekend, which had been like one long slumber party with the three of them becoming fast friends. As Susan had anticipated, Paige was kind of off-the-wall, dramatic, a bit of a sex kitten, but she was not in the least bit insubstantial. There was a raw gutsiness about her that Susan admired, the way she took charge, the way she said what was on her mind. There was also a winsome exuberance that made her impossible not to like.

"Tori, you look sensational," Paige exclaimed, stretching a lacy white garter belt up over her hips, then going over to help Tori with a button she was having trouble reaching on her dress. Susan turned curiously to regard the long-legged brunette who was now, with Paige's assistance, the first one ready. Her short dark hair was styled sleek and very European, accenting her almost oriental eyes, which were slate-colored and seemed to smile mysteriously up at the corners. Stepping into cornflower-blue pumps that matched the background of her dress, Tori whirled around for her friends' inspection. The bare-shouldered pastel chiffon floated up above her knees as she spun in a smooth circle, looking more like a southern society belle than the fast-climbing real estate executive she was.

Always the bridesmaid and never the bride. Damn you, Mother, for joking about it, if, in fact, it was only a joke. And damn you, Travis Walton, for making it so hopelessly true. Tori Mitchell stood out of sight of the large chattering crowd, close behind Paige and Susan under the umbrella of a lush pink cherry blossom tree, waiting in silence for the wedding coordinator to give them their cue. The orchestra had already begun playing warmup music, and Tori took a deep breath, struggling to lose herself in the restful baroque sound as it rose serenely into the summer air.

She was fighting for composure, trying to strike Travis from her thoughts, trying to quell the resentment.

Lately weddings were having this effect on her. All of her friends seemed to be getting married, and a good many of them were onto their second kids. Tori felt as though she were watching a drawbridge making its gradual ascent. If she didn't make it in time, she would fail to make the crossing altogether. With all of her heart, she wanted to make it with Travis, but there was that alarming sense of time moving too swiftly past her.

"You're throwing good money after bad," was her mother's stock phrase when issuing unsolicited advice on her daughter's relationship. There was that, along with a battery of other comments, none of them ever terribly original, but all of them hardhitting.

Tori felt her eyes burning and she swallowed deeply. She had tried so hard over the weekend to be cheerful, but it was impossible to get him off of her mind. The constant disappointments were getting out of hand—his broken promises, his bullshit. He had said he would fly out from Atlanta with her for the wedding. He had said a lot of things. And she knew after living with him all these years that she was an idiot to believe him.

Travis Walton wasn't even divorced. She had fallen for a *salesman*. When Tori first met Travis, she was just twenty-two, fresh out of college, applying for a job at one of Atlanta's prominent single-family tract home developers. Travis, with his devastating good looks and his beguiling charm, was already the superstar salesman there, upholding a record that in the fifteen years since he had been at the company hadn't been beat. He had started in on Tori right away, and of course she fell for his line. He was a pro. At the time Travis had been in the process of filing for a divorce. And now, seven precious years later, aware that he had come no closer to concluding that process, Tori felt duped. Her own rocketing rise within the corporation to her now prestigious position as director of marketing didn't compensate for the frustration in her personal life. Certainly that kind of success was exciting, even heady at times. But it wasn't enough. Travis's friends had known all along. He wasn't ever *really* going to get a divorce. Supporting his estranged wife and sharing his income with her were worthwhile insurance against *having to marry again*. Those were the casual warnings she had heard over the years and then discarded, believing misguidedly that *she* could succeed with Travis where her predecessors had failed. So far it looked like there were no rewards for hanging in there. Just a trail of wasted time, she thought, feeling her eyes beginning to burn again and that familiar fullness at the back of her throat. Determined not to cry, she took a deep breath and held it. In a few short moments a thousand eyes would be upon her. And she had that fifty-dollar makeup job to preserve, as well as appearances.

Oh, yes, appearances. Tori knew she was accomplished at that. Her mother had instilled in her dozens of little tricks to make the rest of the world think that everything was great—everything was grand. She had learned to stand tall, keep her head held high, and her chin and nose tilted up toward God. Well, even if only temporarily, Tori could at least draw strength from that posture. And she did so now as an au courant arrangement of

Romeo and Juliet sprang ceremoniously from the orchestra. As the wedding procession stepped into motion Tori noticed a tightening not only in her own shoulders but in Paige's and Susan's as well. What potential groom were they each thinking of? she wondered. What doomed romance or wishful fantasy was being disturbed now by the rush of music and the stern-looking woman in the prim Saint John knit suit who was signaling to them all to begin? Billy Donahue from Stockton for Susan? Someone new from Beverly Hills for Paige? Tori was surprised to see the tears in their eyes when they both turned to share a last look with her before moving forward and into view. She was even more surprised to find herself reaching out and squeezing both their hands. It was an intense moment for all of them, and her pulse skipped a beat when it was her turn to grace the aisle.

Airy exclamations seemed to mingle with the traditional music as she moved solemnly through the garden ceremony. Her cheeks were aching from the pull of a frozen smile as she continued across the festooned bridge, down the regal white runner, across the expanse of bright green grass, and then over to the designated bridal area, which was set up beneath the vast spread of a Japanese elm.

A pause in the music then summoned everyone's rapt attention, and the guests stood in honor of the bride. Kit was breathtaking, and Tori tried to hold back her tears as she watched her cousin, who looked like a dream as she glided down the aisle, dressed in a cloud of white tulle. More than anything else in the world, Tori wanted Travis to be there with her as he had promised he would, to feel the beauty of the moment and to be seduced by it. Then she cursed herself for banking such high hopes on him.

Feeling a pair of familiar eyes upon her, Tori looked out into the sea of smiling, misty-eyed faces and locked gazes with her mother. *What a wedding. What a catch. Leave it to Kit to do things in such elevated style.* That's what her cool, aristocratic-looking mother was thinking. She was absolutely undone that this was happening to her niece and not to her daughter.

*   *   *

I'm in my element, Paige thought, dancing with abandon to the orchestra's lively rendition of the Pet Shop Boys' new hit song, enjoying the loud pulsating music, the glorious moonlight, and all the admiring glances being cast her way.

There was one man in particular with whom Paige had been playing eye contact games all evening, beguiling glances exchanged in an amusing flirtation. He wasn't especially good-looking, but there was something about him that had piqued Paige's interest. Probably that he looked rich and slightly arrogant, she thought, keeping a watchful eye on him as her dance partner spun her around the crowded floor. That type always appealed to her, the way success did. He was smoking a fat cigar, puffing at it with noble relish.

Paige had already decided that he wasn't going to move from his spot. He was obviously accustomed to people coming to him, and it was going to be up to her to initiate an introduction. But how? She mulled over that enigma as she continued to dance, focusing on her fantasy and spinning it into great romantic proportions. She was feeling gay and brazen, infused with a romantic high that was better than champagne—better than any kind of drug she could imagine. After a smooth though dated disco dip, Paige smiled boldly and was rewarded when he smiled back. With a kind of ridiculous rising excitement she found herself envisioning all kinds of things: flashes of intimate conversation, a fast attraction, moving out to L.A. at his insistence.

Marrying one of Kit's millionaire friends and moving out to sunny California had an enticing ring to it. The city seemed to be teeming with rich, available, good-looking men. With or without her mystery man, the idea definitely merited some thought. When the song wound down to its end, Paige decided she would maneuver her way across the dance floor and inspire a conversation.

But it was suddenly too late. Her unknown prosperous prospect had vanished. Feeling deserted, Paige declined another dance offer, then swooped a canapé off the hors d'oeuvre tray of a passing waiter.

The spread was almost too lavish for words, and Paige wandered around, catching snatches of conversation. Set up all along the periphery of the garden were wondrous-looking food stations, manned by chefs in crisp white jackets and tall hats, shucking oysters, fishing live lobsters out of tanks and preparing them to order, basting exotic meats like reindeer and boar over mesquite grills, carving filet mignon, and serving the inevitable caviar from a caviar bar.

Carrying a plate jammed with delicacies, Paige threaded her way through the mass of expensively dressed guests, back toward her table, where she was glad to find both Tori and Susan. They were laughing and enjoying themselves with a friend of the groom's, a debonair adventurer type named Dustin Brent, who hadn't taken his eyes off Tori the entire weekend. Too bad he was leaving the country for a year to go climb mountains.

"You looked like you were having fun out there," Tori commented, her slate-colored eyes full of appraisal as Paige slid into the seat beside her.

"I was . . ." Paige lifted up a heavenly-looking salmon-covered toast point, then, biting delicately into it, turned to peer through the crowd again. Through the thick throng of people her mystery man was still nowhere to be found. "But my well-designed fantasy just went up in smoke." She sighed, brushing a crumb away from the corner of her mouth and smiling ironically. "Smuggled Cuban cigar smoke, I believe."

Tori and Susan exchanged an amused look with the lanky Dustin Brent. Paige liked the sparkle in his warm brown eyes, the deep lines there that suggested outdoor vigor. "Oh, I do this kind of thing all the time," she confessed to the three of them, raising her wineglass and sipping from it as she went on to explain. "There was this man watching me when I was out there dancing. Not gorgeous, but my type. De Niro, fattened up a bit—" She laughed when Susan made a face. "Anyway, I was fantasizing that he would sweep me off my feet, proclaim mad passionate love at first sight, and produce a *large,* impromptu engagement ring to prove it."

Paige raised her eyebrows in mock emphasis. "I'm great at these kinds of scenarios," she joked as Tori and Susan both broke up laughing. "I'd imagined him insisting that I marry him right away—"

"Wait—I'll go round up the minister before he leaves!" Tori exclaimed in her melodic southern drawl, succumbing to a chocolate she'd had her eye on.

"And don't bother going home to pack," Paige added dramatically, still playing the part of De Niro as Prince Charming. "We'll go out and buy you a whole new wardrobe."

Everyone laughed, except Paige, who drained her glass and turned back toward the dance floor again, feeling her mood beginning to slip. She was thinking about going home, and the thought of having to return to reality had her feeling sobered. She was getting tired of the rat race of New York. Tired of being one of the millions of "pretty but approaching thirty" actress/dancers hoping in a faded way to one day land that choice role in a smash Broadway play. All those high hopes and plunging disappointments, both professional *and* romantic. What was so *great* about a career anyway? she wondered harshly, uneasy about the chunk of years she had invested in her own. Careers, sure, they all had them: Tori, who was head of marketing for one of Atlanta's largest tract home developers, with enough responsibility to give her an ulcer, which it had; and Susan, a labor lawyer, stuck in Stockton, of all places, working arduous hours representing a bunch of farmers. Impressive at first glance, Paige thought ruefully, real estate executive, lawyer, Broadway dancer. They were three thoroughly modern, single, entirely self-sufficient women. But the fact was, all of them had come out to L.A. *alone.*

Paige turned to aim a careful look at Tori and Susan. "I think the three of us should move out here," she said, beginning to feel that rush of adrenaline again. *Why not?* That's what kept running through her mind as she thought about her moneyed surroundings. There was a richness here, an attainable privilege that the people reflected in their smooth bronze complexions and their easy smiles. Everybody she had met here seemed so incredibly friendly, so incredibly affluent. Life appeared easy, clean, blessed with happy weather. It was a perfect place to begin anew, and it was definitely time for change. It was time for good old-fashioned marriage and family with someone like Kit's George, she decided, looking around and just imagining what it would be like to have all this day in and day out. So, George wasn't gorgeous to look at. And he wasn't the funniest guy she had ever met. A large net worth could make up for a multitude of shortcomings, could even cover the cost of fixing a few of them. A child of the sixties who marched for peace, wore Salvation Army blue jeans, and put down anything that even smacked of convention or especially materialism? Hell, yes. Paige was ready for a little convention in her life at this point, a little materialistic indulgence. So, if she couldn't find Mr. Right, she could at least find Mr. Rich. And what better place to find him than in Beverly Hills, where a glimpse into that *net worth* appeared to be on vivid display, with magnificent mansions and rolling lawns, lighted tennis courts, and a Rolls adorning the driveway. The city seemed filled with Georges, and if Kit could find one, so could they.

"Move to L.A.," Tori demurred with a little nervous laugh. "It would sure shock Travis," she said. *Maybe that's what I need to get him to get his damn divorce already . . .*

"The best thing that could ever happen to your relationship with Travis would be for you to move and let him know that he can't get away with not getting a divorce," Paige emphasized, noticing Dustin Brent's surprise and curious interest as he regarded the demure brunette.

"Your boyfriend is married?" he asked.

"Separated," Tori explained, fiddling with her napkin. "Yesterday and today and forever."

Dustin let his eyes linger on Tori for an extra beat before turning to Paige. "What about you?" he asked her. "Is there a boyfriend we'd have to worry about back in New York?"

"Several," Paige lied cheerfully, watching him as he laughed and pulled a cigar from out of his tux pocket, then pointed it at Susan. "And how about you?"

"One. But he's ripe for replacement," she acknowledged.

"I have an interesting proposition for the three of you," he said, flicking his gold Cartier lighter ablaze and drawing thoughtfully on his cigar. "You could all stay at my place and look after the house for me while I'm away. You'd have *your* adventure while I was out having *mine*," he offered lightheartedly.

All weekend long everyone had been talking about the mountain climbing expedition Dustin Brent was going on. It had been his fantasy for years to climb the highest mountain in each of the seven continents, Mount Everest being the tallest and most difficult, and this year he was going to do it. He and a friend had hired an English colonel who was an expert climber to organize the ambitious expedition, which was to consist of a team of six experienced climbers and twice as many sherpas to carry their supplies and set up camps. They had estimated the timeframe at one year and the cost for Dustin at one million, since he was subsidizing the effort.

"That's the best offer I've had in ages." Susan's blue eyes sparkled as she laughed and leaned back in her chair.

"We accept!" Paige warned him, serious if he was serious.

"I'm completely serious," he replied, stretching out his long lean legs and crossing them casually at the ankles. "Honestly, ask Kit and George. I've been known to do crazier things. Besides, I've gotten to know you all pretty well this weekend—I'm sure my house will still be there when I get back. If not, it's insured," he joked.

Paige could barely contain herself as he went on. What an opportunity. What a perfect opportunity for all three of them. She felt flushed with anticipation and yet strangely anxious, as though this could be the solution to all that was wrong in her life. Fate was finally bailing her out. It was her turn.

"Listen, six months to a year is a long time to rely on hired help," he pointed out. "You girls could make sure the maid didn't quit or throw too many wild parties. Not only do I have the maid to worry about, but there's the gardeners, the poolman, pest control, the burglar alarm going off, the smoke alarm. . . . I think it's an inspired idea to have you house-sit for me."

"Hey, slow down a minute. I can't really move out here—" Tori looked like someone who had been strapped into a roller coaster seat and wanted to get out, quick, before it was too late.

"Why not?" Paige insisted.

"I haven't had *that* much to drink." Tori's cheeks flushed an attractive shade of pink. She looked over at Dustin, who was smiling challengingly back at her. "Paige is crazy. Tell her we're only joking around."

"*I'm* not joking. You're welcome to stay at my house." Dustin reached into his pants pocket and pulled out a set of European-looking car keys. "You're even welcome to my toys. They're also insured. There's a black Aston-Martin Lagonda, a Bronco . . ."

"Are you always this generous?" Tori asked him, intrigued.

"Why not?" he replied, raking back his wavy brown hair without affectation. "You only go around once."

Paige was liking him more and more. "Tori, I think we should at least consider it," she said. "What have you really got to lose?"

Not about to be seduced, Tori slid Dustin's keys back across the table. "A couple of little things. Like, I'm living with somebody, I have a job," she said.

The order in which Tori had declared her priorities did not escape Paige, and she hesitated, measuring her next words. She herself had lived with so many different men over the course of years that the live-in relationship no longer carried with it all the weight it once had. "There're live-ins in L.A.," she said softly. "Jobs—"

"I like my live-in. I like my job."

"Just for six months," Paige suggested, watching the temptation in Tori's eyes. "Take a hiatus from both. C'mon, Tori, go for it. Who knows, maybe you'll get a ring and a raise, both, out of the whole proposition."

Tori wished it were as simple as Paige was making it sound. Even with all the grief she got from Travis, he did serve a purpose. *Aside* from her being impossibly in love with him.

He gave her the illusion of being married, being part of a coupled society. Kids were the only missing link, and security, if she allowed herself to think about it. What she might have had to gain by leaving him was always tempered by the thought of first having to face being alone. And so her threats were never carried out. To Tori the singles scene was a nightmare, full of hollow relationships, games and canned conversations, questions and answers played by rote, and always the unsettling prospect of disappointment and rejection. At least the disappointment and rejection she experienced with Travis were familiar. Her threshold there was established. And she could anticipate the blows.

"What would you do here, Paige?" Susan, who had been sitting quietly, sat forward, her interest piqued. "Try and get into some film work?" She watched Paige deliberate, stabbing at a chunk of lobster with an ornate silver fork.

"Maybe film. Or maybe something else entirely."

"What about the show you're in?" Susan asked, full of admiration for Paige, tempted in her pleasantly inebriated state to throw caution to the winds and join her. The idea was undeniably appealing, especially for someone like Paige, who had the nerve to do it.

"What's one more show?" Paige shrugged thoughtfully. "It's not doing that much to advance my career anyway."

God, could they really just up and move? Susan wondered, feeling a nice warm sense of light-headedness from the idea. The thought of moving to a big city had always unnerved her before. She wasn't good in crowds. She felt claustrophobic without the wide-open spaces in which she had grown up. And city people were always so intimidating to her.

"Think about how much fun we'd have as roommates," Paige was saying.

Roommates. The last female roommate Susan had had was Kit, when they'd shared an apartment together at law school. Now that all seemed like a lifetime ago. Bitter memories of her divorce and the friction with her family were mixed up together with some of her best memories ever. What a good friend Kit had been throughout it all, unquestionably more fun and less demanding than any man she had ever lived with.

"It's really tempting," Susan said, unable to believe she was actually considering it. "I've never been impetuous, not even once in my entire life. I'm not sure I have it in me."

"What would your family say?" Tori asked her curiously.

Susan winced, wary not of what they would say so much, because they wouldn't say much, but instead of what they would think. "They couldn't relate to it," she said, toying uneasily with the edge of the delicate lace tablecloth, reminded of the rare Italian lace she had wanted for her wedding gown but hadn't been able to afford. The irony struck her as she looked out into the sea of lace-covered tables, acutely conscious of her opulent surroundings, the glitz and sophistication.

Would she change? That would be her parents' primary concern. They were always threatened by the prospect of her changing, as though moving up in educational or income strata meant leaving them behind. Over the years they had interpreted her apparent need to be different from them as an affront.

"What about Billy?" Tori asked, hitting a different nerve.

Billy. The shock value alone made it hard to resist. Susan looked over at Paige and grinned, trying to affect her new friend's stagy manner of speech. "Not doing that much to advance my career anyway," she mimicked meaningfully and was rewarded when they all broke up laughing.

Dustin, who was puffing leisurely on his cigar, regarded her seriously. "Kit could probably get you something over at her firm, now that she's married to one of their biggest clients."

"Oh, right," Susan said, laughing. *"Just like that."*

Dustin snapped his fingers and grinned. "Hey, that's how it works."

"God, L.A., of all places." Susan couldn't help but reflect on how she and her friends had always made such fun of L.A.—looked down her nose at it. All that glitter and sparkle. All of the phonies and the fancy cars. San Francisco was what northern Californians called a *real* city. It was *substantial,* unlike L.A. It was where they went for a fix of culture or good food. L.A. was a joke. Or had it all been envy and curiosity? Susan began to wonder, her blue eyes focused meditatively on the graceful white lilies at the center of the table. Wasn't there, in fact, something deeply seductive about all that fast living and what they perceived to be high-voltage glamour? Certainly she was feeling it now as she sat there too tense to speak.

"Wait a minute. Someone's got to bring some levity into this," Tori started to say. She was sitting at an awkward angle with one arm draped over the back of her chair, looking as if she thought they were all nuts.

"Why?" Susan asked, suddenly convinced. "It really is the best offer I've had in ages. Maybe I'm crazy, but moving out here is beginning to sound like a very practical idea—"

"You're going to just up and move? Quit your jobs?" Tori looked over at Dustin, who was watching them all intently. He shrugged as though to say "Don't look at me," clearly enjoying their debate. Tori, beside herself with frustration, turned back to Susan. "How can you do that with a law practice?"

"I'll give them sufficient notice." It seemed easy enough to Susan. "The truth is, there's nothing holding me in Stockton. If anything, it's a lousy place for a single woman my age. Career-wise, I'd unquestionably be better off in a big city."

Tori was at a loss to refute that.

"If you want my vote," Dustin said, stubbing out his cigar and then regarding Tori. "I think it sounds like a lot of fun. You all seem to be in fairly static situations anyway. You're young. You're beautiful. Paige is absolutely right. So you'd find your-selves new jobs here. There're plenty of opportunities. And as far as men go, you'd be the 'new girls in town.' I could think of half a dozen nice-looking, fun, wealthy guys who would be eager to go out with you."

"Honestly, Dustin, you'd really let us stay at your place?" Paige asked seriously, as though needing to make sure this wasn't all breezy cocktail conversation, wanting to tie the offer down.

"It's all yours if you want it. Six months. Maybe a year. We're talking seven continents," Dustin replied, turning to Tori with a kind of raw smile. "Well, are you in or are you out, Georgia Peach?"

"I need to sleep on it." Tori hesitated, turning warm and then hot under his gaze.

"Oh, be a sport and just say yes!" Paige had impulsively taken Tori's hand. She thought Tori looked like she was back on the roller coaster again, but this time beginning to feel the thrill.

And she was.

He's only using you, came a replay of one of her mother's many low-blow remarks. God knows, she had heard enough of them in the last week. *You think he's actually going to marry you? Why should he? He's got the best of both worlds. You clean the apart-ment for him. You cook his meals. You entertain his friends. You sleep with him. And you even split the bills. You're a wife-maid combined, Tori, dear, without the perks.*

Without the perks is right, Tori thought, her decision suddenly made. Paige was one hundred percent right. To hell with Travis.

To hell with her parents. Why not move out to California and show them all? If she stayed in Atlanta, her life would remain exactly as it was. If she had the guts to pick up and move, she would at least be expanding her options. Her fantasy was that Travis would be so upset at her leaving that he would break down and ask her to marry him. But if he failed to do that, then odds were, after all this time, he never would. Her fantasy would have been just that.

Feeling her first burst of courage, Tori hailed a waiter who was passing by, then, grinning her apologies, snatched a full bottle of champagne from his elegant silver tray. "I want to propose a toast," she said, looking straight at Dustin Brent and feeling encouraged by his apparent amusement at her sudden bravado as she poured out a full round. "To our generous host," she went on, lifting her glass and enjoying the astonishment on all three of their faces. "When do we book our flights out?"

"Tori, you're my kind of woman!" Paige let out a little hoot of victory, accepting the glass of champagne Tori was holding out to her and raising it up in her honor. "You've got more guts than you know about yet, Georgia Peach. To men, money, and sunshine," she saluted with her usual verve, picking up the ball from Tori's toast and moving on to pitch it as some kind of allegiance, continuing to wage her campaign for L.A.

Fact: Kit's life looked great.

Fact: Their lives looked lousy.

Why not move to Beverly Hills to meet and marry rich men as Kit had done? The city seemed suddenly full of promise. The three of them would band together in search of a common goal—to extricate themselves from their lousy situations in their respective cities and to move to Beverly Hills to begin fresh. The town had been lucky for Kit; maybe it would be lucky for them.

Dustin sort of shrank down into his seat as he watched them. "It's a good thing I'm getting out of the country," he joked, "or my precious bachelorhood would be in serious jeopardy. I can see that . . ."

Paige laughed and trailed her finger flirtatiously down the row of black onyx studs fastening his tuxedo shirt. "You're not out of the woods yet, love. If one of us is still 'uncoupled' by the time you get back"—she grinned as she reached his waistband—"you could find yourself on dangerous ground."

Paige let her finger tarry there for a moment longer before she removed it and placed it in between her full sultry lips.

Susan couldn't believe her gall and she wondered what on earth Dustin thought of them.

Smiling broadly, he proposed the next toast, wishing all three of them great success and starting off another round of glass-touching.

With their hopes sealed, Susan found herself filled with a kind of weird anticipation about their futures.

Certainly this balmy California evening was going to be a night upon which they would always look back. But how? Hopefully with gratitude and not regret. It was the eve of opportunities about to bloom as they agreed to uproot themselves from their old, neglected soils to chance their futures in a new, undetermined place.

Rich men—single women, Susan thought loosely, just as the orchestra announced that the bride and groom were about to cut the cake, inviting all the guests to join them there on the upper terrace.

She, Tori, and Paige rose up from their seats, looking significantly at one another, incredulous at what they were about to do as Dustin Brent escorted them away from the table.

Chapter 2

Susan had suspected that their glittery plans made on the crest of an evening high, with champagne coloring their senses, would have dissolved in the sobriety of the next day, headaches replacing wild expectations. But they had not.

Now, the night before she was to leave for Los Angeles, Susan stood quietly apart from the small group that had gathered in her honor, sipping the Harvey Wallbanger her father had made, watching them. Her father, Jake Kendell, a heavyset man in his early sixties, was famous in his small, close-knit circle in Stockton for his tangy "sure-to-knock-you-on-your-ass" Harvey Wallbangers. If he even remembered this little farewell dinner he was having for his daughter, Susan thought, it would be a miracle. His beefy face was already animated from inebriation. And the evening had only just begun. He was acting as though he had just won a ten-thousand-dollar lottery. He was behaving like an ass.

"C'mere, you little defector. This shindig's for you," he slurred, motioning her over with a fat arm. Jake was what Susan would ordinarily call a functioning alcoholic, but tonight he was sloppy and crude. It was Sunday, and he had begun pouring alcohol into himself early in the morning, attempting to anesthetize himself against emotion, and failing. Ever since Susan had

told her parents about her plan to move to Los Angeles, her
father had hardly uttered three words to her.

"Leave her alone, Jake." It was her mother rising quietly to
her defense, her words barely audible, but generally carrying
some impact. Betsy Kendell's only moments of courage with her
domineering husband surfaced at times like these, when she felt
she had to intervene on Susan's behalf. Susan threw her a look of
gratitude. She was going to miss her a lot.

"Ahhh, you still make the *best*, Betsy." Susan turned to see her
old friend Lisa Davis dipping a Dorito chip into a plastic container heaped with guacamole. Her mother smiled, pleased with
the compliment. They were all gathered out on the Astroturfed
patio of the Kendells' mobile home, seated on woven plastic strip
garden chairs, shielded from the still-hot sun by a white metal
awning. Neighbors were engaged in similar Sunday night entertainment, and the smell of meat barbecuing permeated the air.
Three years ago Susan's parents had decided to move out of the
house she had grown up in and into the mobile home park that
had become a retirement mecca for many of their friends. Jake
hadn't retired yet, but there was talk that he was going to be
forced into it sooner than he cared to think. He was one of the
oldest cargo supervisors down at Stockton's bustling port, where
he had worked for years at a large grain facility.

"Just look at those two. You're still like a couple of newlyweds," Betsy Kendell said as Lisa fed her husband a chip she had
prepared for him, sealing her gesture with a kiss. "How long has
it been? Thirteen years?" Betsy knew exactly how long it had
been, and she caught the chain of uneasy glances that her comment had inadvertently sparked. It was an innocent attempt at
just making conversation, and Susan could tell by the look in her
mother's eyes that she wished she'd said nothing.

The two childhood friends had gotten married only weeks
apart from one another. They had been like sisters all through
school, and both thought it was too good to be true when they
dated and married best friends. They were right. It was.

When Susan decided to go to law school, everything changed.
Ten years ago' women born into blue-collar families, raised in
farming communities like Stockton, simply didn't do that. Espe-

cially when they were *lucky* enough to marry a man with potential, as Susan had. Skip was on the dean's list at the University of the Pacific. He was bright and had ambition.

Collectively Skip, Susan's parents, her in-laws, even Lisa and Buzz, tried to make her feel guilty. What was the urgency about going to law school? Skip didn't intend to need her income. So what was she trying to prove? College was one thing. He wanted a wife who was smart and interesting. But he wanted a *wife,* the definition of which brought them into constant debate, since it appeared to preclude anything she wanted for herself. She remembered all those bitter arguments they used to have and how close she had come to giving in. She wasn't the aggressive women's-libber they accused her of being. And it was a nightmare being at odds with the only people in the world who meant anything to her. Nobody understood that all she really wanted was some control, some choice. The thought of handing over the reins of her future to someone else the way her mother had done with her father was simply inconceivable to Susan. And besides, she really wanted to practice law.

Looking back, Susan knew it had been tough on Skip. He had been subjected to endless remarks about how he had better be careful or she would be making more money than he. There were the inevitable "house-husband" jokes that they had both been too insecure to ignore. When she applied for a scholarship to law school and got it, it was as though his competitive instincts had been challenged and their relationship with it. She was no longer his partner but his opponent, in a game nobody would win.

Her first year at University of the Pacific Law School was a disaster. Skip and his cousin were starting a small rice export business, and she was busy studying. He resented that she wasn't there for him, fulfilling his image of what a wife should be. It didn't take him long to find someone who did. She was a friend of Lisa's younger sister's, and oddly enough, Susan came out of all the unseemly mess as the culprit. If she had been home, fulfilling her wifely obligations, minding the store, so to speak, none of it would have happened. So, midsemester, quiet, reserved, not given to confrontations, Susan made the difficult decision of transferring from University of the Pacific to Hastings Law School in

San Francisco, away from her husband. It was the most daring thing she had ever done, up until now—a choice she still questioned every now and then.

She and Skip were divorced within six months of her leaving him. He remarried only three months after that, and she always wondered if he ever looked back, as she did, and what he thought. Probably she would never know. Those times when they did run into one another he was careful and distant.

Susan moved in to join the rest of the group. She sat down on the one unoccupied chair and leaned forward to dip a celery stick into the guacamole. "Cuts down on the calories," she kidded lightly, looking fondly at her mother, who had a chip loaded with dip in each hand.

Lisa, who was always rail thin and ate like a horse, stuck her tongue out at Susan. "Oh, go for it, Betsy," she said jauntily. "You'll always look petite next to Jake anyway, so who gives a hoot." Going for another chip herself, she turned back to Susan. "So, where's Billy?" she asked gingerly.

Susan's father snorted at the mention of her boyfriend. "Hah!" he said nastily. "He's probably pulling one of his famous no-show acts."

Betsy threw her husband a sharp look. Susan sighed and looked away. There was always so much tension here. She couldn't wait to leave. And why on earth had she invited Billy anyway? Would she never learn?

"Susan, don't get protective of him after all this time," Buzz said, misreading her silence.

"Who's protective?" Susan drained what was left of her drink. "I'm through defending Billy Donahue."

"That'll be the day," Jake sneered.

Susan took a deep breath. *Here they go again.*

"Maybe he'll come by for dessert—" Betsy suggested.

"I don't want that jerk coming over here period!" Jake rose from his chair and went over to the makeshift bar he had set up, where he began putting together another batch of Wallbangers.

"Can we talk about something else?" Susan asked, frustrated, producing a gloomy lull in the conversation.

"Billy's probably going out of his mind," Lisa said finally. "I'm surprised he didn't break down and ask you to marry him."

Susan looked dubious. She had no illusions about Billy.

"What! Are you dreaming?" Jake rolled his eyes.

"Billy's not right for her anyway," Betsy said, putting her arm around her daughter. "Jake, when are you going to stop drinking and start barbecuing the fish?" Jake had caught a ten-pound striped bass that morning, and it was all cleaned and ready to go on a platter.

"When are you going to mind your own business?"

"Mom, Daddy—please knock it off. Can we have one night of no fighting!"

Jake sucked in his gut, attempting to stuff it into his trousers. He was red in the face and his watery gray eyes narrowed bitterly. "What's the matter, Susan? You embarrassed in front of your friends?"

"No . . ." Susan said steadily, feeling thwarted, sorry for him, sorry for her mother.

"Yes, you are. You've always felt embarrassed about me and your mother."

Now Susan stood up to face him. She was tall, but he was much taller, and their awkward proximity had her looking at his barrel of a chest. "That's not true," she insisted, craning her neck to meet his gaze.

"Like hell it ain't."

Susan backed off, astonished at his tone.

"Your mother and me—we break our backs raising you. And you're gonna just up and move away—"

"Dad. I have to do this."

"You have duties here, girl. Your mother counts on you."

Susan was speechless.

"You think you're better than any of us—you always have."

"Jake." Betsy's voice was urgent.

Jake threw a large trembling hand over in Lisa's direction. "What the hell's the matter with marrying someone like Lisa's Buzz? Or ain't he rich enough for you? You just want too much."

"I don't—" Susan started to respond, stung. She turned apologetically to Lisa and Buzz, at a loss for a response.

"You botched up a perfectly good marriage," Jake continued acidly.

"How do *you* know it was a perfectly good marriage?"

"Because I've been around. I may not have your fancy degrees, but I know who's happy and who's not. You goin' to try and tell me that you're happier than Lisa?"

It was true. Lisa probably was happier than she was, if happiness could effectively be measured. With three wonderful kids and a husband who adored her, Lisa practically glowed with contentment. She had a busy life. It seemed she was president of everything: The P.T.A., her son's Little League, assorted local charities. What had Susan held out for? Maybe her father was right. Maybe she *was* chasing rainbows. Always it had seemed to her that her wants were so simple: A job at which she was happy, a man with whom she could share a productive life. But it was true, simple or not, that at least fifty percent of those wants had eluded her.

"Lisa and I are different," Susan said. "Things turned out differently for us."

"Dammit, Jake, leave her alone," Betsy said, going over to her husband.

But he was beyond reprimand, and he shook her roughly away. They were expecting too much from him. Jake was second generation Stockton. His father had worked at the same grain facility at which he now worked, and Jake had always accepted his lot in life. He believed firmly that people ought to stick to their own kind. It wasn't a good idea to begin hanging around with people out of your class. That bred discontentment and envy. Too much exposure was bad. Now everything was changing, getting out of control. His eldest son had also left home and was living in Bangkok as a translator. After flunking out of Berkeley and joining the army, he had gone to study at the army language school at Fort Ord, in Monterey, where he became fluent in Thai, as well as Chinese and German. Jake's middle child was a container engineer, designing and maintaining the standards of containers, boxes, cans, jars, and things of that nature. He still lived in Stockton, but he had Jake's quarrelsome temper and they rarely spoke. It was in Susan that he had placed all of his dreams—small, happy, attainable dreams. Why couldn't she content herself with a life like Lisa's? What was the matter with his kids?

The glass-and-wrought-iron table shook as he slammed his drink down onto it.

Susan could feel him avoiding her glance as he jiggled inside of his pants pocket for his keys, then headed away from them. She thought about going after him, this being her last night. If she had had any idea of what to say, she would have. But with Jake, nobody ever did. His brooding presence was too intimidating. And he left an uneasy stillness in his wake.

The next morning Susan opened her eyes to bright sunlight, striped and glary from under the metal blinds of her parents' mobile home. As she became aware of voices outside she strained to listen, growing tense and alert. All she could make out from the muffled conversation were her father's periodic nos. Most likely her mother was asking him to apologize, to at least say good-bye. He was refusing.

Susan threw off the quilt her mother had made years ago, recognizing many of the little patches as remnants of old clothes she and her brothers had once worn. It was easy to pick out which materials had belonged to her, because her brothers' clothes, by the time they were ready to be discarded, were always more faded, having been passed down from one brother to the next.

Should she brave going outside and facing him, or not? *Yes,* she thought, rising nervously from the squeaky hide-a-bed she had been sleeping in these last few nights. She glanced toward her parents' bedroom, wondering if her father had slept at home or not, or if he had just returned in the morning to change. His lunch pail and hat were now missing from the top of the TV cabinet, where her mother always laid his things. They had been there the night before, before she had fallen asleep.

"Oh, you're up." Her mother sounded surprised as she came into the room through the screen door. It snapped closed behind her as she moved forward, regarding her daughter. Susan's hair was messy around her face, and the old Lanz nightgown she was wearing brought back memories for both of them.

"I wanted to say good-bye—" Susan began tentatively.

"He's his own worst enemy," Betsy said. "Give him time."

Susan looked at her mother, wondering how she had managed all these years with her father.

"You know he's a smart man, Susan. You kids never give him credit for that," Betsy continued, smoothing nonexistent wrinkles from her crisp print housedress.

"He may have been smart at one time, Mom, but he's not smart anymore. He's too busy fighting everything. Everyone. He sounds like—"

Betsy had started to open the blinds, and she stopped, looking hard at Susan. "You just have to understand. You kids intimidate him—"

"*We* intimidate *him*—"

"Yes. That's right. He feels clumsy around you kids. Ignorant. I'm sure he's worried that if you move to L.A., it'll just get worse." The room brightened up as Betsy went back to adjusting the blinds. Susan stood rooted, watching her, wanting to gain strength from her easy wisdom. "It's hard on him—you have to realize that. Whether you like it or not, you kids make him feel like a failure. Dumb. Inadequate. Because you're all reaching for more."

"But shouldn't we be?"

"I'm not saying you shouldn't. I'm saying you need to put yourself in his place, understand how he feels."

Susan's things were piled up on top of her suitcase on the floor, and she went over to begin straightening up, putting to the side a pair of jeans, some socks, and her tennis shoes. "Maybe I should go out to the port to see him before I take off . . ." she said uncertainly.

Betsy bent down beside her to give her a hand. "Let him be, Susan. I know your father." Frowning at the state of disarray of Susan's things, she emptied them onto the floor and began folding them neatly for her. "He loves you," she said as Susan sat hesitating between two shirts, distracted. Betsy pointed to the blue shirt and went on, talking as she worked. "He's going to miss you a lot. But he needs time with this one. The only good thing, as far as he's concerned, is that this cuts Billy out of the picture for a while. But other than that, well, L.A. is a long ways away. And the kind of people you're going to be with are not exactly your dad's cup of tea."

Susan's eyes were moist as she looked at her mother. There *was* a gap, and it was widening all the time. She had a fleeting sensation of her parents coming out to Los Angeles to visit her. The picture she still held in her mind was of Kit and George's lavish home and the opulent life-style she had experienced there. It had been wonderful, exciting. But it was aeons away from the realities that existed in her parents' world in Stockton. What did she want? What was it that she was really seeking? A chill seemed to set in, and Susan shivered, aware that she was driving herself into further conflict. Money? Was that it? For some reason, if that's all it was, she felt ashamed. She also felt confused. Money was enticing, she would be a liar to say that it was not. But inexplicably the images that went along with it made her feel uneasy. They evoked catch words like nouveau riche, plastic. Or was she displaying a form of learned prejudice—more stereotypical brainwashing against L.A.?

Then Susan felt her mother's reassuring hand on her head.

"I think you *should* go. Don't pay any attention to us," she insisted. There were bags below her pale blue eyes, which looked tired and seemed to have shrunk with age. "I'm going to miss the daylights out of you," she said in a choked voice. "But I'll be all right. And so will your father."

Susan sat back heavily onto her heels. Looking gratefully at her mother through a veil of tears, she took her mother's hands in her own and held them. Saying good-bye was a thousand times more difficult than she ever imagined, and it had her feeling torn apart with emotion.

There was that unshakable sadness.

And yet she was so glad to be leaving.

Chapter 3

The truth was, Tori had been hoping Travis would talk her out of going, that he'd finally get his damn divorce and marry her.

But she had had no such luck.

In only three short days she would be on that plane, bidding good-bye to Atlanta—carrying out a version of a threat she had been delivering to Travis for years. It was an ultimatum wagered and lost.

Definitely lost, she thought, dropping mementos of his love into the already full trash can beneath her desk, hesitating over each one and remembering its particular significance. She was at the office, cleaning out her desk, preparing for her departure. Her top right-hand drawer was virtually filled with three and a half years' worth of assorted tokens from Travis with which she hadn't been able to part.

There were notes he had written, photographs, humorous gifts.

Here she was, trying with all her heart to get her life together, her office in order, and herself out of town, and it was typical of Travis to be working on an all-out campaign to wear her down. All week long he had been sending things—extravagant flower arrangements, great stuffed animals, silly bric-a-brac, crazy telegrams.

There were flowers all over her goddamn office, overflowing into her secretary's cubicle, and still more that she had distributed down the hall because she had run out of space.

He couldn't understand why she was ruining what they both thought was a perfect relationship. They had communication, humor, tenderness, just about everything in common, *and* sex that hadn't lost its greatness after nearly seven years.

Travis was forty-three years old. He knew what was *out there.* He thought Tori was making the mistake of a lifetime throwing all they had together away because of some kind of lack of security on her part.

Marriage, what was so damn essential about marriage?

Trust, love, desire, communication, weren't those elements more important, more long lasting, than a lousy piece of paper? Travis had been with Tori longer than he had been with his wife, and he believed fervently that one of the reasons was because they *were not* married.

Tori came upon a picture of the two of them with their arms around each other, slapping a big SOLD sign onto the FOR SALE sign in front of the condo they had bought together only a year ago.

The acquisition in itself had been a big commitment. Tori had seen it as a significant step in the right direction. Travis, on the other hand, had viewed it as a wise investment that he could always turn around.

He needed exit doors that were clearly marked.

Tori lifted the photo out of the drawer, not bothering to block a fresh onslaught of tears, and sat back in her chair, thinking how this all felt like one interminable bad dream. The emptiness she was feeling was so acute that she felt physically ill. Her stomach hurt. Her muscles ached. She felt like she had the flu, when all she really had was a case of being thirty and single, with no prospects toward a goal she suddenly realized she needed to fulfill.

Marriage and kids, it was an American staple. Why did she feel greedy wanting it? Why did she feel as though it would be so difficult to obtain?

Because she wanted marriage, kids, *and* Travis.

Totally out of control, Tori dropped the photograph, now wet from her tears, onto her desk and stared at it. She looked at his wavy brown hair, wanting to run her fingers through its thick mass. She looked at his eyes and caught the lovable, devilish glint that was always there, that always made her forgive him when she had made up her mind never to again. She thought of the Sundays he had brought her breakfast in bed, the tray adorned with flowers he had cut from outside, waking her up by patting her on the rear, then throwing her into the shower and making unforgettable love to her. They had been together for so long, it was as though they were *already* married. If it weren't for wanting children, Tori would definitely have sacrificed a legal union.

A knock at the door broke her thoughts.

Her secretary, Cora Ann, stood sympathetically in the doorway, her newly acquired granny glasses perched on the end of her nose. Cora Ann had been with the company long before Tori. She was an old mother hen, but everyone loved her. Tori followed her glance around the room, where her chrome-and-glass bookcases had been emptied, pictures taken down from the walls, Tori's treasured dhurrie rug rolled and tied into a log behind her desk.

"He's up to thirteen calls today and it's only"—Cora Ann checked the dainty gold watch on her chunky wrist—"twelve o'clock. Good thing he got transferred over to the Peach Tree office, or he'd be sitting on my desk."

Tori looked over at the blinking red light on her phone and felt her resistance beginning to wane. She had been so strong these last couple of weeks, refusing to take his calls, insisting that he move out for the three weeks that it would take to get all of her things in order and wrap up loose ends at work.

She glanced at the phone again, debating, wanting to pick up the line and talk to him.

"What are you gonna do? Not even see him before you go?"

Tori nodded. She was afraid to see him. She had made a commitment to herself, and she couldn't chance breaking down. And yet, in spite of her resolve, she had her hand on the receiver. Maybe *he* was having second thoughts.

Cora Ann buried her nose in a fragrant bouquet of roses and sniffed. "Even *I'm* beginning to feel sorry for him," she admitted.

"He said he's gone back to seeing his psychiatrist again, that he had to call him for Valium, and that he's lost twelve pounds."

Tori looked at her secretary, surprised. "He told you all that?"

"All of a sudden he's my best friend." Cora Ann removed a pencil from behind her ear. "He obviously didn't think you'd really go through with this. Frankly, honey, none of us did."

The red light on the phone continued to flash, urging Tori into submission as she shuffled absently through the neatly sorted stacks on her desk. The light's quickened pulse seemed to match her heartbeat.

"Also, your mother called," Cora Ann said, deliberating through the awkward pause, tapping her pencil onto the pale green steno pad she was always holding. "She wants to know if you can come for dinner tonight. And Mr. Clayton came by just as Travis called. He needs to talk to you about the Clearwater project. He said to stop by his office before you take off today . . ."

Tori couldn't concentrate on a word Cora Ann was saying. All she could think about was picking up the phone and talking to Travis. On top of cramping stomach muscles, she felt a chill and shivered noticeably.

"Just pick up the damn phone," Cora Ann suggested sweetly on her way out the door.

Praying for a capitulation, Tori lifted up the receiver.

She couldn't deny the rush she felt, the unbelievable sense of comfort at hearing his voice. But she held her reaction in reserve. "Travis, *why* are you calling?" she asked him guardedly, her thoughts sinking nostalgically into the past as she glanced down at her crushed white linen dress, which never failed to arouse crazy memories. Travis had bought it for her one evening when they'd been shopping together over at Lenox Mall. They had also bought a fabulous-looking wide belt that slung low over her hips. The belt had cost more than the dress, but Travis had insisted she get it because for some reason the belt turned him on. So did the thought of nailing her in the dressing room.

He had been in rare form that night, following lecherously behind her into the dressing room, ignoring the craggy old saleswoman's disapproving look, which, by the smile on Travis's face, they certainly deserved.

Tori remembered the large three-way mirror and the way he had angled it as he undressed her. First the belt, which he let slip to the floor, then the zipper at the back of the dress, which he undid with his teeth. She hadn't been wearing a bra, only a pair of French net panties he had never seen before, the effects of which had him down on his knees in an instant, moaning his delight as he went straight for them with his mouth. It was all naughty nirvana until their indiscreet foreplay was interrupted by a sharp rap at the door.

"Everything okay in there?" asked the suspicious saleslady.

Everything was fine!

Except now she was on the verge of tears.

"I have to see you, Tori—" Travis was insisting.

"No."

"I have to pick up some stuff at our place anyway—"

"Travis, no. You're not being fair. I can't see you," Tori forced herself to say. She should never have picked up the phone. She couldn't chance breaking down again. "If you need something over at the apartment, go get it now. Anytime before seven o'clock."

There was another long silence. Tori felt as though she could almost hear him thinking.

"How can you leave without seeing me?" he tried again. "Why don't we just have a drink together or something?"

"Travis, I'm hanging up the phone now," she said, shaken.

She looked at the flowers around the room. The gift cards were all the same. "Don't leave me, you silly woman. I love you!" They were *so* Travis—she could feel him saying it as she read each one.

"Dr. Rosto thinks you should give me a little more time, Tori. He thinks you're trying to manipulate me. And that you're making a mistake."

"Screw Dr. Rosto," Tori replied angrily. "I'm not trying to manipulate you. I'm hurt. I love you. I wish things had worked out differently for us. But I feel I'm wasting my time in our relationship. It's a dead-end situation, since I want to get married and you don't. And it's time for me to take control of my life—"

"Eventually I *do* want to remarry—"

"Eventually? We've been living together for six and a half years. More." Tori took a deep breath. She was tired of this conversation. "Dammit, Travis, you're not even divorced yet. Think about that! Why *aren't* you divorced?" Tori was so angry she was shaking. She looked around her office, trying to gain strength from her decision, which was clear in the empty drawers, the vacant walls, the boxes with her personal things. She had made a resolution to move and she was carrying it through.

With her heart breaking, she hung up on him.

The rest of the day passed slowly, uneventfully. There were some final interoffice business meetings, some phone calls, a lot of strained chitchat about how adventurous Tori was to just pick up and move as she was doing.

Only a few days before, Tori had felt indispensable. Nobody at the office seemed to know what they were going to do without her—their young marketing miracle, they called her. The panic about her leaving had naturally been flattering. But now that everything was in order, the machine of the business working smoothly without its missing part, Tori felt as though she were in the way. She felt deflated.

By four o'clock she was considering leaving early, flying out to California tonight. There was no point in coming back to the office to merely hang around. And the sooner she got out of Atlanta the happier she was going to be. She was making a clean break and she needed to do it fast.

"You want me to call the airlines for you, honey?" Cora Ann asked when Tori buzzed her and told her of her decision.

"No. Thanks. *I'll* do it," Tori replied. "I've got nothing else to do."

Then, with her airline ticket taken care of, her farewell hugs distributed, Tori closed the door on that part of her life, got into her car, and headed home one last time, praying with all her heart that Travis would be there to stop her, and then preparing herself in case he was not.

She envisioned dozens of scenarios on the way. One had Travis there declaring how he couldn't possibly live without her. Another had him there with her shouting coldly at him to leave. The possibilities were endless, and she played them all out in her mind as she continued along the lengthy stretch of highway that would take her from the Perimeter, where she worked, to their condo on Lenox Road in Buckhead, sailing against the traffic, since the bulk of the population in Atlanta went the other way. Everywhere she looked there were new developments springing up, many of them ones in which she herself had participated. Highland Estates, that was hers from start to finish. She had even been involved in the land acquisition, since she had gotten the initial lead. The entrance to the models was announced by a big red-and-white banner bearing the company's logo, which she had helped design.

Taking in the bright blue sky, feeling the hot stickiness of the day, Tori let out a deep sigh. It was so strange to be leaving Georgia. The rich-looking red earth that was piled up on the side of the road where another building was going up sent a longing through her. Red Georgia clay; it was like Scarlett feeling connected to the soil of Tara. There really was something about the copper-colored dirt that held a Georgian to his roots, she thought, the red Georgia clay, the dense lushness of the woods that seemed to stretch on forever.

Tori parked her car in the subterranean lot beneath her condominium complex. Then she grabbed her briefcase, maneuvered it on top of the carton she had brought along with her from the office, and with her hands occupied, she shoved her car door closed with her behind. Accustomed to being loaded down with things—her purse, briefcase, groceries, laundry—Tori knew to use her chin to set off the light summoning the elevator. Its great metal jaws opened and swallowed her up.

Travis was sitting on the couch, drinking beer and watching TV, when she opened the door. The sight of him sitting there brought every little nerve ending to the surface. It seemed to be déjà vu from one of the scenarios she had played out during her long drive home, but which one?

Please, God, let it be one of the good ones, she thought, feeling suspended as he stood up and clicked off the set. The twelve-pound weight loss was apparent in the loose fit of his jeans. His love handles had all but disappeared, leaving a smooth line at his waist, making her miss the slight shelf she had found cute and fun to pinch. She hated herself for wanting him so badly, for being so weak.

"Why are you here?" she asked stiffly, using her feet to kick the box inside the door, feeling defensive and wide open for more disappointment. Travis crossed awkwardly over to help her, handing her his beer can, then heaving the box up and over to a clear corner of the room.

"I just wanted to say good-bye—" he began.

"Good-bye," she replied quickly, feeling her heart sink when he didn't go on.

As he walked toward her again she backed away from him. "I'm not going to touch you," he promised, carefully extracting the beer can from her hand without making contact with her skin. The sad part about it was he didn't need to. The air between the two of them was charged with sexual chemistry.

"Please leave," she urged, her voice slightly too high.

"There're a few things we're going to have to talk about and get settled—"

"Talk to Cora Ann. I don't want to have any communication with you, Travis. Not for a while. I'm not ready for it."

"C'mon, Tori." As he put his hand on her arm she felt herself trembling. She wanted him to hold her, to scoop her up in his arms, to carry her into the bedroom and make all this reality vanish. Instead she yanked roughly away from him.

"Travis, I want you out of here," she shouted. "Just leave. Haven't you got any decency? Any inkling of how I feel?"

"I know exactly how you feel!" he shouted back at her.

How? Tori thought. *How do I feel? Tell me.*

"You want to be with me. I want to be with you. This is crazy —your leaving. Give me six months. What's another six months? Let's see how we both feel then—"

"No," Tori said firmly. "If you don't know now, you *never* will."

"It's not that simple—"

"For a *normal* person it would be. You just can't ever make a commitment. You can't ever make up your mind. If you feel like you're going to be trapped, if that's how you view it all, then I don't want to be married to you anyway. I don't want to be in the position of feeling like I'm putting a leash on anybody—"

"Then why get married? Why take the chance of ruining a perfectly good relationship? We've got a better thing going than any married couple we know."

"That's just your arrogant opinion of it, Travis." God, why were they fighting about this again? "I'm not trying to talk you into anything. *I* want to get married. *You* don't. Period. The end. So get out of here, *please*. Leave me alone!"

"Would you want someone to stay with you just because of the obligation of marriage?"

"No. Maybe. I don't know," Tori replied, confused. The truth was, maybe she would. If she were older and they had kids, and he wanted to leave, maybe she would want the security of knowing it wouldn't be so easy for him to leave.

"Look, I know you want kids. And that does change things," Travis said, calming down a bit, his tone turning gentler. "So maybe we would. I don't know. If you really wanted them. I know you'd be a good mother. So if you end up pregnant, then we'll get married. But let's just let it play out naturally. . . ."

Travis had his arms around her waist. His fingers were on that belt he couldn't resist. "God, I miss you so much," he was whispering into her ear, bringing her closer into him. His touch made it impossible for her to respond to the resounding message in her brain that was saying *Back away.*

We are getting nowhere, was all Tori could think. She felt dizzy and confused as he held her more tightly than ever, his cheek pressed against hers, telling her how wonderful she smelled. She fought for control as his large mouth covered hers in a kiss she knew she was desperately going to miss. Then she felt herself caving in as his tongue moved sensually along her neck, making her squirm, pressing on until she was finally kissing him back. There was an alarm blaring in her head and her heart was pounding, but it was nothing compared to this burning-hot desire she was feeling for him.

She wanted to disconnect her brain and *simply feel.* She was crying, and he was kissing her tears, diffusing them all over her face.

Then he did what she had wanted him to do all along. He lifted her up into his arms, cradling her as he carried her into the bedroom, stepping around cartons and then easing her down onto the bed, never separating his mouth from hers, moaning into nearly every kiss.

"Goddamn it, Travis," she managed, completely under the spell of him as a wave of fluid rolled beneath them from the water-inflated mattress, conforming to their shape and movement. She thought fleetingly of her mother, and then her airline ticket, as his hands moved over her stomach, unfastening her belt and casting it off onto the hardwood floor, where it landed noisily. Her parents were expecting her for dinner. Her flight was in two and half hours. What was she doing? His hands were caressing her back now, drawing down the zipper of her dress. She wriggled out of it, sighing as his lips touched down hotly onto her stomach. *God, what's the matter with me?* she thought loosely, intensely conscious of his breath warm and velvety there. He had a physical hold on her, and all she wanted in this instant was to be making love with him.

Forget logic, forget what she was raised to believe she needed. The urge right now was more demanding, more intense. She was helping Travis get out of his pants. She was struggling right along with him, with his zipper, getting the jeans down and off. Now they were one, in sync, wanting the same thing. Pleasure blurred with need, and it existed on a level that wiped out logic because it seemed pure and therefore right.

How she wanted to believe those cons of his, those familiar fragments of comfort imploring her to stay. If only she could surrender to life as it was and love him without complication, without worrying about the future and commitments. If only she were twenty-three again and not feeling pressed for time. Tori fought for control one final time as he pushed aside the quilt and another large wave sloshed beneath them. They were now completely undressed, and she was moving her lips down the length of him, feeling him respond as he angled onto his side, cupping her rear end in his hand.

What a state everything was in. What a cluttered mass of contradiction and confusion. From the partially packed cartons that had taken over their small, always impeccably in order condominium to the crazy myriad of flowers that had also been arriving at home, nothing made sense anymore.

With him hard and urgent inside her now, kissing her with the fever of never seeing her again, she closed her eyes and held on to him, moving with the rhythm of their desire, loving him more than she ever wanted to love anyone again. There was a stillness in the room as their bodies slapped tensely against one another. *Ask me to marry you! Dammit. Get your damn divorce and promise me the rest of your life. . . .* Tears washed down Tori's face as she clung to him, on the edge of climaxing, needing the release. Then as she did, and he relaxed into his own ecstasy, he astonished them both with a proposal.

"You're not going to Los Angeles," he gasped, his body still shuddering from orgasm. "To hell with everything; I'm going to marry you."

Tori was too stunned to reply. It wasn't how she had envisioned a proposal, and she wasn't sure she believed him. There had been too many semiproposals from him in the past. *Semi,* because they had always hinged on some distant slippery detail: money, or his getting a divorce. Gun-shy from a history of disappointments, she pulled away and looked at him, trying to read his soul.

"Tori, I mean it this time," he assured her, propping himself up onto his side to face her and taking her hands. "I really do."

Torn between euphoria and deep skepticism, Tori looked away from him to the ice-blue walls they had painted together, the framed poster art. There were photographs of the two of them scattered around the room. And there were the multitude of boxes marked for Beverly Hills. "I want you to marry me," he whispered, holding on even more tightly to her hands. The loving way in which he said it made her heart leap, and she felt giddy with victory.

"What about your divorce, Travis?" It was a question that made them both nervous.

He punched his pillow, folding it in half and arranging it under his head for a cushion. "Don't worry about it. I'll take care of it."

Tori hedged. The moment was so precious, so fragile; she was afraid of shattering it. "Travis, if you let me down again, I'll *never* forgive you." Her small hand formed a fist of nervous energy that she pressed menacingly into his thick chest.

Lying there watching her, he was the picture of innocence, and she felt guilty for not trusting him.

"How about if I swear on the Bible for you? Huh?" He grinned, tracing his index finger along her hips.

"No good. You're a lousy Catholic."

"Okay, then, I'll swear on my mother's life," he relented playfully, getting up onto his knees and tickling her.

"Last week you wanted to kill her—" Tori protested, squirming as he caught her mercilessly under the ribs.

"All right. I'll swear on my Porsche—"

"Travis, this is serious—" Tori said, trying not to laugh. She watched his brown eyes scan the room, then the length of her, as he calculated what to say next.

"Okay, then, what kind of engagement ring do you want?" he asked after a moment, bounding cheerfully out of bed and crossing the planked wood floor to disappear into the bathroom.

Now, that's serious.

"A big one," she replied, smiling in spite of her anxiety.

He uttered something under his breath, then peeked his head around the door. "How big is big?"

"Big enough that the investment will be too great for you to feel comfortable about backing out."

Travis gripped the door as though someone were strangling him, then collected himself to assure her he would be all right. As he kicked the door shut he let out a loud groan.

"I'm worth it," Tori shouted over the noise of the shower being turned on. It wouldn't be nearly as big as Kit's engagement ring. Kit's husband, George, probably earned in a month what it took Travis a full year to earn. But it didn't matter one bit to Tori. She felt happier at this moment than she could ever remember feeling in her life.

Sitting up and raising her long graceful arms into the air, she let out a quiet little cry of excitement. The mirror across the room reflected her joy, and she smiled at the vision there, feeling young, beautiful, and wonderfully righteous for having ignored her parents all these years when they had told her she was throwing away her best years, wasting them with Travis.

A bad marriage bet? Maybe. But they had underestimated their daughter.

The dozen or so boxes cluttering the room seemed to echo that sentiment, and she glanced gratefully at them, not minding in the least the chore of unpacking that lay ahead of her. The boxes had been her artillery. The flowers had been his. And all thanks to Paige and Susan, for without them, none of this would ever have happened. Funny, she really barely knew either one of them, and yet it seemed today that they were her very best friends. She couldn't wait to call them up to share her tremendous news.

Plucking a begonia from out of an arrangement near the bed, she pinned it into her hair. Then she got out of bed, wrapping the sheet around her naked body and dragging it along for effect to join her fiancé in the bathroom.

Chapter 4

The darkened theater was eerie and magical. A spectacle of cat eyes glittered in the blackness of the aisles that were like dark shadows beneath the lighting designer's pale moon. Scintillatingly, from all over the theater at once, the silent cats began to emerge, scampering forms, prowling toward the huge nocturnal junkyard that was now the stage for T. S. Eliot's flighty Jellicle Cats. As the lights came up, the brilliantly designed set sprang to life, revealing a kind of cosmic playground for cats, a fanciful junkyard with the litter of human consumerism all awesomely scaled.

Outfitted in whiskers, electronically glowing eyes, masklike makeup, and a sleek body-stocking cat costume, Paige slithered across the imaginatively constructed stage set of *Cats,* dancing her way through the collage of junk, slinking around the rusty pots and pans, cast-off cereal boxes, archaic appliances, forsaken mops, dismembered bicycle parts, and giant pushed-in toothpaste tubes.

Bigger. Make it count! Shoulders back. Stomach in. Reach. Stretch. That's it. Saucy now. Leap. Quick turn. Crouch. And hold . . . She'd heard the choreographer's commands so frequently, they played in her head with more force than the words of the songs. Jazz, ballet, acrobatics, these were talented cats indeed, felines of every variety, sending limbs and fur flying in Tony-winning fashion.

Paige was sweating from the hot lights and frenzied exertion, dancing as though she were the only one out there, the focus of the beat, the cat to end all cats. With the ritual of the steps now as reflexive as breathing, she added feeling, more feeling than anyone would ever know.

It was cry or dance, because she couldn't believe this was her last time out there. She was walking out on the dream she had grown up with, only partially fulfilled, and at the same time fighting an insane urge to make this final performance night of hers count. How tempting it was to deviate from the choreographed routine they all did now by rote, to break out of the woodwork of the chorus and perform unrestrained. She thought of the late great Isadora Duncan and imagined the freedom she must have felt dancing out the rhythm that was in her soul, in her mind.

What could they do to her? Paige wondered, now on her knees, swinging her shapely behind for effect. Arrest her? Throw her in jail?

And what about the rest of the cast? It would be a feline fiasco, she mused, as a group of alley cats with dramatically sculpted hair and makeup disguising the faces of eighteen-year-olds, curled around her with a convincing snarl. They were like living celluloid of a younger Paige, when her hopes had been as high as the heavens, her drive fierce. Youth. For them the chorus lines still held promise. Now Paige didn't know whether to envy them or pity them. At thirty, the promise felt like a lie.

Paige hoped Cathy, the pretty one on the end, would make it. Cathy was an outstanding talent, with superb technique, great style. And she was sweet. Of course, in the end, the sweetness could be her downfall. She would need to withstand the harsh and cutthroat elements of the theater, an environment that demanded toughness.

Paige had been tough, and tall, and even talented. She had come *close,* as they say, even made it to second understudy once for a big role in *42nd Street.* But the first understudy had been unforgivably healthy—apparently immune to even the slightest common cold, with muscles that never strained. Paige had spent sleepless nights trying to figure out how to get both the star and the first understudy down at the same time so that she could have at least one shot. She had entertained absurd fantasies like drugging their coffee, having them abducted for a day or two. A slight sprained ankle might have done the trick, but it would have been impossible to trip both of them. She had even envisioned inviting them over for dinner the night before a performance and adding Ex-Lax to their chocolate soufflés which she, of course, would refrain from eating.

Paige plotted plenty. But she never played.

Favorite numbers whizzed by, slipping into memories before they were even completed. There was always a kind of sentimental rush that went along with a final night on a show. But this was Paige's final night on *stage*.

Her thoughts jumped to Susan and Tori, and she wondered how they were handling leaving. Susan had sounded excited, committed, and strangely adjusted to the decision. Tori had sounded as though her leaving symbolized her defeat. She needed bolstering, that was for sure. They had exchanged a few quick phone calls back and forth, mostly talking to one another's answering machines, confirming details, all of them wanting to make certain the others were genuinely going through with this, nobody wanting to quit their job or ditch their boyfriend, to find themselves all alone in L.A. They needed each other.

The closing number in *Cuts* was fast approaching its extravagantly staged finale, with a swell of music and frantically changing lights accompanying the alley cats' ascent into the heavens on a space machine.

That's me, Paige thought drolly, *moving out of this life and ascending into another.* Sure, there would be that glittery presence of stars there, but was Beverly Hills really going to be heaven?

Paige was facing a flood of second thoughts when the house lights came up, signaling the performance's end. It was as though she were being hit with her own mortality, the conclusion of the show marking with piercing clarity the end of her career. As she ran out with the rest of the cast, holding hands, bowing, smiling to the thunderous applause, she realized she was feeling more emotion than perhaps she had ever felt in her life. It was so much sadness welling up inside her, ready to explode.

She was actually reeling with an unfulfilled longing for that last burst of applause, reserved for the star, to belong to *her.* Once and for all *she* wanted to be the one clutching the proverbial bouquet of flowers to her heart and weeping with elation over a performance *well done*—because the audience loved her—because she loved herself. It was a vision that would never come to pass.

As the applause swelled, heightening Paige's anxiety, scattered members of the audience began to rise to their feet in standing ovation. Paige watched as others followed suit, a trend the cast had come to expect.

Her own legs felt weak. They ached, and not from any pulled muscles, but from fear. God, she had been so cavalier about it all up until now. But what had made her so brazenly sure of herself? Was she trading one fantasy for another? *Why can't I set normal goals for myself? Because you're not normal,* was the simple response of a fellow cast member when they'd sat together in the dressing room before the show, Paige applying cat whiskers for the last time. These were her friends, her soul mates, odd and strained as their relationships were, and she squeezed on tightly to their hands as she ran out to take another sweeping bow. She was part of a chain, and she moved more by their motion now than her own. *Stop crying, you jerk,* she told herself, feeling her makeup going all to hell, thick grease paint bleeding together. She couldn't even wipe away the tears with her hands because they were attached to all those other hands.

Earlier today someone had been talking about an opening on a daytime soap. Paige wondered if she should consider postponing her flight a day or two and go for a reading on the part. If she got it, the pay would be good enough to move to the Upper West Side, where she had been dying to live. She could afford to update her portfolio. Enroll in the new Method acting class she had been wanting to take. Maybe go to Europe during hiatus. Get a new wardrobe. And if she got *that* part, there would be others. She would have finally broken in. She would be "network approved."

So long, chorus lines; hello, national TV. She had a *feeling* about this particular part, this show. Maybe it was fate. Maybe just because she was planning on leaving tomorrow and because she was going out for the role strictly on a lark, this time she would actually get it.

The applause was petering out. Paige's heartbeat was escalating. One more reading—what did she really have to lose?

There was her commitment to Tori and Susan. But they could go it without her. And certainly they would understand. If Tori had stayed in Atlanta because Travis had broken down and proposed to her, Paige would have been *happy* for her. Besides, she was doing them both a giant favor, changing their lives for the better. Paige would stay in New York and become a sensation on TV. Susan and Tori would move to Beverly Hills as planned, meet and marry their multimillionaires, and they'd all live happily ever after.

But was that really what Paige wanted? Certainly she could pursue a television career in L.A. as easily, if not more easily than in New York. What happened to her resolve to abandon all that? Paige was having as much trouble letting go of her go-nowhere career as Tori was of her go-nowhere romance.

It was about three in the morning when Paige finally returned home from the farewell party the cast had thrown for her. Her apartment building was dark and hot and smelled from the Chinese take-out joint that was on the ground floor. In the winter the smell was never that apparent. But in July and August the ride up in the shaky little elevator was nauseating, until about the seventh floor. Thankfully, Paige's flat was up on nine.

After unbolting the series of locks on her door, Paige pushed it open and stepped into her now-sparse apartment. Over the weekend she had sold all of her furniture, posters, old clothes, dishes. All that was left in the tiny place was a sleeping bag she had borrowed from the guy across the hall, a pillow, a coffeemaker, the telephone, which was being disconnected tomorrow and was still hooked up to her answering machine, a small pile of clothes, her makeup case, which was open and in great disarray, and two duffel bags packed for L.A.

"I wonder," she said aloud to the empty room, satisfied with her latest plan. She had decided if she didn't go out for that part in the soap, somewhere deep inside she would always believe the part could have been hers, and she would never forgive herself. A friend from the cast knew one of the producers on the show, called him at home, and arranged a reading for Paige. If she got the part, she would stay in New York, and if she didn't get it, she would give up once and for all and be on that plane to California pursuing a brand-new destiny with no regrets.

The red light indicating messages flashed from the answering machine, and she stumbled exhaustedly over to play them back, wrenching off her boots and shedding her clothes onto the floor on her way.

The first message was from Tori, and at the sound of her trusting voice recorded over the crackly long-distance line, Paige felt a fleeting sense of guilt and disloyalty.

But it passed abruptly as she stood there stunned, feeling instead betrayed by Tori's news.

Getting married! Travis had actually buckled and was going to marry her? Paige couldn't believe her ears.

Her first reaction was anger. She was astonished and hurt, as though Tori were deserting them. Then she remembered how *she* was hoping to be the deserter, and she just felt confused, worried about Susan. Susan couldn't move out to L.A. by herself. She would have a nervous breakdown finding herself in that big house, in that big city, on her own.

Paige listened loosely to the rest of Tori's message, which included effusive apologies and then bursts of excitement as she discussed impending wedding plans, struggling to be happy for her. She shoved open the solitary window over where her couch used to be, but the warm dense air offered little relief in the small studio apartment, which felt suddenly more confining than ever.

Great, now what? Paige thought, clicking off the machine in the middle of Tori's cheerful good-bye, wondering if she still had the heart to go for her audition tomorrow. She dropped down onto the bare hardwood floor, missing the faded but pretty Persian rug that had been there. Dammit, why should she feel so responsible for Susan? Susan was a big girl. So if she ended up the only one of the three of them going out to L.A., that wasn't the worst thing either. She was a professional woman, an attorney. And as Susan had said herself, she was much better off in a big city like L.A. than in Stockton.

Sitting cross-legged, stripped down to her underwear, with little beads of perspiration forming on her stomach, Paige felt practically convinced she was going to get the part in the soap. Life worked that way, taking forever to deliver what you were aching to have and then throwing a curve in with it. Tense with the dilemma now posed, she snapped the answering machine back on, wary about what other little zingers might lay in store for her.

"Hi. It's Dustin Brent." Somehow Paige hadn't expected to hear from him again, since they had already worked out all the details of their move, and she held her breath, thinking how strange it would be if he was also calling to bow out. What if he had decided not to go mountain climbing and his house-sitting offer was off?

It was with a start that Paige realized how disappointed she would actually be, and drawing her knees up close to her chest, she listened anxiously as he went on, praying she hadn't jinxed a good thing and triggered this reverse trend.

The sound of Dustin's voice alone made her want to cancel her tryout at the network and head out to California without another thought. It had nothing to do with Susan. It had to do with palm trees, gorgeous weather, and the lure of rich, powerful men like Dustin Brent. A stirring deep within Paige rekindled all that she had been feeling when she had been struck by the urge to move in the first place, and she sighed, deeply relieved when it became clear that he was not calling to rescind his offer.

What the hell had she been thinking?

For the better part of her life she had been pitting herself against the overwhelmingly bad odds of the theater, depositing years into a kind of giant slot machine and waiting for the payout. Small wins, just when she was ready to quit, would sabotage her logic. Broken hopes kept getting pasted back together. But the seams were beginning to show, and she realized now it was time to bow out gracefully while she was still young enough to do something else with her life.

So what if she got this part? The reality was that it was a nice role on a relatively popular soap. But it wasn't going to make her a star.

Paige didn't even *want* to be a star anymore.

What she wanted was a life like Kit's!

"So, I guess tomorrow's the big day," Dustin's voice replayed breezily. "If you let me know which flight you're coming in on, I'll arrange to have you met at the airport. . . ."

With happy resolve Paige replayed the message when it was over.

Susan Kendell Brown had a roommate after all.

As Damon Runyon used to say, "If you rub up against money long enough, some of it may rub up against you."

That's what Paige was thinking as she began to board her flight at Kennedy's TWA terminal, a flight she vowed was going to change her life.

She had woken up that morning feeling great, in spite of only a few hours sleep, liberated from a dream in which she no longer believed and happy because she was finally being entirely honest with herself about what she wanted.

She felt like the million bucks she was looking forward to having as a balance in her checking account soon.

A slender brunette who looked a lot like Tori rushed up to the check-in counter, her arm linked possessively through her male companion's. They were laughing at something, looking enraptured with one another. Of course it wasn't Tori. Tori was in Atlanta, probably also looking enraptured.

Paige had reached Tori early in the morning to congratulate her on her engagement to Travis. She had tried to sound enthused, but Tori had laughed and told her that when it came to real life, she put on an unconvincing performance. Both of them had laughed, feeling a strange attachment to one another, considering the short time they had been acquainted.

"Hey, I hope this guy appreciates what a 'peach' he's getting," Paige had then teased lightly, thinking about how it wasn't going to be the same without Tori.

"I think he does. Thanks to you . . ." Tori had drawled happily in response, her voice trailing off and gaining, in its awkward silence, a more serious note. "Paige, I don't know how to begin to thank you—"

"Name your first kid after me. How's that?" Paige had kidded, moved.

After some more affectionate teasing, they seemed to run out of conversation, each of them wishing the other one luck, wondering when they would meet up again.

It felt odd after having lived her whole life in New York that Paige's only sad good-bye had been to her friend in Georgia.

In New York her friends seemed to be whomever she was working with at the time, and there was always an off-key edge to the friendship because of professional jealousies. Even at the party the cast had thrown for her last night, there had been no teary farewells, no difficult severing of attachments. The relationships were of a different nature; they had to be. They all knew that at any given time they might be up against one another for a role they couldn't live without. The competition was too much to bear and often brought out the worst in all of them. Their closeness would become marred, and although they stuck together, nobody really trusted one another; envy and resentments clung too close to the surface.

The only potentially difficult good-bye Paige envisioned would have been to her father. But, as usual, he was on the road. As a traveling salesman he had represented everything from widgets to eye shadows. Now he was having the time of his life, selling a sexy line of lacy lingerie and, Paige supposed, probably giving half of it away to females he had enticed along the way.

Paige's father, a widower now, was in his late sixties, but still dashing. He was a dreamer and completely irresponsible. Her mother had been the only steady provider in the family, and Paige always knew she should have felt grateful to her, but it hadn't been easy.

For her mother, life had existed as a gray reality. With her father, the color of life was psychedelic, the shades and possibilities endless. While growing up, Paige rarely saw her father because he was always on the road. Yet it was those memorable visits that had always kept her able to see the bright side.

When Paige was eleven, her mother died of a bleeding ulcer. Paige's father said she had worried herself to death over things she couldn't change.

It was on the issue of change that Paige decided she was somewhere in the middle of their genetic pool. She was dreamer enough to believe in her ability to change just about whatever it was she wanted and pragmatic enough to change courses when the dream no longer appeared practical.

Right now Paige believed in change. The challenge was knowing what it was she wanted on the other side.

Being propelled forward and into the airplane by the bulge of passengers, Paige contemplated the series of well-heeled, mostly male passengers settling into first class. She zeroed knowledgeably in on the quality of their shoes and their briefcases, letting her glance ride up critically to assess the tailoring of their suits. One way to insure falling for a guy with a lot of money was to plant herself in their exclusive midst, she was thinking, beginning to debate how she might maneuver a first-class seat for herself.

Everyone knew about airplane romances—the person one might meet and have a flirtation with, if not more, during the several-hour flight to a mutual destination. Five hours of sitting next to a stranger had been known to produce astonishing intimacy.

If Paige had been assigned a window seat or an aisle seat, she might have stayed put. But because of her middle seat, squeezed in between a guy with a cold and a woman the size of a whale, who liked to talk, Paige felt compelled to try for that upgrade. Her oppressive seat assignment became almost a dare—something to read as fate.

In the midst of calculating her move a pretty blond stewardess greeted her in the aisle with effusive compliments on her wild technicolor earrings, which were shaped like flying saucers.

"I love your earrings. Where did you find them?" the stewardess asked as Paige stepped aside so as not to block the flow of passengers still entering.

"Bloomingdale's," Paige replied.

"God, my layovers in New York never seem to be long enough for me to go shopping anymore," the stewardess lamented, looking longingly at them while Paige looked longingly past her into the first-class section, where she noticed passengers already being supplied with French champagne, magazines, and other upgraded service. "Oh, well. Maybe in my next life."

"What about in this life?" Paige suggested shrewdly, turning back to her and looking around to make sure they weren't being overheard. "I'll make you a deal. You get me a seat in first class and the earrings are yours—today."

Paige watched the stewardess laugh, amused, trying to decide whether Paige was serious or not. When she saw that she was, she went over to check what Paige imagined to be a schedule of seating assignments.

Then, eyeing the proposed collateral with obvious temptation, she told Paige she'd be right back. There were two other attendants manning the first-class section, and Paige watched as the pretty blonde whispered something to them, causing them to look her way. Their smiles indicated the kind of "why not?" mentality that appealed to Paige as they signaled her over to a vacant seat.

When the stewardess brought Paige a diet Coke and a menu for the flight, Paige pointed to a familiar-looking man seated across the aisle from her and down a couple rows. "Who's that man? I know I know him from somewhere," she asked, trying to place him.

"Kareem Abdul-Jabbar," the stewardess whispered discreetly, bending down.

Paige actually hadn't noticed the seven-foot-tall athlete seated by the window and she peered around, impressed, thinking she would be even more impressed if she knew anything about basketball. "Not him. The guy sitting next to him," she replied.

"Oh. That's Jerry Buss. He owns the Lakers." The stewardess grinned knowingly at Paige. "Single. Supposed to be a great guy and lots of fun. Want any more profiles?"

"That'll do for now," Paige said, wondering about Buss. Too bad he was so absorbed talking to Jabbar. Once he turned and looked her way, but that was that. It appeared to be a working trip.

The earrings turned out to be a worthwhile exchange anyway.

While the five-hour flight failed to produce a worthwhile airplane romance, it did yield two interesting L.A. contacts who made a point of giving Paige their business cards, along with a gentle easing into the kind of first-class life-style to which Paige planned to become accustomed.

Chapter 5 ～

Dustin Brent's house stood like a monument to Paige's goal.

It was a large Mediterranean-style house set up on a knoll, with a grand Hollywood-fashion circular driveway that was palm lined and had a heavily populated stone fishpond built into the center of it.

As the heavy wrought iron gates spread open, Paige sat back smugly in the flashy black Aston-Martin in which she had been picked up from the airport, finding it hard to believe she was *really* here—that she had maneuvered fantasy into reality—that this amazing palatial spread was to be her new home.

Throughout the lengthy ride she had been playing with different images of what her new *residence* was going to look like, creating vivid pictures in her head. When Evonne, Dustin's secretary, had announced that they were almost there, Paige had tried to guess which house it was going to be. She wouldn't have dared to guess this one. It was too perfect.

In a large round mirror positioned for viewing traffic, she caught sight of herself driving through the posh gates, seated inside the flashy sports car, and she thought, with a little thrill, how so far *everything* was perfect. Aside from the mild disappointment that Dustin wouldn't be there to greet her.

On the drive over, Evonne had told her how she and Dustin had passed somewhere over the Continental United States, where she was flying west and he was flying east, on his way to wind up unexpected business in New York before his departure for Nepal.

Single, loaded, and soon to be out of the country. Too bad!

"I have just enough time to give you a quick tour," Evonne apologized hurriedly when they were inside, her pale saffron skirt and blouse swinging attractively as she walked. With the giant natural clam shell buckle on her belt and her smart silver-and-topaz jewelry, Dustin's pretty red-headed secretary seemed to blend with the soft California decor of the house, which was so much more "done" than Paige would have imagined, considering its inhabitant was a bachelor.

The house looked to be straight out of *Architectural Digest,* and in fact, she was amused to learn a moment later that it was. Angled on a unique fossil-studded stone coffee table in the living room was a copy of the prestigious magazine, a photo from this precise view gracing its famous cover.

Pale pimiento paver tiles on the floor connected the grand-scale rooms, which were monochromatic, the walls painted an earthy sensuous color reminiscent of southern Spain. Expansive uncurtained windows opened out onto luxuriant landscapes. The furniture seemed to be scaled up to accommodate the vastness of the room, solid without being overbearing. There were rattan armchairs, plumply cushioned in white linen, an airy chaise of rattan and cane, and two bold chairs with rolled upholstered arms in subdued shades of melon with white. Along one wall Paige noticed a collection of rare-looking Indian baskets. And then on the other side of the room fishtail palms caught her eye, soaring high into the lofty beamed ceiling, bent as if caught in the middle of gale-force winds.

The Spanish-speaking housekeeper, introduced to Paige as Maria, headed upstairs with the only earthly belongings Paige had retained packed into two new canvas duffel bags, and Paige watched as they disappeared from sight.

"Think you can get used to this?" Evonne teased, moving swiftly past a fat marble sculpture that Paige almost bumped into. A tiny plaque designated the clean Mexican-looking work as *Zuniga.* Zuniga *almost shattered,* Paige thought with nervous relief, trying to absorb everything in one elongated glance as she followed alongside her elegant tour guide. "Stop me if you have any questions."

"Hmmm. Thanks," Paige said, more than just a little overwhelmed as they passed through the living room and into the equally impressive den, where one full wall was devoted to photographs.

It was an interesting glimpse into Dustin's life, featuring her host, who was practically a stranger, with a variety of friends, celebrities, politicians, and also a number of travel shots. There were photographs of Dustin skiing in Gstaad, Dustin with his arm around an exotic girl in a deserted-looking beach cove, Dustin in Japan with an army of Japanese kids, all grinning deliriously.

"What are you going to do, with Dustin out of the country for so long and his company sold? Are you going to continue to work for him?" Paige asked Evonne curiously.

"As you may have already guessed, Dustin's a pretty unusual guy, and extraordinarily generous . . ." Evonne smiled, glancing fondly over at a photograph of her boss where he appeared to be smiling back at her. "First of all, he sold his company—but he still has a lot of business interests I'll be keeping an eye on. There'll be some minimal correspondence. But for the most part he says *he's* getting a vacation, so *I* might as well get one, too. When he gets back, we'll both go back to the *grind.*"

"Was he ever married?" Paige asked, noticing how many different females were represented in the gallery of photo memories. On closer examination there appeared to be a recurrence of only one.

"Yes. Jana." Evonne's eyes seemed to gravitate to the pretty brunette.

Just as Paige was thinking it was odd that he would have so many pictures of his ex-wife hanging on the wall, Evonne began to explain how his wife had died in a plane crash about five or six years ago, while taking flying lessons. There had been some kind of mechanical failure and the plane had gone down over the Santa Monica mountains. "Dustin didn't even know she was taking lessons," Evonne said, frowning. "She was doing it as a surprise because *he* was into airplanes and loved to fly. Can you imagine?"

Paige looked over at another picture of Dustin, seeing him differently, the gaiety diminished. "How long had they been married?"

"Just a few years. She was really special. Looked a lot like Jennifer O'Neill."

"Did they have kids?"

"No."

"I wonder why he never remarried."

"Jana was a pretty tough act to follow," Evonne said quietly.

They were both looking at a wedding photograph that was off to one side. The simple look of joy on their faces sent a chill through Paige.

Then, changing the subject, Evonne pointed a long manicured finger at the bar, where a bottle of champagne was angled into a silver ice bucket, arranged beside three fluted champagne glasses. "Dustin left that for you and your friends, although I understand there's just to be two of you now. He said since he couldn't be here to toast you all in person, he was toasting you in spirit."

He's going to be a tough act to follow, Paige thought to herself, noticing the expensive Cristal label. Generous was an understatement—giving Evonne six months to a year's semivacation, lending near-strangers his house, his cars. From what she had heard from Kit, he was even subsidizing the other climbers in the mountain climbing expedition. She was dying to ask Evonne if he'd been this generous *before* he sold his business for fifty million dollars. Something told her the answer to that question was yes.

Definitely impressed, Paige followed Evonne into the kitchen, where Dustin Brent's extraordinary taste was also in evidence. Everything was sleek, high-tech, and efficient-looking with black granite countertops, gleaming white cabinets trimmed in stainless steel, and industrial ovens and refrigerator.

One section of the kitchen was devoted entirely to Indian cooking, and Paige poked about, intrigued, as Evonne told her how, after he had spent some time there, Dustin got frustrated with the American preparation of what had become his favorite food, and he flew a chef out from New Delhi to give him private cooking instruction—even installed an authentic tandoor oven. *What a life,* Paige thought as Evonne toyed with a silver-framed topaz earring, then gestured her over toward a wall of cookbooks, explaining how half of them were translations of prized Indian editions.

"He is so obsessive that he once fell madly in love with a Picasso and, cash short, sold a building because he couldn't live without it," Evonne related, grinning, as they mounted a back set of stairs that led up to the second floor. "He loves watches," she added, as though to further prove her point. "Has a hundred and two different kinds, some of which are so rare, I need to keep an updated inventory for insurance. He loves sweaters—has literally pounds of cashmere . . ."

They had entered Dustin's bedroom, which was probably the sexiest bedroom Paige had ever seen. It was plush, large, and masculine, opening up onto a private office, a handsomely furnished gym, a steam room, a Jacuzzi, two huge walk-in closets, and as Paige pointed out with an amused chuckle, there was even a *bed.* There was something sensuously pleasing about the sheer extravagance, the pounds of cashmere sweaters piled neatly one on top of the other in every imaginable color, and the endless rows of shoes, from buttery leathers and snakeskin to sneakers.

Paige envisioned borrowing a couple of those heavenly cashmeres, belting them and sticking in shoulder pads, adding an oversized blazer, and rolling up the sleeves. He even had a couple of interesting hats.

But after a brief tour through Dustin's bedroom, Evonne told Paige that it was to be the only off-limits portion of the house. There were four other bedrooms upstairs, all of them also exquisitely furnished, with bathrooms that seemed larger than her apartment.

Her *former* apartment, Paige reminded herself with a satisfied grin, still considering snatching a cashmere.

Later, standing under a rich spray of temperature-controlled water, lathering her hair in a sumptuous shampoo that smelled of fresh, tart California lemons, and not having to bump her elbows as she did so, Paige decided she was in love.

She was in love with her new life, with this house, with Beverly Hills. She was in love with the endless possibilities that appeared to await her here: Men, money, and sunshine. The recurrent theme prevailed. Something deep inside Paige made her feel like she was going to have it all. And for the first time in ages she felt focused. Focused and optimistic.

Paige stepped out of the shower and wrapped herself in a plush peach-colored towel. Peering into the steamy mirror, rubbing it to create a smudge of visibility, she found herself thinking about Tori and how perfect this particular guest suite would have been for her. It could have aptly been called the Georgia Peach Suite. There was silver-and-peach wallpaper in the bathroom, soft peach suede walls in the bedroom. Even the bed fittings had luxurious sprays of peach-colored palm fronds silkscreened onto them. As Paige entered the spacious peach-perfect room, enjoying the swankiness of it, she heard the doorbell ring.

Susan, at last, she thought, letting her towel drop onto the floor and snatching up her robe. She was only partially into it when she ran out to the staircase landing and saw Maria opening the door.

Looking bedraggled from her long drive from Stockton, Susan walked tentatively into the house, wearing jeans, a preppy-looking T-shirt, tennis shoes, and a look of complete awe on her face. Paige watched as Susan smiled self-consciously at the housekeeper, taking in her surroundings with great curiosity as she handed over her two modest-looking suitcases.

"You must drive like a snail . . ." Paige shouted down, welcoming her friend with a roguish grin. It was a little like being the first roommate to have arrived at the college dorm. Well, on second thought, *not quite.*

Tori caught a glimpse of herself in the mirror as she passed through the lobby of the Ritz Carlton Hotel on her way to meet her mother for lunch. She was glad to see that she looked as good as she felt. The image she reflected was tall, demure, and positively radiant. She had on a pale pink buttery leather pantsuit, the sleeves on her large extensively padded jacket pushed up to just below the elbows, an ivory silk Charmeuse sleeveless shirt, and a chunky silver necklace. Her skin-tight leather pants squeaked quietly as she walked, creating a rhythm to the tune in her head—a jaunty strain from "I'm Getting Married in the Morning." Of course, she wasn't really getting married in the morning, but she was getting married soon. *Soon.* God, it was still so hard to believe.

As she approached the dining room she was greeted by the tinkling sounds of fine china, silver, and crystal. It was one of those electric days, and she could feel heads turning to watch her. She met each pair of eyes with a confident smile, sharing her joy, knowing how infectious it was. Then, as she looked through the plush cactus-toned room that was architecturally high-tech but classical in decor, she spotted her mother already seated, regarding her menu through a pair of tangerine-colored granny glasses that matched her smart tangerine linen suit.

"Hi," Tori issued cheerfully, sliding into a rosewood-framed chair that was being pulled out for her by one of the many hovering waiters.

"Don't you look beautiful," her mother commented, looking up from her leather-bound menu and over her glasses, which were perched on the end of the same fine aristocratic nose that Tori had inherited.

"Thanks," Tori replied. "You look great, too."

Amanda Mitchell always did. Even when she went to the market she looked perfect, hair and makeup done. That was just her way. She believed in always looking one's best. To her, it was a matter of pride and self-respect. Looking especially striking today, her mother glanced down one last time to muse over a selection on her menu, then set it decisively aside, removing her glasses and moving on to the business of her daughter.

"Well, you did it," Amanda said in a congratulatory manner, taking a bite of her celery swivel and saluting Tori with a bright red Bloody Mary. Her elegant face was a mask that Tori had never been very successful at reading. Her mother had sounded pleased when she called to tell her about her engagement to Travis, but her happiness always seemed so controlled.

"Miracle of miracles, right?" Tori smiled. What the hell, she herself was sublimely happy and it would take more than her cynical, frustrated mother to crush her spirits. A waiter came over, and Tori ordered a Mirassou chardonnay that was available by the glass.

"I hate to bring this up, Tori, but when does Travis's divorce become a fait accompli?"

Tori had been waiting for her to bring it up. "He's at his lawyer's right now," she answered, prepared.

Amanda's thoughts seemed to be running in high gear. "Have you set a date?"

"We're hoping for sometime in December. It depends on what Sam says—his attorney."

Amanda's eyebrow arched.

"Look, I know you and Dad aren't exactly crazy about Travis, that you don't trust him. But just be happy for me, okay?" Tori realized she had been wrong about her uncrushable spirits; they were definitely now on the decline. In only a few short moments Amanda had managed to burst her beautiful bubble. Tori sat up straight and looked over toward where the waiter had put in her drink order, suddenly needing it. She studied a porcelain fruit arrangement on the wall.

"We like Travis." Amanda's voice was silky and composed. "It's just that his track record doesn't exactly make me want to run out and bet my life savings on him."

"You never were the betting kind," Tori joked, intent on keeping things light. But Amanda didn't even smile. "Look, Travis takes getting remarried *very* seriously. He made a mistake with his first wife—we all make mistakes—and he's being very cautious this time around."

Amanda opened her mouth to say something, then stopped herself, emitting a clipped sigh. Tori knew it was a trap. That's what Amanda did when she wanted to say something that was most likely out of line.

"What?" Tori asked, in spite of her better judgment, aware that she was falling for old bait.

"Nothing."

Like hell. "C'mon, Mother, what?" Tori insisted impatiently.

Her drink arrived and she took a soothing sip of it, noticing how at all the other tables people seemed to be having such a wonderful time, chatting gaily, waiting for the Ritz Carlton's Friday luncheon fashion show to begin. Anxious for the distraction, she glanced around to see if there were any models yet on the floor. Then, in response to her mother's pregnant silence, she asked tersely, "What is it you're *dying* to say?"

"Do you really think Travis loves you enough?"

Tori felt like standing up and walking out. She looked at her mother, more astonished than angry. "What do you mean *loves me enough*? He wants to marry me—"

"He didn't initiate a proposal—"

"Maybe he's not the initiating type—"

"You gave him an ultimatum, Tori. Marry me or I take off for California—"

"I didn't mean it as an ultimatum, and I didn't present my leaving that way. I had a terrific opportunity to move to California, and I thought why the hell not." Tori fingered the lion-and-crown logo on her wineglass, trying to contain herself. "What did you expect me to do? Just stay? Leave the relationship as it was? *You're* the one who was always complaining about it."

Amanda took a deliberate sip from her drink, not replying right away. "You could have broken up with him but still stayed in Atlanta."

Tori thought, *Why am I even arguing with her? I'm getting married. I'm happy. Who cares what she thinks?* Then she went on anyway. "I still think it would have been the best thing for me to move to California, if things hadn't worked out with Travis. New surroundings, new people, and I'd have been too far away from him to cave in, as I've been *known* to do in the past."

It was a fact that aggravated Amanda to distraction.

"Travis needed a good kick in the pants," Tori went on more tolerantly, since in the end things had worked out as she wanted. It was just going to take a while for the security of that to sink in. "He may *never* have taken the initiative," she continued. "He would have left everything as it was, comfortable. He doesn't care about getting married. *I* do."

"How can you marry someone who doesn't want to marry you?"

"I think he *does* want to marry me."

"He doesn't want to lose you; that's all you really know for sure. He's making this decision under duress. . . ."

Tori couldn't have felt less hungry when their waiter reappeared to take their order. She listened to her mother requesting the cold veal roast with tuna sauce and *viande de Grissons.* It was exactly what Tori had thought she wanted, but her appetite had vanished along with her joy. "I'll have the fresh fruit and cottage cheese," she said, not because it sounded good, but because it was light. Then she decided that her mother was simply being her usual negative self, that Travis did want to marry her, and that she was allowing herself to get psyched out. The purpose of this lunch was to talk about the wedding, not to analyze Travis's motives. After lunch they were on their way to select an engagement ring. That had been Travis's idea. And that's what Tori wanted to focus on. She wanted to go back to feeling elated.

What happened next made it possible. Like a messenger from the heavens above, the waiter returned with a frosty silver ice bucket containing a bottle of Travis's favorite champagne. "Miss Mitchell," he said with a warm smile, as though appreciating the romantic gesture immensely, "compliments of Mr. Travis Walton. He said he'd see you all later at Tiffany's. And something about going easy on a guy. Keep the rock moderate."

Tori let out an audible sigh of relief, thanking the waiter with more gratitude than he could possibly understand. Her confidence flipped back into place, and she eyed her mother, feeling happy and even a little powerful from the win. She wanted to kiss Travis for not letting her down.

Chapter 6

Paige and Susan were already taking full advantage of their gracious new habitat, ensconced in the swirling mist that rose up and out of the steamy outdoor Jacuzzi into the pleasant evening air.

It was a warm lazy summer night, and they had had the best time out at dinner, celebrating their arrival in their new city, talking about the lives they had left behind, speculating about the new lives that lay ahead of them.

"Cliché or no cliché, I think it's really happened. I think I died and went to heaven," Susan said, adjusting her shoulder blades down to the hot rush of water penetrating from the jet, sipping blithely at the champagne Dustin Brent had left for them. She closed her big blue eyes for a moment, sighing pleasurably, then quickly reopened them, half afraid this perfect picture might have vanished. Happily Dustin's immense, breathtakingly landscaped backyard hadn't just been an alcohol-induced hallucination.

Probably enjoying themselves as much as she was, she thought, punchy by now, were the army of crickets who appeared to be out in full force tonight. She watched them darting capriciously in and out of the glow of opalescent lights spread throughout the luscious grounds, where there were lovely beds of flowers, a couple of great old trees with massive branches that looked ripe for climbing, and a large rectangular swimming pool, which gleamed invitingly beneath the moonlight, making it look tempting enough to jump into as soon as the heat from the Jacuzzi got to be too much.

Paige yawned and drained what was left of her drink, reaching over to the nearly empty bottle of champagne and refilling her glass. "I'm getting spoiled. After Kit's wedding, and this, I don't think I'll be able to go back to the cheap stuff," she said, tasting the Cristal with emphasized relish. She maneuvered her bare chest back down beneath the water, grumbling that her breasts weren't large enough to warrant above-water status.

Susan laughed, embarrassed, unaccustomed to Paige's brashness but assuming she would get used to it. Her own breasts, which were certainly smaller than Paige's, were in clear view, and now, self-conscious, she too slid deeper into the water. How could Paige, who had such a ravishing figure, even dream of complaining about it? *It must be hell being an actress and having all that sort of thing count so much,* she thought.

"So, are you going over to Kit's law firm tomorrow?" Paige asked her.

Susan had set up the appointment the moment she had made up her mind to move, and she nodded yes. "Kit also recommended a couple of other firms. I'd like to stay in labor law, and they really don't do that much of it over there. Her firm is mostly entertainment, some real estate . . ."

"Yes, but her firm is *lucky,*" Paige pointed out, grinning as she brought her glass back up to her lips. "It produced George. Don't forget, we've moved out here to upgrade our *personal* lives. Jobs are easy to come by, but I'll wager Georges are not. What do we want to do, meet a bunch of poor laborers?"

Susan laughed again. Paige had had her in stitches all night. "I could represent the other side, you know," she quipped, feeling a little like a traitor as she said it. In Stockton she had always gained such great satisfaction representing people upon whose lives she felt she had a real effect. Her father had often worked under unsatisfactory conditions out on the docks, and even though she had dealt primarily with agricultural labor organizations, she felt a particular zeal about her work.

Paige meanwhile cocked her head to the side as though she had forgotten about the possibility of the other side, and now approved. After thinking about it for a moment longer, she sighed with a distinct look of regret. "I wish I'd gone to law school or business school . . ." she said.

"Why?" Susan asked, amused.

"It's so easy for you," Paige replied levelly. "I have no idea what I'm going to do. I have experience in only one area, and it's an area in which you get almost no credit for your dues paid. Either they like the way you look for the role or they don't. You're so dependent on luck."

"It's not too late. Go to law school."

They were talking through a cloud of alcohol.

"First I'd have to go to college." Paige eyed Susan with a tough little laugh that seemed almost defensive, repositioning herself in front of another jet. "I'd always thought it was a big waste of time," she explained. "I knew exactly what I wanted and I thought sitting in a classroom, fooling around with all that sorority shit, wasn't going to get it for me. I wanted to get out there and work. Money was another factor, since I wasn't exactly an ideal candidate for a scholarship," she conceded woozily.

"So, go back to school now," Susan advised.

But Paige only laughed again. "Can you picture me sitting in a classroom for the five or six years it would take to get a degree that would be of any value?"

Susan couldn't, but clearly neither could Paige. Her green eyes narrowed thoughtfully. "I haven't changed," she admitted honestly, wringing out the wet ends of her long honey-colored hair and twisting it all up into a thick knot. "I still can't sit still like that. It's a function of genetics. You're either born a student, or you're not. Even talking about it for this long makes me feel claustrophobic. *Confined.* Which is how I always felt at school. Like a racehorse being held back and made to wait through a set of tiresome directions when all I wanted to do was run."

Susan watched as Paige let her hair tumble back down beneath her shoulders.

"That was one of the advantages of being an actress," Paige
went on, polishing off what was left of her champagne. "You
could be a lawyer, doctor, head of some exciting empire, without
the dull grind of school or the job itself. You'd get to wear the
look, play the role, even speak the language. Then by the time
you were good and sick of it, you'd get to throw that identity
away and pick up a new one."

"In that case, I guess you must have really gotten into the cat
persona, hanging on to it for four and half years," Susan teased,
draining what was left from her own glass, then ducking as Paige
delivered a curtain of water, fast and hard in her direction.

"Very funny," Paige admonished, laughing and squinting as
the wave of water sprayed in both their faces. "As long as you're
going to be my roommate, you could be a little more supportive,
you know . . ."

"Sorry, I couldn't resist," Susan replied tipsily, still blinking
water out of her eyes. She snatched up the bottle of Cristal just as
Paige was going for it.

There was a brief silence as Paige waited to reclaim it, seemingly lost in thought. "Oh, hell, I don't want to work anymore,
anyway," she said, watching as the last few drops of champagne
detached themselves from the neck of the bottle and dribbled into
her glass.

"Why? What do you want to do, besides snare yourself some
terrifically rich guy?" Susan asked her. Things were definitely
starting to get blurry, and she realized she was on her way to
becoming absolutely smashed.

"I guess marry him and let him take care of me for the rest of
my life. Acting should be as good a background as any for stepping into the role of a high-society wife," Paige allowed, raising
an eyebrow and smirking.

"Not a very liberated vocation, Paige," Susan chastised.

"Who do you think you're kidding? *That* kind of liberated I've
been since I was twelve years old. Now I'm ready for the ultimate
liberation of not having to worry anymore. I'm ready to hand
over the reins."

"Just make sure you like the carriage you're getting into."

"Do I look like a girl who would get into the wrong carriage?"

Between the champagne, the heat from the Jacuzzi, and all the excitement of moving, Susan thought she was going to dissolve into another laughing jag. She also thought she was seeing things, and she turned to Paige with a low perplexed giggle. "Do you see what I see? Or am I just too drunk for words?"

As she said it, Paige's mouth dropped open, and they both looked over toward the figure that seemed to have appeared from out of nowhere. It was Tori, still dressed in pale pink leather from earlier that day, with makeup smeared around her eyes, and a pitiful expression on her pretty face.

"I'm just so filled with rage," Tori explained to them later in a broken voice, tears continuing to wash down her face, catching on the ridges of her long dark lashes. She tried to blink them away, looking up toward the sky, which had that middle-of-the-night look to it, the blackness gradually diminishing, the spray of stars growing fainter.

The three of them were well into another bottle of champagne, swacked and lying on lounge chairs by the Jacuzzi. They were wrapped in their host's lush terry robes, of which he kept a fresh supply in the pool house, listening to Tori cry her heart out as she told them of the heartbreak and humiliation she had undergone in the last twenty-four hours.

The day had begun with her feeling higher than she could ever remember feeling. That lofty but precarious pinnacle of euphoria had her feeling powerful and victorious. Exalted from her win. She was Rocky, with her hands flung high in the air and cheering. Feeling invincible. Gloating over her mother's lack of faith in her. Feeling eternally grateful to Travis and allowing herself to love him even more than she had ever thought possible.

She and her mother had gone to Tiffany's as planned and, as Tori tried on one beautiful ring after another, even her iceberg mother had melted and was giving in to the joy that had her daughter nearly delirious.

The small white bright stones symbolized a dream come true. Each little flicker that bounced off the precious stone sparked something significant in Tori's heart. One spark for the wedding scene she had always believed she would have with Travis. Another spark for kids. Memories collecting in advance of the events.

But then her whole world had come tumbling down, her hopes and dreams and happy projections, right along with her pride. While she stood before the elegant counter at Tiffany's with a black velvet tray of diamond rings glistening in front of her and the one she liked best sparkling on her finger, Travis phoned to call the whole thing off.

Falteringly, he had tried to pin it on his attorney. But his meandering excuses rang false and all too familiar—the thrust of his plea, as usual, postponement.

Midway through, Tori had cut him off, catching the impact of her mother's look and knowing deep in her heart that she would never fully recover from this moment.

"If I hadn't had you all to come to, if I hadn't had that blessed airline ticket staring me in the face, my things all packed, I don't know what I'd have done," Tori emphasized in a bewildered fashion. Then she laughed for a moment, more as an effort to stop herself from crying than anything else.

"You know those movies you see where the character's completely lost it—" she sniffed, taking a brief breath again. "Where she stays holed up in her once attractive apartment that's now a complete wreck, as she is, collapsed into an alcoholic stupor until she either kills herself or someone comes to the rescue—well that's how I feel. If I hadn't have had you all, that poor stupid fool would have been me—my scenario down to the letter. Only maybe I'd have gone and bought a gun in the middle of it all, and shot Travis right in the goddamn . . ."

"Balls!" Paige finished for her.

Poor Tori nodded in accord. She held absolutely no resemblance to the cool, composed southern belle they had met at the wedding, and Susan's heart went out to her. Even after consuming nearly a whole bottle of champagne, Tori couldn't seem to get anesthetized. She was shattered beyond words, mesmerized by her own anger. She looked as though she really could have killed Travis. Paige, outspoken as ever, said she should have.

"God, when I think of all those years I wasted with him—" Tori said fervently, sitting up.

"Uh-uhhh. You can't do that—" Paige interrupted, rising and swaying a little as she walked. "You can't think about that. It's history—*he's* history. You've got to bury him."

There was something to the concept of Travis six feet under ground that seemed to cheer Tori up, and for the first time that evening she actually smiled. "I'd like to *really* bury him," she said, pantomiming the act of holding a pistol, extending her arm toward an imaginary target. The champagne had restored some color to her cheeks, and contemplating revenge, instead of just feeling sorry for herself, seemed to bring back the sparkle to her dark, exotic-looking eyes. With a steady arm, she pretended to pull the trigger, jerking back afterward as though the gun had a nice kick to it.

"Good riddance Travis whatever-your-last-name-is . . . was." Paige proclaimed, satisfied, her eyes fixed on the spot where Travis's dead body would have fallen.

"The only proper thing to do now is to hold a funeral for him," Susan joked, playing along with them. Then she snickered, wondering where in a swank place like this she would be able to find a shovel.

"Susan, now that's a great idea," Paige said, looking surprised that it had come from her. Completely blotto by now, she tripped over one of the champagne bottles on her way to scout for a burial spot, her speech reflecting a mounting enthusiasm. "I think it would be an ideal form of therapy," she said. "To figuratively bury the bastard. Enact a funeral."

Tori seemed sold on the idea.

Susan, who had only been joking, thought it an absurd one. There definitely wasn't going to be a dull moment living with these two, and she rose to her feet after Tori did, feeling slightly silly, but enjoying herself as she padded along the cold ground behind them.

Paige was the one to finally locate a shovel. It was in a storage shed outside the pool house. There was also a rake, which they took as well.

With everything so beautifully manicured, it wasn't easy to find a spot that they could in good conscience dig up, but after a while of giddy hunting, they decided on a spot beneath a tree.

Tori's only regret was that it was in the shade. She said she would have preferred that he have to bake in the hot sun instead.

Standing barefoot on the cool, grainy-feeling dirt, in their matching robes, the three of them took turns digging.

"I've never presided over a funeral before, but I'll wing it," Paige declared.

Susan chuckled, then glanced over at Tori, who was staring down miserably at the ground they had messed up.

Paige came over to put her arm around the tearful brunette. "Now," she said gently, "first we need to throw something in there—do you have a picture of Travis, anything else that he's given to you?"

Tori closed her eyes for a moment, her lips pursed tight against tears. She took a deep drink from her champagne glass in an effort to ward off the sobriety she felt seeping back in. "I've got a couple of pictures in my wallet—" she offered, going for another strong swallow.

After she had returned and handed over the collection of wallet-sized photographs, she watched Paige and Susan examining them. Some of them had Tori and Travis together, arm in arm, others had him alone. It was a weird feeling. Part of her wanted them to tell her how "darling" he was. After all, she was sharing with them photographs of the man she loved and was only *trying* to hate. She actually found herself looking over their shoulders, repressing an urge to narrate: *this one was taken at the park at a company picnic when we first started dating . . .*

God, was it possible that she could ever really get over him?

"He's cute," Paige admitted, shuffling through the photos a second time. "But he's dead," she reminded them, jarring Tori as she let the precious mementos drop out of her hand and into the appropriated plot.

Tori was infuriated by her impulse to bend down and retrieve them, and instead handed her glass brusquely over to Paige. "Wait a minute," she said, reaching to unfasten the chain around her neck with fresh determination. "Let's do this thing right." Feeling a renewed sense of anger over what he had done to her, she let the thin gold strand slither down in beside the pictures.

It seemed like a brazen thing to do and she felt fortified by the act, by the approval she was getting from Susan and Paige, who she could see saluting her from out of the corner of her eye. Spurred on, trying to ignore the ache in the pit of her stomach, Tori hurried across the yard again, toward her pile of clothes by the Jacuzzi where she snatched up a pair of great-looking white snakeskin pumps Travis had given to her just a few weeks ago. She was about to add them to the heap, when Paige made a fast seizure.

"Now, let's not get carried away," Paige intercepted, wriggling into the stylish shoes, which appeared to fit, pivoting smoothly around in them to flash a B.A. over Travis's grave.

Tori couldn't have been more astonished at the sight of Paige's bare ass posed so irreverently and she laughed, feeling a hot crimson blush invading her cheeks. "God, Paige, you're wicked," she chided breathlessly. "Positively *disgraceful . . .*" They all shrieked with laughter, collapsing drunkenly into one another's arms until there were tears rolling down their cheeks.

Susan wondered out loud if they weren't all going to be punished for their sacrilege.

Paige simply beamed, clearly too crocked to care. "As long as we're at it," she suggested, "We might as well bury all old ghosts. Travis won't mind sharing his plot, Tori, will he?" Unconcerned whether he would or not, Paige went cheerfully about refilling all their glasses, then threw the empty amber bottle, which was the expensive champagne's trademark, carelessly into the grave alongside Tori's jewelry and photographs. "Susan, you could throw in what's-his-name from Stockton, and I could throw in . . ." Paige giggled, peering down. "Gee, I wonder if there's room down there for my menagerie of failed love affairs?"

"Here, dig a little deeper," Susan remarked, stooping down to retrieve the shovel and handing it back to Paige, who obligingly extracted some additional dirt before launching into her solemn address:

"In memory of our dearly beloved Travis-shithead-Walton—"

"She's a natural at this," Tori whispered.

Paige cast a reproachful look their way, then resumed her oratory: "We lay you to rest, beneath the sod . . . ashes to ashes, dust to dust . . . You tried to be a decent human being, but alas,

you failed, leaving in your wake one very distressed individual."
With mock sincerity, Paige looked away from Travis's imaginary
remains, over to Tori for a moment, then back again. "To your
dearly beloved ones gathered here today, I say, 'Rejoice! The son-
of-a-bitch is dead!' "

"What about the other guys in there? We can't forget about
Billy, you know," Susan quipped.

Paige pondered for a moment. Then suddenly remembering
the glass in her hand she raised it up into the air. "Let's toast
them," she suggested expansively. "To . . . Oh, screw 'em.
Let's toast ourselves instead. To *us*! I think we're terrific."

To complete the ceremony, all three women lifted their glasses
and smashed them a bit too heartily against one another's, causing the costly Baccarat crystal to break and fall into the grave.

"I sure hope we find those Beverly Hills billionaires we moved
out here to meet, *soon,* " Paige said grimacing down at the wreck-
age and wondering how much more in debt they were going to
actually be by the time Dustin Brent returned.

Chapter 7

Paige was among the solo diners lining the south wall of Nate and Al's Delicatessen, the crowded, famous Beverly Hills deli where she had been going every day for breakfast since she arrived in L.A. a week ago. It was a good spot for viewing and eavesdropping. Everyone there chatted casually with the waitresses, who zipped back and forth past their tables, with a large percentage of their customers' morning diets committed to memory. Who took decaf and who took regular. Who was supposed to be watching their cholesterol and who their salt. The small individual banquettes were built close together, so it was easy for Paige to pick up interesting snatches of conversation. The atmosphere was friendly, clublike.

By all accounts, Nate and Al's served as a kind of commissary for the two most prominent industries in town—show biz and real estate—congregating beneath one roof, and often at one table. When the movers and shakers of the small inbred community weren't actually making deals, they were "schmoozing," as Paige had heard it called, picking each other's brains before, during, or after a plate of well-prepared lox, eggs, and onions, and several cups of good hot coffee.

Paige found it entertaining to watch as she brought her own

cup of coffee up to her lips, grateful for the rich aroma and smooth wake-up taste. It was exactly what she needed to make it through another day of pounding the pavements of the job market jungle.

Auditions in New York had been rough, but at least she was well known on the circuit there. She had friends and experience, which afforded her some respect. Trying to get a regular job was a different story. For Tori and Susan, looking for a job was a breeze. Armed with college educations, master's degrees, a doctorate of law for Susan, real estate credentials for Tori, they were exploring all kinds of interesting-sounding alternatives. But Paige was starting at the lowest rung of the ladder, discovering that making a career change without the passport of a college degree or job experience made her practically unemployable. Nobody cared that she had been in this musical or that. This was Hollywood. An out-of-work actress was an out-of-work actress.

Thinking she might meet a steady flow of executive types who occupied the dozens of high-rise buildings in sleek, clean-looking Century City, Paige had begun her search at a Century City employment agency.

Expecting to take them by storm, she had breezed in, looking spectacular, anticipating a surplus of options. Who wouldn't want to hire her? She was bright, attractive, dynamic. She felt capable of doing anything. Just teach her the role and she would play it.

But to her great dismay, she found it did not work like that. If anything, her looks and energy seemed to antagonize the woman processing new applicants. Paige was handed a pile of paperwork, and then herded off into a room filled with other applicants, where she was instructed to fill out the lengthy questionnaire and, afterward, to submit to a ghastly examination.

Full of problematic spatial-relations puzzles, ambiguous multiple-choice probes, the test made her feel like an idiot. It was absurd; she wasn't applying for a job as an aeronautical engineer. So why start examining her on complicated mathematical equations, multiplication and division of percentages and many-figured fractions? Nor was she trying to pass herself off as a historian. After the math portion came the requisitioning of dates of historical events, names of particular battles, where they had been fought, and who had led them. Part three veered off into her absolute worst subject, geography, where they caught her up short on capitals, lakes, even topography of mountains. Who gave a damn about which body of water connected this state or that, or what the capital of Turkey is? Her only concern with mountain heights was in respect to a growing phobia she had developed lately about any kind of heights.

Through a glass window, she had been able to see another group of applicants hunched over typewriters, being tested for speed. After that they would be expected to demonstrate their shorthand skills, as would Paige, even though she had already told them she didn't know shorthand.

Staring helplessly through the window, watching all those fingers flying across the typewriter keys, and positively mortified that she didn't at least have a pocket calculator to cheat a little with on the math portion, Paige slipped the mostly unanswered test papers into her purse. She had been far too embarrassed to leave them behind when she walked coolly out of the room, feeling very "un-cool" inside.

The classifieds had proved equally futile, most of them bogus employment agency plants looking to lure prospective applicants into their offices so they could make commissions off them. The tantalizing job descriptions you *saw* listed and appeared to qualify for just happened to be taken. . . . However, they had others, if you could just come in and interview.

Paige had had it with their interviews. She was perfectly capable of finding a job on her own. Her focus being, exclusively, where to meet rich men.

Today her plan was to hit Rodeo Drive. If she failed to meet a score of rich men there, while working in one of the more pricey boutiques, she figured she could at least befriend some of their rich female clientele who might fix her up.

She was also thinking of interviewing at a couple of the higher-end health clubs to teach dance and aerobics. At least the rich men there would be on the young side and in good shape.

"I still don't know what I'm gonna have," said an elderly man in loud plaid slacks and a short-sleeved yellow shirt, who had

been sitting in the booth beside Paige's for a while, browsing
through the sports section of the newspaper.

"Have *hope,*" the waitress said, hurrying past him toward
someone else, who was signaling for his check. It was probably a
line she used all the time, but Paige was in the kind of mood in
which it felt meaningful. *Hope.* What did that mean to her? Finding a job today? Or, better still, finding a wealthy prospect who
would eliminate her need to do so?

After parking at Bonwit Teller's, where she was assured of
wrangling a free parking validation, Paige crossed Wilshire Boulevard, heading north on Rodeo. From the prominent corner
there where Dayton met Rodeo, Giorgio's blinding yellow-and-
white striped awning announced the shopping landmark, and
Paige decided to make it her first stop.

Could Judith Krantz really have been alluding to this when
she wrote *Scruples?* she wondered, disappointed as she entered
the cluttered emporium and looked around, sneezing immediately from all the Giorgio cologne being sprayed out into the air
of the store's entrance. There were two pretty black girls, dressed
alike, standing at the doorway smiling promotional smiles and
spraying the heavy scent. Paige smiled back at them. When
you're applying for a job, you smile at everyone, just in case they
carry some weight in the hiring process. Though it was doubtful
the perfume girls would. Over at the counter, to her left as she
walked in, were two more perfume girls, and Paige approached
them, allowing another couple to edge in front of her, and then
hanging back patiently.

The place was jam-packed.

There was glitz all right, but missing was the aura of elegance
and haut monde she had expected to see. It wasn't anything like
the chic-looking boutiques Kit had taken them to when they had
been out to L.A. for the wedding.

The very yellow shop was overflowing with hordes of shoppers
who looked to Paige like they had just been dropped off by a tour
bus. She half expected to see racks of souvenirs and postcards,
sets of Giorgio coasters. Instead, she saw racks of three-thou-
sand-dollar dresses, all squashed together, as though there were a
sale going on, but there wasn't.

It was true, everything she had heard about the swank institution existed; there was the long, gleaming oak-paneled bar serving up cocktails and cappuccinos, the famous pool table, the glittery fashion accessories, the astonishing price tags.

But for Paige, the glamorous myth of Giorgio was definitely dispelled, and she walked out without bothering to go any further.

Collecting a series of discouraging No—but do check back's, she maintained her pace, heading doggedly north up Rodeo, refusing to let her confidence erode.

After all, this was something she was doing just for the money, she kept reminding herself. It was temporary; it wasn't a career. So she couldn't let it get her down. It was an interim thing.

It was just that she hadn't counted on it being so tough, she thought, exiting another shop, with her sixth rejection, deciding the next time if they asked her if she had any experience she would lie and say yes.

Then she started debating if she wouldn't be better off taking her portfolio around, getting an L.A. agent. She could try and do some commercials, audition for some soaps, sitcom work . . .

Paige was in the middle of an old but updated daydream, when she strode past Jerry Magnin, Polo, and then another men's store called Mr. Guy. It struck her, as she nearly collided with a good-looking man walking out of the last shop, carrying an armload of packages, that a high class *men's* clothing store could turn out to be the best her yet. She and the gentleman smiled apologetically at one another, then with renewed spirit, Paige retraced her steps and went to inquire about positions inside all three. The expensive merchandise ranged from hip to designer high-styled, indicating that the men buying them might just gorgeously fit the bill.

Things were looking up; she collected two applications, and then a third at Ted Lapidus, which was for men and women.

On the other side of the street was a striking complex of small individual designer boutiques such as Valentino, Maud Frizon, Krizia, and even a baby boutique sporting big labels and big price tags for little people.

Kit had taken Paige, Tori, and Susan there, on their first day

visiting L.A. Paige remembered it specifically because the name
of the shop was Tori Steele, and they had teased Tori at the time,
that this could have been hers, if she had been lucky enough to
have snared the flamboyant tycoon before the other Tori did.
"It's just a shame," Kit had joked. "Look at all the great dis-
counts you could have gotten for us."

According to an article Kit had read just last week in *Women's
Wear Daily,* the money behind this enterprise came from a fabu-
lously wealthy Texan who married a woman twenty-five or so
years younger than he, and then financed all this as a plaything
for her, not caring at all if it made money or if he dropped a
million bucks on it a year.

It was just the kind of fairy tale Paige envisioned for herself, as
she browsed her way through the series of in-vogue boutiques,
passing from one into the other through connecting interior
doorways. With a tinge of impatience she fingered the luscious
merchandise, regarding the other women in there who were casually trying things on, accumulating great piles of the fine apparel,
culling through their selections. *Soon,* she told herself, watching
them enviously, smiling evasively at the shop girls who were politely offering assistance.

Just as she was going to ask about a job opening, she spotted a
ravishing red jeweled evening gown that she was dying to try on.
She stole a glance at the price tag and nearly laughed out loud,
feeling something else deep in the pit of her stomach. She had to
have this dress. It was ridiculous, really, because it was fifty-five
hundred dollars, but Paige's thoughts were racing, the way they
did when she had already made her mind up about something,
and was hell-bent on making it happen.

Impulsively, she removed it from the rack, and asked to try it
on. It felt extremely heavy.

"I think this is one of the best things in his collection this
year," said the trim, smartly put-together salesgirl, with a heavy
French accent. The *he* she was referring to was Valentino. "I
think it would look *great* on you!"

It sure as hell should, for fifty-five hundred dollars, Paige
thought dryly. *Fifty-five hundred dollars. She was really out of her*

mind. With the salaries she had been looking at, it would take her
forever to accumulate enough cash to even dream of buying it.

But Paige played along, enjoying being treated as a customer
instead of someone trying to get a job.

Once inside the small, mirrored dressing room, she slipped off
her own tight cotton skirt and blouse, then gazed longingly at the
dress before putting it on. Her shoes were all wrong so she kicked
them off, lest they ruin the effect. Then, as though reading her
mind, the saleswoman peeked inside and asked Paige what size
pump she took.

Moments later, Paige emerged from the dressing room, with
the shimmery gown hugging her long curvy shape, wearing a pair
of red satin pumps they had found for her, and looking positively
dazzling. The fabric was thin as air, and the tiny crystal beads
sewn delicately onto it sparkled as she moved, causing a definite
stir within the shop. The dress was strapless, with a well-con-
structed *bustier* that subtly pushed up the bosom. There were
fingerless red jeweled gloves that stretched up just above her
elbows. And a hip-length, loose-fitting red jeweled jacket with
large padded shoulders.

"It's absolutely divine on you, no?" the French saleswoman
effused.

Paige could not have been more in accord, and she grinned like
the cat who had swallowed the canary. It was amazing what a
fifty-five-hundred-dollar garment could do for you, she thought
giddily, unable to take her eyes off her reflection as she spun
demurely around to catch the gown from all angles. As she did
so, the same man she had almost bumped into in front of Mr.
Guy, passed by the front window of the store, and they caught
each other's eye.

He paused to regard her, nodding his head approvingly, playfully, as though he thought she should buy it.

In response, she tilted her head uncertainly, then narrowed her
sly green eyes, her expression querying You think so?

More emphatically this time, he nodded again, shifting his
heavy load of purchases to the other arm. As he did so, Paige
noticed he had acquired an additional shopping bag, this one
from the baby boutique next door.

Married? she wondered, *or maybe divorced and guilty.* She smiled broadly and decided to take a chance, pointing her finger toward him first, and then toward the dress she had on, creating a sign-language motion that was intended to read—You want to buy it for me?

His smile after that was even broader than her own. And she stood there with her hand poised on her hip, daring him. By this time the saleswoman and a few other people standing around had noticed what was going on. It was rather exciting. Nobody really knew if they knew each other or not, but they were dying to know what was going to happen.

"Is that your husband?" the saleswoman finally asked curiously, as though she somehow had already guessed that it was not.

Paige merely shook her head no. Her adrenaline was racing.

"Your boyfriend?"

"Uh-uh. No." She concentrated on the man's eyes, trying to read what was going on behind them. They were brown eyes, round and intelligent-looking, with deep creases beneath them. He looked to be somewhere in his late forties, early fifties. Was he generous? Was he rich? Was he going to walk away or come inside and sweep her off her feet? She almost fainted when he pushed the door open with his shoulder and walked inside.

By now, just about everybody in the shop was standing motionless, watching, some trying to be more subtle than others. If they had seemed blasé a few moments ago, puzzling over which fifteen-hundred-dollar blouse to buy, they weren't blasé now.

"She'll take it," he said, striding confidently toward them.

Paige stood positively dumbstruck. She was always weaving these fantastic episodes, but they didn't really materialize. She would fantasize the scenario, and then the guy would walk away. More likely than that, he wouldn't stop in the first place. At the very most, he'd stop for a brief moment, smile, and then walk on. Paige didn't know what to say. Everyone was standing around like statues, not sure if he was putting them on.

"She looks smashing in it . . ." the saleswoman ventured at last, clearly feeling ill at ease about saying anything at all, but anxious to make the sale.

When Paige felt his hand come to rest on her bare shoulder, she shivered, a delicious chill traveling from where his skin met hers and then coursing out in all directions. Money and power— an aphrodisiac? The world's most sublime.

Paige, who was always overflowing with gab, could not think of one thing to say. This was the part where they were supposed to fade out, in his gorgeous pad, the dress thrown down carelessly onto the floor, the two of them in bed.

There were a couple of plush mauve chairs over by a steel-and-glass table set up for sales transactions, and she watched as he unloaded his purchases onto them, turning gamely back to her afterward. He himself was dressed as though he frequented these shops. He had on a smart-looking black-and-gray twill blazer of a summer weight, handsomely tailored pale gray slacks, an elegant shirt flecked with gray, and an expensive-looking tie that brought it all together. His buttery rich charcoal shoes were positively scuffless. The only jewelry he had on was a Bulgari watch.

"We'll take the shoes, too," he decided, enjoying a few more moments of the suspense he was creating. "Are they comfortable?"

It was the first time he had actually addressed Paige and she swallowed awkwardly, clearing her voice, which seemed to have dried up on her.

"Hmmm. Very," she managed with surprising composure. Inside, she was a flurry of nerves. Who was this man? And why was he playing this game with her? He was like an apparition of her own creation, who had accidentally dropped into her real life. Most bizarre for her was that there were other people observing. Her daydreams had always happened in a bubble of privacy, but this was a daydream occurring out in the open.

Caught up in it, she smiled her most beguiling smile and walked across the room, modeling for him. The dress hugged tight across her hips and rear end, and she caught him appreciating the effect, regarding the shimmery fabric that draped down toward her ankles, restricting her stride somewhat, even though it was slit rather high in the front. The deeply cut red pumps made her legs look incredibly sexy beneath the gown, as they clicked across the black slate floor.

"What about an evening bag?" he asked, winking at Paige, then proceeding to roam the shop in search of one that might satisfy him. There were quite a few scattered around, displayed to accent different outfits. He went over to a particularly pretty one, which was shaped like a large egg, with variegated red-toned rhinestones covering its contoured surface. "Here, catch . . ." he said to Paige, raising his arm up and back, feigning a pass with the jeweled bag, as though it were a football and causing everyone to loudly catch their breath.

Paige broke up laughing. She thought he was the strangest but most intriguing man she had met in ages.

Please don't be married, she thought. The absence of a wedding band was a good sign, but inconclusive.

The saleswomen, from the looks they were exchanging with one another, clearly had to put up with a lot of crazy clientele, rock stars, brat-pack movie stars, the eccentric well-to-do from all over the world. The Frenchwoman assisting Paige hurried over to delicately retrieve the jeweled egg, as though it were a time bomb that needed to be detonated. "Judith Leiber," she said, naming the purse's renowned designer, presumably in justification of its undoubtedly dear price tag. "We just got this one in."

"Would you like that one or a different one?" he asked Paige considerately, maneuvering close enough for her to be able to breathe in the pleasant fragrance of his after-shave. His eyes were only several inches above her own and she felt them studying her, raising dozens of tiny goosebumps as they trailed down her neck, exploring the provocative cut of her neckline, and lingering on the daring exposure of skin there.

Feeling a tremor of excitement, she pursed her lips, considering, trying to sound nonchalant. "Goes great with the dress."

He grinned, then went over and got the purse again, arranging its gold strap over the curve of her shoulder, stealing a touch of flesh from where he shouldn't as he did so.

Her head was swimming by now, and she caught him with a sharp look that was more sportive than discouraging, as she watched him ease innocently out of the gesture. It was time for one of them to make the move. She took the plunge. "So, where are we going?" she asked him offhandedly, looking as if it were a crime not to be going somewhere divinely special indeed.

Their eyes met again, bold young green eyes connecting with savvy, more complicated brown eyes.

She nearly swooned when she saw him reaching into his pants pocket, pulling out a smart snakeskin billfold, and opening it up. "Carnival Night at the Nicky Loomis mansion," he replied with equal offhandedness. "As far as I'm concerned, it's L.A.'s main event."

For Paige it was definitely going to be.

Five and a half grand, phew! The price of his toys was rising sharply. He watched the skinny French broad nonchalantly tallying up the other items. Tack on another twelve hundred for the purse and an even four hundred for the Maud Frizon shoes.

What the hell, this sexy little bombshell in the hot red dress looked like she was going to be worth it. He didn't really give a damn what the total came to; it couldn't touch the kind of dough his wife shelled out regularly for her insatiable clothing appetite. She had a closet the size of this shop, and even with frequent recycling it was crowded. This little number was for him, for his pleasure, a fuck-toy for his frequent business jaunts to L.A. His father-in-law had at last done him a good turn when he expanded their operations to include California.

He never used to tell them he was married. But now he generally did. It wasn't the obstacle it used to be, so why bother with lying? With the proportion of single women to single men so unjustly balanced, women appeared to have a whole new mindset. There was a tough new breed out there bearing little or no conscience about man-stealing. He offered the surplus of single women, if not a serious relationship, a great time, great sex, and always great gifts. This one, like all the others, would probably think she was different, more special, that she could eventually get him to fall in love with her and leave his wife. That methodology seemed to be built into the female psyche. Marriage and kids. If the money didn't come from his wife's family, he might have been susceptible, vulnerable, he had to admit. There was grave temptation in a young, curvy thirty-year-old instead of Alicia, a gorgeous bod like this one, day in and day out, in bed and out of bed, causing other men to lose their minds with envy.

Not that Stan Parker had any right to complain. Already his situation was enviable. His wife, Alicia, was still reasonably attractive, intelligent. She made very few demands on him. And with her inherited wealth he had been accorded power, prestige, and a life he liked a great deal.

This was indeed one of the perks, he thought, enjoying that impressed look on Paige's spectacular face, as he peeled off one bill after another, telling her more about the big annual charity bash he was inviting her to. The party's host, Nicky Loomis, prided himself in throwing the most-looked-forward-to event in L.A.

Raised poor in Omaha, completely self-made, first as a National Football League star; then in his early thirties, taking over a beer empire; and then later going on to fulfill his grandest goals, owning important sports teams and building them into even bigger ones, going against the tide and constructing his own private sports arena for their games, Nicky Loomis had become a kind of living legend in the sports world.

His press dubbed him a wild man, always a girl on each arm wearing miniskirts because he was known to have a thing for miniskirts. His flamboyant ways were tolerated in the highest social stratum only because of his equally flamboyant charitable contributions. Such as this affair, which he held annually on his own private grounds, an estate made famous years ago by its original hotel baron owner. It was an event for which all stars showed up.

Movie moguls. Politicians. Other sports heavyweights and team owners. It would not be at all surprising to see Donald Trump or George Steinbrenner, Jerry Buss, or even Marvin Davis. People flew in from all over.

Since Nicky was a night person, the evenings were known to go on until four or five in the morning, when he would have set up a big breakfast buffet. He loved to party, probably had the best time of anybody there. And what the heck, two thousand bucks a head, a swell time, and the proceeds went to funding research for curing cancer.

Too bad the big bash was a couple of months away, Stan Parker thought, lamenting, watching this remarkable-looking woman watching him.

Too bad he had a plane to catch in a couple of hours and was on his way back home to Philadelphia, not scheduled to return to L.A. until then.

Those daredevil green eyes of hers were teasing him beneath a thick curtain of lashes. She had great-looking thick eyebrows, sandy colored, like her wild mane of hair that touched down almost to her ass. Rich, honey-colored skin, made for touching.

She would *definitely* think she was different from the others, more special, more clever, more capable of luring him away from his wife. Maybe she was.

When she headed for the dressing room to change clothes he decided to add a mysterious touch and leave before she reappeared—or before he broke down and spent the night, missing Alicia's father's birthday party. He would scribble a quick note on the back of a business card, instructing her to hold August sixth.

God, what a great ass she has, he thought as she kicked off the pumps with a rare flair, and then sashayed into the changing room. *Great ass and a great walk. Ol' Nick would probably try to snatch her for himself; she was just his type. Gorgeous and flashy-looking. The only thing missing was the cut-up-to-her-crotch mini-skirt.*

Although Nicky was single and Stan married, Stan still felt she would fare better with him. Nick was strictly only good for a one-night stand.

On a last impulse, he told the salesgirl to wrap up another Judith Leiber evening bag for him to take home to his wife. A couple of little Judith Leiber pillboxes also, the ones shaped like bunnies, with all the rhinestones, for his daughters.

Chapter 8

Travis Walton is sitting on the toilet, with his pants draped down below his knees, his underwear binding his calves, reading a Superman comic book. The elastic on the underwear is worn, stretched out, full of holes. He looks absurd, still wearing a shirt and tie, with a stupid smile on his face from something he just read in the comic strip. The tie has spaghetti sauce on it.

Tori felt a slight but encouraging pull of amusement, as the image of her former lover shifted. Now she had him wearing only his underwear, sweeping the pathways in front of their condo in Atlanta, with all the neighbors outside, watching him and laughing their heads off. A ferocious little mutt begins barking at him and he fights it off, scared out of his wits, holding the yelping animal off with the broom and hollering for help as the dog zips around behind him and takes a hungry bite out of the cotton Jockey shorts stretched across his buns.

"Laugh at your lover. Picture your lover in an absolutely asinine situation. See him sitting on the toilet reading a Superman comic book or cleaning streets in his underwear while the whole world laughs at him."

Bravo, Tori thought to herself, deep into the book Paige and Susan had picked up for her called *Breaking Free: 20 Ways to*

Leave Your Lover. It was a behavioral approach to getting a lover out of one's system, written by a Hollywood hypnotherapist who had treated endless cases of heartache. The author posited that feelings are learned and could thus be unlearned by employing certain behavior modification techniques he had developed.

The point of the section on laughing at your lover was to get the lovesick to see their lovers in a ridiculous and inferior light, to knock them off their pedestal.

Tori had the book positioned discreetly in her lap, on top of a magazine, so that nobody could see the title. She was sitting in the reception room of Bennetton Development Company, waiting to be called upon for a job interview. She was about ten minutes early for her appointment and killing time, trying to exorcise Travis from her heart.

Burying him had helped only temporarily. Then his ghost rose up from its impromptu grave in Beverly Hills to haunt her, invading her soul with memories, conjuring up still vivid sensations —the way she felt when he kissed her, when he held her in his arms, when he made her laugh. Every time the phone rang, she would race to it with that flutter of excitement, her hopes strained, praying that it was him. She went through all these complicated machinations, conjecturing what she would say, what kind of position she would take, the deal she would propose. Her intricately conceived scenarios changed every other minute because she was thinking about him every other minute.

"Act the part of someone who no longer loves their lover," the book advised.

I can't, Tori thought futilely, *I do love him.*

"Imagery is at the heart of many behavior therapy techniques. Imagine you are falling out of love . . . You *are* falling out of love. Imagine it. Think as if it's happening. Pretend you no longer love this person. Images have great power. It's images that put you in love in the first place. The thought of how wonderful he is, how right for you, how appealing, how sensitive, how open, how considerate . . . Change your imagery! Change your self-image. You are a person who is not in love with anyone. See yourself that way . . ."

Tori was trying with all her heart to absorb the words like

medicine, to drink them in and find herself healed by the clear
and astute messages contained within the pages.

But as the book said, it wouldn't happen overnight.

"Tori Mitchell?"

Caught by surprise, Tori looked up, self-consciously snapping
the book on her lap shut as she did so.

"You're hired."

"What?" Still startled, Tori looked up into the eyes of a tall,
divinely attractive man, somewhere in his late thirties, with un-
styled hair the color of straw, which touched down in back to the
collar of his pink polo shirt. He had a thick, rugged neck, a deep
tan, a strong chin, good mouth, a small nose, and sexy peacock
blue eyes, which sparkled with arrogance.

Before Tori had a chance to slip it into her briefcase, he was
leaning down, examining the book she was trying to conceal in
her lap.

She was so embarrassed, she could barely think straight. He
laughed, showing off perfect teeth and terrible manners.

His lack of decorum worsened as he swept the book away from
her and began leafing through it, regarding her intermittently
over the pages as she attempted to snatch it back from him. She
knew she was blushing beet-red; her cheeks felt hot as coals, and
her pulse was going haywire.

He was chuckling, thoroughly entertained.

"Do you mind?" she asked mortified, finding herself wrestling
with him, a perfect stranger, a perfect jackass.

Before she knew it they were standing in a corridor, where he
had maneuvered out past the receptionist, through the door, and
into the maze of offices. The company was large, occupying a full
floor. Tori had followed him, seizing her things and hurrying
after him. She had not missed the receptionist's look, and she
wondered if this kind of thing went on often. Who was this jerk?

People nodded deferentially to him as they passed by with
assorted greetings, checking Tori out, curious.

"By the way, you have a *great* accent," he said, grinning at her
as he mimicked her southern lilt. Then he shook his gorgeous
head, indicating disapproval. "He's not worth it. Whoever he
is . . ."

Tori had calmed down somewhat, aware that she wasn't going to get her book back until he was good and finished with it, anyway. She smiled, a tight, tolerant smile. "Are you finished?"

" 'Make love in your lover's most unflattering position . . .' " He laughed vigorously, his broad athletic-looking shoulders rising up with amusement, the pink knit material accommodating the movement as he looked Tori up and down. "My guess is you don't have an unflattering position," he leered. " 'Recall all abuses . . .' This is pretty kinky stuff."

He was way out of line, and Tori was about to turn and leave. He could keep the damn book, for all she cared.

"I'm sorry. I don't know what happened to my manners," he apologized expansively, stopping her, taking her hand, and introducing himself with the same impetuous air. "Richard Bennetton. Successor to the throne of Bennetton Development Company. You're very pretty."

Tori gave him an icy once-over. He would not release her hand, and she was forced to continue to stand there under his toying gaze. Richard Bennetton. Son of *the* Bennetton. So, this cocky lunatic was the owner's son. It figured.

"Do you conduct all your interviews this way?" she asked him acidly.

"I never do anything the same way twice. It gets boring. So when could you start?"

Tori laughed, in spite of herself. "I don't think we've played out the interview part yet," she said, in a crazy way intrigued by him. He was spoiled but cute, giving a little boost to her badly bruised ego.

"Interview, schminterview. I have uncanny instincts about people. Especially gorgeous brunettes. You want the job? You're hired."

Tori was incredulous. Her résumé was good. But she would wager a week's salary that he had not even read it. "Just like that? Just because I'm a *gorgeous* brunette?"

"I was wildly impressed by your résumé."

Tori laughed again. "Yeah. Sure you were." A disturbing thrill passed through her as he tightened his grip on her hand and drew her closer. Warning signals went off in her head as she thought of

Travis and how impossible it had been working with someone
with whom she was involved. Working *for* someone with whom
she was involved would make for triple the madness.

Still holding her hand, Richard led her past his secretary's
vacant cubicle and into his office, directing her into a seat.

It was a large corner office with a spectacular view of the city.
The one wall that did not offer a view was covered in corkboard,
with blueprints and attractive color renderings of housing projects pinned to it. Richard went over and sat down in his plush
leather chair behind his big black granite desk that was cluttered
with paperwork. The only photograph Tori saw was one of Richard standing somberly beside an older man whom he resembled
so strongly that Tori presumed it was his father. There were no
framed wives to indicate he was married, no evidence of kids.

Richard was leaning back in his chair, twisting a rubber band
around his fingers. Her book he had tossed down onto the heap
of papers in front of him. "That's the old man," he stated, following her glance over to the picture on the wall, swiveling his chair
to get a good look at him. Then he turned back to Tori with a
little smirk that was hard to read. "You'll meet him. He still
drives us all crazy around here. If you want the job that is . . ."

"I'd like to hear about it first," Tori said, as two lights on his
phone lit up at the same time. Leaning back in her chair she
could see his secretary still had not returned to her desk, and she
wondered how long he would let the phone ring before he picked
up a line. Then she heard an out-of-breath female voice mutter-
ing to herself, "Hold on a minute," and then a more professional
sounding: "Richard Bennetton's office," as the calls were finally
answered. Craning her neck, Tori could see his secretary looking
completely harassed as she set down onto her desk a mountain of
brochures. Cradling the phone against her shoulder and stretching the extension cord, she moved to shut Richard's door, afford-
ing the two of them some privacy.

"Your background is in marketing, right?" Richard was saying, ignoring the momentary commotion. "You'd join our marketing department. We've got a new project that's pretty incredible, if I do say so myself." He was leaning so far back in his chair,
it looked as if it were going to break. "Our approach is brilliant.

No one's ever done it before. A prospective buyer comes to our showroom, which is on the site, sits down in front of a video screen complete with joy stick, and cruises the property where we're building a series of private, all-custom estates. We've simulated what it'll look like after it's built, using famous estates from Beverly Hills and Hollywood as prototypes. We've got mock-ups of the old place of William Randolph Hearst's mistress, Marion Davies. Douglas Fairbanks. Walt Disney. The Harold Lloyd estate. The Playboy mansion. The Kirkeby estate, where they used to film *The Beverly Hillbillies*. So it's actually a kick. The parcels are all between two and five acres, and the idea is to give the buyers a chance to see what kind of amazing spread they could have on their lot, if they wanted it. We whet their appetite, like you've whet mine."

Tori was trying to take all this seriously. She had heard a great deal about the project and thought it would be exciting to work on. It was Richard who was going to be difficult.

"So, can I buy you lunch?" he asked, rising restlessly to his feet, business abruptly concluded.

Tori hesitated, leery to say the least. "I've got plans," she lied unconvincingly.

He laughed, reading her loud and clear, then tossed her book back over to her. "If you want the job, it's yours," he told her, coming up behind her and touching her hair. "Just don't wait too long. You know how the saying goes: He who hesitates . . ." Richard completed his warning with an insinuating wink that solidified why she would be out of her mind to accept this job.

If she were the client, she would be wondering where all the money came from to pay for all this. Two floors of brand-spanking-new office space on a prime floor in one of downtown Los Angeles' new gorgeous skyscrapers located on recently renovated, prestigious Bunker Hill.

Nothing about Susan's new life in L.A. resembled her former life in Stockton. She had even had to go out and buy all new clothes. Paige and Tori had insisted that she dress for success. They told her she looked like a country bumpkin, drab, dull. No minced words. Plain Jane. Polyester Paula. So now she looked worse still, in her crumpled linen suit they had talked her into. "There's status to wrinkles," Tori had assured her. "The more wrinkles, the better the fabric. Silk, cotton, fine linen. You show me someone without dozens of creases, and I'll show you—"

"Synthetic Sue!" Susan had finished for her, getting the message loud and clear. Starch was out. You can take the girl out of the country, but you can't take the country out of the girl.

She couldn't believe that she was working here, in one of California's largest, most influential labor law firms, representing the enemy. She was going to have to be doing a lot of justifying to herself in order to sleep at night, a penalty for having switched sides from labor to management. She was in the camp of big business now. In a way, it erased some of the hypocrisies she had had to deal with before, the holier-than-thou contention of representing the *people,* when, in fact, often she was merely working with the other corrupt, out-to-conquer kingpins. Labor organizations may have originally begun for the good of the people, but everyone knew the union guns could be as bad, if not worse, than the business guns. In it for their own gains anyway, they were no longer altruistically fighting to help the workers. So who was she kidding; there were bullies on both sides. At least on the side of management, they made no bones about it. They were in business, out to net as much money as possible. Sweatshops were a horror of the past.

There! She sounded like management already. After only one day on the job.

The simple fact was, management paid more than double. In Stockton, representing labor, Susan earned around twenty-two thousand dollars a year. Now her salary was closer to fifty. Plus perks. The reason for this was that union lawyers worked on yearly retainers, whereas management traditionally billed clients by the hour. Hence, the fancy offices, the expensive cars the partners drove, and the first-class travel arrangements when travel was necessary.

So why did she feel so ambivalent, she mused, as she lifted her crumpled linen blazer from the hook on her door and worked it on, catching the shoulder pads on the shoulder pads of her wrinkled silk shirt. Her office was small but nice, infinitely prettier and neater-looking than any office she had had before. It had white grasscloth walls selected by the attorney before her, modern chrome and laminated made-to-look-like-oak furniture, a scaled-down sofa, occasional table, and two chrome upholstered occasional chairs on which clients or colleagues could sit. Susan's only design decision was going to be what poster art to buy for her bare walls, a task she planned to take care of now on her way home from work.

There was a poster shop in Westwood Village that her secretary had recommended, and Susan drove past the wide-stretching campus of UCLA, and then down crowded Galey Avenue trying to find it. The streets were already spilling over with students and devotees of Westwood, and it was not even dark yet. By eight o'clock, the village hangout would be a frenetic urban youth jungle, teeming with teenagers hanging out of loudly honking cars that ranged from their parents' fancy European models (Rollses and Ferraris not being at all uncommon), to beat-up Buicks and VWs from the other side of town. Susan caught sight of a parking spot being vacated and cut over toward it. Good parking spaces, when they were difficult to come by, always made her feel lucky. And she threw on her parking brake in a good mood.

There were some mimes, their faces painted white, lips, cheeks, and eyes done in exaggerated clown-fashion, holding court before a large crowd. Susan edged in to get a closer look. They were quite good, actually, and she laughed, caught up in the show as they acted out a jealous lover routine. One of them played the harmonica, and when the act was over he broke into a playful medley while the other two passed around a hat, collecting money. Susan took a couple of dollars from her wallet and tossed them in.

Feeling a warm glow from having done so, she negotiated a path through the ever-increasing mob and headed up the street, hungry from the various aromas of hamburgers, pizza, and falafel, while keeping an eye out for the poster shop. Dinner wasn't until seven, and the delicious food smells assaulting her senses tempted her to stop for a snack. She, Tori, and Paige had all been invited over to Kit and George's house for a casual barbecue. Afterward the three women were going to a polo match. Not that any of them was particularly into polo, but Paige had decided she was into polo players. If the event proved disappointing, she had culled an extensive itinerary of nightspots for them to investigate over the course of their evenings in L.A. The purpose of doing so was partially to have a good time and meet interesting men—partially to bring Tori out of her slump.

Miraculously, Susan had gotten over her own inamorato, Billy Donahue, the moment she made up her mind she was leaving town. She had felt nothing when they said good-bye, not even a tinge of the triumph she had been certain she would feel when she left him in a cloud of dust from her Mustang, driving off to a new life they both seemed to sense would be far more exciting than the life he led now. She was moving on, changing tracks, growing, stepping boldly into a vast spectrum of challenges that she was eager to meet. Billy Donahue's mold had been set somewhere in his late teens, when he thought he had it all. Maybe he did—then.

Susan suspected Tori's Travis Walton was not all that she had him cracked up to be either, but Tori was blindly obsessed with him, so much so that Susan kept expecting the doorbell to ring and him to be standing there, engagement ring in hand, marriage proposal and apologies spewing forth. The fantasy was so strong within Tori that it seeped from her very being, connecting into those around her. Susan ached for the stunning brunette who, for all her effort, just could not pull herself together. All fantasies should have come to an abrupt halt when Travis had the nerve to instruct his lawyer to call Tori and propose a low-ball offer on her share of the condo the two of them owned.

The poster store was not at all what Susan had expected. It was closer to an adult toy store and she meandered in, browsing, curious about all the imaginative gadgetry. There were molded black-rubber race cars that functioned as telephones, erotic body parts that functioned as erasers, silverplated paperweights that functioned as five-pound dumbbells, Igloo cold-food containers that doubled as stereo speakers for Walkman units, and even speaker telephones with memory dial and radios designed for use in the shower.

There were so many posters on the walls that Susan did not

know where to look first. They were arranged from about knee level clear up to the ceiling, not missing an inch of usable wall space. She could take her pick between the pretty ones, the funny ones, the more avant-garde, as well as the expected reprint staples, Miró and Hockney being the most heavily represented.

Susan was trying to decide between a couple of David Hockney swimming-pool scenes and a Stella racetrack, calculating the cost, when she noticed a set of stairs leading up to a small studio-type loft. Putting her decision on hold, she mounted the floating staircase that was off to the rear of the store and was surprised to find a delightful display of work created by local artists. There were whimsical ceramic pieces, some exquisite glasswork, interesting sculptures, and a long narrow case of expensive-looking handcrafted jewelry. But what made her actually catch her breath and think seriously about making a purchase were the large and colorful works of one artist hung spaciously on the toast-colored walls. The material the artist had used looked to be plastic-coated chicken wire, painted in vibrant colors and formed into abstract designs. Wondering if she might be able to eke one out of her budget which only moments ago had seemed more than adequate, Susan toured the lot of them, trying to determine which one she would choose. Instead of buying a room full of posters, she could buy one special painting and add to it, if need be. Good God, Paige's extravagance was already rubbing off on her.

Standing facing one of the wire collages was a youngish-looking man in worn, tan-colored cords and a UCLA sweatshirt, with old-fashioned wire-rimmed glasses framing his intense blue eyes that seemed to be looking through the piece in front of him. There was something about the way he was standing there, looking so critically at the work, that made Susan think that he was more than just a browsing student, that perhaps he worked there. When he went and lifted the heavy-looking work off the wall and rehung it to his satisfaction, presumably going for perfect alignment, she concluded he was obviously not just a student.

"Excuse me, I was curious how much these go for," she asked him, uncertain if he had even heard her.

He took off his glasses and rubbed his eyes, completely distracted. "Pardon me?" It was a definite double take.

Now that he had spoken, there was a kind of distinguished quality to his voice that caught Susan by surprise and made him seem markedly older. On closer examination there were lines beneath his small but deep blue eyes, a slight setback to his curly blond hair. He had the kind of flared nostrils that she had always found sexy, and she looked away, aware that she had been staring at him. "Do you work here?" she asked, questioning why, if he did not, he had been lifting and rearranging the painting on the wall.

"Oh, no. Well, not really." He smiled pleasantly, appraising her, nonplussed at how confusing his reply had come across.

Susan smiled back at him, feeling awkward, waiting for an explanation. He did not look the part of someone who went around straightening paintings on walls; he did not look that fastidious.

"I'm the artist," he explained with an unassuming shrug, the dimple on his left cheek growing more pronounced. Susan's eyes traveled down to the worn kneecaps of his pants, which looked as though he played ball in them frequently, and did a lot of knee-slides. His being the artist certainly explained his behavior.

"Are you really?" she asked, just to be sure.

He grinned and nodded.

She was definitely intrigued. "I love your work. It's really terrific," she said, looking up at it again with even more enthusiasm. "I was just wondering if I could afford to buy one," she added wryly. "But I suppose I should be talking numbers with someone who works here, not with the artist himself." To her amusement she realized she was flirting with him, which was completely uncharacteristic for her. The funny thing was, it felt good.

"*If* anyone works here," he corrected her, looking around at the nonexistent salespeople, setting off that wonderful dimple again. There were some typed sheets of paper on top of the jewelry case, cataloging the inventory and he picked one up, scanning it briefly before handing it to her. "They're a little lax here," he explained, though unperturbed. "I guess when I'm rich and famous I'll be in a position to complain. Then again, if this keeps up, it's not very likely I'll ever be rich and famous." He laughed as though he could not have cared less about attaining that status. "Thankfully, I don't have to count on their obviously absentee sales force to pay my rent," he added matter-of-factly, indicating the gold-and-blue letters on his sweat shirt. "I'm an economics professor at UCLA."

"Economics?" Susan said, caught by surprise once more. "Not art or art history?" She had come to the conclusion that he was definitely too old to be a student, but a professor would not have occurred to her. Now it seemed befitting.

"I'm a closet artist. It's how I relax. The fellow who owns this place kept seeing my work at the sidewalk art fairs they hold every year in Westwood, and asked me to show here." He leaned in closer to Susan, dropping his voice. "They're asking a ridiculous amount of money. It's embarrassing. If you're really serious about buying something, cut what you see on the page there in half and negotiate with them from that point. But don't say I told you so."

"You may get famous, but I'll wager you're not likely to ever get rich," Susan laughed.

"Oh, I'd just blow it anyway. Besides, did you ever meet anyone rich who was happy?"

"Is that what you teach in your lectures on economics? Must go over real big."

"I teach the science of money, not the philosophy of it."

"I see." Susan chuckled. *Paige would not approve,* she thought, amused. Then she remembered that she was supposed to be meeting Paige and Tori over at Kit's and she glanced anxiously at her watch, having to squint repeatedly in order to read what time it was. Paige had talked her into contact lenses on their second day out in Los Angeles, and the left one felt as though it had slipped. The damn things made her eyes water all the time, and they were a nuisance to put in. The hell with vanity; she was going back to her glasses. This artist professor looked alluring enough in his. Besides, years ago she had talked herself into liking the image of herself in glasses. They made her feel more serious.

So much for posters. So much for this adorable professor. "I've got to run," she said regretfully, wishing she could stay and talk to him or see him again. "I guess I'll be back to negotiate—"

"Hot date? Or a husband?" he asked, fishing.

"Hot date," she replied, happy about the way he had asked. She stopped herself from adding that it was with her girlfriends.

"Well, that's certainly less disconcerting than a husband," he replied. "If you're interested in poor, starving artist-professor types, I'd like to call you. We wouldn't exactly be doing Chasens, maybe something more on the order of a picnic by candlelight at the beach, or something like that . . ."

Chasens was where Kit and George's rehearsal dinner for the wedding had been held. It was beautiful, expensive, a key restaurant in town, but candlelight at the beach sounded much more enticing. She looked down at the Xeroxed sheets of paper he had handed her, trailing her finger down the page. "Mark Arent," she read aloud, locating his name, then grinning at him.

Neither of them had been aware that they had neglected to even exchange names, and now Mark asked her for hers.

"Susan Kendell," she said, automatically extending her hand and then feeling foolish for having done so.

"*Can* I call you?" he reiterated. "We can talk about me giving you a good deal on some of this overpriced stuff here . . ." His tone was joking; his eyes were sincere.

"Sure," Susan said, already imagining Paige's mocking reaction. For lack of any scratch paper, she gave him a deposit slip from her checkbook, a quick smile good-bye and then fled.

She felt him watching her all the way down the stairs and out the door. Her cheeks were pink with pleasure, and her smile intensified as she wondered just what she was getting herself into. So much for her Beverly Hills multimillionaire.

Chapter 9 ~

Kit and George's marriage set up a perfect paradigm embodying all they were striving to find, love and money harmoniously coexisting beneath one grand roof. Their new marriage was going swimmingly. The two newlyweds appeared to have it all: challenging careers, interesting friends, an exciting life-style, and, now, the added thrill of a baby to look forward to. At dinner that night Kit had announced to them that she was pregnant.

The Dom Perignon had not yet ceased its flow.

"If all else fails, *then* you can swoon over this bum artist guy, but give yourself a chance," Paige was saying to Susan as the three girls stepped out of Dustin Brent's Aston-Martin, turning it over to the valet parking attendant at the posh Los Angeles Equestrian Center, on their way to attend the polo match. They were all three dressed to be noticed, having been forewarned that an evening at the popular Equidome was as much a fashion event as it was a sporting event. It was also a premier social event, and by Paige's account a perfect place to meet the kind of men they were hoping to meet.

There were the polo players and the polo partyers, all part of the well-to-do horsey set. In the course of her research on where they should go in L.A., Paige had read an article which described

a polo player as equal parts machismo and money—an image
that immediately caught her interest. A dashing figure in helmet,
skintight pants, and knee-high boots who played a fast and furious game while mounted on a horse at swiftest gallop, swooping
down to chase a billiard-sized ball lying seven feet from his shoulder in the most dangerous team sport in the world, where half a
ton of man and horse were smashing wildly into six other horses
and players on a thirty-five-mile-an-hour collision course. That
dashing figure, who maintained a high-goal rating, a string of
polo ponies, and liked to play within the sport reputed to be the
"king of sports, the sport of kings" seemed like a choice candidate.

"*No* artists," Paige asserted, sweeping past her friends,
through the bold white arch at the entrance, past the bright white
fences that lent the appropriate horsey feeling to the sprawling
complex. She was dressed all in white, wearing a tight, ankle-
length skirt that opened in front as she walked, showing off her
long, tan, bare legs, her new boots. Her blouse was a crisp white
cotton man's-style shirt, with big shoulder pads, lots of rhine-
stone-and-stud work, closed at the throat with a sparkling rhine-
stone bolo tie. She was the only one of the three of them who had
dressed equestrian-style. Tori was wearing a new icy pink linen-
and-lace skirt outfit. Susan was in the new black pants and
T-shirt Paige had helped her to select at a shop on Melrose. The
snug-fitting pants were tucked into boots that were the black
variation of Paige's white ones, which they had bought together,
and she had on a loose-fitting golden-poppy blazer. "Not even
successful artists," Paige maintained. "Because they're too insane. *I* ought to know. I have an extensive history of artist fiascos
from which we can all take note. They can't hold on to their
money or their success; they're self-destructive; and, most impor-
tantly, *you* can't hold on to them."

"He's not an artist. He's an economics professor," Susan said
defensively, taking a good deep whiff of the familiar horse scents.
Some people complained about the smell, while Susan, associat-
ing it with pleasure, loved it. She felt right at home with the
barnyard smells, which evoked feelings of happy anticipation
within her, made her think of the long, exhilarating rides, the

freedom of a good gallop. With it all she found herself growing increasingly excited about seeing her first polo match. Paige was making such a big deal about Mark Arent. You would think the man had proposed to Susan. Who knew if he would even call? Although she hoped he would. She looked over toward Tori for support, but derived not so much as a glance. Tori had been in her own world all night long, and still was. The two job offers she had received today had done little to cheer her, although the first one, with the erratic playboy-son conducting the interview, did not exactly sound kosher to Susan.

"Well, you know the old adage about professors: Those who can't *do,* teach—" Paige had replied smugly, her mean green eyes on a guy wearing a deep-brown leather bomber jacket, a faded blue denim-colored shirt beneath it, and a sexy hairy chest beneath that.

Susan thought he looked rich but dumb. "That's bullshit, Paige," she said. "Some people *like* to teach. It makes them feel good."

"That or they're afraid of going out there, into the real world, and having to compete," Paige countered. They had reached the ticket booth and were standing in line. The arena was in clear view and already crowded. Off to the side was the private bar and grill restaurant they had heard about, with a lovely outdoor patio overlooking the polo field. "It's *safe* within the confines of a university. The students look up to you. You can *profess* all you want and never risk being put to the test. I think you should concentrate more on the stockbroker George is fixing you up with, counselor, *and* on tonight—"

"Yes, I noticed how you gave *me* the stockbroker and maneuvered the producer for yourself," Susan chided lightly, winking at Tori, who had, in turn, been assigned the surgeon.

"You want the producer?" Paige replied, with that smartass smile of hers. "He's yours!"

"What, we're going to swap blind dates?" Susan thought Paige probably would.

"Why not?" Paige answered, as though the thought amused her.

"Because the stockbroker is going to call up expecting to get

Susan-the-lawyer, and the producer is going to call up expecting to get Paige-the-dancer, and what are we going to do, tell them we switched?"

"You could make it all a lot more fun by *not* telling them," Tori commented, letting out a long deep breath as though she had been holding it for several days. "Susan, you could be Paige; and Paige, you could be Susan. That's the beauty of a blind date. They have no idea what you look like, other than that George probably told them that you're both tall and blond, which you both are. I'm the only one who couldn't get away with it."

Paige laughed, glad to see Tori looking alive again. "She just doesn't want to have to throw her doctor into the grab bag."

"Travis hates doctors. It would be so great to go home engaged to one."

"That's the spirit," Paige commended her, jumping topics and leaving Susan with the stockbroker, after all. "Did you see Kit's necklace and earrings? God . . . all those sapphires make getting disfigured for nine months sound appealing," she went on, referring to the gift George had given Kit to celebrate her being pregnant.

"You're not doing half bad yourself, on that score," Susan reminded Paige. "Jeweled designer gowns, et cetera . . . without getting knocked up."

"Without even a first date . . ." Paige threw in, preening.

"What's so bad about getting knocked up? Sounds good to me." Tori opened up her purse and took out her wallet. They were next.

"Nothing, except that I wouldn't fit into that gorgeous dress," Paige remarked.

Susan looked squarely at Tori. "Let's get things rolling with your *doctor* first, huh?" she suggested.

"It wasn't the doctor I had in mind," Tori frowned. The tone of her voice indicated that she had meant it as a joke, but it fell flat.

"Travis is six feet under," Paige reminded her. "Dead and buried. If you're carrying his kid, save your news and tell the doctor it's his."

"I don't want to marry the doctor. I don't even know the

doctor. He probably has buck teeth, and comes up to my belly button. You heard George say how funny he was. Have you ever met a funny, good-looking doctor? They're either good-looking and full of themselves or funny, short, and overweight. Maybe I'll buy a blond wig, and take your producer, Paige."

"Three, please," Susan said drolly to the man behind the ticket counter.

Looking for seats, they passed a series of private boxes. Did the names designated actually sound rich? Or was it just because she expected them to, Susan wondered, reading the little printed signs as she trailed behind Paige and Tori, heading up toward the bleachers. Harold Tanner. John B. Colligan III. *Mark Arent,* she thought to herself with a little squelched chuckle. *Wouldn't that be something?*

The game was actually thrilling to behold, with all the massed tonnage of horses and men charging with breakneck fury up and down the length of the football-sized arena in hot pursuit of one small ball, about as big and elusive as a round bar of soap. With each tenacious *whack* of a mallet, the ponies would slow, stop, change direction, then shoot out in full racing spirit, legs stretched, hooves pounding, at times accelerating to speeds of forty miles an hour in a matter of seconds, sending up billowy clouds of dust in their wake. Attempting to bring a sense of order to the frenzied stampedes and the raucous cheering was the announcer enthusiastically calling out the plays over a loudspeaker, his booming voice competing with bell signals and intermittent organ music. The players wore cotton T-shirts in their team colors. Tonight it was green against blue, sleek-fitting white breeches tucked into high leather boots capped by thick ribbed knee guards and spurs at their ankles.

Tori was thoroughly caught up in the game, cheering out loud, rooting for the team in the green T-shirts because Paige had decided she liked the green team. With the violence of ice hockey, the velocity of racing, the tension of football, the precision and challenge of golf, and the teamwork of basketball, polo was quite a game. Fundamentally it was played a lot like soccer or ice hockey, each team wrestling to gain control of the ball, to finesse it across the playing field and into the goal. But the feroc-

ity with which it was played—astride horses reeling and charging
at furious speeds, the players dipping crazily into a melee of
flying hooves and flashing sticks to take a shot—made it all that
much more enthralling to watch.

They had brought along a pair of binoculars, which George
had lent them, and Tori was peering intently through them when
the blue team began a sudden and surprising comeback. A player
from the green team overconfidently sliced the air with his mallet, intending to finish off the ball, which was only an arm's
length from the goal, but missing it entirely. His error was com-
pounded when a player from the blue team surged forward,
scooping the ball smoothly off the ground, propelling it in an arc
into the air. There was a rough and tumble scuffle as the other
players rallied to intercept, but the same "blue bomber," as Tori
came to call him, continued to chase the ball, driving it in a
relentless volley of forehand strokes, seemingly unstoppable. At
full run, a player from the opposing green team angled to the left
over the horse's withers and propelled the ball backhand, stealing
it away and sending it back again in the opposite direction. But
not for long, as the blue bomber pivoted sharply around, catching
up to the ball in advance of anyone else. Thrusting his left shoulder forward, employing a scythelike movement, he swung his
upraised mallet in a mighty blow, sending the scampering ball at
least fifty yards. His mare whinnied and shied uneasily as he
prodded its sides, charging maniacally off after the ball again in
relentless pursuit.

Up until now, the announcer's commentary had merely
blended in with the lively and colorful scenery. But when the
name *Richard Bennetton* was repeated several times in connection with the play, Tori nearly fell out of her seat.

The players' heads were protected by wide-rimmed pith hel-
mets or the newer shiny plastic models, while their eyes and faces
were shielded by narrow guards, making it difficult to see what
anyone looked like.

Which was why it took Tori until the fourth and final chukker,
or period of the match, to discover Richard Bennetton was
among the players.

Paige must have recognized his name at the exact same moment because she grabbed onto Tori's arm and looked at her with wild bemusement. *Couldn't be the same Richard Bennetton. Or could it?* When his name resounded again loud and clear through the house speakers, Paige yanked the binoculars from Tori's grasp, nearly strangling her with the narrow black cord from which they were hanging.

Trying to pick him up, Paige scanned the field, lingering for a brief moment on the attractive redhead, also riding on the blue team, whose fiery mass of hair tumbled loosely down her back, beneath her bright blue helmet, distinguishing her as the only female player on the field. Paige moved on, studiously roving the field through the lenses of the binoculars until her intended subject entered the frame. Tori was torn between watching Richard, who had just brought the game to such a thrilling climax, and watching Paige, who was smiling as if she had just fallen in love. "Why the hell didn't you go to lunch with him?" Paige whispered under her breath. "He's gorgeous. Rich. And what a great ass," she continued, gesturing toward the tantalizing view of his rear end rising up and out of saddle in a smooth rhythm as he stretched forward to scoop up the ball, the tight white riding pants accentuating his incredibly sexy bottom. "I'd have gone to lunch, taken the job, and we'd be married by now."

"Sure you would have." Susan laughed at Paige's audacity, swiping the binoculars from her to get a look at this Adonis. With all the elaborate headgear, who could tell whether he was gorgeous or not? What she did pick up was an intensity, the way he was going after the ball at full gallop, leaning out of his saddle in order to make shots that appeared to call upon a gymnastic agility just short of trick riding.

Tori, seeing her two friends gaping at him like that, reclaimed the binoculars just in time to see Richard finish off the game in an arresting maneuver. In a vaulting catapult, he drove the ball straight between the posts, making the goal, and winning the match for his team in one swift shot. She turned bright red when she realized that she was on her feet, cheering louder than almost anyone else in the crowd.

* * *

"Horse people—why do they always look wealthy?" Paige asked after the matches, as they edged their way through the crowd, on their way to the disco there.

When neither Susan nor Tori bothered to reply, she answered herself. "They look wealthy because they're horse people, and horse people just look rich."

"Brilliant, Paige," Tori said, giving Susan a look, feeling incredibly nervous at the prospect of running into Richard. Paige and Susan had said they wanted to go dancing at Horses, the Los Angeles Equestrian Center's restaurant-disco they had passed on the way in, or to check out the private club, maybe get some dessert. All Tori wanted was to sneak out as inconspicuously as possible.

Already she was beginning to see some of the polo players coming through, beer in hand, mingling with their friends.

While all scruffy from the field, their team shirts sweaty and clinging, wet towels tied around their necks, their white pants streaked with dirt, they looked far more appealing than the guests who had not played. Maybe it was the invigorated glow coloring their complexions, sending off a raw sexuality, a hearty, rustic radar. She was a bundle of nerves, though she didn't know why. She hadn't even *liked* Richard. He was cocky. Way too arrogant. He had seemed like a jerk. It was just this game that made him seem so alluring, the competence with which he had handled the horse and the reckless danger that at times approached the edge of lunacy.

So why was her heart racing, as though *she* herself had just been out there, her pulse double the rate it should ordinarily be? Why was she rehearsing in her head what she would say to him if they did run into one another? Curt little remarks occurred to her that made her smile. Not that she would ever really deliver any of them. Witty, smartass pearls rarely materialized when she needed them.

Probably he was here with a date. A girlfriend. Probably he was screwing the redhead on his team. She was savage like he was, loved danger like he did. *Paige* could manage a man like Richard Bennetton. But he would make mincemeat of Tori, and Tori knew it.

The entrance to Horses was spilling over with the mob that was too large to contain inside its doors. Paige determined that it was too college-rowdy here anyway, and began steering them away from the noise, and back over toward the arena to the sign which announced Riding and Polo Club—Members Only, where a more subdued, sophisticated-looking crowd was gathered.

"Members *only,*" Tori reminded Paige, deciding Richard Bennetton was more likely to be here than at Horses, and that she would die of embarrassment if he were to come by and see them trying to sneak in. She could not have been more relieved when Susan pointed out an additional sign, set up on a pedestal over by the door, which read Private Party Tonight. Standing only a few feet away from it at the doorway's threshold were two young men with navy blazers, checking names against a printed guest list. Paige watched them for several moments, as though contemplating how to get in anyway.

"May I help you?" asked one of the men, looking over the three of them. Tori could see Paige trying to read the guest list from her upside down perspective as she stalled, smiling at him.

"We were just catching some fresh air before we came in," she replied smoothly.

"Oh." He looked as if he were debating whether to ask her for her name or wait, when a group of people walked briskly up, rattling off their names, and distracting him.

Tori looked past him, into the room, growing more and more curious about Richard, wondering if he was there. There was a brass railing separating the bar area from the dining area. Hors d'oeuvres were being passed by waiters wearing white shirts, black bow ties, and green butcher-style aprons, which matched the hunter-green-and-burgundy decor of the room. It was all very rich-looking, with roomy burgundy leather armchairs arranged by the fireplace, light oak-framed French windows opening onto an outdoor dining patio. Lush green ficus trees with braided roots sprang from bamboo baskets. And the smoky essence of steaks being barbecued could be inhaled all the way outside. It was so crowded it was difficult to see if he was there or not, and just as she was about to give up, half-relieved, half-disappointed, she glimpsed him standing by the bar with his arm around his red-headed teammate, both of them laughing amidst a large group of friends.

"C'mon, let's get out of here," Tori said brusquely to Susan and Paige, raising her voice a notch so as to be heard over the din of band music.

Paige hesitated, then intuitively followed Tori's gaze inside the doors. "Is he in there?" she asked, standing on the toes of her new white cowboy boots to improve her vantage point.

"Yes . . ." Tori nodded distractedly, her eyes glued to him as he took a swig of beer, lustily wiping his mouth afterward with the back of his hand, then winking at the redhead. It was the same wink he had given *her* just this morning.

"Hmmm. With the redhead . . ." Paige observed, frowning upon locating him. "You sound jealous . . ."

Tori shrugged, surprised to find that she was. "Crazy, isn't it?"

Paige looked past her again, into the room. "All depends on how you look at it. What was it that book said on how to get over your lover? 'Find a new lover. . . .' Could be, dear heart, that things are looking up. I'd say ol' Travis is fading from the picture already."

It was the first time Tori had gone a full hour without brooding over Travis, and she smiled at the revelation. Richard Bennetton had his attractive head tilted back while consuming the balance from his beer bottle in one long luxurious guzzle, making her think of a sexy beer commercial. Instead of feeling stung by the queer sense of jealousy she had experienced only a moment ago, she felt oddly released by it.

Maybe Paige was right. Maybe things *were* looking up.

Chapter 10

It was not altogether unlike performing, gyrating her svelte hips to the loud, pulsating music. Only instead of being on a big stage she was on a tiny one, and the bursting-to-capacity audience was on a significantly smaller scale. They were exhausting their limbs, grunting and sweating right along with her, following her expert lead through an intensive workout geared to help them maintain their already extraordinary shapes.

Paige had ended up getting a job at Sports Club/LA, one of the city's more fashionable and expensive health clubs, teaching aerobics classes. After a couple of weeks of hard-core searching, money and hopes wearing thin, a job opened up for her there and she accepted it with relief. One of the other instructors had quit, and Paige had jumped at the position.

"On your stomachs," she cried out now, over the blare of music.

A quick glance at her watch told her that she had only a few minutes more to go before stretching her students out and winding up the class. Twenty more counts to finish off this position, another sequence pressing in the opposite direction, and their glutei maximi would be killing them for the next forty-eight hours each time they went to sit down, making them think reverently of Paige and her wonderful workout. What Paige really hoped to accomplish was to establish some good contacts so she could teach privates, clearing a tax-free sixty-five dollars an hour instead of a pre-tax ten dollars an hour.

Beethoven's Fifth was perfect cool-down material, and Paige led the relieved class through a series of final soothing stretches. Ahhh, time to go home. The pushing-to-the-max stuff that left them short of breath and ready to drop was behind them. Time to unwind, to think about what they were going to do this lovely Friday night, the prelude to their weekend. The old T.G.I.F. still applied.

Paige knew what she was going to do. Tonight was the night she, Tori, and Susan were all going out on the blind dates George and Kit had set up for them, Paige with the producer, Susan with the stockbroker, and Tori with her surgeon.

The three women had already concluded that the best part of these dates was probably going to be the getting each other dressed and ready, and then the comparing-notes session afterward when they could collect like college roommates and laugh, even if they felt like crying. God, it was nice having such good girlfriends again, not just fellow cast members, but real friends. So far, the best part about moving to Beverly Hills was unquestionably Susan and Tori.

When Paige arrived home from the health club, feeling all grimy from her workout and in a quandary over what she should wear that night, she found a massive bouquet of flowers sitting on the entrance hall table.

"From 'Philadelphia' again." Susan had come out of her room and was calling out to Paige from over the elaborate wrought-iron banister, which wrapped dramatically down around the paver-tiled stairs, concluding its spiral in an exotic indoor cactus garden. She was in that horrible old bathrobe of hers again, rubbing her just-washed hair with a towel.

Paige plucked the white gift card from out of the arrangement, trying to suppress the gnawing doubt as to Philadelphia's bachelorhood. He had been sending flowers and gifts of remembrance at least once a week since their encounter on Rodeo. No phone calls, just a steady stream of extravagant tokens accompanied by short, suggestive notes. This one said "Can't wait to see you, beautiful, all wrapped up in that divine red dress, like a Christmas package."

"What he means to say is that he can't wait to unwrap you." Susan had come downstairs and was standing behind Paige, reading the note over her shoulder, smelling of Ivory soap. "Don't you think this man is a little obsessed? All these presents and innuendos?" Susan remarked, pushing her oversized glasses against the bridge of her nose with her index finger. "What did you do to him? Are you sure you told us the whole story?"

"Down to the last detail," Paige reported, lifting up the bouquet and carrying it into the den, where there was another arrangement, slightly wilted, positioned in the center of the coffee table. Removing the old one, she replaced it with the new.

"Sure would make me nervous," Susan said, dipping down to filch a chocolate from the Steuben candy dish beside the flowers. "Let's see, silver handcuffs from Tiffany's . . ." she rattled off dubiously.

"They're not handcuffs. They're wrist-cuffs. They're sterling silver Elsa Peretti bracelets—"

"A snakeskin whip . . ."

"A Judith Leiber *belt!*" Paige laughed, correcting Susan, eyeing the chocolate, which she finally popped into her mouth. "So, the man's into Judith Leiber. The purse he bought me was also hers. You're the perverse one, Susan, reading all these lewd things into very classy designer gifts."

"How about the silk stockings with the red lace garter belt?" Susan queried with a smirk. She had her head tilted to the side, her wet hair spilling down to one shoulder, as she continued to towel dry it. Paige thought her beat-up terry robe looked as if it would disintegrate if it were run through the washing machine one more time.

"Valentino. To match my dress," Paige replied demurely, not missing a beat.

"And what's *his* present?" Tori chimed in, also in her robe, only *hers* was satin-and-lace Dior. Having gained both their attention, Tori swept down the stairs. Of the three of them, this house suited her the best. Susan belonged in something more

earthy, ranchlike, less *done.* While Paige felt she belonged in
something *more* done, preferring the fun of flash to quiet chic.

"Like the man said, *me.*" Paige derived a kick out of shocking
the two of them. "And you need a new robe, kid," she said
snidely to Susan. "If you decide to spend the night at the stockbroker's, better borrow one of mine."

"What—sleep with him on the first date?" Susan cried with
mock gravity, flipping her hair the other way to dry the other
side. "And besides, I like this robe; I like the cut. I've never been
able to find another one like it."

"Time to give up, dear heart," Paige teased, poking her finger
through a small frayed hole on the side, and tickling Susan.
"God, I'm starving," she announced, taking a bite out of a
square-shaped chocolate, hoping it was a caramel and not a nou-
gat. "Since I can't eat before my classes, all I've had all day is a
glass of apple celery juice. Mr. Producer's not scheduled for another hour and a half—"

"Oh, bad news, Paige," Tori interrupted grimly. "He called
about an hour ago to say he can't make it tonight. They're having
some problems with the film he's shooting, and he says he's going
to be stuck out there until late. He said he'll call tomorrow to
reschedule."

Paige went over to dump the older flower arrangement into the
trash can behind the bar, pausing as she did so. "Well then,
maybe I'll take the stockbroker, after all," she kidded Susan,
smiling to hide her disappointment. She was in the mood to go
out. Not to stay there all alone in that great big house. Curling up
with a good book sounded like internment. Suddenly restless, she
tugged open the bar's small refrigerator, looking for something to
drink. "I thought he had a rather sexy voice when I talked to him
on the phone," she said slyly, relinquishing the cork from an
already open bottle of chardonnay and pouring herself a glassful.

"So did I," Susan replied, pointing her finger at Paige, then
looking over at Tori. "I think we should lock her in her room
until our dates leave. The girl is not to be trusted."

Paige laughed. "Go ahead. Leave me all by my lonesome.
With nobody to have dinner with or keep me company . . ."

Eyeing the two of them, she brought the cool glass of wine to her lips.

"I'm sure Maria would sit down and eat with you," Tori joked, referring to the housekeeper, who seemed to be scared to death of the three of them.

"Muchas gracias por nada," Paige replied unsmiling. "Maybe I'll go to a movie. Or brave a nightclub on my own—" The phone rang and she snatched it up.

Maybe it was the producer and there was a change in plans. Maybe it was John Lester, the man whom she had met on her flight out to L.A., whom she had already gone out with a couple of times. Maybe it was the mortgage broker she had met today at Sports Club/LA. "Hello," she said smoothly into the receiver, winking at Tori and Susan, hoping it *was* for her.

The cheerful male voice on the other end did not sound the least bit familiar. "Hi."

"Hi," Paige said back to the undetermined voice, shrugging at the girls. "Who is this?"

"Who's *this*?" Whoever it was, he was a tease.

"You called *me*. So who's *this*?"

"I like a woman who takes a stand. Okay, I'll give you a clue—"

"Is this an obscene phone call?"

"That could be arranged."

Paige removed the phone from her ear and put her hand over the mouthpiece. "Some screwball—"

"Hello . . . hello . . ."

"I'm still here," Paige reassured him, laughing. "Okay, what's my clue? Who the fuck are you, already?"

"This can't be the sweet innocent I met at my office last week —employing such language."

With a vague sense that she might be speaking to Richard Bennetton, Paige shot a look over at Tori. "You're damn straight it's not," she said, her mind rushing ahead. Office? Had she met anyone in an office who would call her? No. "Let me guess. You play a mean game of polo," Paige ventured, not missing the stunned expression that had overtaken her brunette roommate.

"Polo—" Tori's delicate hand flew up to catch her gasp.

"Very good," he said, sounding impressed. "So has she been unable to get me off her mind?"

"I doubt it, but why don't you ask her yourself?" Paige answered, rolling her eyes as she handed a faint-looking Tori the telephone.

Tori was shaking her head. "No, no, no," she whispered, her stomach all in knots. "Take a message. Tell him I'm not here."

But Paige just kept shoving the phone at her. Tori had no idea what to say to him. If she could call him back, she could get her thoughts untangled. Stymied, she watched as Paige and Susan deserted her, heading up the huge staircase, leaving her in the lurch.

"So you're a polo fan as well," he began the conversation. His voice immediately triggered a picture of him in her mind, sitting behind his huge desk, looking up at his father, then looking penetratingly out at her.

"Yes. Well, not really," she answered foolishly. She was trying to get this straight in her mind. Had he seen her at the polo matches? Or was he referring to what Paige had said? If he had seen her there, why had he not come up to her? Then she remembered the redhead. "Paige, my girlfriend who answered the phone, is into polo," she said awkwardly. *Into polo players, anyway.*

"How'd you like the way I saved the day for my team Friday?" he asked, and she wondered if he was intentionally addressing the question she was mulling over in her head. So he *had* seen her. She wondered when. A shiver of excitement passed through her.

"I was impressed," she replied, trying to concentrate on their conversation so that she could respond with some lucidity, some intelligence. *Relax,* she told herself. While it was starting to dawn on her that she should be flattered that he had called, she was having a hard time regaining composure. She was rusty, out of practice. Living with Travis all those years was like being married. It was ages since she had been on a date.

Thankfully, Richard made it easy on her, carrying the conversation with a polish that indicated *he,* clearly, was *not* out of practice. They talked about polo for a while, the warm July weather they were having, the position at his office he thought

she should at least be considering, his recent trip to the south of
France, and then finally he asked her out on a date.

Replaying it all in her head afterward, she practically floated
up the stairs, giggling to herself because their conversation could
not have gone better. First, there was tonight's dinner with Kit
and George's friend, Dr. Jeffrey Wallerstein. Then next week she
had a date with Richard Bennetton, handsome playboy polo
player who, from their conversation, she had garnered to be
bicontinental, bicoastal, bilingual, but hopefully not bisexual. It
all felt like great revenge against Travis. It felt so great that she
went directly up to her room to tear up a picture of him that she
had been hanging on to, like a recovering alcoholic who stashes
away reserve bottles just in case. No more on-the-sly fixes when
she opened her wallet, she thought, gaining momentum as she
ripped the photo to shreds.

There was one last picture of Travis hidden in the zipper compartment of her suitcase beneath the bed, and she figured she
would know she was completely cured when she was able to tear
that up as well. *"Destroy all photos,"* the book had said. She was
getting there. "Find a new lover." She was trying.

Richard had sounded nicer on the phone than he had at their
interview, more congenial, less full of himself. She was actually
looking forward to seeing him.

"Well?" Susan asked, standing at her open door, all dressed
and looking terrific. Her ash-colored hair fell like a soft mist
around her shoulders, and she was dressed in an outfit Paige had
lent her. After two failed attempts at wearing something from her
own wardrobe, a dress Paige said looked "too prim," then a pair
of pants Paige said looked "too Stockton" (even though she had
bought them at Macy's in San Francisco), Susan hadn't known
what to wear. Her new Melrose outfit was at the cleaners, and
she hadn't thought to pick it up. Her other recent L.A. acquisi-
tions, Paige told her, were appropriate for work, but not for evening.

As their resident wardrobe consultant, Paige insisted Susan
borrow the new Karusai outfit she had just bought. Although
Paige made the least amount of money of the three of them, she

definitely had the most clothes, which she was happy to throw
into a kind of joint pool for all of them to share.

"Don't you look chic," Tori said to Susan, who spun around
uncertainly for a second inspection. *If she would only stand up
straight and hold her shoulders back, she would be guaranteed to
turn heads,* Tori thought, then decided she probably did anyway.
The featherweight silk pants and oversized jacket, each silkscreened with different sweeping, artistic-looking designs, bil-
lowed as she turned. Beneath the jacket she was wearing a simple
black scoop-neck shirt.

"You don't think it's 'too Paige'?" Susan worried.

"I think it looks great on you," Tori insisted, feeling so high
right then that probably anything would have looked great. Giving it a firm second appraisal she decided the outfit looked at
least as good on Susan, whose taller frame lent an added elegance.

"So tell me what happened . . ." Susan came inside Tori's
bedroom and flopped down onto the bed, watching Tori rush
haphazardly around the room, getting dressed with giddy distraction. In the trash can she noticed Travis's torn-to-shreds photograph, and she wondered about it but didn't ask.

"We're going out next week . . ." A pretty flush colored
Tori's pale skin. "He *did* see us."

Susan was thrilled for Tori. She had never seen her glow like
this. Not that Susan thought it was Richard specifically, more
that he had buoyed her confidence. And after that rat in the trash
can, boy, did she ever need it. "When? Where?" Susan asked,
envying Tori's petite, graceful frame as she slipped into a Matisse-like print silk tank-dress, then bent over searching in her
closet for a pair of shoes. The pair Susan suspected Tori was
looking for were on the floor right beside her. Susan picked them
up and waved them in the air for her to see.

"Thursday night. To a big black-tie birthday party at this private club called Neon. Oh, thanks," she sighed, gratefully taking
the high-heeled pumps and wriggling into them. Continuing her
conversation with Susan through the mirror, she added a pair of
sleek, quill-shaped African ivory earrings, two thick ivory ban-
gles, and an ivory-and-gold ring.

"So are you going to take the job working for him?" Susan asked playfully, adjusting a pillow beneath her arm as she leaned into a more comfortable position. Her date wouldn't be there for another fifteen minutes or so.

"You never know—" Tori replied breezily, finishing herself off with a couple squirts of cologne. "Versace. Want some?" she asked, turning toward Susan.

"Just in case they arrive at the same time, wouldn't want to clash," Susan replied, rising to her feet and accepting the bottle. Closing her eyes, she gave her neck and wrist a quick dousing, then handed the bottle back to Tori, who was standing beside her, the two of them reflected side by side in the opalescent seashell-framed mirror. "Great team, aren't we?" Susan said. Tori took her hand and gave it a tight squeeze. Susan, smiling, pointed to the discarded remnants of Travis scattered in the trash can.

Tori laughed. "As Paige would say, 'Fuck him!' "

When the doorbell rang they both shot glances down at their watches. "I'm not nervous, are you?" Susan asked facetiously, drawing a quick breath. This stockbroker guy was probably a creep—most blind dates were—but she had a nervous flutter in her stomach nevertheless. It was getting so "dressed," she thought, that produced the anxiety. It made her feel as if she were about to be on display, as if the stockbroker were shopping and she were the merchandise.

When Susan went downstairs to answer the door, she was stunned to see her artist-professor, mostly hidden behind one of his enormous paintings, standing there waiting for her to invite him in.

"Hi," she said, feeling that nervous flutter intensify. "What is this? What are you doing here?" Her excitement was impossible to contain. *No artists.* Paige's mandate echoed in her head. *Sorry, Paige, this could be love,* Susan thought, looking at the top of his curly blond head.

Mark came into the house and, after some maneuvering, set the painting against a wall. Tori had appeared at the top of the staircase and was watching. Susan signaled for her to come down.

"You look sensational," Mark was saying, unable to take his

eyes off Susan, who felt embarrassed, way overdressed. She wished that she could run upstairs and throw on a pair of jeans like he had on. Wash off all this makeup. No frayed knees this time, she noticed, taking stock of his stiff, new-looking Levi's jeans. In fact, he looked all cleaned up, as though he had gone to a fair amount of trouble for her, wearing a fresh shirt, smelling as if he had just gotten out of the shower.

"Thanks," she replied, full of questions as she looked into his deep blue eyes that were slightly magnified behind his glasses. She wanted to be wearing *her* jeans and *her* glasses, and *not* to be wearing her contact lenses.

"I'm a real sucker for pretty women who like my work," he began almost shyly.

Susan glanced over at Tori, feeling completely overwhelmed.

"I decided I'd rather you have it than let it sit hanging up on a wall in a gallery where nobody was even bothering to try and sell it anyway," he explained.

"Mark, I can't accept this," she said, though she was dying to. Her astonishment at the last few minutes fused with an uneasiness as to what she was going to do when the doorbell rang and the "creepy stockbroker" and the "fat-but-funny surgeon" arrived. Paige, she decided, could have the stockbroker after all. In a daze she remembered to introduce Tori to Mark.

"Nice to meet you. I've heard so much about you," Tori was saying, all southern charm and smiles as she shook Mark's hand. She was genuinely impressed with his work and stepped back to admire it, telling him how terrific she thought it was. Susan could see by Tori's expression that Tori was surprised that it *was* this good, which pleased Susan to no end.

Mark looked flattered, not at Tori's compliments about his work, but that Susan had told her about him.

"Really, Mark, I can't accept this," Susan said again, though she was already imagining how wonderful it would look hung up in her office.

"Well, then how about if you just keep it for me for a while? The truth of the matter is, I have no place else to put it," he teased, the quick dimple on his left cheek giving his sculptured face a friendly warmth that enveloped Susan. "I figured you had wall space in your office and, since you like it, could hold on to it for me."

"What happened to the wall space it occupied only a week ago?" she teased back, shifting her gaze from him to the colorful piece. It was the one she had liked best from the show, the one he had been rehanging.

"After the earthquake, the damn wall shrank," he replied with a funny shrug.

"I see. What earthquake?"

Mark looked over at Tori. "Is she always like this? Are we taking a deposition or something?"

Susan took a deep breath, tempted, but not sure what to do. She wanted to say, At least let me buy it from you, but she also didn't want to insult him. "Look, I feel kind of funny about this. Originally, you were talking about a break on the price. Why don't you just give me a great deal on it?"

"Some guys bring over flowers—I bring paintings. Just say thank you." Mark looked at her quietly, she thought, conscious of Tori's presence beside them. "Actually, I was on my way to see a friend of mine perform at this nightclub out in Trancas Beach, just past Malibu. You both look like you're going out but if you're not, why don't you come along? The place is kind of a dive, but my friend's a great saxophonist, and I'm kind of partial to dives anyway."

As he said it, Susan knew she was going to have a terrible time with the stockbroker. They were going to some supposedly "in" restaurant, where they would probably consume more gourmet pizza and pasta (that's all anyone in L.A. ever seemed to eat), when she would much rather go with Mark to the dive and listen to his musician friend play.

"Uh, we can't," Tori was saying, looking sympathetically over at Susan. "But that's very sweet of you. Maybe a rain check."

Susan thought he looked disappointed. She had to hold herself back from jumping in and saying she would go with him anyway. She was envisioning the beach as a backdrop in all its moonlit splendor. The romantic dive. She would concede just about anything if Paige would go out with the stockbroker in her place.

Tall and blond . . . Help, Paige! Where are you when I need you? Pretend you're me, and go out with the stockbroker—please.

"Oh, listen, it's a Friday night," he was saying. "I figured you'd be busy. But I thought I'd try. And by the way, no strings with my painting. I'm just an eccentric artist who can't resist giving something he's created to someone who is so terrifically enthusiastic."

"Eccentric artist or distinguished professor—how do you keep the identities straight?" Susan kidded, about to veer back to the rain check.

"So, *this* is the professor!"

Susan couldn't help but cringe at the sound of Paige's low, sexy voice. Her cringe intensified at the sight of Paige making her entrance in a hot pink satin kimono that barely covered her ass, wearing matching pink slippers and a saucy smile. So much for Paige saving the day. She was standing at the landing, her hair dripping wet, heightening her appeal. "Sorry for the way I'm dressed," she added. "I didn't know we had company." *Like hell she didn't,* Susan thought to herself, immediately guilty for her quick, jealous reaction. She hadn't missed Mark's speechless look, the way his eyes kept going to Paige's long bare legs. "I didn't hear the doorbell; I must have been in the shower."

"Paige, this is Mark Arent. Mark, Paige Williams," Susan said stiffly, looking over at Tori, who returned her look.

"*The* Mark Arent . . ." Paige emphasized. Then she headed over to his painting, the hem of her kimono swinging precariously, clearly tantalizing him as she moved about surveying it. "You really did this?" She looked innocently up at Mark, her theatrical moss-green eyes trained to captivate. Paige, who never went out of the house without wearing makeup, had on none. She looked Cover Girl-natural and, unjustly, more his type than Susan herself at the moment, when, God knows, she wasn't at all.

Mark nodded self-consciously, her slave.

"It's fabulous," Paige enthused, flashing that magic smile of hers over at her roommates. Susan wanted to shove her into a closet. Here she should have been feeling grateful to Paige for lending her her clothes, always bolstering her, making her laugh, when now all she felt was a burning resentment that bordered on tears. Paige was reducing the very articulate professor to a bumbling adolescent.

"Thanks . . ." he floundered, gaping at her. His eyes went from Paige to Susan, who accepted his gaze with relief and attempted to hold on to it.

"Do you make a habit of that practice, giving away your work to pretty girls who admire it?" Paige asked him flirtatiously. Susan thought If he did, she did not want to know. She had a horrible, sinking feeling that tonight *she* was going to end up with the stockbroker, Tori with the surgeon, and Paige, the femme fatale, was going to end up with the professor. It was sheer agony waiting to see how Paige would maneuver that.

"Actually, this is a first," Mark answered, and Susan chose to believe him. There was a momentary silence, which he filled by taking stock of his surroundings for the first time. "So who lives here?" he asked with belated curiosity. "All of you?"

"We're house-sitting," Tori answered.

"Pretty nice place," he observed, continuing to look around, perusing the art on the walls with a keen interest. "Who's the owner?"

"A man named Dustin Brent."

Mark had never heard of him. "Where's he now?"

"Off climbing mountains for about nine months or so," Paige said.

"The lives of the rich and famous," Mark remarked, not looking particularly impressed. "Well, sorry you all couldn't make it to see my friend. He does this rock-and-roll-style blues that makes you *need* to dance. Maybe another time."

"Mark . . ." Susan jumped in. This whole thing had turned sour. She knew she was overreacting about Paige and told herself she should just feel flattered that he had come by to see her. It was a great compliment that he'd brought her one of his paintings as a gift. "Listen, as long as you're parking this thing with me," she teased, "couldn't you at least help me hang it? Let me buy you dinner afterward to thank you."

Mark smiled at her. "You name the day," he said.

"I don't even have your number or anything," she said. "Let me get a piece of paper."

When Susan was out of the room, Paige asked Mark, "What friend?" Far from subtle, she went on to elaborate on how much she *loved* rock and roll *and* blues, and how she was the only one of the three of them who was staying home that night with nothing at all to do.

Susan returned just as Mark was suggesting that Paige go get dressed, and join him. Tori frowned at Susan and shrugged. Mark looked completely innocent. And in the midst of it all, the doorbell rang, like a time's-up signal, with the fate of the evening indelibly sealed. Susan and Tori's dates had arrived at exactly the same moment, the pairs less than perfect, but irreversible.

Chapter 11 ⤳

Dan Sullivan, Susan's stockbroker blind date, had his hair slicked
back à la *Miami Vice*. He was wearing a crumpled black, red, and
gray linen jacket, fashionably oversized. He had a perfect tan and
a build that unquestionably required hours of dedicated mainte-
nance at a health club, probably Paige's Sports Club/LA. The
two of them were so hip-looking that Susan barely recognized
that she was part of the couple when they passed by a mirror
while being led to their table at the fashionable Ivy at the Shore,
one of the pricier indoor–outdoor cafés bordering the Ocean
Front Promenade in Santa Monica. She, Susan Kendell Brown,
didn't belong to that picture, that image she saw reflected in the
swank, mirrored wall. That slick Hollywood-looking couple
walking in step with her appeared only vaguely familiar. It was
Paige's chic Japanese outfit that seemed to go with his, as though
they had coordinated it all in advance, black and gray, stylishly
large and flowing, that had caused her to do a double take. A
handsome couple indeed, but uncomfortably alien. Susan wanted
herself back. She wanted Mark back. She wanted to kill Paige.

She didn't consider herself a violent person, and yet she was
enraged, sitting here at the white linen-draped table lit attractively by twinkling votive candles, amidst the Casablanca decor,

the thick bamboo furniture, the whirling paddle fans, the Palapa straw ceiling, nodding every now and then to what Dan Sullivan was saying, pretending to study her green-and-pink menu, while instead possessed by an ungovernable stream of elaborately conceived, extremely violent fantasies about what she would like to do to her conniving, sexpot roommate. Strangling her seemed infinitely more satisfying than shooting her. The physical act might at least provide some relief from the fury that was consuming her.

After Paige had so artfully inserted herself in Susan's spot, she had pulled Susan aside to ask her if she "minded." *Do I mind? I'd like to kill you with my bare hands.* That's what Susan had wanted to reply. But instead, coward that she was, she had answered with a frosty "No, I don't mind," hoping, foolheartedly, that Paige would possess some modicum of conscience, decency, loyalty, or merely a simple grain of sensitivity, and bow out. Paige was clever enough to have engineered it so that Susan could have gone out with Mark, and she with Dan-the-stockbroker. Clinging to that hope, Susan had kept stalling, waiting for Paige to save the day for her, throwing unsubtle glances intended to suggest the switch. But Paige either didn't pick up on her hints, or didn't care to. They had been standing in the hallway, where there was an antique African blowgun hung on the wall as art. Susan had been tempted to take it down and shoot Paige right through the heart . . . if she had one.

The coup de grace was that the two of them were directly across the street, right at this moment, over at the Santa Monica pier. Mark had said he was taking Paige there to kill time and maybe grab a bite to eat, before heading off to see his friend perform at Trancas.

God, this had to be one of the worst nights of Susan's life. She couldn't even hope to enjoy herself or give Dan Sullivan a fair chance. She wanted to be out on the ratty but romantic-looking pier, eating French fries and sno-cones and winning stuffed animals at game booths, with Mark.

"So what are you going to have?" Dan asked benignly.

A heart attack, she thought gazing across the street at the bright neon sign that wouldn't let her think of anything else but

Mark. The famous old art-deco archway looked brightly alluring in purple, yellow, and green neon, its lively letters conjuring up images of Paige and Mark, walking hand in hand, laughing, flirting, leaning against lampposts and kissing through the sheer fun of it. She pictured Paige abandoning her manic search to find a rich man, falling head over heels in love with love, in love with Mark. The scenario continued bleakly, with Susan marrying someone like Dan, ending up wealthy but miserable. He would probably cheat on her because she wasn't glamorous enough. She would find out, try to live with it for a while. Then, unable to do so, she would divorce him, winding up with some token settlement, a couple of critical years older, and lonely all over again.

"All that?" joked the would-be groom when she forgot to answer. "You must be *really* hungry."

Susan was too full of anger to be hungry. She looked away from the pier and across the table at her date. He had a nice smile that made her feel suddenly weighted with guilt. She smiled back at him, wanting to connect, then looked down at her menu, reading it for the first time. "I was thinking of having the . . ." It was a blur of food descriptions. Why was she so undone over this? She had only just met Mark. Maybe she wouldn't even like him. For all she knew he was boring, self-righteous, a professorial snob. For all she knew Dan Sullivan was the best catch on the West Coast. She and Mark weren't dating, so why shouldn't Paige go out with him? Paige wasn't interested in someone like Mark, anyway. She just hadn't wanted to stay home by herself. And she did love to dance. "Capellini . . . or maybe something from the mesquite grill," Susan replied with effort. Really, what she needed was a drink. The wine Dan had ordered was chilling in a bucket beside the table because, upon tasting it, Dan had decided it wasn't cool enough. Susan eyed it, content to drink it warm. So she would put an ice cube into her glass.

"They're both good choices," Dan said, seemingly intent on her having a good time. "You may want to start with the capellini, then get the lime chicken over mesquite." His smile was boyish. It cut through some of the studied sophistication.

Susan closed her menu. "Would you mind if we traded seats?" she asked. This wasn't working. She wanted to concentrate on him, and it was impossible with the pier looming larger than life right in front of her. He looked at her peculiarly, rose up politely from his chair, and she let out a short sigh of relief, blaming the move on cigarette smoke from the table behind her. Facing the painted brick wall was infinitely better than facing that damn neon sign all night long, illuminating where she wanted to be but was not. She was going to have a good time if it killed her, she vowed, inching around the table and switching places with him. They passed nose to nose through the tight spot, brushing against one another. Then as she slipped into her seat she caught the same stubborn green-and-purple reflection bouncing off her water glass, flickering at her like an inexorable tease. With firm resolve she moved it as far away as possible, into the dimness of a shadow.

Dan Sullivan was forty-five years old. Grew up in Beverly Hills. Went to Beverly High the same time as Richard Dreyfuss, Albert Brooks, Rob Reiner, and assorted other superachievers whose names she didn't recognize, but probably should have. She tried to sound enthusiastic as he continued rattling off his credits as though delivering a prepared speech. She gathered he went on a lot of blind dates. After Beverly High, he went to the University of Southern California. His father owned a stock brokerage firm, which was how he happened into the field. He skied, played golf and tennis at his country club, had an extensive repertoire of "in" restaurants and movies, saw a shrink once a week, did recreational drugs, and drank Corona beer with a twist of lime. The two of them had nothing in common.

When Susan masochistically asked him if he would like to go across the street to the pier after dinner, he looked at her as if she were nuts. He literally laughed at her suggestion as if it were a big joke. "What? Mix with the element?" The pier was "sleaze city," he told her, a rundown, ramshackle eyesore, a crime magnet that would have done the city of Santa Monica a big favor if it had fallen into the ocean during one of the big storms or earthquakes. Seemingly amused by her out-of-town naïveté, he went on pompously to cite that, according to the police department, the crime rate in the dilapidated pier area was five times that of the rest of the city. Then he laughed again, preening about his élitism with a superior smirk, raking his fingers through his *Miami Vice* hairdo, and adding that if perhaps she had brought a gun along with her, or a switchblade, they could conceivably reconsider.

Susan drew her water glass back over into the light again, positioning it to recapture the colorful neon that appealed to her but clearly not to him. Gaining sort of a sick solace, she planned to stare at the glass for the duration of the evening.

They were leaning against a lamppost, kissing like a couple of teenagers. The ramshackle wooden pier beneath them was vibrating from all the people dancing and jumping around to the great fifties' vintage rock-and-roll music being pounded out by the band housed within the three-sided blue-and-white striped tent. Glittery letters on the drum set identified the group as Li'l Elmo and the Cosmos. Their pompadour hairstyles, dark shades, and slick suits were in keeping with their doo-wop mode. "Shake It Up Baby . . ." reverberated through the seaboard air, mixing with the crashing surf just below, the cheering appreciative crowd that was so large it spilled outside the bounds of the tent, onto the crummy, wood-planked walkway. The young, scruffy-looking crowd was in constant motion, infected by the music, dancing, swaying, hands up in the air, bebopping to the can't-stand-still sound of another era. It was so much fun.

"Dance with me," Mark said to Paige in the middle of the best kiss she had had in ages.

"Hmmm, my two favorite things," she murmured breathlessly into his mouth. He tasted like a cherry sno-cone. He looked cute, kind of silly, with his lips stained cherry red from the sweet icy mound. Hers were probably purple.

"Two favorite things? Hmm, what's that?" He put his hands over her head against the ribbed green lamppost, pressing his body into her incredibly seductive one. What a strange night! He had had Susan on his mind all week long, since he met her. And now he was behaving like a teenager with her roommate, completely intoxicated, swooning the way he hadn't done in years. He reminded himself of one of his students. And he kissed her again, with a hard-on that wouldn't quit.

"Kissing and dancing," she replied. "Are you as good at dancing as you are at kissing? Do we have to stop kissing in order to dance?"

"I don't see why," he answered, taking her gaily in his arms and spinning her onto the dance floor.

"You're good," she laughed, her eyes bright as the moon.

"At kissing or dancing?"

"At both!" she conceded as he brought her down deep to the ground in a daring death drop that drew applause.

They were John Travolta and Olivia Newton-John, and the sea of dancers parted to make way for them, whistling, hooting, and clapping their approval. Inspired by having an audience, Paige tried to take over the lead, but Mark overpowered her effort. He was good. Strong. Better than a lot of men she had danced with onstage. *Please, God, don't let me fall for this guy,* she prayed, giggling with delight as he held her close, playing out a scene from some corny musical as he whirled her around until she became so dizzy she had to collapse in his arms. After another outburst of applause, the mobbed and frenetic dance floor closed in on them again. Burning hot and feeling fantastic, they went at it once more, dancing until they were ready to drop.

"Hungry?" Mark asked her as they headed back up the pier, past various restaurants spotted between game booths, past the dozens of pushcart vendors plying the boardwalk, selling everything from hot tamales to baked potato skins to sno-cones. All they had eaten all evening were the sno-cones.

"Hmmm, am I ever," Paige answered, walking backward in front of him, feeling wildly energetic, wildly sexy. How could she do this to Susan? Susan was her roommate, her friend. She just wanted to sleep with Mark one or two times, screw to their hearts' content, and then she would give him back to Susan, for keeps if she wanted him. It was a concept Susan wouldn't understand or forgive in a million years. Paige just wanted a fling with him. To run her fingers through that curly blond hair, to lift the glasses off his sexy, neoclassic-looking face, and put them on the nightstand beside his bed.

She wondered what his bedroom looked like. It was probably small. Sparse. Except for a lot of books. He probably had a small, adjoining studio where he painted. That would be fun too. Maybe they could paint each other.

Paige, you're a terrible person, she told herself. The kimono had been intentional. She just couldn't stop herself upon hearing the male voice emanating from downstairs. There was something fun about teasing, arousing the innocent buck. When she had gotten out of the shower, she had put on her man-sized terry, which she kept on a hook on the back of the bathroom door. Then, when she had emerged from her room and heard Mark, she had run back into her room and hunted for her more provocative hot pink satin number, hoping he wouldn't leave before she made an appearance.

It was nasty. She should feel guilty. She did. A little, but not enough to stop herself from teasing his neck with her tongue until she made him squirm as he pulled her over to a game booth.

For fifty cents the carny hustling the game booth promised the thrill of a lifetime. The gimmick was to slam a sledgehammer down hard onto a metal seesaw-type gismo that had a sickening-looking rubber frog perched on the opposite end. As the hammer made impact with the vacant metal disc, setting the seesaw off-balance, the rubber frog would go flying, hopefully not onto the floor but into a pond of sorts that had plastic lily pads floating about as receptacles. If the frog landed by chance on one of the lily pads, the player won one of the crummy stuffed animals lining the wall. It was a feat Paige knew, from her numerous excursions to Coney Island, to be nearly impossible.

For her maybe, but not impossible for Mark. It turned out he was a whiz at carnival games. Like Paige, he had grown up in New York, and his hangout had been Coney Island where he had set for himself the goal of learning to outsmart the carnies running the always rigged booths. After Paige's frog leaped onto the floor, Mark handed the carny another fifty cents and told her to take note. He bent down low, eyeing the set-up from counter level, then went on to win five efforts out of seven.

Loaded down with prizes, the two of them continued on, touring the booths with far more enthusiasm than the larkish games warranted. Paige came close to winning several times, just enough to keep the thrill alive, and Mark was definitely winning enough to keep the carnies leery of him.

There were all the usual gimmicks, tossing the football through a tire, throwing darts at balloons, pitching coins into glass plates, shooting water pistols into painted clowns' mouths to inflate a balloon and make it pop, throwing balls at stuffed cotton-calico cats, balls at old-fashioned lead milk bottles, and still more balls at a big round metal knob that was rigged, once hit, to dunk a T-shirt-clad woman into a giant tub of water.

After watching for a while, Paige went up to the man running the dunking booth and whispered her impulsive request in his ear. He looked at her as if she were crazy. He could not possibly do what she wanted him to do. Then she handed him a five dollar bill and he changed his mind.

A moment later, Paige had replaced the waterlogged lady and was sitting on the bench herself, challenging the rapidly increasing crowd who, like Mark, most of all, couldn't believe their eyes.

She watched as Mark dropped two quarters into the carny's hand, astonishment registered in his cool blue eyes, determination registered on his mouth as he took in her new cotton dress, following the off-the-shoulder ruffle, down to the tight, dropped waist that hugged her hips. She was barelegged, having cast her shoes off to the side, and she dropped a toe down toward the water, wondering how cold it was.

Bang! The ball missed, although Mark aimed carefully and threw with all his might. Paige almost fell in from surprise and she grasped on tightly to the wooden plank beneath her, regaining her balance and staring reproachfully at her armed attacker. *Bang.* The ball missed again. A shudder of nervous excitement passed through Paige and she smiled, then ducked as the third ball swerved an inch or so from her head. "Sorry," he apologized, then procured another ball and aimed again.

"Hey, give someone else a try," an overweight guy in shorts and ribbed undershirt called out, pressing in front of a hell-bent Mark, and snatching the baseball-sized rubber ball he had just paid for from his hands. "Back of the line, buddy," the guy stated flatly, returning to Mark his fifty cents. If only she had a camera —the look on Mark's face was priceless.

Paige laughed at his reaction. She waved at him, watching as he acquiesced, appraising the line that had grown to be considerable, gamely counting the ranks of noisy contenders while he made his way to the end of the line. Paige was about to climb down, when she was sent shrieking into the water from a ball hurled by the fat guy in the shorts.

She arose blinded by a veil of water, soaking wet, teeth chattering, and thoroughly stunned. Her clothes were plastered to her body. They felt cold against the warm night air. She felt her nipples taut, erect, pressing against the soaking wet cloth of her dress, and she started to look down but then stopped, embarrassed. It was easy enough to imagine the effect. It was registered in the eager eyes of the men waiting to see her get drenched all over again, waiting for a shot at her themselves, their lurid fantasies ignited. She reddened when she realized hers were as well, then quickly sought out Mark in the crowd, signaling for him to help get her the hell down from there. She found him with his arms folded over his chest, looking at her with a strange, knowing smile that made not just her clothes feel transparent but her thoughts as well. This time *he* waved at her.

"Mark," she shouted, teeth still chattering, folding her own arms across her own chest, needing his help in order to get down. But Mark just burst out laughing when someone else purchased three balls and prepared to throw.

"Hey, wait a minute, this is a *joke*—I don't really work here," she said, turning from Mark to the skinny youth about to bomb her, and then to the carny. She couldn't believe what was going on. She was a lunatic for having gotten up here in the first place.

Bang. Paige was released down into the water a second time. And yet she could have sworn the guy missed the knob by yards! As she came up gasping for breath, she eyed the carny, sure that he had somehow maneuvered the drop himself. "Am I going to at least get a cut?" she remarked snidely, laughing herself this time while flipping a curtain of wet hair away from her face. After all that dancing, the water actually felt refreshing. She had given up on being dry.

"You want a cut, you've got a cut," he said, his shifty brown eyes converting to slits as his smile broadened. Tonight could be a windfall for him. His wife was standing nearby, probably already counting the coins in her head. She had a big beach towel wrapped around her husky shoulders. Her platinum hair was beginning to dry. *Break's over, honey,* Paige started to say, when Mark at last decided to come up beside her.

"Had enough?" he teased, removing his glasses and rubbing those gorgeous blue eyes of his.

Paige glared at him in response. But he was so cute that she couldn't keep a straight face.

Reinstating his glasses, he took in her arousing state of dress, and smiled appreciatively until she actually blushed.

A variety of whistles and hoots rose up from the restless crowd.

Paige, ever the performer, looked out at her audience with actressy composure. What the hell, her *Cats* costume had been more revealing than this. She extended her forefinger up into the air and said grinning, "All right, guys, one more shot at this. Better make it count." Then she turned back to the carny, and said playfully under her breath, "But no cheating this time, mister. Mark, watch this guy's hands."

Bang. Midspeech, Paige was sent shrieking down into the water again.

The carny brought both hands up into the air, looking genuinely surprised, declaring his innocence. Paige turned from him over toward his wife who was chuckling away, as though dunking Paige was the most fun thing she had ever done in her life. Still laughing, she went and got a fresh towel and gave it to the soaking wet stand-in. Her husband went and got a big plastic sack filled with stuffed animals and handed Mark, already laden with junk, the whole bag.

The natural thing to do after that seemed to be to walk along the beach, shoes in hand, arms around each other, listening to the surf and falling under its seductive spell. They had taken a couple of blankets from Mark's Jeep and had wrapped themselves in them for warmth. Paige had slipped off her wet dress and borrowed a baseball jersey of his to put on instead. He remarked that it was longer than the little robe number she had been wearing earlier, and she laughed. It was true.

The beach for Paige was soul-stirring. The huge waves of the Pacific exploding, retreating, swelling again, creating a sense of expectancy beneath a moonlit sky as they walked on and on, the noise from the pier growing fainter and fainter until it was only a memory. The smell was salty, fresh. The air felt thick and moist. The sand beneath her bare feet felt soft and tickly, with its surface giving way, conforming to her steps.

Rarely out of Manhattan, Paige was lucky to walk on grass let alone sand, and she reveled in it now, promising herself a seaside residence one day, envisioning the beach as part of her own backyard, the ocean her private wading pool. Drifting off to sleep to the rhythmic sound of the ocean, being transported by it to another world. *Ahhh, what soulful slumber,* she thought. And how convenient for the sandman's faithful delivery, the customary souvenir of a good sleep.

"I'm getting kind of used to you with wet hair," Mark said, his voice gently interrupting the silence. "Second time in one night. When you came downstairs. And now."

"Yeah?" Paige turned to him, lifting the wet mass all to one side, and letting it cascade provocatively over her shoulder. It was getting chillier outside, and she wrapped the blanket more snugly around herself.

"You too cold?" Mark asked, stopping and wrapping himself and his blanket around her for additional warmth.

"Not now," she said, and it was true she was not. His body acted like a heater, infusing her with a splendid warmth, melting the chill, disarming her resolve to not respond to him. He couldn't afford that idyllic place for her at the beach, she reminded herself lamentably. He couldn't afford *her.*

"You look great with wet hair. It's very sexy." Those eyes again as they bore into her own. That exquisite chiseled nose.

Their thighs were touching, her naked icy one against his warm denim-wrapped one. It was so quiet, so still. There was not a soul in sight. She was hot. She was cold. She felt vulnerable and intensely turned on. "Oh, yeah," Paige said again, tracing his cheek with the still chilled tip of her nose. "How sexy?"

"Pretty fucking sexy—" he answered in a low voice. His blanket was like a tent around them.

"Fucking sexy enough to do it right here?" Paige asked.

An exceptionally powerful wave erupted on the shore, causing her to jump. He drew her closer, sinking down onto the sand, spreading out one blanket for them to lie on, the other to cover them up. They were completely entwined beneath it, toasty warm, kissing roughly, then gently, still tasting faintly of sno-cones.

Paige felt another wave of guilt, thinking about Susan, her large blue eyes so innocently reproachful. But then Mark's hand was traveling up her thigh, and she could barely stand the plea-sure. His other hand was rising up beneath the baseball jersey, caressing her stomach, her breasts. She, in turn, was struggling with the zipper on his jeans, undoing his shirt, and caressing him.

It figured that his skin would be so damn soft, like the finest silk velvet, so that she couldn't stop touching him. It figured that *his* touch would exceed perfect, gossamer strokes arousing her to new heights, beyond control, beyond any desire to control.

If he were rich, he would climb on top of her, explode in two seconds, and it would be over, with a quick gratuitous peck on the lips, and her left wanting. But Mark was taking his time. He was leisurely attentive, a superlative lover, making her fall deeply in lust with him. Both their heads were hidden beneath the blan-ket now so that it was pitch-dark, the blackness amplifying the rhythmic sounds of the surf, their luxurious kissing. Her own moan blended exquisitely with his as his soft full lips found her absolute favorite spot to be kissed.

Should she tell him now? Did she dare? Did she dare not? She was dying to make love with him, but eventually she had to set the record straight, explain to him why she had moved out to L.A., why they couldn't possibly get involved. Their sexual in-dulgence would be for the sheer pleasure of it, but nothing threat-ening that broached commitment. They could be lovers, friends, intimate friends, but he must be completely aware that she was undeflectable in her intent to meet and marry a rich man and that, for once in her life, come hell or high water, she was going to score a triumphant ten on her goal.

She was fast losing her train of thought. And yet her train of thought was contributing to the excitement. There was something sexual and offbeat about her predicament, reckless and bad. She felt guilty and wildly turned on. She was trembling and quivering all over. God, if she stopped now to confess all this she would be missing the climax of a lifetime. As he lifted the blanket for a moment and let in a chill rush of air she felt herself falling over the border of reason. His warm tongue, the intense heat of his body disturbed by the frigid gust caused her to cry out in utter delight.

Fuck it, she'd tell him later.

Why were the broke ones always the best in bed?

Chapter 12

"When we went into the restaurant all he did was talk about how short he was. By the time we left the restaurant, I thought I was out with a midget," Tori said drolly to Susan.

It was just after four in the morning, and the two of them were sitting in the den drinking coffee and Armagnac, and eating pistachio nuts. Both were still wearing their clothes from the evening before, shoes deposited somewhere in the room, hair and makeup wilted. Their respective blind dates had brought them home around midnight, Susan's a little before, and they had been sitting up talking together ever since. The only one who had not yet made it home was Paige. A fact that had Susan drinking considerably more than she should.

"Oh, c'mon, Tori," she said, helping herself to another glass of the rare, aged Armagnac. The powerful brandy stung as she brought it to her lips, but the taste and the heady feeling it rendered afterward were delicious. "I met him. He wasn't *that* short."

"He was pretty short," Tori argued, yawning, curling up onto the couch with her head resting on a pillow she had fluffed up. "But most of all it was how short he kept *saying* he was. Maybe if he had spent all evening talking about how tall he was, he would have given a more towering impression. By the time dessert arrived I was picturing him requiring a telephone book or one of those kiddie stools in order to be able to reach the surgery table to operate on one of his patients." Her dress was carelessly hiked up so that her long slim legs were in full view, red toenail polish vivid through her stockings as she flexed and then pointed her toes.

Susan chuckled tipsily.

Tori smiled at her own joke. Could it be she was regaining her sense of humor? Please God! It was Richard Bennetton's phone call that had elevated her mood. She was feeling gay and somewhat sought-after. Even the short surgeon had pressed her for a second date. "Better go easy on that stuff, Susan; it's pure firewater," she advised her friend, who was sitting on the adjacent white duck couch, feet crossed at the ankles on the coffee table, bottle still in one hand, shot-glass-sized liqueur glass in the other.

"Tomorrow's Saturday. I can get as drunk as I please," Susan protested, planning on drinking herself into oblivion.

"Not to mention that our liquor tab here is mounting steadily," Tori added, taking the bottle from Susan and pouring a shot of the Armagnac into a fresh cup of coffee. She preferred her firewater diluted.

"Dustin's postcard said to drink and eat whatever we wanted—"

"Even so—"

"Evonne said we would be doing him a favor, clearing room to afford him the pleasure of acquiring more."

"Sounds more like something Paige would say. Are you sure that really came from Evonne?"

"Are you asking *me* to comment on Paige's reliability, trustworthiness, credibility, or character?" Susan slurred, looking miserably at the clock as one of the graceful stainless-steel arms swept forward to indicate 4:14 A.M. She was tempted to call Trancas and find out if they were even still open. In L.A. nothing was still going full swing at four in the morning.

"Maybe they went out with Mark's musician friend afterward," Tori suggested.

Or then again, maybe Paige has gone back with him to his place and they are screwing their brains out, Susan's thoughts countered unhappily.

They both reached over for another handful of nuts at the same time.

"That was such a nice note Dustin sent. Why can't we meet someone like him?" Susan sighed.

Tori sipped her drink, regarding Susan from over the rim of her cup. She was accustomed to thinking of only one man. Now her head contained a menagerie of men. Richard Bennetton. Still ol' Travis, of course. The seemingly short surgeon. Susan's Mark Arent—or was it Paige's Mark Arent? Paige's mysterious gift-bearing suitor from Philadelphia. And not to be left out, Dustin Brent. "We did meet him."

"So which one of us is he swooning over, missing terribly? Which one of us had him tempted to cancel his trip and stay behind to pursue love? Which one of us is he hoping will still be single when he returns?" Susan wondered dreamily, cracking the natural-color shell of a ripe pistachio with her teeth, then dislodging the nut into her mouth.

"Paige!" They answered in aggravated unison, as Susan dropped the remains of her shell into a crystal bowl marked expressly for that purpose.

"I've never really hated anybody before in my life," Susan said. "Not liked them, sure. But never *hate*. I *really* hate Paige. I mean really hate her." Susan tore off the brass clip-on earrings Paige had lent her and threw them down onto the coffee table. "She gives with one hand, then takes with both of hers. I don't care about these clothes. I don't care about these earrings. I feel like such a jerk. Like I can't get mad at her because she's been so bighearted about all this. But how bighearted is she really when she stays out all night with a guy that comes over to see *me*?"

"There's the good news about Paige. And the bad news," Tori rationalized. It was true. There was something so spirited and fun and actually giving about Paige. If you had a problem, it was her problem to tackle as well. She was as intent on solving it as you were, maybe more so because she was so stubborn and had so much energy. The bad news about Paige was that you couldn't quite trust her. She was a true sybarite, completely self-centered.

If stealing your pleasure granted *her* pleasure, she was prone to doing so, as evidenced tonight, probably not at all aware that she had even done anything wrong.

"Yeah? Well I'm real familiar right now with the bad news. Better remind me about some of the good."

"If it weren't for her, we all wouldn't be here now—" Tori said truthfully, her Georgia accent sounding especially pronounced as she rose to Paige's defense.

"What's so great about *here*?" Susan sipped gloomily at her glass of Armagnac, staring down into the deep tawny color as though it contained answers.

"Would you rather be back in Stockton with your life as it was?"

"Now *you* sound like Paige!"

"Getting the runaround from what's-his-name—" Tori pressed on.

"I'm trying to forget—"

"Not caring. And yet wishing you *did* care. You said so yourself, most of the other eligible men there were ex-husbands of the girls with whom you went to school, guys you wouldn't give a second glance to then. It's not just *men* opportunities. Look at your career jump. Look at how much more money you're making here and the possibilities there are for you," Tori continued, overriding Susan's next interruption. "Would you rather be back in your small-town community, going to barbecues at your parents' mobile home? Look, I have nothing against mobile homes, but I just can't picture you content in a small town like that, getting ridiculed for your ambition rather than encouraged and admired for it, stuck in a rut, when there's clearly so much more opportunity for you out here."

Susan felt tears stinging in her eyes and she blinked them back. Maybe she *was* getting a little too drunk. She felt tired and overwrought. She both missed her family and resented them at the same time. Every time she called, they were so aloof, so distant. They didn't want to hear about L.A., her job, her friends, the house in which she was living. Even though she was calling them from the office, not paying for the calls herself, they kept cutting her off, using the long-distance business as an excuse. She was fine. They were fine. That was all they needed to know. Their conversations were more like telegrams, clipped, abbreviated sentences getting to the heart of the message and then out of it just as abruptly. Didn't they care at all? Didn't her mother care? When she had called Lisa and Buzz, her only real friends in Stockton, she had been stung to find a remoteness there as well, cutting remarks about "Tinseltown," digs about her life there. Upon confronting them, she was told that what she was facing was an inevitability that she would have been naive to not have considered. She had moved, which to them translated as moved on. Her life was different from theirs. And therefore she was now different, changed. *What! Overnight? I'm me. I'll always be me.* But even with her oldest and dearest friends, she was butting up against an unforgiving brick wall. And it naturally hurt.

Content—is that what Tori had said? *Content* was such an ambiguous word. Who was really content? If one were healthy, one was supposed to be content. If not, then one was greedy. Susan's mother and father would claim to be content. But Susan would argue that they were not. One could be content for a fraction of time, but not for any duration. It went against the grain of human nature. Even children were incapable of being content for long. Children offered the purest example of contentment as mere illusion. Take an ice-cream cone. It provided pure, sweet, creamy contentment, but then it was either devoured or it melted away, and the child was left no longer content. Contentment was a passing phenomenon in which people put altogether too much stock. Susan could not say that she would rather be back in Stockton, back in her old life. It may have been okay before, but it was definitely not okay now. "What am I supposed to feel, gratitude toward Paige?" she asked resentfully, chugalugging the rest of her brandy, then reaching over to set the empty glass down onto the table. "When she downright steals the man of my dreams—"

Tori looked at her compassionately, running her fingers through her short dark hair, her dark eyes warm and probing. "C'mon, Susan. You don't even know the guy. What kind of a person can he be anyway, to come over to see you, then go out with your roommate and stay out all night, huh?"

"Human. Paige is probably raping him."

Tori opened her mouth to argue, but then had an apparent change of heart and shrugged.

"I hope she contracts herpes. Or something worse."

"Susan!" Tori had to laugh at Susan's uncharacteristic vitriol.

"Well, okay, maybe not something worse. But a mild case of something would serve her right."

"If he's so perfect, why is it you think she could *catch* something from him? Perfect men come with a clean bill of health. Anyway, he's obviously an easy lay," Tori asserted swiftly.

"Thanks to Paige we've established that one. So maybe he has an overactive libido—"

"I *see*. An enlarged libido," Tori intoned. "Now, that can be a real problem—chronic in fact."

"A bigger problem is a guy with a libido that doesn't operate properly. I'd rather have to contend with an enlarged libido than one too weak to get it up," she volleyed.

"We're concentrating on his weaknesses, Susan. *How to Get Over Your Lover and Survive*—remember that? *Weaknesses,* you all kept insisting to me. *Concentrate* on his weaknesses. Now I've given you one to work on; let's focus on it."

"Like you're cured—"

"I'm *improved*. I'm counting on time and Richard Bennetton to cure me. My affliction was born over the course of years," Tori declared dramatically. "It was a fire, raging wild and out of control, definitely destructive and difficult to extinguish. Your little flame should require just a Dixie cup sized dousing of water, then *poof*, charred a little, but otherwise like it never happened."

Susan laughed, in spite of her frustration, watching Tori gratefully as she leapt up from the couch and strode over to find the manual they had given her. "This *colossal* libido problem of his," Tori continued—tripping over one of Susan's strewn high heels, then recovering with giddy grace—"could make your life miserable. Now, wasn't that what's-his-name's problem, your lawyer-boyfriend in Stockton? I think there might be a pattern emerging here—"

"Billy Donahue," Susan coached this time. She had to laugh because the two men could not have been more different from one another. But she nodded her accord, smiling and submitting to the game. She had never seen Tori so loose, so plucky. Maybe she *was* getting over Travis, miracle of miracles.

"*That's* right, Billy Donahue. Here's another one for you. Mark wears glasses," Tori recalled. "You want your kids to grow up with defective eyes? Bad eyes are genetic."

"Half of that genetic order is already a go, Tori. *I'm* blind as a bat without my glasses."

"Oh, that's right," Tori yielded with an easy laugh. She had to admit, coming up with "weaknesses" for Mark was a strain, but she was trying. His height was good; his build was good; he was obviously bright and talented. So forget the gene arguments. He wasn't terribly loyal, but they had already covered that ground. What they had not covered was that he wasn't exactly in the income bracket they had allegedly moved out here to enter.

Susan, meanwhile, smirked. "You're having a rough time, aren't you. He's pretty nearly perfect, isn't he?"

"Not *so* perfect. As my mother would say, 'he doesn't even have a pot to piss in.' "

"Your genteel southern-belle mother would say that?"

"She would manage to *say* it genteelly. Anyway, there you go. Can't live off love forever. You're making at least twice the income that he is—you think that's good for a relationship?"

"I don't care about that—" Susan really didn't.

"Aha, but *he* would! Don't forget he has that enlarged libido and ego problem. He would care. They all do. They get bitter and nasty and resentful. Like it's your fault you're more successful than they are. They cheat on you to console themselves. Especially the ones with—"

"I know . . . enlarged libidos."

"You *are* catching on. So there's your focus. He's sweet and sexy, but broke and soon to be bitter, out philandering, maybe even gambling away your money, to try and rescue his own situation. He's a dreamer. All artists are dreamers. He'll be dreaming about that big win. And as he loses more and more of your hard-earned money, he'll keep dreaming that he's getting close to Lady Luck. Lady Luck will take the form of a mistress. An adoring, sympathetic student, soft, blond and voluptuous. There'll be a

whole slew of them, in all colors and sizes. Tack on the burden of
guilt, which he's surely already been carrying around. And then
he'll start to drink. It happens to the best of them."

By now Susan and Tori were both laughing uproariously. They
had started working on the brandy again, and Tori was grinning
and bearing it, and drinking it straight.

"You ought to pass up real estate and consider a writing career," Susan said.

Tori wrinkled her small patrician nose, her eyes welling up
with tears from the brandy. "No way. This is wretched stuff. It
would never sell," she replied, referring to her story, not the
brandy. She was beginning to like the brandy.

"Why? I'm buying it," Susan countered. "And I'm an intelligent, eighties woman. A discriminating, successful lawyer."

"You are that," Tori agreed, sitting beside Susan now, bump-
ing her affectionately with her shoulder. "Okay, so now you want
to hear the revenge part, the just-deserts conclusion to my little
yarn?" she asked, clearly anxious to finish what she had begun.

"By all means," Susan said, toasting the so far unuttered conclusion in advance.

"Paige gets the broke-but-talented artist-professor she stole
from right under your nose. *But,* your revenge is that you end up
married to some rich guy you fall for after you recover from
Mark, which shouldn't take too long, married with your gorgeous Russian lynx-belly coat, your nanny pushing your divine
little baby in the park in a romantic-looking English pram, while
Paige ends up barefoot and pregnant, trying to buy caviar with
foodstamps!"

It was in the middle of another passionate interlude that Paige
finally decided to set the record straight.

Back at his apartment, which was ironically at the beach, in
the quaint canal district of Venice (romantic, but more bohemian
than Paige had had in mind), after a couple more memorable
rounds of lovemaking, Paige set forth the ground rules and the
boundaries of their relationship.

They were lying in his romantically proportioned double bed,
an antique that had belonged to his grandmother, listening to one

of Mahler's later works, when she broached the subject. As envisioned, Paige had removed his glasses, set them on the small, also antique table by his bed, beside a small brass clock. They had passed on Trancas altogether. Paige was too wet to go anywhere and, besides, they were in the mood not to listen to other people's music but to make their own. Mark's room was painted a quiet white, with some drawings framed and hung on the walls. It looked like the sort of bedroom a professor would inhabit. Small, French, and poetic-looking, a fishtail palm flourishing in an attractive clay pot atop another antique piece in the corner, tapestry pillows arranged on a partially upholstered love seat, and books battling for space on the étagère. But it seemed incongruous for an artist who painted bold, vibrantly colorful canvases like the one he had given to Susan.

Still glowing in the aftermath of their lovemaking, Paige touched his brow with her lips, imparting the speech she had been planning.

When she had told him everything, including the part about her admirer in Philadelphia, the charity gala he was taking her to at the Nicky Loomis mansion, he rolled onto his side to face her, tracing her full breast with his forefinger until the nipple rose up hard and taut, taking on a life of its own. Luxuriating in his touch, his presence, the rich, marvelous music of Mahler, she wound up giving vent to far more than just that information. In a pleasant state of frank abandon, she went back to unwrap fragments of her life in New York (it turned out they had grown up within several miles of each other), her mother dying when Paige was only twelve years old, her friendship with Kit, the bride who had been the impetus for the rich-man hunt, her relationship with her father, and her struggle to make it on Broadway.

She talked. He listened, asking questions every now and then, the kind that inspire long, revealing answers, inserting reminiscences of his own. While she spoke more candidly than she ordinarily did, owing probably to his intelligent, easy acceptance, his nonjudgmental interest, he continued his sensual probing of her skin.

He was passing his fingers exquisitely over her arms, massaging her back, stroking her legs, her stomach—fluid motions voluptuously orchestrated with the music that simultaneously turned her on and relaxed her.

At some point, and she was not sure when, their touching became more intense, more sexual, more urgent. They were both up on their sides, thigh to thigh, chest to chest, toes toying with each other's.

The curly blond hair that grew like wild silken vines over his chest felt sublimely sensuous as her fingers wandered through its depth. The words were out, and they were contemplating a kiss, a long passionate one.

Mahler had also grown more intense, provoking their passion further, charging Paige with an electriclike current that shot through her very being. Their tongues were entwined, tasting, teasing, their lips pressing softly together, wiping out any extraneous thoughts.

In her mind, she and Mark were back on the beach again, feeling the damp, salty air, listening to the ocean imparting secrets to the dark, isolated beach, the whispering lull of the waves drawing them into a satisfying void where no one else could follow drowning them in pleasure.

Paige had already discerned how he loved to be stroked, fingertip caresses that aroused his already swollen private parts, inciting him further, while her hand encircled and moved against his shaft, causing him to moan to the swollen crescendo of sound that stirred the air.

He climbed on top of her thin time, drawing both of her legs up to his mouth, kissing them alternately, lovingly, as he moved deep inside of her, while her hands slid down to envelop his bulbous underpart, massaging the warm, moist, flaccid skin nested there with those everloving golden curls, moving her hips to keep pace with him.

Every moan of his coursed through her, his excitement ushering her excitement until they were one, seeking the same motion, the same rhythm, the same end.

She could feel him holding back, delaying his momentous outburst, taking her further and further, until she was breathing more erratically, breaths that were harder to grasp, and she had let go of control and thoughts, and was climbing higher and higher, lost in primal sensation. She started to cry out just as he did, their friction increasing until they were both bathed in glorious sweat, fervent in their movements, needing this orgasm to be the best of them all. And it was.

Savoring the feeling of his weight upon her, watching daylight break through in a filtered illumination that edged the curtains, which were not quite wide enough, Paige was torn between being delighted about Mark's facile acceptance of what she had told him, and feeling stung.

In a way, it granted that she would be able to have her cake and eat it, too. She and Mark could sustain an intimate friendship, great sex, support, and fun while she looked around for her rich man to marry. On the other hand, his position wasn't exactly flattering. She wanted it all. She wanted him to adore her, to crave her. And yet to let her be free.

Paige straggled in about ten in the morning. She found Susan asleep on the couch in the den, the book she had been reading surrendered onto the floor beside her. Tori's shoes, linen blazer, purse, and abandoned jewelry were also still downstairs, but Tori herself appeared to have made it upstairs to her bedroom.

The haphazard state of the elegant room told of a long, late night: brandy bottle down considerably, liqueur glasses left out, lipstick-stained coffee cups, drained-to-the-bottom coffee pitcher, the mountain of pistachio shells spilling from out of the crystal bowl over onto the table, and the gallon-sized carton of ice cream that had been polished off.

From the zipper compartment of her purse, Paige brought out a joint she had been squirreling away, since it was so hard to get good grass nowadays, and succumbed to smoking it. Taking a profound drag from the small yellowed-with-time cigarette, she bent down to pick up the book that lay just below Susan's dangling hand.

How to Get Over Your Lover and Survive read the familiar title. *No, not another one,* Paige thought, dismayed. "Susan, you silly jerk, you don't even know the man," she said reproachfully, looking down at Susan's innocent face breathing peacefully from under the cloak of sleep. When she noticed Susan tensing, hugging herself as though she were cold, Paige lifted the pretty, Indian-looking blanket from the arm of the other couch and drew it gently up over Susan while continuing to regard her with aching regret. How could she have done such a thing, she thought, filled with self-recrimination as she stared down at the friend she had betrayed. Growing more and more uncomfortable, Paige squirmed, taking another intense hit of grass, hoping to dull the guilt.

What was she going to say to Susan? *I'm sorry?* She kept struggling to think up an apology, an explanation, but each one she devised sounded more lame, more inadequate than the next. It was like breaking someone's heart and then offering a Band-Aid.

It reminded her of that awful Christmas when Kit had gotten a beautiful china doll from her parents. Paige had been eaten up with jealousy because all she had gotten from her parents were some Colorforms, a plastic egg containing Silly Putty, and a slip because her father had been selling slips that year (and it had been a particularly bad year for him). She still remembered with a nagging clarity how she had pulled Kit's doll away from her and broken it. "Let me just see it. Don't be such a hog," she had shouted, yanking and yanking until she not only pulled the doll away from Kit's tight grasp but had caused it to drop onto the unyielding black-and-white tiled floor that had been in Kit's parents' den, where the Christmas tree was, and it had shattered into a million pieces. Paige had been gripped with guilt for weeks. She used to dream about it. And she remembered how she had cried at the time—they had both been crying their eyes out—while she kept saying she was sorry over and over again. She remembered how helpless she had felt on her knees beside the minute fragments, trying with all her heart to piece them back together when it was clearly an impossibility, yearning to turn back the clock so that it would have never happened and the beautiful china doll would be back as it was. Kit had been heartbroken, but forgiving. It was Paige who had never quite forgiven herself.

Taking a deep drag on the marijuana cigarette, still studying Susan's sincere and lovely face, Paige slumped down into the chair that had Tori's jacket draped over the back of it, experiencing that same sense of futility and helplessness.

What kind of a terrible person was she to have done such a thing? First she tells Susan not to go out with Mark. Then she not only goes out with him but she ends up in bed with him. Never mind that it was just for the fun of it, that her original position on Mark remained intact—he was not the "catch" she was looking to marry. Susan would never understand. And she would certainly never forgive Paige.

Paige considered denying it. Saying they had just been out all night together, fooling around at the pier, then Trancas, jumping from spot to spot. She found she was nearly panicking, trying to think of a way to repair the damage she had done, to redeem herself. For the first time in years, really since Kit had moved to California, Paige finally had girlfriends again, not the kind she had had in the shows, but real friends and she desperately did not want to lose them.

Chapter 13

Someone's birthday party.

Only Madonna's.

All throughout the evening, Richard had been pointing out different celebrities, names and faces which eluded Tori. The guy in the leopard-skin bow tie—he directed *Star Fire*. The girl in the gold lamé Halston—she was in the new Wier film. The guy with the yellow sneakers that matched the yellow flecks in his bow tie and tuxedo cummerbund had just won an Emmy for his appearance in the new musical *Brash Baby James*.

But a birthday party for Madonna, who was romping around quite "unlike a virgin," with true star cadence, who had been cajoled into giving an impromptu performance, had Tori admittedly awed.

The party Richard had taken her to, being held at Neon, the very exclusive, strikingly appointed private club, was unlike any she had ever been to, with everyone dressed to kill in what could only be described as "black-tie hip." Hairdos were extreme, even weird, sculpted and sprayed to sustain their daring shapes. Clothes and jewelry were also avant-garde, some gorgeous to look at, some unique but too bizarre, some vampish and cheap. Variety and high spirits abounded.

Tori's gown fell into the gorgeous category, thanks to Paige, who had pressed Tori into wearing her new, smashing, red Valentino that Philadelphia had bought for her. It was a bold offer, considering the Nicky Loomis affair she was attending with him was scheduled for the following night. Tori was a wreck, fearing she might spill something on it or snag the delicate fabric, but Paige, still zealously trying to make up for what she had done to Susan last week, wouldn't hear of Tori not wearing it.

The first few days after Paige's all-nighter with Mark had been strained, to say the least, with Susan broodingly quiet, Paige nervously noisy, and Tori uncertain how to act, feeling uncomfortably stuck in the middle. After Paige had apologized for the hundredth time, Susan had finally exploded and told her to shut up already. Paige feebly proposed to help repair things with Susan and Mark, resolving not to see him anymore, but Susan maintained that she didn't care.

On Sunday the four of them—Paige, Mark, Susan, and Tori—had all gone together to Susan's law firm to hang the painting he had brought her. A mistake, Tori had thought at first, with Paige and Mark exchanging private looks, Susan trying to act like nothing hurt, and Tori, still in the middle, striving to keep everything light.

After they had finished at Susan's office, Mark had invited them all out to a favorite falafel stand of his in Venice for lunch, then sailing on a friend's boat, which was really far too small for the four of them.

The cramped quarters served to break down the tension, with everyone nearly getting smacked in the head by the boom as the wind changed courses, and they tried to duck and maneuver themselves out of the way. By the time the sun went down, they had arrived at a sort of tentative peace, all of them punchy from being in the sun so long, the motion of the sea imposing a soothing lethargy, so that they were all surprisingly relaxed, laughing, and having a good time.

Susan had burst into tears later, when they arrived back at the house, but Paige never knew that. "I'm just washing it all out of my system," she had said to Tori, looking completely heartbroken. "It probably wouldn't have worked out, anyway. I don't think we have a lot in common. And I've always preferred dark, swarthy men." There was music floating upstairs from an album Paige and Mark had put on. Mark was having dinner there with the three of them, and Susan assured Tori that she could handle it.

Over the course of the week, Paige and Mark had gone on to become an item. "Just friends," she kept telling them, but Tori wondered. Paige was obviously sleeping with him, and, Tori thought, leading him on. But then again, maybe Mark was smarter than all of them. Maybe he glimpsed a side of Paige that they did not. Maybe he was unconvinced by her brash airs and perceived his best strategy to be patience. Wouldn't it be ironic, Tori thought, if her prediction, called in jest, which had Susan ending up with her millionaire and Paige with her penniless professor came to pass?

While Tori was in the midst of getting dressed, Paige had appeared in her doorway, cradling in her arms her entire ruby red collection—gown, gloves, jacket, purse, shoes, plus the earrings, necklace, and bracelet that had followed by UPS—all compliments of Philadelphia. She stood there for a few long moments surveying the scene before her. It was about twenty minutes before Richard was to arrive, and Tori's room looked like "the big one" California was expecting had finally struck, with Tori's bedroom having been at the epicenter of the massive earthquake. Clothes, lingerie, jewelry, shoes, purses, and makeup were strewn everywhere.

Tori herself was standing wearing only a pair of bikini panties, rummaging through what was left in her closet and feeling completely distraught over what to wear, when she heard Paige saying, "What the hell, maybe this will help to soothe my guilty conscience. Though I think I'll have to come up with something a hell of a lot more than just an outfit for Susan."

Caught by surprise Tori turned around, speechless with relief and gratitude as Paige shrugged and said, "I'm repenting any way I can." Before Tori could muster up the will to protest, Paige dropped the whole lavish load onto the bed, issuing an eager, "C'mon, Miss Georgia Peach, hurry up and try it on before he gets here!"

The effect the dress had on Richard had Tori feeling eternally grateful to Paige. Red was unmistakably her color, the way it contrasted with her pale skin and jet-black hair, which was more spiked and more extreme tonight than she ordinarily wore it. And while the cut of the dress was sophisticated, it was also audaciously seductive, the way it molded to her shape, pushing up her bosom, showing off a lot of leg, making her feel both self-conscious and wickedly alluring at the same time, making her flush the same color as the dress when Richard arrived and she opened the door for him.

He had stood there appraising her for what seemed a long time, his eyes full of amused admiration, as though he had been expecting something far more conservative than the skintight red jeweled gown that left little to the imagination. "You're really full of surprises," he had said, approval in his voice as he circled smoothly around her, appreciating the drama of the red creation from all angles. The one thing Tori had wanted to pass up at the last minute, feeling doubly self-conscious, the red jeweled fingerless gloves, which rose up past her elbows, were what he seemed to be the most bowled over about. As he helped her on with the matching red jeweled jacket, his hands grazing her bare shoulders sent a shiver down her spine, which she could have sworn he felt.

He looked divine in his smartly cut tuxedo, as handsomely appealing as he had looked, still sweaty and invigorated, just off the polo field. He had that same luminous glint to his pale blue eyes, she thought, as he escorted her out to his candy-apple red car, enthusiastically identifying it as a late fifties' model four-door Facel Vega, a recent acquisition for his extensive vintage car collection. Polo was only one of his passions, he assured her, as he opened the door for her to climb inside, eagerly pointing out how the car's unique body design had been so avant-garde for its time that in its era it was a magnet for cops. Built near to the ground in front and in back, it created the illusion of going one hundred twenty miles an hour, even when it was standing absolutely still.

A little showy for her taste but interesting, she thought, ducking into the streamlined classic, taking in the gleaming sterling silver appointments inside and the Baccarat crystal perfume bottles mounted in the back sporting fresh pink-and-white speckled tiger lilies. She immediately thought of Travis because he was mad about old cars.

They had gone to dozens of classic car exhibits together, and she recalled how he used to swoon over the various models, making her laugh as he wished aloud in that funny way of his that a fairy godmother would come and perch herself on his shoulder, wave a magic wand, and grant that the car of his choice would be his. Ironically, the object of Travis's fantasies last year had been a silvery gunmetal Facel Vega.

Impulsively, Tori found herself wishing that Travis could see her stepping into the four-door model that would have made his head spin, wishing for the vision to sting him, to cause him regret. Then she sighed, her pleasure of a few moments ago waning because she was the one bearing the regret.

As Richard chivalrously closed the door for her, seeing to it that she was securely inside, she gazed out through the window and up at the sky, struck by how few stars were visible in contrast to her black and glittery sky in Atlanta. Employing a childhood rhyme, silently wishing upon the largest star she could find, which was probably a planet and not a star anyway, she wished solemnly that she would stop caring *what* Travis thought.

Then for just the briefest second, Richard put his hand on her thigh as he slid into the car beside her from the driver's side. It was a strange sensation, considering where her thoughts had been, and she realized this was the first prelude to physical contact that she had had with another man since Travis. Not feeling any sexual attraction to the surgeon, the concept hadn't occurred to her when he had benignly kissed her good night. But Richard's touch was striking another chord, a responsive one, triggering some deeper intuition, a precognitive vision of the two of them together in bed making love. The image was bizarrely clear, a fragment of time, unsettlingly real, playing in her head like a movie trailer in advance of the act, leaving her both excited and at the same time scared to death.

Richard's friends looked a lot like he did. They were gathered around a festively adorned table, which had a tropical-looking

centerpiece fashioned in keeping with the dining room's aquari-
umlike design. The elliptically shaped room evoked the sensation
of being in water, aqua neon reflecting off birds of paradise,
painted glass walls the color of the Caribbean, illuminated by
tubes of flowing neon gas, aqua, raspberry, red, and violet, all in
bright and fluid motion.

Traveling the length of the long oblong wall, framed in the
center of it almost like a living painting, was a tropical garden
containing giant birds of paradise and lush, verdant trees.

It was all very elegant, as were Richard's friends, who seemed
to stand apart from the rest of the crowd.

They were all youngish, jet-set wealthy types, tied to Madonna
through business transactions instead of rock and roll, talking
casually about their Cessnas, their polo, their high-powered investments.

Only one of them was dressed eccentrically. He was a film
producer friend, an old Columbia chum of Richard's who had
just returned from shooting a film in Tibet and was entertaining
the table with horror stories of the erratic endeavor.

Madonna was to be starring in his next film. He was hoping it
would be shot somewhere more civilized, like in Paris, London,
or New York. Or that the cast would at least behave in a more
civilized fashion.

Tori learned that Richard too had tried his hand at producing
several years ago, though, she guessed, not too successfully. She
was getting the impression that if you had money and lived in
L.A., at one time or another producing was a phase you went
through.

"I'm a guy who needs to run fast," Richard confessed to Tori
when a couple of the guys were kidding him about the T and A
picture he had produced a few years back. "Life has a boredom
factor that keeps me always in two places at once. The day after
production stopped, I was already in the real estate business."

The man sitting on the other side of Tori overheard Richard's
comment and laughed. He reached into the breast pocket of his
tux and brought out a buttery leather pouch containing Cuban
cigars. Passing them among his friends, he remarked, "Yeah, be-

cause his old man told him the well was going to run dry if he didn't get a *real* job."

"Hey, give me a break. *Summer Sensation* made money. My old man was just jealous!" Richard cheerfully defended himself, accepting one of the cigars and then drawing it beneath his nose to inhale the aroma.

"But you blew more than it made," the cigar donor admonished. Then he looked directly at Tori. "Richard's idea of producing a picture is he flies everywhere first-class, stays in first-class hotels, *suites* yet, has the most expensive restaurants in town cater the sets, generally marries the star, buying her jewelry that ups the budget by at least forty percent—"

"Fuck you, Jordan. I only married one star—"

"You also only made one picture," laughed a woman who looked like a younger Candice Bergen. "You want to know about Richard? This is a typical *Richardism:* The picture takes place on the beach, right? A good place for a T and A flick, admittedly. But does he shoot it in Santa Monica, like any sensible person shooting a low-budget film? No, he shoots it in the south of France."

"Hey, they have better T's and A's in the south of France," Richard replied, his hands up in the air by way of a disclaimer, a grin on his handsome face. "Sorry, I couldn't resist," he apologized afterward to Tori. "These guys always like to give me a bad time."

"Ah, poor Richard," another one of the women said, blowing him a kiss across the table. "You want to hear another Richardism? He's on the board of our tennis club. As are all the gentlemen seated before you," she added, patting the tablecloth in front of her in a designating fashion. "He happened to miss a board meeting and they made him president."

"Does that mean you're popular?" Tori asked him lightly, not really getting the so-called Richardism.

"No, it means I'm a schmuck," he said laughing. "Administering the fucking club takes up as much time as my real job."

"You *have* a real job?" Someone else chimed in.

"Now come on, guys, you're going to give Tori all the wrong

impressions," Richard said, being a good sport about the whole thing.

"He works very hard," the producer said solemnly. Then he put his hand up in front of his mouth and pretended to choke.

The roasting was brought to an abrupt halt by a parade of white-gloved waiters boasting trays of tall rosy-colored soufflés, the sweet fragrance of the piping-hot confection trailing behind them as they began depositing them in front of Madonna's guests. Silver bowls of rich whipped cream followed. And then a boisterous chorus of "Happy Birthday."

Madonna, laughing gaily, stood up on her chair to take a bow and throw kisses. She was dressed in a black jersey number that fit like Saran Wrap.

"So who wants to go to Argentina next month?" Richard asked, a second spoonful of soufflé poised in front of his mouth.

"What's in Argentina?"

Tori glanced across the table at the two women who had asked in unison.

"Polo ponies," Richard answered, winking at Tori and then leaning in thoughtfully toward her. "See, if you come to work for me, you can do crazy things like take off for three weeks to go to stay on a gorgeous sprawling *estancia* in exciting Argentina," he said in a voice this time that included only her, describing the rambling Spanish-style hacienda that belonged to a friend of his.

Tori laughed, feeling a warmth from his sparkling eyes that were a paler version of the aqua on the walls. "How's that?" she asked, her voice matching the tenor of his, giving in to the flirtation.

"You'll be my assistant. I'll *require* your assistance."

"Hmmm, I thought I'd be working in the marketing department."

"Yes. But for me. I'm thinking of using a South American theme on the next phase of Bel Air Estates. We're putting polo fields onto some of the estates and I thought it might be a clever idea to market them as Bennetton's *estancias,*" he joked. "I'd need you there with me to pick up ideas. We'll want authenticity . . ."

Tori laughed. "Authenticity," she reiterated, smirking as a

waiter refilled her wineglass, waiting for him to finish and depart. "All part of the job—"

Richard lifted his refilled glass and tilted it toward her as she raised her own. "Sounds intriguing, doesn't it," he said, touching her other hand, toying with the small paved-diamond ring on her finger that looked like kids' jewelry in comparison to the rocks the other women were wearing.

"I think I'm looking for something more—" Tori hesitated, watching his tan muscular hand closing over her pale delicate one.

"More *what*?" he asked, interrupting. She felt her chest swell and her cheeks color. He grinned, taking it all in, calculating. "Bennetton is known for its top-flight salaries and perks, you know."

"I think it's the perks that have me alarmed," she noted.

He was moving his hand along hers in slow circular motions. "We have excellent medical insurance. You'd get a car—"

"Vintage, like yours?"

"If you like."

Tori laughed again, feeling little electriclike waves all over.

"We're a great company to work for. We take over Disneyland once a year—just for our employees. You want to go back to school to take certain classes? We bankroll you. Tax season get you confused? We hire a slew of extra accountants during tax season to help out anyone who needs it. Did I show you our gym? Separate men's and women's. Our Christmas party is un paralleled . . ."

The dizzying currents continued. Tori put down her wineglass, afraid to drink any more. Then she picked it up again, not sure what to do with her free hand. His steadfast gaze had more effect on her than one of those fast spinning rides at an amusement park.

"I'm still waiting for you to say yes . . ."

She was tempted, unnervingly tempted. *Yes, yes, yes.* The reply rolled around in her head. The job she had finally decided to accept was for a stuffy Canadian-based firm. But it was a stable job, and a choice career move. The job for Bennetton could turn out to be a whim. Richard was clearly erratic, and the job itself so undefined. The sensible thing to do would be to say no to Richard. To tell him, thank you very much, but that she held fast to not mixing business with pleasure, that she was already a veteran of that error, and that she had accepted something else.

"I have an idea," Richard exclaimed mysteriously, rising abruptly from his chair before she had managed to say anything at all. In seconds he had taken her hand and was whisking her up from her chair and out of the party, offering only the faintest of good-byes to his pack of puzzled but not surprised friends.

How strange to be in the arms of a man who had grown up with Kennedy, Sinatra, and Andy Warhol at his family dinner table, Tori thought looking out over the view that was a three-hundred-sixty-degree sweep from the beaches of Santa Monica to downtown Los Angeles.

They were standing on the property country-and-western singer Kenny Rogers had purchased for his new home, staring out at the magical city view aglow in a sea of bright, twinkling lights, broken only now and then by random patches of blackness. Richard had driven Tori up to see the three-hundred-twenty-five-acre site for Bennetton's Bel Air Estates in hopes of selling her not only on the job he was offering her but on himself.

The multi-million-dollar private estate community was both opulent and rural at the same time, set up high above the city in its own majestic mountain-carved haven. For 3.5 million dollars, the discriminating customer could acquire a spacious two- to three-acre site overlooking Century City and Beverly Hills, complete with luxuriant landscaping, security, stone streets, and a pad for a tennis court, Richard told her. For the equestrian-inclined, horse facilities and polo fields were also an option.

The detail work that had gone into the project was mindboggling, from the four-thousand-square-foot Italian granite gatehouse, which housed the unique laser-disc video selling devices, to the custom-designed curbs, gutters, and sidewalks, all done in a stamped concrete with a stone pattern finish and laid out in meandering curves, to the streetlights, fire hydrants, and Stop signposts painted with a verdigris patina to look like weatherworn copper. The exceptionally lush landscaping, which had a

European look, principally evergreen shrubs and plants accented with plump stalks of powder-blue-and-lilac delphiniums, had been put in ahead of the construction of the homes themselves. This was done to establish the exclusive environment into which a prospective buyer was buying for upward of three million dollars for a piece of raw land. And that was without the house.

Standing on top of the world in their formal evening wear, a faint breeze stirring the late-night air, with Richard seeming suddenly more vulnerable than arrogant, Tori knew that she was indeed sold.

True, Richard was the overindulged son of a powerful real estate magnate, spoiled, as one would imagine, growing up rich and gorgeous to boot. But there was something else about him hidden beneath the cultivated veneer of his privileged roots, some brooding sensitivity, a hurt that made her want to embrace him and make everything perfect, as it looked to be on the outside. He was honest, cut right to the heart of things, and she liked that. He said what attracted him to her was that she was not afraid of him. She thought that was pretty funny since, in fact, she was scared to death of him.

She had never personally known anyone with wealth on this scale. Vintage car collections. Private jets. Being invited to rock stars' birthday parties, with half the guests arriving in chauffeured limousines, was hardly an everyday occurrence for Tori. She would have to stand in line for hours in order to get only average seats to see Madonna in concert, let alone go to her birthday party. Traveling across the world on a whim, the way Richard and his friends apparently did, staying in only the most swank accommodations, needing bodyguards, as he said he had at one time—it was a lot for Tori to take in.

Richard's mother had died when he was twenty-two, when he was away at Columbia University, smoking a lot of dope, snorting a lot of cocaine, dating a lot of international-beauty-queen types, driving fast cars, and living under the silver-spoon delusion that the world was his oyster.

He used to fly back and forth between coasts and had what he described to Tori as a first-class operation within first class, making himself a curiosity factor for the stewardesses because of his youth and quiet vulnerability. By the end of each flight, he would have picked up at least one of them, offering a ride in the limo that was awaiting him. From the limo he produced great tapes and dope and then from there seduced his new "friend" into coming back with him to his great brownstone on the Upper East Side, an invitation which no one ever turned down.

Richard's simple joyride life came to an abrupt halt when his mother died. He was too young and too self-centered to have even considered mortality, that she might not always be there for him. He had been in bed with a couple of the stewardesses, as it happened, when he had gotten the news. They were all so ripped out of their minds they ignored the telephone's incessant ringing for the first several hours, hoping in their drugged haze that it would go away, feeling too out of it to be able to carry on any kind of coherent conversation. He almost didn't even answer when he did, except that he couldn't stand the infernal ringing any longer.

His father's secretary had been the one to call, something he had always wondered about, but even to this day never confronted. The words seemed completely unreal; they kept coming at him over and over again, cutting through a thick fog. Maybe it was the drugs; maybe it was just the shock. He had been more out of it than this before, but he had never felt more out of it. A heart attack, had been the shocking news. But there was nothing wrong with his mother's heart. It was the strongest heart he had ever encountered. Maybe it was his father who had had the heart attack, he remembered thinking in a flight of panic. He could have handled it if it were his father.

The painful irony of it was the fact that he would have had an opportunity to see her before she died if only he hadn't been so messed up when the calls had started coming in. By the time he got the news it was too late to get a flight, and he'd had to wait until the following day. That handful of hours had been critical. His mother died only two hours before he reached the hospital and, to this day, he hadn't ever gotten over the guilt and sense of being cheated at never having gotten to say good-bye.

Richard's relationship with his father remained complicated, fraught with anger, competition, and awe. Tori still remembered the way Richard had sat studying his father's picture in his office, the remark he had made about Tori meeting him, as if he were God there at Bennetton.

In retrospect, the remark now seemed razor-edged. It took a lot of fight to amass the kind of wealth Richard's father had amassed, to reach the heights he had reached, and she imagined he was still there presiding at Bennetton Enterprises, exercising his iron will, running the show with his dukes up, proving himself even at the expense of his son. While Richard referred to everything as *his*—*his* property, *his* concept, *his* sales force—Tori suspected that with a father like Elliot Bennetton, Richard was afforded little autonomy. High-powered men with big egos rarely just handed the store over to their sons.

Tori also learned that Richard had been married twice and had twin daughters, age six. His first marriage had been an act of rebellion, carried out when his father became engaged only a year after his mother's death. Richard had wanted to throw a monkey wrench into his father's marital bliss, so he had showed up at their huge wedding with a bride of his own, turning the affair into an unexpected double ceremony. "Guess what she did for a living," Richard had asked Tori sardonically. Tori got it right on the first try. She was a stewardess.

Wife number two was more in keeping with Richard's image. While for a long time he avoided glamour, cover girls and makeup, he wound up falling in love with and marrying a beautiful French actress. She was starring in his T and A picture his friends had been ribbing him about earlier. Along with her beauty, she had that great French style and arrogance. And of course she had great T and A. They had a whirlwind romance, which ended the day of the wedding. After that it was clear she was on a gold-digging expedition. She was very French, very spoiled, and very moody. On the set they had dubbed her the enfant terrible. She tamed down for a while when she became pregnant, but then after she had given birth to her twins, she went right back to the role of spoiled French bitch and played it to the hilt. After a year and a half of this, Richard threw her out. The problem, of course, was the twins. Richard tried to gain custody, but in the end he relented because, with his life-style, being a single father was just too difficult. Chantal, his wife, took the babies back with her to France, where they lived now, taking long vacations to the United States to stay with Richard as part of their custody arrangement.

"So you see I'm not really the best marriage bet—I don't have the best history," Richard told Tori, and she couldn't decipher how he meant it. A warning to detour her from entertaining any nuptial designs on him? Or was he just stating a fact? *Or* was he embarrassed about his record and trying to make light of it?

"I stand forewarned," she replied, disappointed because the sense of intimacy seemed to have been shattered. They were still standing looking out over the city. The temperature had dropped. She had his tux jacket draped over her own gossamer jeweled one.

He drew it tighter around her, lifting her chin to meet his lips. "I didn't mean it that way," he said, kissing her.

Mean it which way? She wondered why they were discussing marriage on a first date, anyway. He had said that he liked to run fast, and she felt suddenly anxious. Which direction was he running? Toward her or away from her? Kissing him was definitely easier than pursuing this confused line of thought. *Kiss me and transport me far, far away, up to a place where thoughts cannot touch me,* she reflected, eager to blot out anything cerebral, craving a release to pure unguarded sensation. But interference from the workings of her mind prevailed, interrupting sensation, breaking it down.

Richard's lips were thinner than Travis's; they felt different as they pressed against her own.

His kiss was not as smooth, nor as leisurely, and she found herself growing frustrated, melancholy, missing Travis's kiss, the way the two of them could stay joined like that for hours, kissing, teasing, touching.

Richard was moving his hand inside her jacket, over the fabric of her gown, cupping her breasts.

She wanted to feel excited, to stop thinking . . . to stop thinking of Travis, but she had no control.

Feigning arousal, she murmured appropriately, touching him back, running her fingers along his neck, which was thick and warm, letting her hand drop down to his elegant white shirt, feeling his form beneath it.

Richard Bennetton was perfection. What on earth was the matter with her?

The pace of his breathing had quickened, and she realized he had no idea how wooden she felt. This should have been so sexy, so romantic, standing on this plateau above the city with its rare and private vantage, their exquisite formal evening wear stirringly incongruous with their earthy surroundings, the rich earth beneath their feet. The fragrance of wild flowers growing up from the still undeveloped plots of land clung heavily in the darkened night air. There was a faint rustling sound from the trees and the activity of crickets, which punctuated the silence.

It should have felt like a dream come true, Tori with her multimillionaire, confiding in her like a little boy, kissing her, wanting her. But whose dream? Was it hers or was it Paige's?

"God, I want to make love to you," Richard said huskily in her ear, his breath hot with desire. She wondered how many women he had taken up to this exact spot and then seduced. It occurred to her that this might just be a variation on the airplane-stewardess maneuver. The thought bothered her and she had to let it out.

"So where's the tapes and the great dope?" she asked warily, though trying to appear playful as she pulled away. "The brownstone on the Upper East Side—" she reminded him.

He looked at her for a brief puzzled moment, then burst into laughter, sweeping her up in his arms and carrying her rather unsteadily toward his gleaming car of another era. Her dress shimmered, caught by the beam of his headlights. "Why, in the auto, of course," he joked, awkwardly opening the door and depositing her inside, then reaching across her to switch on the radio. "Actually they didn't have tape decks in the fifties," he recalled, "and I'm too much of a purist to put one in. I hope this will do."

A news update flashed across the broadcast, and Richard turned the dial until he came upon a song that suited him. They both laughed when they realized it was an old tune of Kenny Rogers'.

"He must know we're here, on his lot—" Tori kidded, running her fingers through the back of Richard's straw-colored hair, which grew low down at the nape of his neck, as was the latest fashion. Short on top, sensuously full in back, very eighties with a touch of nostalgic sixties. She felt him responding as he rolled his head back and closed his eyes for a brief moment, taking thoughtful pleasure in her touch. Not having moved from his position, he was still stretched across her while holding himself up slightly on one elbow so she wouldn't be crushed. They were both listening to the song on the radio, looking into each other's eyes and sharing the irony. If it *had* been a tape, she would have known it was planned. Instead, it felt like a strange and wonderful message of fate. "I remember this song," she said, feeling the need to say something. He seemed to be penetrating her soul through her eyes, recapturing what she had felt for him earlier. His fingers were keeping time with the sultry country-and-western rhythm, lightly grazing the swell of alabaster skin which rose up from the *bustier* of her gown.

Now she was aroused. Now she could feel the pace of *her* breathing quicken, an excited moistening between her thighs. She was aware of her skin heating up, melting, growing sexy and restless for his touch.

"I think you're going to be in trouble," he observed ominously, the corners of his mouth subtly upturned as he continued his study of her.

She didn't know what he meant, but she felt herself blush. There was something very intense, very intoxicating going on here between the two of them, some connection that had her feeling all out of kilter again. It was puzzling because she was unable to grasp the logic of it. There was a smile rising up from deep inside of her that she could not hold back.

"I predict that within three months you're going to be *taking* that bad marriage risk you stood forewarned on," he said, his fingers roaming dangerously lower, tracing deep into her cleavage, trailing down as far as her dress would permit. She could feel her heart pounding, but he wouldn't let her interrupt.

"Here's another warning," he said, leaning in still closer. "When I want something, I always get it. Nothing stands in my way. Nothing at all. I don't have any feelings about what you want. I wouldn't care if you were married. With a boyfriend. I'm aggressive *and* obsessive. I don't stop until I get what I want. And from the moment I laid eyes on you, sitting there reading that stupid book, I wanted you. Boyfriend or no boyfriend, I predict there's going to be a rock on that finger before you even know it." He was holding her left hand up to his lips, forming a band around her vacant wedding-ring finger with his kiss. She blushed, she smiled, she probably turned as red as her dress. His tenacity was heady, challenging even, flattering because it was now directed at her.

Was this another line of his? Or was it for real? She couldn't tell because her already spinning thoughts had picked up still more velocity. He had driven her up here to beguile her into accepting the job offer. Now it appeared the position might be as his wife. A thought passed fleetingly through her mind but evaporated before any words could be formed. He chased the words off with a lingering kiss, smoother than the kisses before, then maneuvered out of the car, coming around to the other side, clearly enjoying her stupefied reaction. "Careful. I warned you that I like to go fast—" he teased when he was in the car beside her behind the burnished rosewood steering wheel.

"You don't even know me," Tori cautiously pointed out.

Grinning, he inserted his key into the ignition and started it up. "Oh, yes, I do," he said, cocksure, as they swayed from side to side, unable to maintain their balance, and certainly unable to maintain hers, as the four-door Facel Vega passed over the gravelly unfinished surface of the famous country-and-western singer's mammoth lot, peeling out onto one of the many roads that he personally had christened.

Then she thought of Travis, and her heart slammed into her chest like a heavy lead gong, causing her to lose touch with how she felt altogether as Richard drove the few blocks leading up toward his just-completed house on a hill, one of the first to have been erected in pricey Bennetton Estates.

Chapter 14

"This is the most fucked-up world—everyone's always in love with the wrong person!" Paige observed later, when Tori had returned home from her evening with Richard. It was after having gone up to Richard's house where Tori had made an empty kind of love with him, consumed with thoughts of Travis the entire time, feeling acutely as though she were cheating on him by being there in bed with Richard.

Richard's body had been like aspirin when she needed Demerol: over-the-counter stuff when she needed prescription.

Her whole being literally ached for Travis, a gripping need that had invaded the very essence of her so that each thought she had was overlapped, joined with a thought of him, the concept and the face of Travis unyielding. He was a drug from which she was experiencing painful withdrawal, the high she required in order to feel alive, in order to feel at all. Being there in bed with Richard only heightened her distress, her craving, his unfamiliar naked presence merely producing a more frustrated awareness of what she needed and didn't have.

Damn him. Straight-as-an-arrow Tori, who smoked grass only occasionally but had never experimented with cocaine or anything harder, felt as though she had gone and gotten herself hooked on a drug far worse, a drug infinitely more devastating. Her addiction had her feeling strung out, frantic for her fix, ready to concede to anything in order to get it.

With Richard naked in his big luxurious bed beside her, moaning from her touch, trying to initiate pleasure, *she* remained far away—plea-bargaining with her psyche in a humiliating effort to ward off total trauma. She needed to feel high, to float away in waves of mind-releasing orgasm and promise.

And she did promise. She promised herself—the hell with everything—she was going to call Travis tomorrow. Maybe tonight. She was going to sneak into Richard's football-field-sized bathroom when this was all over and call Travis to tell him exactly how she felt, how she needed him, and how he also needed her.

The hell with marriage; the hell with her pride and babies and all that she had ever imagined for herself. She couldn't take this anymore. Her heart was breaking for the thousandth time, dealing a death blow to her judgment. It had taken two months of seeing Travis nearly every day before she had felt comfortable enough to make love with him. And now on her first date with Richard she was in bed with him, living out some sort of perverse revenge against Travis and feeling as if it had backfired. All she wanted was to move back home to Atlanta, back to Travis. Back to their condo that he was trying to sell. He could keep his blessed marriage to his wife he hadn't seen in years. He could do any damn thing he pleased. She would never harass him about marriage again, never even mention it.

She was reformed.

It had all just been foreplay until now, with Richard trying to make her come, trying to ready her for his eager entry, but his voice beamed her back to earth, back into his bed.

"You're so wet," he had said thickly, in a voice that sounded as washed out as her thoughts, coming in only distantly familiar, passing through the roadblock that was Travis. His body felt even more unfamiliar, looked unfamiliar, golden skin, golden hair, golden boy, when she was accustomed to dark, macho, and middle-class. "You ready?" he had asked considerately, sucking softly at her shoulder, his long, athletic form pressed up against her. They were both up on their sides, facing one another, their thighs tangled as he held one small but shapely breast cupped in the palm of his hand, while she trailed her fingers along his skin, bronzed from so much sun, silky to the touch.

"You're exquisite," he pronounced, repositioning himself so that he could encircle her breast with his mouth, moaning with relish as he drew his hand down again, passing over her stomach, causing *her* to moan.

He was right—she *was* wet, needing the consummation as much as he. She tried to pretend he was Travis, then stopped herself, stubbornly, as she held his rock-hard penis between both hands, creating a double friction that made him cry out.

Tori wanted nothing more than to feel profoundly turned on by Richard, to lose herself in the power of his high-velocity brand of courtship, and to lose *Travis* in the upheaval of its wake. Even if it were all to be a wild and crazy, impetuous mistake, if it wiped out Travis whatever bruises she incurred would be worth it.

And as he flipped her over, onto her stomach, and entered her from behind, she vowed to try.

"God, you feel so fantastic, I'm going to explode," he whispered after about thirty seconds, and then did.

Not exactly the most romantic position, she thought, for their first time together. But at least she didn't have to face him.

"It's just so classic," Paige reflected, watching as Tori somberly switched off the flood of outside lights. "Susan's in love with Mark. Mark's in love with me. I'm in love with the prospect of being filthy rich, which Mark will never be. Richard's falling in love with *you*. But you're stuck in a rut in love with Travis, who's dead and buried in the backyard anyway. Everyone always seems to be facing the wrong way."

"Richard's hardly 'in love' with me," Tori corrected her, walking into the powder room and picking up the entire box of Kleenex. "He's used to getting whatever he wants. And since he doesn't *have* me, he wants me."

"I thought you said he *did have* you," Paige teased, noticing Tori's makeup that had looked so perfect a few hours ago when she had helped her apply it, but was now smeared into a charcoal mess around her pretty eyes. When Richard dropped her off she had walked into the entry hall and seen Paige standing there, book in hand, even though it was two in the morning, waiting to see how it all went. In that instant the floodgate had burst, and Tori had dissolved into tears.

"Only my body, not my soul. I guess he wanted both."

"Funny," Paige said. "When you're younger you give your soul and guard your body. When you get older, you give your body and guard your soul."

"I guess when you marry a rich man you're not in love with you give your body and *sell* your soul," Tori philosophized ruefully, pulling out a fistful of Kleenex and blowing her nose.

"Not me. A prostitute sells her body. A fool sells her soul. I sell nothing."

"You sell your body *and* your soul."

"I share my body, and I always guard the hell out of my soul," Paige insisted, laughing. Then she asked sympathetically, "God, was it that bad?"

Tori thought about it for a moment, looking up at Paige from over the shield of Kleenex concealing the rest of her face, looking a little like an Egyptian belly dancer as her dark eyes smiled in a kind of surrender. "No. Actually, I liked him a lot. I'm just all screwed up, that's all. Thanks for the dress, though. It was a show-stopper." Unable to unzip it by herself, she turned her back to Paige for help.

"Yeah, well let's see what kind of magic it works tomorrow night," Paige said, carefully gliding the zipper down the delicate jeweled fabric of the gown.

"I hate to tell you this, but your party's *tonight,*" Tori corrected her, pointing to the predawn hour appearing on Paige's shiny gold counterfeit Rolex. Wishing she were more like Paige, Tori leaned over and gave her a peck on the cheek. Paige always knew exactly what she wanted. She didn't flounder. She was pragmatic. She had a glow about her, even now in the middle of the night, a clear-headed, scrubbed kind of glow in her white terry robe, her lush, honey-colored hair swept up off her face into a ponytail. "Thanks for being here for me," Tori said gratefully to her, "but go on upstairs and get some sleep. Actually, your dress did work magic for me tonight," she added on second thought. "I'm just too dense to appreciate it. And anyway, *you're* always magic—with or without a Valentino." Holding the unzipped red gown up so that it wouldn't slip off, she gave Paige a light shove in the direction of the staircase. To Paige's lingering look, she replied, "Thanks. It was perfect. I know tonight will be perfect for you. Now get the hell out of here and get some sleep!"

Already imagining the pleasant sensation of her head meeting her pillow, eager to drift off into sweet dreams of this evening's much looked forward to affair—her date with the mysterious Philadelphia—Paige grasped sleepily onto the cold wrought iron of the stair rail, envisioning herself as the belle of the ball, the new girl in town who would turn heads—*Paige Williams, the Enchantress.* Using the stair rail for support, she swung around to head dreamily up the stairs.

Paige Parker, she thought, drowsily trying on her date's last name and smiling because she had always liked alliterations.

Her near-slumber rapture was caught up short by Tori's brusque but unsurprising announcement. "By the way, I accepted the job at Bennetton," Tori offered without expression.

"Good girl," Paige replied, turning to give her friend the thumbs up sign. If only her friend didn't look so desolate, heading over toward the bar, toward the bottle of Armagnac they had *all* been using to numb their bouts of excess emotion. "It takes time, you know," Paige noted encouragingly.

Tori nodded, wishing she could put that interminable stretch of time on "fast forward" and get it over with, already.

The Beverly Hills Hotel crowned Sunset Boulevard like a big pink cake, full of sweet legends, conjuring up lofty expectations. It was pink and green and grand. It stood like a marvelous old tribute to the era when Hollywood reigned supreme.

Paige drove up to the hotel in Dustin Brent's shiny black Aston-Martin Lagonda feeling very gay, very chic as she handed the expensive toy over to the parking attendant and flashed him one of her more beguiling smiles. It was a gorgeous day, the sky a deep blue, the sun a vivid yellow ball, like a kid's crayon drawing where, in the background, you would expect to see purple mountains rising up into proud peaks.

Mountains are not purple. They're brown.
Says who?
Should we teach them reality? Or let their imaginations flourish
without boundaries, without imposed censors? It had been one of
the arguments of the day when Paige was a kid, freedom versus
control, nobody certain, Spock preaching one thing, then later
trying to take it back. And what they had ended up with was an
entire generation counting on the power to paint mountains any
damn old color they chose.

Speaking of color, Paige was wearing a scribbly slipdress that
had vivid strokes of boysenberry run wild on tawny tangerine. It
was vibrant and very revealing, dipping to a very low V in back.
She hadn't known what color shoes to wear and had finally decided on a pair of high-heeled black patent pumps she had
bought on sale at Charles Jourdan just before she had moved out.
They didn't quite go, but they didn't clash either.

Catching glances from all directions, she swept through the
lobby of the old hotel, appreciating the airy California decor, the
bustle that activated her senses. She thought back to her initial
impression of the hotel, when she had arrived there in June to
stay for Kit's wedding. *June, July, August—what a turning-point*
summer. Thank you, dearest Kit, she thought, feeling eternally
grateful to her old friend as she headed past the bank of phones,
exchanging flirtatious looks with the men there presumably conducting *deals*—"taking" meetings by phone.

There it was, the Polo Lounge. And from inside she saw her
date waving to her. Handsome Philadelphia looking like a dashing Don Juan. He was as smooth as three-star French vanilla ice
cream.

She hadn't been certain that she would even recognize him. It
had been at least a month since they had met, and their bizarre
but memorable exchange had been only about fifteen minutes
total.

"Hi," she said cheerfully, slipping into the booth beside him,
liking his oatmeal linen suit, his crisp white shirt, and his tie that
seemed to blend with her dress. They made a handsome couple
and had drawn stares from the neighboring tables. Now that she
was sitting face to face with him, it all came back. The round,

intelligent-looking brown eyes. The thoughtful creases beneath
them that she imagined could make him look kind or tough,
depending upon his mood. He had a good head of hair for his
age, which she had estimated to be about forty-five. His teeth
were capped; she could tell by the color differentiation when he
smiled. She also noticed that he still wasn't wearing a wedding
band and that there was no tan line there to indicate that he had
taken it off for her benefit.

He was taking her in, just as she was taking him in. So she
looked past him, through the window and out to the courtyard
set up with green-and-pink flowered tablecloths, tempted by the
sunshine, musing that she would have preferred to have sat outside in the garden.

"You look gorgeous," he said, placing his hand on her back,
reacting to the absence of fabric there. With a faint smile reflecting his surprise, he ventured further, curiously trailing his hand
the length of her spine, all the way down until it intersected with
the crazy fabric of her dress where he would have had to negotiate with the nylon zipper to go farther. It was all done with the
utmost of discretion, his wandering hand protected from view,
sandwiched between her young blooming body and the shiny
vinyl booth. "Now I know what I want for lunch," he asserted
brashly.

She smiled coolly, deciding to play it remote for a while, thinking he appeared a little too eager to collect on his gifts.

But now came the difficult part, what to say to each other.
Flirting was easy. Screwing was easy. Carrying on a conversation
required work. She had no idea what he was interested in, what
he even did for a living. Straight out asking him would sound
forced, contrived, idiotic, and maybe even beside the point. She
had to set the tone but she didn't know which keys to strike first.
Her opening line began to take on blustering proportions, as
though her first words would set her into a category in his mind
from which it would be impossible to ever climb out. It occurred
to her that she was probably already in that category.

Thank goodness the waiter appeared to requisition drink orders just as she had embarked on some fatuous sentence and
spared her from having to complete it. Drink talk could be the

beginning of small talk, which could lead them into big talk, and then they could relax and have sex. *God, the pressures of first dates.*

Even the simple task of ordering seemed to present an obstacle. What if she ordered alcoholic and he ordered nonalcoholic? She would feel like a lush, drinking at twelve in the afternoon. On the other hand, something alcoholic seemed appropriate, more festive. She considered champagne, then decided it would look too put on; a beer would look too casual. A Bloody Mary seemed like just the right thing if it weren't too potent, but then she determined the high would probably do her good.

"What about you, Mr. Parker? Your usual?" the waiter asked, while making note of Paige's order. The unexpected familiarity with Philadelphia's name and drink caught her by surprise since he had told her that he didn't stay here.

In their one brief telephone conversation (all other communication had been through telegrams and gifts), he had gone on with such elaboration about how he preferred staying at the old Château Marmont, explaining how he liked it because it was more intimate, more romantic, more bohemian, hidden up in the Hollywood Hills, and commenting how over the years it had become known as a kind of a dormitory for Left Bank artists. Screenplays for *The Color Purple, Butch Cassidy and the Sundance Kid,* and *The Day of the Locust* had all been written by writers in hibernation there. Whoopi Goldberg had whooped it up in the lobby there. Garbo had slept there. Belushi had died there. Sting had once stayed up all night performing a concert for the hotel staff.

Not that Stan Parker seemed like the bohemian type. But his plan was for the two of them to go back to the old Château after lunch (he said they didn't have much of a restaurant), relax by the swimming pool, "get to know each other," as he had put it, and then get dressed and go to the affair together.

It sounded like a good plan to Paige.

"So. Tell me about *you,*" Philadelphia said, inching in closer to her after the waiter had disappeared.

The line coming from her would have sounded inane, but she was grateful that he had broken the ice. From him it was fine.

Not clever, but definitely fine. Paige laughed. Her nerves some-what mollified. "I'm a heart surgeon," she teased. "I work with research and rare species—"

He laughed, his eyes bright with amusement, his appreciation of her humor putting them both still more at ease.

The waiter returned with her Bloody Mary, and Stan's "usual," which looked like bourbon on the rocks. Paige tipped her glass toward his. "What? You don't believe that I'm a doc-tor?" she asked, looking at him with mock reproach over the rim of her spicy red drink.

He shook his head no.

"There was just a big article about me in *Newsweek,*" she de-clared, as though incredulous that he hadn't read it. "About a breakthrough I made in developing a new kind of laser technol-ogy that helps transplant an obscure variety of Japanese gold fish hearts into Brazilian parakeets, keeping the parakeets alive for at least two more years. Can you *imagine* what that's going to do for mankind . . . ? What do *you* do?"

"Me?" He looked as if he would try to top her. "I'm a leader of a little-known religious sect in New Guinea."

"I thought you said you were from Philadelphia."

"I was born in Mongolia. My father was a fan of W.C. Fields, so we relocated. Though by the time we got there, W.C. was already off in Hollywood. Then when I was about eighteen, I got the word from upstairs and set out to enlighten pygmies."

Paige was all ears. "On what?"

"Vegetarianism—" They both cracked up.

"This is going to be fun," she predicted, wondering what he really did, grinning at him over the rich green leather-bound menu the waiter opened and placed in front of her.

And it was. Stan Parker was a lot of fun. He was impulsive. Funny. Easy to talk to. She learned that he was in the import-export business and judged that he did exceedingly well. But unfortunately, the demands of high-powered corporate life pre-sented themselves with a little too much clarity when an un-timely phone call interrupted their lunch, demanding his pres-ence at an unforeseen meeting.

He couldn't have been more gracious about it, finishing the meal without hurrying through it, attentive to her, making sure she had had enough. Did she want dessert? Another cup of coffee? After they were all through, he gave her the key to his room at the Château and told her to go on ahead without him, promising that he would join her there just as soon as he could manage to escape.

Paige was pleasantly mulling the whole thing over while lying out by the sparkling blue oval-shaped pool at the Château Marmont, dark shades over her eyes, drinking diet Coke by herself, oiled and soaking up what was left of the midday sun.

"Miss Williams. Telephone for you again."

It had been an hour since Stan's last call, and Paige shielded her eyes as she looked up at the young handsome man attending the pool area. "Thanks," she said, rising up from the low peach-colored chaise and heading over to the house phone, which was contained in a small brick alcove.

"Well," she asked in a silky voice, snapping her bikini into place over her behind from where it had hiked up, grinning with expectation.

The pool attendant, watching her, also grinned. Another one of Stan Parker's gorgeous little numbers. With this one he had truly outdone himself. She was as close to a "10" as they came. He sighed, thinking it must sure be great to be rich and capable of buying anything. Barely able to tear his eyes away from Paige's beautiful ass, he took the bill she had signed, which from her oil had the faint scent of coconuts, dumped it into the trash, and rewrote another, per Mr. Parker's usual instructions. The bill was still charged to the penthouse, but under the timeworn alias "Joe Smith" so that there would be no record for any prying private eyes, should his wife ever get suspicious. God, didn't these stupid chicks smell that the son of a bitch was married? Or did they know and not care?

"I'm going nuts here, thinking of *you there*—" Stan was saying apologetically to Paige. "We're at a stalemate on this thing. Neither side will budge. Are you doing all right?"

"Fine. A little lonely, but very relaxed—"

"Save some of that relaxation for me."

"I think you should just give in already," Paige teased. "What's another million or so? Compared to an afternoon with me—"

She could feel him smiling over the line. "You probably have on one of those really sexy, French-cut bikinis, with the cheeks of your undoubtedly perfect ass in ripe view," he said.

"I do," she replied playfully.

"God, I knew it. And I'm stuck here with a bunch of stuffed shirts. What color is it? Tease my imagination into a complete frenzy."

Paige looked down at her skimpy gumdrop-orange suit, the revealing top, her sensuous hips swelling softly over the sides of the bottoms that were about the width of a licorice stick. "Gumdrop orange," she answered harmlessly.

He sighed again. "You've probably got a great tan. Your skin is probably the color of caramel and just as smooth."

She cuddled in closer to the brick wall. "And you can't have your lawyers take it from here?" she cooed.

He sounded suddenly distracted, as though there were someone else in the background. "Sorry, beautiful, break's over. I ordered up some champagne and caviar. If you're hungry when you get back up to the room, go ahead and open it," he directed hurriedly. "I'll see you just as soon as I possibly can." And abruptly he hung up.

With her hand lingering restlessly on the phone, trying to kill time, Paige decided to call Tori and Susan, hoping to find someone in. The machine picked up and, disappointed, Paige left word telling them how things were going, about Stan's cute sense of humor and his *un-cute* premature departure and delayed return. Then she left the time, telling them to call her back if they got this message within a half hour.

With the sun's power diminishing, the air growing chillier, Paige collected her suntan oil, her magazines, threw on the shirt she had brought along with her and followed the quiet garden path back over toward the castlelike edifice of the Château.

Killing time before heading up to the suite, she passed idly through the grand, recently renovated, European-style lobby, feeling the red tiles of the floor there cool beneath her bare feet.

In any other hotel, she would have felt self-conscious walking around dressed as she was, barefoot. But the Marmont *was,* as Stan had claimed, *different.*

She looked up to the cathedral-like arches looming over the entry arcade, the chandelier swaying there, ghostly, reminiscent of old black-and-white movies, a clock striking midnight, the scampering of unseen feet. It was made of heavy wrought iron fitted with amber-colored glass and it was genuinely eerie, hanging almost precariously from a ceiling painted in bright, fresh shades of aqua, lavender, green, yellow, and orange conceived in a Matisse-like design.

To her right was a sunken lobby, with cathedral windows, Moorish arches, robust blue furniture, like the furniture in Stan's suite, a marvelous old rolltop desk and a mahogany baby grand piano, where a frail, weirded-out-looking guy wearing wire-rimmed glasses and a deep scowl sat agonizing over the keys. He would play a series of notes, frown, then pick up the bottle of beer he had on the seat beside him, take a swig, then start up again. Next to the beer was a yellow pad of paper and a pencil, and she realized that he was composing. Curious if he were somebody famous, she watched for a little while longer. He had to have felt her standing there looking at him, but he didn't turn around even once.

Growing bored, she headed back toward the room, past the small receptionist desk, pausing in front of the antique vitrine that displayed a variety of Château memorabilia behind glass doors. Its contents ranged from Château Marmont postcards, matchbooks, small stacks of *The Hollywood Reporter, Variety, Rolling Stone,* an unexpected collection of antique dolls with painted porcelain faces, and, surprisingly, the flowered jams and Château Marmont T-shirts she had noticed the moody pianist wearing.

After mounting the couple of flights of stairs leading to the penthouse, Paige proceeded into the plush four-room suite, wondering when Philadelphia would call again. He was true to his word, she was glad to see. Set up attractively on the coffee table, along with flowers and two crystal candlesticks, was an unopened tin of Iranian caviar on ice, a plate of miniature toast squares, and, alongside that, a silver ice bucket containing champagne. It was already six o'clock and the sight of the spread made Paige suddenly ravenously hungry. Weak with temptation and nothing in her stomach, she eyed the tin of caviar, debating, but in the end was unable to disturb the perfect picture.

Instead, she decided to bathe and get dressed.

Just as she was measuring a couple capfuls of fragrant oil into her bath, the telephone rang and she rushed across the icy marble floor of the expansive bathroom to catch it, wondering if it was Tori, Susan, or Stan.

"Hi." Her ebullient, sexy reflection bounced off the mirror as she answered the phone, relaxing into friendly disappointment at the sound of Tori's voice on the other end.

"Got in just under the wire—exactly twenty-seven minutes since your call . . . Is he there yet?" Tori asked, a touch of southern-style sympathy in her voice. It was definitely not the distraught, melancholy voice of last night, Paige was glad to note, and she wondered what had caused the change.

"No, this meeting of his sounds like it could go on forever," Paige complained, keeping an eye on her snowy white bath water, which was rapidly filling up, airy bubbles climbing higher and higher under the force of the water.

"Goes with the territory, Paige. You want a rich guy—this is what you get. A lot of absenteeism while they're out keeping those seven figures rolling in—"

"There's always inheritance cases, like your divine, polo-playing Richard Bennetton—"

Tori laughed brightly. "And speaking of whom—guess who's coming for dinner? Guess who happens to *also* be going to Kit and George's little dinner party tonight?"

"No—you're kidding! Oops, hold on a sec." Through the mirror, Paige had caught sight of the tub about to overflow and dropped the phone in order to shut it off in time. She returned a split second later, eager to hear the rest, thinking no wonder Tori sounded so cheerful. "How did that happen?"

"I mentioned to Richard last night that I was going there. He knows them. But only peripherally—"

"And he had the nerve to call them up and invite himself?"

Tori laughed in cheerful confirmation.

"That's pretty flattering," Paige approved, arranging the various gels and creams from her makeup case along the counter, examining her face in the mirror to be sure she hadn't caught too much sun.

"I knew you'd like that. I just got back from Kit's. She's busy redoing her seating arrangements."

"What did George think—"

"I don't think George is too keen on Richard, but Kit said he's just jealous. He wishes *he* were six two, gorgeous, and loaded without having to lift a finger."

"He's got a point. I think I'm jealous, too. So who's Susan's dinner partner?"

Tori started laughing again, southern-style sympathy creeping back into her voice. "I'll give you two clues: *Brylcreem* and . . . Commodities."

It took Paige a moment; but then she groaned as she got it. "Oh, no. Not the *Miami Vice* stockbroker—"

"Kit said she never gave him a fair chance. And you have to admit, it was a pretty tough night for her," Tori charged.

Paige paused quietly at the reference to Mark, who, though practically living at the house, and everyone's "friend," remained a sensitive subject, since he disappeared routinely into Paige's bedroom after hours. Paige had vowed to herself to make it up to Susan. Even to stop seeing Mark, but she couldn't get herself to break it off. He was the other side of what she needed right now. He made her feel good. He made her laugh. And she seemed to fulfill all that for him. Instead she kept hoping Susan would meet and fall for someone else. Someone more in keeping with the prototype they had moved out here to meet.

"Who knows, maybe she'll like him this time around," Tori offered lightly. "Now, listen, go make some more magic with that red dress of yours. It obviously casts powerful spells . . ."

"That was you who cast the spell last night," Paige said, hanging up the receiver with an amused grin.

When her bath was all steamy and ready, she climbed inside, letting her robe drop into a puddle on the floor. All she was missing she thought, closing her eyes and sinking deeper into the hot bubbling depths, inhaling the exotic almost Oriental fragrance of her Opium bath oil, was a glass of champagne—and, of course, her date, the mysterious Philadelphia, who was growing ever more mysterious still.

An hour and a half later, with Paige lying on the bed, dressed, hair and makeup done, attempting to watch a rerun of *The Waltons,* there was still no sign of him. Not even a phone call this time. Every little noise she heard had her fluffing out her hair, altering her position, primed to greet him.

Growing more and more impatient, she got up and began wandering around the suite, straightening up.

The maid had already been in to turn down the bed, but Paige added her own finishing touches, taking her new, bought-for-just-such-an-occasion Dior gown from out of her overnight case and laying it suggestively across the covers, plucking a couple of flowers from one of the vases and arranging them artfully across the pillows. After that, she retrieved her perfume from her makeup case and sprinkled some judiciously over the sheets and pillows until they smelled subtle but wonderful. Then she moved on to lower the lights to a romantic dim, turned on some music, and finally adjusted the draperies to show off the dazzling panoramic view that made the suite so spectacular, especially at night.

Perfect, she thought, canvassing the suite, pleased with her efforts as she made her inspection of it.

When she couldn't think of anything else to do, she crossed restlessly back over to the window, contemplating the garish but still vital Sunset Strip, with its star-spangled glare of visual metaphors, seriously beginning to wonder what had happened to her date. The telephone had remained queerly silent after Tori's call. It was seven-thirty, and she knew the party had already started. Searching for some sign of him in the silvery stream of traffic that hissed around the bend below, she found herself growing increasingly anxious.

Was she being stood up? she speculated uncomfortably, finding the possibility doubtful. After all, she was in *his* room.

Or was it his room? She was beginning to wonder about everything. He had given her the key, true, and she had been signing the incidental drink bills she had charged to the room. But something was off.

When she had gone to lay out his toilet articles, there had been none. When she had opened the closet to take out his dinner jacket and make sure it was pressed, she had found all the closets bare, except for her own few things, which she had put into one. She had been taken aback at this at the time, since her initial understanding had been that he had arrived the evening before. But then she just presumed that she had misunderstood, that instead he had come in early this morning and that his luggage was simply still in the limo.

But now, considering the myriad of small but gnawing puzzles, she wondered. She wondered about all those people addressing him by name at the Beverly Hills Hotel, the formal, almost self-conscious way in which he had said good-bye to her there.

Starting to analyze everything, she flashed back on the way he had slipped around her question about where his meeting was to take place, as though afraid that she might call him there. The way he had evaded just about everything having to with his personal life. The gifts, the telegrams, even dodging giving her his office phone number.

While she realized she might be letting her imagination get the better of her, she couldn't help this feeling that things were not quite adding up, and it struck her with a disheartening jolt that probably he was *married*. "Paige, you idiot," she scolded herself, "What's wrong with you? You move out to California and, all of a sudden, you've lost your grip." It killed her that she had been so unwilling to face up to this now obvious conclusion earlier, that consciously or unconsciously she had been so intent on protecting her fantasies.

Admittedly, Paige had been out with her share of married men, slept with her share of married men, but it was the prospect of his not being forthright with her, snaking around the issue and not saying anything, that shook her. Lying was the one thing she absolutely wouldn't tolerate. If she wanted to fool around with a man who was married (and since she had moved out to California she specifically did *not* want to), it had always needed to be a conscious choice, a fair, joint decision. Right or wrong, *that* she had been able to accept. At least a relationship was possible in that context; there was a straightforwardness, the terms all laid out on the line. But this outdated, male-chauvinist garbage—*let the dumb broad think you're single and she'll put out for you*— infuriated her. Who did he think he was? What kind of *games* did he think he was playing? *Well, just let him discover exactly who he was playing them with,* she thought, fingering the luminous ruby fabric of the gown he had bought for her, catching the glint of her jeweled evening bag on the couch.

Disappointed, feeling like a complete dope, if her hunch was right, and definitely wanting revenge if it was, Paige opened the desk drawer in the living room and pulled out the telephone directory, looking for the telephone number for the Beverly Hills Hotel. When she found it, she picked up the phone and punched out the number, glancing uneasily toward the door. As long as he was this late she hoped he would be a few moments later. She wasn't looking for an overly dramatic confrontation. And that's what she would get if he came in now and heard her on the phone checking him out. If her hunch was correct, she needed time to compose her response.

As the line began to ring, and then the hotel operator answered and put her on hold, she took a deep breath, watching the door through the gilded antique mirror over the desk, finding her thoughts drifting off to Mark. She resisted them immediately, feeling embarrassed, hurt, and immensely frustrated as she stuffed the telephone book back into the drawer.

Did she really want to know? Of course she wanted to know. She had promised herself: *No more married men.* She had moved out here to get married herself and they had to be strictly off-limits, *verboten.* They were a waste of time, a waste of energy, and all too often a waste of heartbreak. Yet she was going to be dammed if she wasted this evening. She had been looking forward to it for too long, had too many hopes banking on it. If Stan Parker was married, she would use him exactly as he planned on using her. She would go ahead and go to the party with him—but she just might *leave* with somebody else. *Thanks for the introduction, darling, it's been swell.* That would be in lieu of *him* having the opportunity to say *Thanks for the fun fuck*—"Good evening.

Beverly Hills Hotel." At last the operator had returned back on
the line.

"Yes, Mr. Parker's room, please. Stan Parker," Paige requested, drumming one of the engraved hotel pencils on the desk,
bracing herself. It was a game of roulette. The little silver ball
was spinning, and she was waiting for it to land. Black meant
there would be no Stan Parker registered there. Red meant the
phone would begin to ring.

What a shit, she thought resentfully when it did, when her luck
rolled into the red, setting her on alert. One ring, two rings . . .
at the eighth ring she heard him call out her name. Only she was
too bummed out for it to register right away that his voice was
not coming in over the telephone, but that he was actually there
turning the key in the door.

"Hi, beautiful. Paige, darling—"

Reacting like a shot to the dull ringing that persisted like bad
news in the background, and at the same time to the voice at the
door, she touched the receiver down into place just an instant
before he appeared in person in the room, disarmingly handsome
in an exquisitely tailored tuxedo.

Chapter 15

Miami Vice stockbroker Dan Sullivan was just as dull as Susan remembered from her blind date with him a couple of weeks before. But the dinner partner Kit and George had seated on the other side of her, Jack Wells, was a different story.

He was an anomaly in the otherwise homogeneous crowd of slick, upwardly mobile types seated around the large rectangular dining-room table. There were thirteen of them (uneven because of the last-minute addition of Richard Bennetton), all nattily dressed, chatting casually over flowers and flickering candlelight. Tori was seated directly across from Susan, between Richard Bennetton, who couldn't keep his eyes off Tori, and a husband of one of Kit's friends whom Susan remembered meeting at the wedding. All of Kit's female friends, Susan noted with interest, were professional women. There was Jane Triperton, a photo-journalist who worked for *Newsweek,* Leslie Cravitz, a pediatrician, and Brenda Locke, a literary agent. Susan and Tori were the only unmarried women there. And three of the six females were pregnant—Kit, Jane Triperton, and Leslie Cravitz. A sign of the times, Susan thought, looking down at her own flat belly and trying to imagine it in bloom. Leslie and Kit were on baby number one. Jane was embarking on baby number two.

Jane and her husband, Lance Triperton, had been leading most of the "baby talk" conversation, offering advice on which Lamaze class to take, which doctors were said to be "too quick to cut," pros and cons on nursing—did it or did it not mess up the mother's breasts and *insure* needing a postnatal boob job?— where to find unique baby furniture, the best scientifically designed stimulus toys and apparatus, scaled-down Ferraris for one-year-olds, and finally the exchanging of baby-nurse gossip. Jane had compiled an extensive list of private nurses, their phone numbers, and vital statistics and told Kit and Leslie to have their secretaries call her secretary for a copy of the information.

Having babies in upper-crust L.A. was certainly different from having babies in Stockton. Susan glanced across the table at Tori, wondering if she could possibly relate to any of this because *Susan* certainly could not. Postnatal boob jobs, live-in baby nurses, father-and-son Ferraris, Italian cribs . . . She tried to calculate what the cost of having a baby in Beverly Hills must run. No doubt as soon as the live-in nurse moved out, a live-in nanny would move in to take her place.

It was impossible to catch Tori's eye. She and Richard were oblivious of the entire discussion. They were talking softly between themselves, smiling private smiles, sharing private laughs. *Good for you, Tori,* Susan thought, happy for her. Susan liked Richard. Probably he was spoiled—but that wasn't *his* fault. He was charming and obviously intent on wooing Tori, who, Susan thought, was far too skeptical of his attentions. Why shouldn't he be taken by her? She was down-to-earth, smart but not on the warpath to prove it, beautiful without having to try too hard, and aloof. She wasn't falling all over him, as he was probably accustomed to. Plus that southern accent of hers. . . . Susan could see its disarming affect in Richard Bennetton's handsome face.

Jack Wells caught Susan looking and gave her his own private smile, a quiet communication that seemed to link the two of them and, at the same time, mark them apart from the others at the table. It was as though he had read her thoughts, inferred that she was different, and in the same glance communicated to her that he was different as well, and glad of it. She was sure that he had seen through her high-styled floaty silk dress, Paige's bronze leather jacket and boots. He had probably noticed her worrying that she was going to dribble soy sauce on it during the Japanese hors d'oeuvres they had been served sitting around in the den, and probably caught her gagging on the big squishy coral-colored fish eggs. Kit and George had hired a Japanese caterer, and the caterer's native culinary theme was being carried out to the letter, down to the dragon-emblazoned plates, the tinkling background music, the lyrical arrangement of the flowers, the colorful paper lanterns, and the fancy, ivory chopsticks; everything, except that Kit had passed on actually requiring her guests to sit on the floor to eat. Maybe because half the female guests were pregnant.

Susan and Jack had barely spoken to each other all evening, other than to exchange a few pleasantries. *Oh, so you practice law. Oh, so you manufacture surfboards. Good salmon skin roll, isn't it? Super house.* But she had gleaned a sense of him just by watching. There was a bad scar across his left cheekbone. On anyone else at the party she would have assumed it was from a racing car wreck or a bad skiing accident, a trophy-wound inflicted from one of the rich man's sports, something daring and glamorous. But on Jack Wells the keloidal gash brought something tougher to mind, a rough and tumble street fight, the cutting edge of a knife. Like Susan's, his hip California look was strictly camouflage, she was positive, adapted so that they might blend in when they wanted to—just as long as there wasn't another alien there, sensing the difference. She saw it in his moody brown eyes, his gaunt angular cheekbones, the cautious set to his jaw, the way he had stood around earlier taking everything in, absorbing, measuring as though he were, by choice at times, invisible. Although he wasn't conventionally good-looking, she found she was drawn to what she imagined to be his come-up-the-hard-way brand of elegance. He would be smart, maintain few illusions. No silver spoons or prep schools for this hard-core American male. It was marked in his guarded manner, in his wide, hooded eyes which seemed to carry something raw behind them. He was very nearly the definition of cool. And Susan smiled back at him.

"I'd love to have a kid," he volunteered, surprising her, even though it was "baby talk" that had been dominating the general table conversation for the last twenty minutes or so. He put it to her like a wry proposition, his grin friendly, inquiring. "Maybe ten of them."

"Ten kids!" she laughed, picturing bedlam, wondering if he had been an orphan, and therefore craved an enormous family, or a deprived only child. "I hope you're exaggerating," she emphasized, sipping through a smile at her still-warm sake.

"Why? Did I scare you off?"

"Maybe," she replied, giving him a sidelong glance as one of the pretty, kimonoed waitresses slipped between them for a moment to remove her plate, which contained just the barest remnants of vegetable tempura, a few artichoke leaves that had been dipped and fried, and the lone stem of a zucchini flower. "At these rates . . . with a private nurse per baby, ten Italian cribs, ten private school tuitions from nursery on . . . ten reconstructive breast surgeries. Ouch!"

"Ouch! is right," he proclaimed. "I don't know. Where I come from, *drawers* work as well as cribs. They're cozier, even."

He had made her smile again, as she imagined a whole big chest of drawers, each one containing a cute little blanketed baby. Blue for the boys. Pink for the girls. "And where's that?"

"Minnesota."

"Really? I've always imagined Minnesota to be incredibly beautiful."

"Incredibly cold, anyway." He frowned and she wondered what the frown meant. Apart from his not liking the cold.

She moved aside as a fresh plate was set in front of her, accepting a warm, fragrant towel to clean her hands.

"What about you? Where are you from?" he asked.

"Stockton. It's north of San Francisco—"

"I went into a real estate deal up there once. You know, you *look* like a country girl."

"Hmmm . . ." It was her turn to frown.

"It was meant as a compliment."

"You can take the girl out of the country, but you can't take the country out of the girl?" she inquired, looking at him askance. "What sort of real estate deal?"

The face he made indicated that it was not one of his better ones. His shrug implied a casual acceptance of the loss. "So, did you practice law there? In Stockton?"

She smiled fiendishly, knowing that her reply would get the goat of a manufacturer, an owner of a large plant. "I represented the unions—" she revealed.

On cue, he grimaced. "That's the wrong side of the fence to be on."

"It all depends upon whom you happen to be sitting next to," she replied demurely.

"Well, I doubt you'd be sitting next to a labor activist at a posh little dinner party such as this."

"True." She smiled, sizing him up. "Actually, I'm on *your* side of the fence now. Not because of any philosophical conversion," she was quick to add.

"What then? Money?"

"It pays the bills."

He grinned, looking at her with what she took to be tough respect. He was a realist and he liked other realists. "So how does it feel to have switched sides, to be representing *management* now, instead of the *people*?"

"The *people*—" she mocked lightly, knowing he wouldn't believe for a moment that the *union* could ever really be synonymous with the *people*. "The truth?"

"The truth."

"I miss the action of being out in the fields. It's a far cry from reviewing employment contracts for executives, negotiating their perks, their deferred payments, their golden parachutes, and poison pills, which is what I seem to do all day. You can hardly compare going to bat for some executive wanting a Mercedes over a Cadillac versus someone wanting running water or a toilet that he doesn't have to share with thirty other workers."

"Is that what you used to do?" She couldn't tell if he was intrigued or making fun of her.

"That's exactly what I used to do," she said somewhat defensively, thinking back to her old gutsy tactics. "I used to go out to the farms, the nut orchards, with my court order in hand, and argue with these big-gutted field foremen, who'd get angry as hell when they'd see me. But I loved it, chasing down the trucks, getting the poor, uninformed, frightened workers to realize that they could expect and fight for more humane conditions for themselves and their families."

Jack listened quietly, appraising her. She wondered what he was thinking.

"You can't believe how pathetic the conditions are," she went on. "The workers live in filthy sheds or in these dormitorylike structures with twenty to thirty beds all crammed together. One toilet. One wash basin. They're lucky if they have hot water. They're lucky if they have running water, period. Not to mention no health insurance, that they can be fired indiscriminately if they get sick or if someone higher up doesn't like them. No time off for funeral leave. Sure, most of the union leaders aren't really out to make life for the workers more bearable; they don't care if they have hot water or that there are little kids working the fields. But I loved that in the course of serving their *business* interests, I was getting to see a difference being made. It assuaged my sixties' conscience."

"How much *difference* do you really think you made?" Jack asked a touch too condescendingly. "Did you ever go back afterward and see what exactly had been done, not just talked about or promised?"

"Nothing happens overnight. But there were changes. And *yes,* I did go back and see for myself."

He looked doubtful that the changes could have been significant. He also looked as if he had had plenty of problems with the union guns himself, and she sympathized, knowing how miserable it could be on the other side, the kind of harassment he would have undergone. The truth was, she felt she wasn't naive, just that it was an extremely complex issue about which she herself was plenty ambivalent. Just looking at the last several Teamsters' presidents, they had all been in jail, with the exception of Jackie Presser, who had been under investigation for years but had been spared having it go any further because he was an informer for the FBI and on the FBI payroll. Former Teamsters' president Ray Williams had been indicted, tried, and convicted for trying to bribe a senator. Jimmy Hoffa for bribing jurors . . .

Jack refilled both their sake cups with the individual porcelain containers that were at each of their places, then took a thoughtful sip of his own. "Unions are archaic at this point. They served their original purpose, but for the most part they just exploit those whom they originally set out to serve. I say in fifteen years or so there will be no more unions."

Susan raised an eyebrow, studying her dinner partner, noticing the heavy shadow that was developing along his jawline and finding it sexy. He looked like a cross between Dustin Hoffman and Billy Joel; he had the same intense, wiry characteristics. They were even about the same height. "So how did you happen to get into surfboards? You don't look like the surfboard type," she asked, changing the subject.

"I'm not. I hate the ocean—"

"*I* know," she ventured gamely. "It's too cold—"

He pointed his trigger finger at her and smiled, friendly again. "Plus all that sand. You can never get rid of it. It stays in your trunks and between your toes—" His smile broadened and she laughed. "*My* trunks, anyway."

"I love the ocean," she said.

"Well, we must have *something* in common," he joked.

"Horses?" she tried.

"Nope. I'm allergic."

"Tennis?"

"No time."

"Me neither. There, I knew we'd find some common ground," she said, catching a glimpse of what looked to be a tattoo on Jack's forearm, only faintly visible through the fine white cotton of his shirt. It was a hot night, with the arid Santa Ana winds in full gust, and the men had been given clearance from their host to remove their jackets. Curious, but lacking the nerve to stare or ask him about it, she averted her eyes. "What *do* you like to do?"

"Make money," he responded easily. But he put his hand over his forearm, massaging it there as if the muscle were sore, and she wondered what he was thinking—if he had noticed her trying to make out what was beneath the fabric, if there was anything even there.

"Oh, so that's why you like L.A. The land of money worship."
She took another sip from her sake cup.

"A god that pays off at least," he remarked with a steely smile.
"A tangible deity that you can put in your pocket, make multiply, do any damn thing you want with. Buy hot running water
. . . Even use it to help feed poor starving kids or fund research
drives to cure cancer. It's a productive belief. Which god do you
worship?"

She regarded him curiously, not quite able to get a handle on
him. "That's a very serious question," she replied.

"You can worship *me* if you want," he said, this time without a
trace of seriousness.

The conversation all around the table paused as a bowl for the
next course was slipped in front of each guest, the flower vases
rearranged to accommodate hibachi-type cooking units, one set
up between each couple.

"I want you to know that this dish is especially for you, Jack,"
Kit interjected from her end of the table as the petite Japanese
waitresses brought out a series of steaming iron pots that smelled
absolutely mouth-watering. "Those buckwheat noodles you've
told me about . . . *soba,* well, Haruko makes them and they're
divine. At least I think so, but what do I know? I never lived in
Kyoto—"

One of the waitresses giggled and glanced at her cohort. "Neither did Haruko," she confessed.

Susan, growing ever more curious, looked at Jack. "Kyoto?
You lived in Kyoto?"

"After 'Nam," he said casually, seeming to enjoy the awkward
silence his answer produced. Whether it was intentional or not,
or for her benefit or not, he unclasped his hand from his forearm,
and she decided there was definitely some kind of tattoo there,
though she couldn't distinguish what.

Dan Sullivan leaned over to say something to her, and she
nodded, without bothering to really listen. It was something
about having been in Kyoto himself, but she wasn't interested.
He was boring and his experience there would have been boring,
a carbon-copy nonadventure.

Jack Wells, on the other hand, with his scar that lent him

character, his tattoo glimpsed beneath his shirt sleeve, his seemingly out of character money worship, *he* interested her plenty.

As the thick *tanuki soba* noodle soup was served, Jack identified its various ingredients, the seaweed, or *kobu,* the fishcakes,
called *kamaboku,* and a couple of the more exotic Japanese
spices. He also expounded on the etiquette of slurping, how the
appropriate way to eat soup in Japan was to slurp; the louder the
slurp, the greater the compliment you were sending to the chef.
Everyone at the table laughed at the loud, ill-bred sound of him
consuming his favorite dish the Japanese way, with noisy gusto.

But Susan was glad when he subdued his intake of the rich-
tasting dish and directed all of his attention back to her, elaborat-
ing on the portion of his life that he had spent in Asia. After
Vietnam, having fallen under the mysterious Eastern spell, Jack
had stayed on in the Orient, living in Singapore for a while, then
moving on to Japan. Still undergoing emotional aftershocks from
the chaotic violence of Vietnam, where he had served as a member of a little-known U.S. Army unit known as Tunnel Rats, the
Asian aura of tranquility, the feeling of restfulness, of absolute
serenity, acted as a medicinal balm.

For eleven long months, his responsibility had been to ferret
out Viet Cong in a nearly paralyzingly effective and ostensibly
impregnable network of subterranean redoubts, where the VC
had built an astoundingly advanced tunnel complex humming
with factories, hospitals, flag-making workshops, printing plants,
theaters for USO-type entertainment, and strategically placed
subterranean command posts. He had done combat in this underground maze, armed only with a flashlight, a knife, handgun,
grenades, and sharp animal cunning. Not bothering with false
modesty, Jack told her how most enlisted Rats lasted only four
months and that, in the four-year history from discovery of the
tunnels until the end of the war, no more than one hundred GIs
were even qualified to wear the TR badge and the jungle fighter's
bush hat that distinguished them. The criteria for the treacherous
volunteer mission had been compact stature and gargantuan
courage. Only five seven, lean and sinewy, Jack said he had been
an ideal candidate for the Rats.

The history of the thriving tunnel complex Susan found particularly fascinating since it was ongoing long before the war against which she and her generation had marched. The Reds' triumph over the Americans, Jack explained, was in actuality the culmination of a thirty-year war going all the way back to the forties and fifties when ground was originally broken for these tunnels by the Viet Minh, predecessors of the Viet Cong in plotting a revolt against their French colonial masters. Almost all the tunnels had been excavated by hand, by peasants using spades or hoes, and the power had been generated by pedaling a bicycle. Remarkably, some of the underground structures were four stories deep.

From these tunnels, which were entered by intricately engineered trapdoors, Communist cadres infiltrated the South Vietnamese capital more or less at will, making the American war effort futile and leading inevitably to the fall of Saigon. It was of little consequence that the Americans had the greatest firepower of any army under the sun, because while our U.S. troops were invading, defoliating, and destroying the land above, they couldn't possibly prevail with the Viet Cong manning their base camp from under the earth below their feet, in a two-hundred-mile tunnel complex that, at the peak of the war in the mid-sixties, stretched from the gates of Saigon all the way west to Cambodia.

Jack didn't spare her any of the details. He told her about how they had approached the camouflaged trapdoors as if walking on scorpions, which was too frequently the case, taking unthinkable risks to pump tear gas or napalm into the complex labyrinth, and succeeding only in wiping out a fraction of their target because, every hundred yards or so, the VC had constructed special water traps rigged to seal entire tunnel sections into separate compartments so that only a single sector could be affected. She shivered from the too-vivid pictures he was creating in her head, reacting to the fear and futility he must have felt.

After the war, Jack said he knew he couldn't face going back home. The reality of his life back in the States was too unreal, too jarring. He said he needed an Asian existence for awhile in order to successfully make the transition. And Japan was where he thought he had found his enlightenment.

Even Japanese art was soothing, their music, their design, their immaculate bonsai gardens, which were at once austere and serene. Those eleven months had been too long, too intense, too full of death and insanity. So he had lived in Japan for a couple of years, healing himself, working odd jobs, mostly in hotels catering to American clientele, learning the language, trying to break through the mystery enshrouding the complex and age-old Japanese customs.

But the tranquility wore off in short order, once he had moved back to the States, replaced by a reckless anxiety to make money fast, to catch up. He felt the blow of inflation both in the economy as well as in his age, finding himself a quarter of a century into his life with no money, no college education, no work experience, and nothing hopeful on the horizon. He wanted the art, the beauty, the grace, but he wasn't going to get it without ample cash to first afford him food, shelter, and self-respect. It had to do with a person's worth being measured by dollars, in his mind, because it would buy power and control, an essential he had had to live without in 'Nam, something he would never live without again. Power and control didn't exist in that jungle. You needed wits and brawn and also a hell of a lot of luck in order to survive.

Nobody escaped a war like Vietnam unscathed, and Jack Wells wasn't any different. He didn't lose any limbs, walk with a limp, or lose his sanity, but he was unquestionably a veteran, a veteran who had traded his Lutheran God for the almighty dollar, becoming a devout workaholic, a Wall Street fanatic.

Kit and George's dinner party was a great success, and when the evening broke up Susan had been in great spirits, waiting for Jack to ask her for her telephone number, sure that he would want to ask her out since they had enjoyed talking to one another so much. When he didn't, her ego seemed irreparably wounded and she left crushed.

First Mark, then Jack. What was the matter with her? Maybe she just wasn't in Tori and Paige's league. Maybe it was time to face the music and alter her expectations. What *were* her expectations, anyway? At this very moment, as she slipped into her car alone, without Tori, because Tori had gone with Richard, she decided she had no clue whatsoever, and she burst into tears.

Instead of going home, she decided to drive back to the office. At least there she could feel in her element, in control. *Successful.* The ever-present piles of work on her desk were something she could manage without this painful insecurity, something in which she could thankfully lose herself. Thank God for work, for her career. If she was bombing out socially, at least they loved her at the firm. They found her to be quick and capable, a creative thinker, good for accumulating those extra billable hours because she was often the last to leave at night.

As she pulled out of the driveway, Susan looked at herself in her rearview mirror, more dissatisfied than ever, wishing she looked more like one of her roommates.

Chapter 16

Paige was burning.

But still cool enough to have not confronted him yet. Her arm was looped through Philadelphia's as they threaded their way through the opulent room, through the gay, elegant crowd toward the dance floor, where he whirled her deftly into his arms, a smashing dancer, humming into her ear along with a tune Frank Sinatra had long ago made a household classic. She hadn't solved the puzzle yet, but she would, soon and with flair.

The party was only the most gorgeous she had ever been to. The legendary estate within which it was being held warranted its status. It was a formidable house, where it would be no trick at all to lose five hundred people, with one huge room opening into the next, ad infinitum, where no amount of furniture could possibly make the place look cluttered, let alone cozy. It was full of crystal, candles, and beautifully dressed guests, milling around, dancing, eating, having a grand time. The Carnival Night theme was carried out subtly, lending a festive mood. Paige half expected the thirty-foot ceilings to produce an echo-chamber effect, probably if one walked through the house alone, there would be one. She could imagine the theatrical resounding of footsteps reverberating through the cavernous rooms, unobstructed.

The house felt very forties, conjuring up images of the hotel baron who had once lived there, at the time Hollywood's reigning party giver, and the glittering, glamorous affairs he was known to have held.

What an era, she thought nostalgically, as Philadelphia drew her closer to his tuxedoed chest for a samba, breathing into her ear how exquisitely she moved. He felt so good up close like that, and she almost relaxed. He looked so sublimely handsome in the black-and-white attire that was de rigueur.

If only she were wrong; if only there were an explanation for his being registered at two hotels at once, she reflected, staring out through the romantic series of French doors, which lined the ballroom. They had been left open so that the guests could flow freely out onto the terrace, down the graceful tier of steps, and out into the spectacular stretch of garden, which Paige likened to a miniature Fontainebleau, even though she hadn't yet been to France. Out past the sparkling, brightly lit fountains, which were housed in long, colorful flower beds, was a second dance floor. While the orchestra inside was playing big band sounds from the forties and fifties, outside there was a disco company blasting current hits. Both were loads of fun, and both dance floors were packed.

The popping of flashbulbs interrupted Paige's train of thought, and both she and Philadelphia turned to see which celebrity was being made immortal on film.

Dancing just a few feet away from them she noticed a tall, imposing-looking man with broad shoulders and thinning dappled gray hair. Dancing with him were two women who may have been his daughters, but who she suspected were not from the way they were dressed, both in jazzy miniskirt outfits, one of satin and lace, the other smothered in emerald green sequins. The three of them stopped dancing just long enough to pose for the photographer, each of the two women cuddling in to plant a kiss on each cheek.

"Who's that?" Paige asked curiously.

"Your host," Stan whispered in her ear.

Anxious for a better look, Paige maneuvered in closer. Bulky and bursting with energy, he looked every bit the part of the

flamboyant ex-football star. On the way over to the party, Philadelphia had given Paige the full rundown on her sports-mogul
host, telling her all about his football career, about how in his
early thirties he had gone on to earn his fortune taking over the
beer empire for which he had been hired to do sales, then hurled
himself right back into his true love, sports, in a way that would
put him on the map forever. Acquiring sports teams with only
average records, he built them into championship ones, and then
constructed his own private sports arena for their games. Paige
thought she should have guessed it was he by his doe-eyed, miniskirted dance partners, since he'd been dubbed by the press "a
wild man—with a fetish for miniskirt-clad girls half his age, one
on each arm."

The illustrious Nicky Loomis was known as much for his flamboyant antics as he was for his sharp business acumen. He was
big and powerful-looking, an ape with a brain and an unquench-
able sex drive. He was imposing but still boyish, as though he had
never really outgrown his football days, which he probably
hadn't. She guessed his age at somewhere in his late fifties. He
had small lively eyes, slightly bloodshot from too much fast living, and a prominent nose that looked as if it had been busted a
couple of times, enhancing his looks rather than detracting from
them, adding another layer of character.

When he noticed Paige studying him, he gave her a flirtatious
once-over—a ladies' man, cool and secure, good for a one-night
stand and a small diamond bauble as payoff. She returned the
look, equally cool, trying to establish in a glance that he had met
his match, that he would be missing the time of his life if he let
this brief eye contact encounter end there.

As Philadelphia steered Paige off in another direction, she felt
Nicky Loomis's eyes on her back, tailing her as they sambaed
through the thickening crowd, away from him.

It was a sign and she smiled, pleased, a back-up plan beginning
to take form in her head. It was time for the unveiling of the
facts, time to find out whether or not Philadelphia was single,
married, an innocent charmer, or just a snake.

Why would a man take two hotel rooms? She could think of
one reason only. If he were married. That was an easy one—no

untimely phone calls from the wife and kids coming in when he was in the middle of receiving a blowjob from his mistress.

On the other hand, maybe there was another Stan Parker registered at the Beverly Hills Hotel, Paige thought, remote as the possibility was.

"You want to take a walk?" he asked her, that horny smile appearing on his face again. What did he think? He was going to get laid in the gardens? Not if there's a Mrs. Stan Parker, you're not. Think again.

"It's so incredible out—" he said with that silver tongue of his, taking her hand, and leading her out through a pair of the French doors, out onto the patio, down the stairs, and then in the opposite direction from where the party was set up. Just out the door, she caught Nicky Loomis still watching her and she drew a quick fix of strength from his unmasked interest, slipping him another cool smile with her eyes, allowing just the faintest curve to her lips.

The backyard was positively mammoth, easily large enough to accommodate his own private football field, *with* bleachers, Paige thought, as she and Stan roamed out of sight of the others, accompanied only by the voice of Whitney Houston serenading them through the state-of-the-art outdoor speaker system, the words of the popular song getting to Paige.

It was chilly and he put his tux jacket over her bare shoulders, since she had left the jacket to her dress back at her seat.

They walked for a while not talking, very close together. Paige's brain felt scrambled and she wondered if men, relationships, love, or any offshoots thereof would *ever* be easy for her, if she would ever be lucky.

She wondered if she could ever fall in love with someone who was simultaneously falling in love with her.

She had meant what she had said to Tori, about life being all messed up that way—everyone always in love with the wrong person. Or the *right* person at the wrong time. All she wanted was what Kit and George had found—both of them unattached, available; *him,* rich, fun . . . Like in the movies. Like in the ever-present scenario of her daydreams. Romance, sexual attraction, safe happy love. And a bankroll to weather the storms.

No more struggling with the likes of cute and good-in-the-sack Mark Arents. She had had dozens of Marks and knew only too well how when the sexual feast wore off, all that was left was just another guy who could only barely afford to take her to dinner.

If only Stan Parker would whip her around, take her into his arms, assuage all her worries, tell her it was love at first sight, tell her that he knew by instinct that he had never met anyone like her before and knew he never would again—that they were symbiotic; this was kismet; they were meant for each other.

She wanted him to tell her that he understood the deeper level of her soul that she kept carefully hidden away, the vulnerabilities she masked with such bravado. That he understood why. That he understood her past, without her even having to utter a word.

It happened so frequently and so convincingly in so many books and movies that she knew the whole thing by heart and couldn't accept it not happening in her real life, if she willed it so, if she waited long enough. God knows, she was due. She was thirty. She was tired. She was running out of lines. She needed him to make it simple, to be her Mr. Right.

This is not a play, Paige; this is real life, she told herself, feeling her hopes plunge as she reached down into his tux pockets for warmth and came upon the shapes of what felt like two different hotel keys. One of them she recognized from the Château. The other one she couldn't figure out.

"So what did you think of the Château?" he asked, the timing of his question catching her off guard, causing her to let the keys drop back down into the bottom of the pocket.

"It's great. Terrific," she replied, stumbling distractedly over her answer, not about to remove her hands from their satin-lined position. "You stay there often, you said?" Her question sounded strained, and he looked at her queerly. She smiled to cover up.

"Yes. Fairly often . . ." As though in imitation of her fantasy, he stopped in his tracks and whirled her around so that they were facing one another. Only now, naturally, it all felt false. "God, you look beautiful in that dress. It made me crazy then, and makes me crazy now," he declared, fondling the expensive fabric proprietarily.

Her hands remained shoved down deep in his tux pockets, her hand clenching the keys as she fabricated a smile. She was stumped, trying to think of a way to confront him.

He started running his finger down her cheek, along her chin, then over her lips. *She* wanted to use her lips for talking right now, not for kissing. They were definitely not symbiotic, she decided as he leaned in to kiss her anyway, which she let him do, her thoughts crowding her brain and blocking sensation.

"Warmer?" he asked, stopping to take a breath, his eyes glazed over with longing, his hard-on affecting his speech. He had her tomato-red lipstick smeared all over his mouth.

"Yes," she lied, her heart racing from anxiety. Just ask him flat out. *Are you married? Are you married . . . ?* But the words wouldn't come out. They kissed again, this time with his hands taking liberties, roaming beneath his dinner jacket, over her breasts, down her waist, her hips, slipping down to her thighs.

"God, you do make me crazy," he breathed, filling her mouth with his words. "You have the sexiest body. I was going nuts at those meetings today. I kept thinking of you in your little bikini . . ."

He tugged lightly at her wrists, removing her hands from the safety of his pockets and relocating them onto his swollen erection. "How am I going to go back out there like this . . . ?" he murmured, grappling with her gown, struggling to lift the heavy jeweled fabric up and out of his way so that he could maneuver his hand down into her panty hose to grab her ass. Then groaning and nodding more, he lowered his hands down beneath her red lace panties until they were getting at the wetness of her crotch, playing there, and it felt good, even though she had to make him stop.

She was so moist, she knew he was reading that as a *yes, go on.* She tried to wrestle his hands away, but he ignored her effort, probably interpreting it as token resistance, kissing her harder than ever and pressing up against her until she could barely breathe.

Before she knew it he had unzipped his pants and had pulled his very red, very hard penis from out of the opening there, grinning with lustful pride. Her dress was up at her waist now. He had cornered her up against a massive magnolia tree.

With her mind spinning in a thousand different directions, unable to comprehend how this had happened so fast, afraid to flee and afraid not to flee, Paige ducked down, accidentally brushing her cheek against his penis and slipping awkwardly around him. She was breathing erratically, trying to get control of herself, of him, of this tricky situation. "Excuse me," she managed with miraculous calm. She was sweating now. But she held on to his coat because she had to check out the keys in the pocket. "I have to go to the ladies' room," she blurted out.

He looked at her stunned, out of breath, appearing ridiculous with all that lipstick smeared worse than before on his face, his cock at attention standing out from the metal jaws of his zipper.

She let out a nervous chuckle, feeling every bit as ridiculous as he looked as she backed away, wriggling her dress back down into place, trying to correct her own lipstick. "I'm sorry, Stan, but I have to pee."

She moved fast, fearing that he might come after her.

What if she were wrong? What if there were an explanation? Would all this then be funny?

It wasn't easy, hurrying warily down the rock path of the garden in her high heels. But she made it, emerging as inconspicuously as possible, seizing a glass of champagne from the tray of a waiter, trying to appear composed.

Inside the house, looking for a bathroom, she spotted Nicky Loomis again. The miniskirted miracles, she noticed, were gone.

They turned up again, however, in the powder room, fixing their makeup, chatting, taking a break in front of the long stretch of makeup mirror, addressing each other's reflection instead of bothering to turn and look at each other.

On the far side of the ornate pink room, in the corner, there was a sitting room arrangement, with a couple of pink satin love seats and a small, attractively accessorized table between them. Paige sat down, literally gulping her champagne. She brought out the two hotel keys from his pocket and set them down on the table. And there it was, the Beverly Hills Hotel confirmed in engraved gold script.

Not surprising, but not enlightening either, Paige thought, staring down at the two keys, trying to figure out what to do.

In hopes of learning more, she reached into his breast pocket and discovered the smart snakeskin billfold that triggered an instant recall of their romantic, madcap meeting, then a pang of regret that things had turned out this way. Cautiously, she opened the wallet, turning first to see if the two miniskirted miracles were watching her.

They were oblivious. Good.

Swallowing deeply, Paige began examining the wallet's contents, discovering the family photos she had been afraid she would discover smiling through the small transparent jacket directly behind his driver's license and gold American Express card.

She looked closely at the picture of his wife, finding her to be fairly attractive in a prim, expensive, unimaginative sort of way. The Halston suit, the pearls, the smug smile, standing beside her adoring husband, one kid on either side of them. They looked like the perfect family. *Flawed,* she thought, the picture of Philadelphia standing in the garden, saluting her with his erect cock, still fresh in her mind.

Probing further, Paige came upon only more credit cards and a few hundred dollars in cash.

Well, now what?

Now she had to handle this mess and, at the same time, preserve her dignity. Or, anyway, her pride.

"Do you think he can even get it up?" cracked the redhead in the green sequins, standing up and spraying a final cloud of hairspray onto her perm. Paige turned curiously around.

"Honey, I don't think he can get it *down!*" the other one giggled. She couldn't have been older than eighteen. When she caught Paige staring at her, she giggled again and waved a giddy hello. Paige had no doubt of whom they were speaking. Her only surprise was that they didn't already know firsthand.

The redhead had pulled a vial of coke from out of her purse and was twisting off the cap. There was a small spoon rigged to the side, which she removed. "One more for the road—" she explained, dipping the tiny spoon inside and then casually snorting the powder. Some dropped onto her lipstick, and clung there.

"Great dresses," Paige said to them both, taking another swallow of her champagne, thinking.

This time both girls giggled. "Thanks," they said, one just after the other. "Our date's into miniskirts. In case you haven't heard." Paige assured them that she had. The blonde took a couple of snorts of the proffered cocaine, then held it out to Paige, her young eyes bright, alert. "Want some? It's real pure—"

Paige declined. Coke made her too wired; she didn't like the feeling. "Your date . . . You mean your mutual date?" she posed with a smile.

The redhead put her arm around the blonde. "We share everything," she confessed suggestively. They were obviously trying to shock Paige, so she intentionally didn't react.

"So do you two go to a lot of parties like this?" she asked, stalling them off as they were about to turn and go.

The redhead looked at her as if to say *Are you nuts?* "This party is Geritol city. We met last night at a real 'happening' party at the Playboy Mansion."

Even at thirty, Paige felt suddenly very old.

"We'd never even heard of *Nicky Loomis,*" the redhead went on in a slinky voice, "but our sources say he's *only* 'Mr. Sports King.' Like he owns just about all the sports teams you can think of here. The StarDome. Anyway, I think he's kind of hot myself—"

"She has a father complex," the blonde explained with a titter, pulling the coke out of her purse again, sharing it, as she had said she shared everything, with her friend.

Paige's eyes went to their hemlines again and she laughed, on the brink of a wild but great idea. It had to do with getting back at Stan. It had to do with getting together with "Mr. Sports King." Paige thought he was rather "hot" herself. She liked this big old house. She liked the fact that "Mr. Sports King" was single. He would be nearly impossible to rope and tame, but, oh, what a catch, if she caught him.

"Listen, would you two like to make some money and have some fun at the same time?"

"Hey, like you just hit on our two favorite things," the redhead said, snorting eagerly at the cocaine and then returning the vial to her friend. "Add in, maybe, sex," she decided.

"Thanks. As a matter of fact, I just might," Paige retorted shrewdly. She had figured out a way to get rid of Philadelphia gracefully, and she was all smiles and good cheer in anticipation. She took his billfold from out of his pocket again and opened it, extracting two one-hundred-dollar bills to help pay for the execution of her plan.

Step one had the blonde running off to get Paige a pair of scissors and a silver domed tray, while she sent the redhead off for a pen, a sheet of paper, and a discreet retrieval of the sequined jacket she had left at her seat.

Once alone, the smile gone from her face, Paige set to work composing the appropriate notes.

The note to Stan, she decided, would say "Sorry you weren't straight with me. As it turns out, I *do* mind that you're married, but my double-your-pleasure stand-ins don't. I'm sure you think of us all as interchangeable units anyway, so have fun. And by the way, don't embarrass yourself or me by coming by the Château Marmont tonight . . . Happily, you do have somewhere else to stay."

The note to Nicky Loomis would simply say "Less is more." What she planned to send along with the note would say the rest.

When the two stoned-out-of-their-minds, bubble-headed teen-agers returned carrying the goods, Paige went to work. Appealing to Nicky Loomis's penchant for miniskirts, she had decided to cut off the bottom of her evening gown, and she took a last lingering look before having the nerve to rip into it. The mirror was not a full-length one, so she had to stand on a chair and let the girls help her. All the coke they had consumed didn't exactly help to steady their hands.

"Hey, this is a Valentino. *Concentrate!*" Paige ordered, unable to believe what they were doing to the dress she had never even really dreamed of being able to buy. It was some consolation, as she saw the scissors tearing into the sumptuous fabric, that at least Tori had had a chance to wear it, too.

When they were all through, Paige laid the shimmery jeweled remains of the gown out across the silver tray, adding a huge stalk of red ginger, which she pulled from a flower arrangement, along with the note she had written to Nicky Loomis, which said it all. The shiny domed lid crowned it perfectly.

After the girls had gone—carrying with them the domed tray and some crisp bills for the waiter who was to deliver it, plus the jacket complete with wallet and credit cards, to be returned to Philadelphia—Paige took a final glance at herself in the mirror. It was a good thing she still had great legs, she thought, standing up on her toes so that she was able to view her fifty-five-hundred-dollar miniskirt creation from the knees up. Coping with familiar symptoms of stage fright, she crossed her fingers for luck and headed out.

Partially concealed by a primitive African sculpture, she stood rooted near the doorway, watching as Nicky humorlessly regarded the waiter handing him the domed tray. He eyed it as though there were a bomb planted beneath the cover. Relief flooded through her when his apprehension turned into boyish pleasure as the glitter of material was revealed and he scooped up the note, hooting unselfconsciously to the friends circled around him. This man was all mischief himself; Paige could see that, as he hooted again after reading the inscribed message, holding on to the big stalk of ginger, the remnants of her gown, and looking around for the balance of it.

When he saw her, sort of in hiding, there was a click of recognition. Paige felt her heart do a flip, and she scooted out through the entry, past pedigreed antique paneling, which she felt compelled to touch, past magnificent carved corbels, exotic paintings, colorful Chinese porcelains, and mounted ostrich eggs, tripping over an upturned corner of an Aubusson rug, recovering and floating out the door, out past the power of personal treasures demonstrated on a scale she had never before seen. A glance over at Philadelphia already out on the dance floor gesticulating with the two replacements Paige had sent him served to reconfirm her decision.

In no time, Nicky Loomis was outside beside Paige. His eyes
took in her face briefly, then cut down to her revamped gown,
pausing there with keen interest. It wasn't often she had to crane
her neck to such a degree, but he was so incredibly tall. So incredibly powerful-looking. His bullish looks made Philadelphia
appear too tame, too suavely handsome.

"I think I'd like to get to know you better," Nicky said softly.

"Not here," she replied, feeling bold and happy with her exchange thus far.

He was amused but careful. "The Bel Air Hotel's convenient—" he said, gesturing with his large hand, a heavy star
sapphire ring on his finger catching a glint of light.

But Paige smiled cunningly, reaching over to intercept the rest
of his sentence, touching her index finger to his lips. "Tonight's
my treat," she said with that same sultry smile, well aware that a
man like Nicky Loomis was not used to being "treated," certainly not by his dates. He would be used to taking care of everything, initiating everything, paying for everything, but that was
all part of Paige's strategy. She wanted to throw him off, set
herself apart. The miniskirt was going to be her only concession.

And that was different, a ploy, a brash and daring statement
applied to arouse his interest, which it clearly had. She wanted to
be careful not to fit into any of Nicky Loomis's patterns, particularly the one-night-stand pattern about which she had already
been forewarned.

Playfully, Paige snatched the car keys from his hand and
helped herself into the driver's seat of his Rolls-Royce. Before he
could even say *boo,* she had completely taken charge and she
drove out of the private gates of his fairy-tale castle, with him
silent by her side, heading down Sunset, down the Strip, toward
another castle, toward the Château Marmont.

He wants to lay me so badly that he's letting me call the shots,
she thought gloating behind the steering wheel, at least for now,
anyway.

The look on Nicky Loomis's face as he walked through the
penthouse, noticing the caviar, the champagne, the flowers, the
music, the dimmed lighting, the bed turned down, the spectacu-

lar nighttime view illuminating the suite through the open drapes, made Paige's heart leap.

He was positively bowled over. She could see it in his expression as he turned to her. "Did you plan this?"

Her mouth curved into an involuntary grin. Thank God for Philadelphia, she thought, forgiving him completely. Thank God he had popped for the penthouse, ordered up this incredible spread. Thank God he had been tied up all day and been too late to partake of it. Thank God he had brought her to Nicky Loomis's party. And thank God for the ruby red dress . . .

"Who else would have?" she teased, joining her beloved Philadelphia in the sin of omission, joining Nicky on the couch.

Heady with success, Paige opened the bottle of champagne herself and filled up the two fluted glasses. He just sat back watching in open astonishment, relaxed, enjoying whatever game it was she was playing, and letting her play it to the hilt. He had his big arms spread over the back of the couch, one thick leg stretched rigidly out, close to hers, the other bent at the knee, in slouch jock fashion. He had loosened the bow tie at his throat and unbuttoned the first couple of buttons of his elegant white shirt. "I think I like being seduced for a change," he observed, accepting the glass of champagne as she handed it to him, filling the room with his presence.

Paige smiled again. *Less is more,* she reminded herself, believing that to be her best course. She wanted to say very little, keep him at bay, and not blow the image she had extemporaneously lucked into, seeing how he obviously liked it. Instead of struggling over a reply or another line of conversation, she busied herself with opening the tin of beluga caviar.

"So . . . I have some questions—" Nicky began, biting into the beluga-smeared cracker she had prepared for him.

"You do?" she asked, using her bottle-green eyes to get to him, to maintain control.

He laughed. "About a dozen of them."

She sipped innocently at her champagne, still not taking her eyes off of him, cooperative. "Fire away," she offered, prepared to dodge.

"Who were you with at the party tonight?"

She gave him a smug, noncommittal smile. "Stan Parker."

"Stan Parker," he reiterated, mulling the name over for recognition. Paige could see that he was coming up blank. She had already known from Philadelphia that the two men had happily never met. "He was your *date*?"

"Hmmm," she nodded. "And now he's with *your* date . . . or, rather, dates, plural."

Nicky's already small eyes appeared to grow smaller as he appraised Paige, studying her as she scooped out another good-sized dollop of the caviar and smeared it onto a second cracker for him. "Should I ask you how you arranged *that*?" he inquired, vastly entertained.

"If you like—"

He considered for a moment, hesitating before popping the second canapé into his mouth. "Did this Stan Parker guy *know* you were going to ditch him? Did he know about your . . . *designs* on the evening—"

"You mean my designs on you?" Paige interrupted, savoring the unique taste of the caviar, squishing the little eggs up against the roof of her mouth with her tongue and relishing the exquisite flavor that oozed from them as they burst.

He looked flattered. "Have I ever met you before? Have *we* ever met before?"

"No," she answered simply, the champagne cool and bubbly as it went down her throat, then fizzed up to her brain.

"Are you interested in sports?" he asked next.

She wasn't sure what to answer there. She found sports unbearably boring. But they were his whole life. "How could I be interested in *you* and *not* be interested in sports?" A neat dodge, she thought, aware that she had her work cut out for her. Tomorrow, after work at the health club, she would make a beeline for the library and studiously inhale everything to do with sports that she could get her hands on, including looking *him* up in the periodicals. She wondered what year he had played for the Green Bay Packers and what position.

"You *could* be interested in money," he replied somewhat crudely.

"Who *me*? Oh, I hate money," she declared with mock emphasis, not about to let him make her squirm. "And *you* could be interested in sex—" she noted, mimicking the kidding-on-the-square accusation.

"Who *me*? Oh, I hate sex," he rallied back with a great belly laugh. They were sitting closer together, trying to out-smartass each other, enjoying the heat.

"Hmmm, so I've heard," she shot back.

"What *have* you heard?"

An I'll-never-tell sort of smile appeared on her lips.

"So why *am* I here? Why me?" he asked, eyes narrowed again, kicking off his shoes. Waiting for her answer, he unfastened his bow tie and cast it aside.

It was a tricky question. She decided the wittiest response would be the truth. "I just moved out here from New York and I'm shopping for a husband. By all accounts you're lousy husband material, but I kind of like what I see, and I like going for the long shot."

He had just taken a mouthful of champagne and he nearly choked on it. She could imagine him hurrying to put his shoes back on, grabbing his bow tie from the chair and flying out the door before the marriage monster grabbed him.

But instead he merely picked up a cocktail napkin, dabbing at what he had spilled, while continuing to study her with even more amusement than before. She felt a happy thrill because, for some completely intangible reason, she felt her proposition wasn't wholly impossible. Maybe she felt that way because he *didn't* run, and he didn't appear mad or panicky. "Marriage, huh," he was smiling, composed again, taking another sparkling swallow of champagne.

"What the hell, it's in style again," she assured him, not missing the way he was taking in her legs.

"You want to rope me down the aisle, huh?"

"Like a bull." She winked demurely.

"I suppose I should be nervous," he said, indicating the way things had been set up with a sweep of his hand. "When you want something, you go after it, no holds barred."

"You can walk out now," she told him, slipping off her heels,

drawing her legs up onto the sofa and curling in closer to him.
"Now that you know how reckless and dangerous I can be."

"No. I think I'll hang around for a while," he said, clicking his
glass to hers and holding her in his gaze as they both sipped to
the challenge.

His lips were thin and she focused on them, pausing for effect
before kissing them. She wanted to stay in command, to do the
seducing.

And yet when she went to kiss him she was surprised to discover that he had stored up a mouthful of champagne that he let
spill into her mouth as they joined together, creating a sensation
that was at once funny and sexy as hell. He was letting her know
that she could not take over completely. He was reckless and
dangerous himself. He was making her skin tingle and her cheeks
hot. Without breaking the kiss, he maneuvered himself on top of
her on the couch, her cut-off gown rising up still higher on her
thighs. The music was mellow and romantic in the background,
and it all felt fabulous with the candles gleaming on the table
beside the flowers, creating a lovely glow.

"What an exchange. You make the Bobbsey Twins look like a
Big Mac instead of filet mignon," he said, abruptly breaking the
mood as he reached for his wallet and indelicately removed a
little blue capsule that contained a rubber. "So everyone feels
safe," he explained tactlessly.

She was too out of breath, too stunned, to reply. Romance
detonated—gone, she thought bleakly, as he hopped off of her.

Before she could even manage to lean up on her side, he had
practically finished stripping off all his clothes and was tossing
them casually onto the lap of the same plush wing chair where
his bow tie lay. He was smiling boorishly, his extremely fit body
reflecting a strong degree of vanity. "Especially nowadays, one
can't be too careful," he added coarsely, before swaggering off in
the direction of the bathroom.

So much for her perfect evening, Paige thought tightly, fuming. When would she ever stop dreaming? She was just another
lay for this guy, not any different from the miniskirted miracles
with whom she had swapped places. And why should he think
any differently? Hadn't she confirmed his impression when she

snipped off fifty percent of her brand-new dress and then presented it to him?

Worse, she was a decade older than the twosome had been.

Refusing to blur into his interchangeable parade of one-night stands, even at the risk of never seeing him again, Paige pushed up from the couch and grabbed a lipstick pencil from her purse.

He thought he had it made in there, the smug son of a bitch, about to slip his little protective seal over his precious cock, ready to screw. Well, tonight, guess who was going to be the screwee?

He wanted safety. She'd give him safety. But as for his sexual release, he was on his own.

Looking for something upon which to write, she snatched up his tuxedo shirt, hastily scrawling onto the back of it her second note to him this evening, simply reiterating her first: *less is more.* If he had done less talking and more kissing, he'd have most likely gotten laid.

Burning mad, Paige scooped up the balance of his evening clothes, leaving his inscribed tuxedo shirt laid out for him on the chair to ponder, his wallet, and money clip. Grabbing her overnight case from the closet, her glitzy Judith Leiber evening bag, her overpriced Maud Frizon high heels, she walked out on him. Damn Nicky Loomis. And damn Stan Parker, too. Damn them all.

Hurrying dispiritedly down the stairs, one shoe on, one shoe off, feeling embarrassingly conspicuous with his heap of evening clothes and her own cut-off Valentino gown, she caught her plight reflected, mimicked, in the mirrored wall that wrapped along the staircase. The picture she saw of herself chasing down the flight of stairs like that was more funny than sad, she told herself as she felt some of her anger beginning to fall away. Erratic, crazy, and funny. What was she so depressed about?

Her goal this evening had gained a face, a name, a persona. And that was progress. She had definitely set herself apart, she thought with a grim, nervous laugh. This was one little screwing session Nicky Loomis wouldn't be so likely to forget.

It was *lucky* she had been jarred into her senses. Joining the scores of fun-time lays would have only sabotaged her case, which she had, by chance, stated flat out for him. Feeling more and more hopeful, Paige reviewed her position, concluding that, in the end, the evening may have just turned out to be a smashing success.

Her objective had been to make him intrigued enough to set her apart from the multitudinous others, and to make him want her. She thought she may have accomplished both.

On the other hand, she hoped she hadn't overdone it. She didn't want to leave him so stripped of his pride that he wouldn't want to see her again.

Not to mention stripped *literally,* she thought, looking down at the load in her arms.

Passing the antique vitrine displaying a neat stack of the Château Marmont T-shirts alongside a stack of flowered jams like the pair she had seen the pianist wearing earlier, she abruptly backtracked, deciding her dilemma was solved.

The picture that had appeared in her head of *the* Nicky Loomis, Mr. Sports King himself, slipping out of the Château Marmont thus dressed struck her as one for the records.

"Can I help you?" asked the desk clerk, looking dully up at her from the paperback he was reading.

Experiencing the same rush of excitement she had felt earlier because the challenge, in some way, was still on, Paige took him up on his offer, pressing a couple of bills into his palm and sending him off to execute another fragment of her still-evolving plan. She instructed him to knock on the door of the penthouse and, if nobody answered, to slip inside, deposit a set of the jams and a T-shirt onto the blue wing chair, and then slip back out. As an afterthought, she handed the desk clerk Nicky's shoes and socks.

One round for me, she thought, climbing into the Aston-Martin Lagonda and ripping out the driveway, feeling a great gush of exhilaration and pride.

Chapter 17

It had all happened so fast. But then she presumed that's what life with Richard Bennetton was like, and the way things were going she had better get *used* to it fast.

Fast, like the shocking velocity at which Richard's private Gulfstream jet was now traveling, ripping through the heavens high above the Amazon, just bounding Bolivia, after stopping for fuel in Panama, en route to Argentina.

Overnight, Tori's life had changed. It was exciting and she relished the speed, which kept her lost in the stratosphere, zooming, gaining altitude, defying gravity. She was a kite, and Richard was directing her course higher and higher, clear of the chronic tug of Travis, until her hard-to-shake Georgia love was a mere nostalgic speck on the red-clay horizon of another life. It was wonderful and completely unreal.

Work wasn't work at all. As opposed to working her tail off in Atlanta, twelve-hour days, pushing to meet project deadlines, responsible for an entire division, plus a significant hike in pay, Tori's job, so far, appeared to be merely to amuse the senior vice president of Bennetton Enterprises—namely, Richard Bennetton. That could have sounded boring, trivial, unrewarding, or un-worthwhile compared to the high-powered position she was used to. But at the moment it was just plain fun.

Besides, boring meant doing the same thing day in and day out, and life with Richard contained not even the suggestion of sameness. It was an adjective he avoided like the plague.

At the moment, all his attentions were being lavished on Tori and she was reveling in it for however long it lasted, though he kept assuring her it was going to last forever. What he felt for her was different, he claimed; *she* was different. He was totally flipped out over his little Georgia Peach. He loved her accent, her perspective on the world, her straightforwardness, and the way her skin smelled after making love. He loved the brand-newness that his world held for her and her intelligent appreciation of it. She wasn't indiscriminately "gaga" over everything, and yet she wasn't in the least bit jaded. Instead, she treated everything as a curiosity, something to try out, to regard, to taste, to like or dislike, simply depending on how it struck her own selective palate. He was thoroughly unconcerned about her apprehension that he would grow tired of her as he seemed to do with everything else—once conquered moving on to meet the next more interesting challenge—insisting that he wanted to meet new challenges *with* her. For the first time, he felt secure, happy, as if he had someone on his team, someone spectacular, whom he could genuinely admire and respect, whom he wouldn't be embarrassed to take to dinner at his father's house.

That's when he had caught Tori's attention and she had let herself begin to believe him. Elliott Bennetton, the senior Bennetton whose picture inspired fear among his legion of employees, Richard being no exception, was off sailing on the *Royal Viking* near India right now with Richard's stepmother. Tori hadn't yet had the opportunity to meet the legend face to face.

Dreaming of what her Latin adventure was going to be like, she relaxed, sinking deeper into the softness of the luxurious suede seat of the private aircraft, staring out the window at the cloudless sky, trying to make out the utterly foreign continent that awaited her below. In preparation for the trip she had already read Isabelle Allende's stunning book *House of the Spirits,* seen *The Official Story,* and rented a videotape of the old Argentine classic *Camila.* With her imagination thus fueled, she felt primed and eager, already envisioning the great *estancia* where they were to be staying as special guests of one of Argentina's premier horse breeders, Alejandro Carballo.

Richard's latest extravagance was sponsoring a polo team for the upcoming season in Santa Barbara, and he had wanted to go to South America to procure not just the finest and most expensive polo ponies bred in the world but the most sought-after riders as well. Alejandro himself was included in that exclusive inner circle, his presence alone on a team insuring a sponsor immense status. Richard had already decided he was prepared to pay an astounding quarter of a million dollars to get Alejandro to ride with him, a coup that he said would have him the most envied sponsor in the tournament. Beginning the sport practically before they had even learned to walk, Argentine polo players were known to be in a class of their own. The experience, Richard promised Tori, would be unforgettable, with every imaginable courtesy being extended to the rich American guests, since the sky was obviously the limit on what a prospective buyer could spend on such a venture.

After their stay on the *estancia,* Tori and Richard were jetting off to Buenos Aires for a few days, then Rio, where they were meeting up with an old friend of Richard's who was taking them island-hopping on his yacht. From there they would hit Peru, picking up the intrepid Death Train, given its name because of the precarious path through which it traveled, following the more adventurous route through to Machu Pichu where they would get to wander among the historic Inca ruins.

And for this Tori was getting paid. *Take notes,* Richard had told her, playfully justifying the expense. She couldn't help but wonder how he was going to justify it to his father, however. Or maybe they were just so rich that his father wouldn't care. Whatever, Tori was way beyond her ken.

The Carballo *estancia* was indeed like something out of an old Argentine movie. It felt as though time had stood still here, no traffic, skyscrapers, or urban litter to connect her to the present. The ranch house was a rambling pink stucco structure with a dark green tiled roof and dark green shutters, built all on one level on rolling green acreage that stretched as far as the eye could see. It had been built by Alejandro's grandfather, also a polo pony breeder, in the early nineteen twenties and all the original details had been painstakingly preserved. In addition to breeding horses, his family also raised cattle on the *estancia,* and there were tall, billowy fields of wheat and corn harvested for export. The stables were huge and neatly kept up. There was also a polo field on the property, an amenity Richard told Tori that was as common as tennis courts in the backyards of the houses in Beverly Hills. There was also a tennis court.

The interior of the old house was elegant but extremely masculine, with dark tiled floors, dark wood around the fireplace, dark green leather furniture, dark massive wood tables, everything oversized and heavy. The kitchen served exclusively as a workplace for the servants, big and functional-looking, with huge slabs of meat, all blood-red and incredibly fresh, laid out on the dark green tiled counters, eerie to Tori because they comprised the limbs and flesh of animals that had been raised right here on the ranch. *All grain fed, with no hormones,* boasted their host.

After their tour of the *estancia* and a light lunch, Tori and Richard were shown out to the lovely guest house where they were to be staying, and left alone to relax and rest up until evening. Horse business would begin the following day, with an exciting and probably exhausting agenda, they were assured. But after their hosts had departed, tempted by the crisp fresh air that smelled of clover and lush lolling pastures, Tori and Richard set out by themselves on a leisurely walk, taking along some of the fruit that had been left for them in the cottage.

Tori was anxious to know what to watch for when viewing the horses the next day, and she asked Richard dozens of questions, curious as to how the animals would be shown and for exactly what characteristics he would be looking.

He explained that they would be working the horses first in figure-eight formations, to demonstrate how they handled, and after that in a straight line.

The trainer would ask them for speed, then bring them back very quickly into a halt to show how nimble they were. How they moved was critical for polo, where they were required to stop and turn, stop and turn erratically, at a wild pace.

He told her to pay extra attention to the horses' hind legs, which had to be strong for stopping; they had to be very strong behind but nimble for quick turning.

If the animal was fast, could stop quickly, and be able to turn on virtually no notice, it was a perfect horse, he asserted, as they strayed farther and farther from the cottage, passing the stables, training areas, the garages housing farming equipment, and on out into the wider open spaces, where various crops were growing and livestock were grazing in the fields, until it was just them and great stretches of silky green pasture beckoning them for a nap.

"Also the size and shape of the horse's neck is important," Richard added, stooping down to rip a yellow wild flower from its roots and tickle her with it until she grabbed it from him, tucking it behind her ear and smiling at him as he went on with his explanation.

"*Why* should the horse's neck be flat?"

"So that it doesn't obstruct the polo player's view. You want a short, flat neck, also a soft sensitive mouth for turning and handling well," he stressed, guiding her over toward a big oak tree that looked to be a thousand years old, pausing to put his arms around her. "Let's see how soft and sensitive this mouth is," he suggested, kissing her and murmuring accolades, going back for more.

"But not so easy to handle," she warned him.

"Good," he answered, approving.

"What about the size . . . the height, the weight—" she asked conscientiously, while kissing the tip of his nose.

Running his hands all over her in desirous assessment, he declared, "Perfect—"

"The horses," she reminded, backing only momentarily away.

He sighed, giving in, but reluctantly. "Not too big—there's a height limit for good polo ponies. They should be only fifteen hands high. Big horses are difficult to turn. And they must turn with both sides—" Then with a growl of frustration, he wrestled her down onto the grass below the tree, concluding that she now knew *everything* that he knew about what to look for in buying polo ponies.

She told him that she seriously doubted it, as they stretched out close to one another, finally feeling the seventeen-hour flight catching up with them, happily expired from their walk. Lying on their sides, snacking on juicy pears and kissing between bites, they fell lazily asleep in each other's arms, hidden from view by the tall, grassy fields. They slept like that for over an hour until a ruddy brown-and-white-streaked calf, who had apparently strayed from its mother, startled them awake, contentedly licking their faces.

After returning to the guest house to continue their *siesta,* then bathe and dress, it was time to join the ensuing barbecue party their host was holding in their honor out in the courtyard.

Standing around on the bricked-in patio, laughing, talking, drinking red wine from short, sturdy-looking glasses, was a crowd of about twenty guests, all around Richard and Tori's age, the women tan and fashionable-looking and, as was the custom on the old *estancias,* the men wearing the traditional gaucho out-fits called *bombachas.* It looked like a lively South American costume party.

Although Richard himself had opted for jeans, he had already predicted to Tori what the other men would be wearing, explain-ing how Argentine men loved to dress up, that they were like peacocks who liked to strut and show their stuff. The effect, she had to admit, was debonair and rather sexy, with the baggy-style pants tucked into sharp-looking riding boots, white shirts show-ing off their dark, healthy-looking complexions, and *rastras,* which were wide, interestingly-fashioned belts weighted down with silver coins, slung low on their hips, handsome silver knives wedged into the back. It was part of the old country pride, the celebration of customs they still held dear.

Over to the side of the courtyard, were a dozen or so gaucho-outfitted servants, only less flamboyantly so, attending to the cooking for what was going to be an elaborate, traditional feast. Skewered on a spit in the center of a huge pit was a whole baby goat, a *chivito,* and surrounding the pit were ranch hands contin-

uously shoveling fire around the animal to cook it and char it to
perfection. Another group of workers attended the bricked-in
barbecue, cooking other parts of various animals, sweetbreads
called *mollejas;* small intestines, *chinchulines;* veal kidneys, *ri-
ñones;* and blood sausages, *morcilla.* There were also skirt steaks
and beef ribs. The smoky aroma was rich, kicking up Tori's appetite.

It was a chilly September night, spring in the southern hemi-
sphere, and Alejandro's wife had piled high up onto a table a
selection of brightly colored shawls for all the women to use in
case they got cold. Tori, wearing tight white jeans and only a thin
cotton sweater, happily accepted the one Alejandro held out for
her as they stepped into the group and he went about introducing
the two of them, making sure they were each given a glass of
wine as he did so. Richard, with his arm linked through hers,
gave her an amorous squeeze.

"Tori Mitchell and Richard Bennetton, please meet our good
friends," Alejandro said warmly in that melodic Spanish accent
of his. He was tall and dark-complected, with jet-black hair and
flirtatious eyes the color of Tori's. The guests were introduced far
too quickly for her to catch all the names, so Tori just smiled
politely, glancing from one to the next, shaking hands. It was a
blur of Spanish anyway, lilting names like *Mariana, Clara, Lita,
Esmerelda,* and, for the men, *Aldo, Clemente, Maximo, Angel,
Ignasio,* and *Hector.*

The name that both stood out and shocked her, was the name
Dustin Brent. He was the last to be introduced, and they remained engaged in their handshake for a prolonged period of
time, both equally astonished, and yet unsure as they appraised
one another, both thinking that it couldn't possibly be.

"Not mountain-climber-adventurer Dustin Brent who lives at
13288 North Summit Drive?" she asked, laughing as he began to
laugh.

"Not Tori Mitchell who lives at 13288 North Summit Drive?"
he said in response.

"My English may not be so hot, Ricardo, but something
strange is going on here," Alejandro chided Richard, enjoying
whatever coincidence was transpiring.

Tori laughed again, feeling her cheeks flush. Like Richard, Dustin was also in jeans, wearing the *American* costume. Only she noticed that he was on crutches, with a clumsy plaster-of-paris cast on his left foot.

"I can't believe this," he exclaimed, catching her off guard with an exuberant embrace, crutches and all. It was great to see a familiar face and she hugged him back, delighted, wondering what had happened to him and what he was doing here. After living in his house, among his personal possessions for the last couple months, she felt a strange and satisfying bond with him.

"I can't believe it either," Tori cried, turning quickly to Richard to explain and repeat the introduction, but he had already caught on. After all, he too had been in Dustin Brent's house, heard the story, or a modified version of it anyway, on how the girls had come to house-sit for him.

The two men shook hands, Dustin friendly, Richard less so.

"So who's looking after my house, with you off playing in South America?" Dustin queried lightly, when the introductions were all finished and Alejandro had led Richard off in another direction to talk polo.

The warm brown eyes fixed onto her own, causing her to recall the various photographs of him she had been seeing daily throughout his house, lived with. It was weird to be with him suddenly in person again, the three-dimensional Dustin Brent, laughing, talking, as vibrant as she remembered him. "Paige and Susan," she answered.

"Wait a minute, weren't you the one who *wasn't* going to be coming out, who got engaged?"

It was a touchy question and Tori didn't quite know how to field it. "It was a twenty-four-hour engagement, or something like that. A long, boring story," she assured him, careful to disguise the wound.

"Oh, I'm sorry," he said kindly.

"No, look, those things happen. It was for the best."

There was an awkward pause in which they busied themselves with their wineglasses. Her eyes were level with his cream-colored cashmere sweater, which he had pushed up at the arms, and she flashed on what his secretary Evonne had referred to as

his "pounds of cashmere" sweater collection, wondering lightly
how Paige had managed to restrain herself from digging into it
all this time. "So, it looks like you got over him pretty fast anyway—" Dustin posed after a moment or so, with a sly gesture
over to where her handsome date was standing.

Tori smiled in response, looking over at Richard. Richard
caught her eye as she did so and winked affectionately, mouthing
an I love you.

Tori winked back at him, slightly embarrassed, then returned
her attention to Dustin. "It's been an eventful summer," she explained, grinning self-consciously. "Thanks to you. Your house is
wonderful. We really appreciate—"

"Hey, I appreciate that you're all looking after it for me," he
interrupted graciously.

"No, but you've been incredibly generous—"

He smiled, shrugging off any further thanks. "So catch me up
on all the gossip. What's going on with all of you? Did you all get
jobs?"

"Yes. Susan got a terrific job working at a big downtown law
firm. Paige is teaching exercise at a health club, Sports Club/
LA."

Dustin grinned as though revisiting a picture of Tori's bombshell roommate in his head. "I like Paige. She's got guts. Great
guts, great energy, and a great sense of humor," he said, both
with amusement and admiration. "So, has she found herself her
rich catch yet?"

Tori blushed, unable to recall exactly how much they had told
Dustin. Knowing Paige, Tori figured she had told Dustin everything, unabashed and unabridged. Tori wondered if Dustin didn't
have a slight thing for Paige. She remembered thinking so at the
time.

"Not yet," she answered, thinking of Nicky Loomis, sure that
Dustin would know who he was. "She's still dropping her bait."

"She'll probably draw up five at once," he kidded.

"Probably. But, meanwhile, the guy she's seeing every day is
an economics professor at UCLA, who knows all about her rich-
man agenda and is amused by it. Obviously he doesn't qualify,
but he's hanging in there."

"Who knows, maybe love will triumph over money. What about you? I've heard this Bennetton character you're with is plenty loaded, here to purchase a couple hundred G's worth of polo ponies. Flew in on his own private jet—"

"I'm looking for love *and* money," Tori cut in, thinking she would be a whole lot better off if she were only kidding.

"And have you found it?" he persisted.

That was the million-dollar question—or billion-dollar, if she were to keep up with inflation. Who knew? She smiled, considering, glancing over toward Richard again. Was she in love? Could she be in love with him? Could he *stay* in love with her? He looked like the quintessential Marlboro man tonight, hard to resist in his faded jeans, work shirt, and cowboy boots. Tori definitely wanted to be in love with Richard, to be able to toss fate to the winds and let the pieces of her life fall wherever they were meant to fall. But it wasn't her nature. Her nature told her it was just too early to tell.

"Actually, I'm working for Richard. Bennetton Enterprises. They're in the building business—" she said, sidestepping his question, then smiling because she could see he was not going to let her off the hook so easily.

"Interesting job—" he observed. "Handsome young boss. Trips to South America. Y'all doing a housing project here?" he asked, plainly joking.

Tori just smiled again, raising an eyebrow. "Looks like you got put out of commission from your mountain climbing trek. What happened?" she asked, wisely rerouting their conversation.

"I shot myself in the foot," he said, frowning down at the injury.

"You *what?*" Tori broke up laughing, then felt bad and put her hand to her mouth to try to stop. "I'm sorry. That just sounds so—"

He shot her a mock dirty look as she continued to laugh, helping her out with the balance of her sentence. "Klutzy. Clumsy. Totally unmacho."

"Hmmm. *Totally,*" she agreed, still chuckling, sipping her wine while looking down at his cast. "It does sound pretty absurd, you know. Here you are off on this macho expedition, climbing the highest peaks across seven continents, and how do you get injured? You shoot yourself in the foot—"

"Well, I'm glad you find it so amusing. But it hurt like hell."

Tori winced. "I know. I'm sorry. I'm sure it did."

"Uh-huh—"

She watched as he took a thoughtful swallow of wine.

"You were climbing the Andes, I take it?" she said.

"About to. We had just flown in from Santiago a couple weeks ahead of schedule, and there was this raging blizzard going on. Everything was covered in snow.

"One of the guys suggested we wait out the brunt of the blizzard, hunting for guanacos in Mendoza—that's the wine country at the bottom of the Andes—and hold off on the climb for a day or so."

Tori wrapped her shawl more tightly around her shoulders. "Bad idea?" she asked, trying to imagine.

"Terrible idea. You couldn't see a thing through that blizzard. I was scared to death I'd end up shooting one of the guys instead of a goddamn guanaco. So I aimed a lot, just to amuse myself, but I never fired. Except once, accidentally, when I heard a gun shot that sounded too close for comfort, and I threw myself onto the ground to avoid getting hit and, in the process, managed to send a bullet from my own rifle whizzing past my ankle, fracturing the bone."

Tori apologized, grimacing. "God, I'm sorry I laughed," she said. "Poor you."

But Dustin was laughing right along with her. "Served me right," he said. "I'm a mountain climber, not a hunter. I should have stuck to mountain climbing."

"So are you going to have to go back to the States?"

"Hmmm, and move in with the three of you?" he considered with a lingering grin. "It's tempting, but I think I'm here for the duration. Another couple of days and this thing comes off."

"The doctor said you could continue climbing?" Tori was surprised.

"No, but Alejandro's *vet* said to go for it. I figured if he's good enough for Carballo's twenty-thousand-dollar polo ponies, he's good enough for me."

Tori thought he was a little crazy, but she liked his spirit. "How do you know Elena and Alejandro? You a polo player too?"

"No. We met years ago in Egypt—"

A loud *gong* resonated through the air from where a ranch hand sounded it, signaling them all to dinner, creating a hungry stir.

Dustin, inhaling the rich barbecue aroma that pervaded the air, put his arm around Tori again and escorted her, hobbling, toward the table. "California definitely agrees with you. That, or I'd just forgotten what a knockout you are. Maybe I *should* give my poor little ankle a rest and head straight back for the States. If it weren't for Bennetton, I'd be booking my flight home right now."

Tori flashed him a dubious look. He was funny, cute, down-to-earth, and she liked him.

"So you haven't told me, how're my good friends Kit and George?" he wondered.

"Great. Kit's pregnant," she informed him excitedly.

He smiled broadly, looking genuinely pleased. "That was fast work."

"What did I tell you about keeping an eye on these two?" Alejandro mischievously reminded Richard, as the four of them came together, awaiting seating assignments by their hostess.

Richard, only feigning concern, put his arm around Tori's waist, displacing Dustin, and kissed her proprietarily on the lips.

Dinner was served out on the courtyard, around one long table, with the cooked meats arranged on huge platters, being passed around by the ranch hands. There were also big plates of crusty bread for them to make their own sandwiches, big rustic bowls filled with colorful medleys of salads—tomatoes and onions, green salad, celery salad, shredded carrot salad, everything served vinaigrette. Perfect-tasting ears of corn, handpicked that day from the fields, were also brought out to the table, along with a big basket of fruit with bowls of water to wash it.

Everyone was very friendly, and the general table discussions were all spoken in English for the benefit of the Americans present. Tori was seated next to her host, Alejandro, while Richard

and Dustin flanked Alejandro's wife, Elena, down at the other
end of the table. The conversations were lively and spirited,
heated at times. Especially on the subject of inflation, which Alejandro leaned over to inform Tori was a subject that was never
absent from a single meal.

"Doesn't it give you indigestion?" Tori wondered, biting into a
delicious-tasting *chinchulines,* the size of a finger, curled.

"Always. There's no excuse for it. We have the best natural
resources here, you know. The best. Cattle, wheat, corn, miner-
als. Our country should be wealthy, our economy flourishing.
And instead, the whole thing's a disaster.

"The budget is perpetually out of balance and to correct it the
government just keeps printing more money, devaluating it, giving it new names. They took the peso, and changed it to something called a *peso ley,* took the *peso ley* and changed it to *peso
nuevo,* on and on until it got so completely out of control that a
million-peso bill became worth only two American dollars. After
that, the geniuses decided to chop about four zeros from the peso
and change the name of the currency altogether, calling it an
austral instead of a *peso.* For a while we felt like we were making
a comeback. A great economic recovery. The *austral* was at
eighty cents to a dollar, and everyone felt optimistic. But that
was only temporary. The *austral* is sliding back down, and God
only knows what it will be worth next week. The government is
trying to do something about it, but—"

Alejandro threw up his hands, as though to say, what could he
do. "The military flunked the test, so now these fellows are trying
to strengthen the economy, but it's an uphill battle."

"And take a wild guess at who's going to get squashed in the
battle. Lousy leftists—" Alejandro's cousin Clemente complained, referring to Argentina's present constitutional government and its civilian president. "Alfonsin went to school with
Mitterrand. He's a socialist. We were better off with the military
in control."

"Never better off with the military," someone else put in.

*"If only we could have a civilian president . . . if only we
could go back to the military,"* Elena mimicked. "I'm so bored
with this. We vote a government in and then about three weeks

later everyone is already turned around and against them. As soon as they try to tighten belts, *poof,* then nobody likes them."

"Do *you* like them, Elena?" Alejandro teased his wife from across the table. "They're raising our local and export taxes on meat again. That cuts directly into your shopping budget you know—"

"No, darling, anything but that. Quick bring back the junta," Elena sparred playfully with her husband, her hazel eyes flashing in a bewitching contrast to her ginger-tan skin. Like all the other Argentine women at the table, she was an ardent sun worshiper, tan for them being almost as significant as money. "And speaking of shopping, Tori, when you get to Buenos Aires, don't bother with Florida Street. It's way too touristy now. Richard, darling, take her into the *La Recoleta* district—"

"Oh, are *you* in trouble!" Alejandro empathized. A few of the men at the table snickered their sentiments.

Elena gestured to her husband to mind his own business. "It's expensive, but they have great things. Also some great antique shops—"

Tori caught Dustin Brent looking at her, raising his eyebrows in a knowing way.

"Thanks a million, Elena," Richard joked, hitting his palm to his forehead in mock concern.

From shopping tips they moved to travel tips, talking about the mystical and daring Death Train excursion Tori and Richard were planning on taking. About Brazil. What was happening in real estate there now, in São Paulo. Back to complaining about the government, and finally into the most sobering topic, about the *desaparecidos,* the missing people. A couple of days ago there had been a bombing in one of the banks in Buenos Aires, and there was fear that terrorism was starting up again.

One of the guests at the table had lost a sister and an infant niece a couple of years ago, during the last military regime, and the family was still looking for the baby, believing that, like many of the other children whose parents had disappeared, their niece had been taken and given up for adoption. It wasn't an uncommon story, unfortunately. Apparently, the sister had worked at the university, associated with a lot of radicals, and it had been no surprise when she had suddenly vanished. But of course that had been under the military regime. The same regime so many of the wealthy Argentines now wanted back in power.

After dinner, during dessert and coffee, the tone changed and became partylike again. Alejandro brought out a few guitars, and everyone sat around in the courtyard, away from the table, singing regional folkloric songs, swaying to the music, laughing, and joining in. It was a spectacular night, full of music, stirring Latin love songs and more stars in the sky than Tori had ever seen before. The moon was an awesome round ball. Sharing a hammock beneath its soft light, propped up by pillows, Tori and Richard lay together with their arms around each other, drinking and feeling happily swept into the mood. Although neither of them spoke Spanish, they were at least able to join in on some of the more redundant refrains, singing gaily along and probably butchering the piece. Dustin's Spanish seemed to be flawless as he sang right along with the others, even accepting a guitar at one point and playing as well.

"Alejandro thinks you're *la máxima,*" Richard whispered into her ear. He had the faint scent of whiskey on his breath. It filled her nostrils, smelled sexy, nice.

"Yeah. He's got good taste." Tori felt contentment wash over her as Richard squeezed her hand.

"Marry me," he murmured softly, nuzzling her neck with the tip of his wonderful nose. "They've got their own private chapel right here on the ranch, a service tomorrow morning. We'll borrow the priest and have him marry us."

"We're not Catholic," Tori reminded him, shimmying involuntarily as he kissed her behind the ear.

"So, we'll convert."

"I don't want to convert."

"So, I'll offer him some *pesos.*"

"You can't buy off a priest."

"Watch me."

"Richard, you're crazy."

"Hummm. I know. But marry me anyway."

"We don't even know each other."

"That's part of the excitement. And I know I'm going to love every new phase of you that I unravel."

Tori laughed, high again, her head in a cloud. Speeding faster and faster, too full of wine and good food. Too full of steamy Latin music and fantasies, when she was a die-hard realist at heart. While she didn't trust his impetuousness, the offer was powerfully heady.

"Okay. What do you need to know about me first?" Richard asked cooperatively, shifting up over onto his side so he could see her face.

"I don't know," she said.

"Ask me anything. It can be as personal as you want. *But marry me.*" His deep marine eyes flickered and made her smile, evoking paradise, a hidden cove of water somewhere in the Caribbean, warm, safe, and full of unimaginable pleasures. *I want to love this man,* she thought. *I want to trust him.*

"How many other women have you proposed to?" she asked.

"*Before* my sixth birthday, or *after*? Between four and five I was really into marriage," he admitted.

She played with his hair that was growing long and sexy at the nape of his neck. "Then what happened?"

"I got into dinosaurs."

"And then?"

"Space."

"And then?"

"Model cars."

"And then?"

"The Beatles."

"And now?"

"*You,*" he said kissing her sensuously on the lips. "Will you marry me?"

"If this still feels this good in Machu Pichu I might have to," Tori answered, scaring herself half to death at the recklessness of her words. She felt Dustin Brent's eyes on her as Richard whispered in her ear that he couldn't wait to get back to their room and make love to her. God, what if she came home from this trip married? Mrs. Richard Bennetton. Tori Bennetton. Or would she keep her own last name? Babies? Did he want more kids? What was she even thinking? She honestly didn't know him, other than what he wanted her to know about himself. She still wasn't over Travis. And she hadn't discouraged Dustin Brent from sending a raft of flirtatious glances her way all throughout the evening. She was plainly screwed up.

"You think too much," Richard told her, and she couldn't help but wonder if he didn't know her better than she thought.

"Anyone up for a midnight ride?" Alejandro asked, setting down his guitar and rising up to his feet to take a count. "My horses are in their glory at night during a full moon—"

There were a few incurable romantics who couldn't pass up the offer, Richard among them. Tori was surprised when he slipped out of the hammock and whisked her up into his arms, volunteering the two of them. It was a wildly romantic notion and she felt charged with excitement, renewed as she watched the ranch hands armed with jackets and flashlights, distributing them. She looked to see who else was going. Ignasio and his wife, Lita. Mariana, Clemente, Alejandro. And, she had to give him credit, Dustin Brent, cast and all.

The more energetic guests mounted the gorgeous animals, which the ranch hands brought round for them, and they all took off, equipped with flashlights and silver flasks provided by their host, riding off into the wondrous moonlit Argentine night.

Chapter 18

Susan had been working such grueling hours that she had fallen asleep in the library at her law firm, her head supported by a thick stack of computer printouts, her glasses lopsided at the tip of her nose. There were legal volumes, pulled from the rich walnut bookshelves, spread in every direction across the immense conference table, her clients' files, her own notes, her dictaphone, and about a dozen pencils, all of them worn down because she had been too lazy to keep having to sharpen them.

A hand on her shoulder jarred her awake, and she had to squint at the early morning sunlight disorienting her as it imposed itself into the plush, oval-shaped room.

"Susan?" It was Mr. Kreegle, one of the letterhead partners, a short, funny man without much hair but with the warmest smile. "Good God, what are you doing here? You've only been with the firm a few months—you bucking for a raise, an early partnership—or did you get into a fight with a boyfriend?" he asked sweetly.

Susan looked up at him, pushing her glasses back into place, feeling herself turning crimson. "First I have to *find* the boyfriend," she lamented. "No, I just wanted to get through this Mutual Cable case and I knew I wouldn't be able to sleep until I'd finished."

"I guess you were wrong. You were sleeping like a baby."

Susan looked down at the mess in front of her, just to be sure she hadn't only dreamed that she had finished it. "As a matter of fact," she said with a sleepy smile, indicating the work in front of her. "Mutual Cable contracts—done!" Feeling groggy but content with accomplishment, she looked at her watch and winced. "Seven-thirty. Time to run home for a quick shower." Then as an afterthought she added, "Hey, what are *you* doing here so early, Kreegle? Bucking for a raise?" she teased the senior partner.

He smirked and announced that his gorgeous wife, who was leaning against the door behind Susan, looking radiant, untired, unharassed, wearing chic chamois western-styled jeans and shirt, was on her way to rest up at the Golden Door health spa. "Susan, you've met Liz," he said, as Liz breezed in toward them.

"Sure. Hi," Susan said self-consciously, feeling like a mess, imagining circles under her eyes, wishing she could at least sneak on some lipstick, swallow some mouthwash. *Oh, the hell with it.*

"Teddy needed me to sign some papers," Liz explained. "We just bought a place in Aspen. You'll have to come skiing with us sometime. Maybe *I* can work on finding that boyfriend for you." She had on a pretty shade of glossy melon lipstick that matched her earrings. Her teeth were perfect, as if she had them buffed at the dentist every couple of months.

"Matchmaking is Liz's specialty," Kreegle said.

Susan smiled politely, feeling exhaustion creep in as the obviously happy-together couple began to walk out of the library arm in arm. Kreegle paused to put his hand on Susan's shoulder one last time and gave her a warm squeeze. "I'd tell you to go home and take a nap, not come in until eleven or so, but I need you out on a strike problem that's suddenly escalated at one of our clients' factories out in Commerce. Dickson was handling it, but his wife just had a baby about an hour ago, and I'm afraid we're going to need you out there today. I'll brief you as soon as you get back," he said. "Oh, and it's best you don't take your own car. Leave your secretary a note to get you a rental. I hear it's gotten pretty rough—"

Susan was used to field-rough, but not factory-rough. His warning made her wonder. But on the other hand, after all the boring paperwork she had been doing, she realized she would welcome the change of pace.

"Teddy, honey, I hate to rush you, but I'm going to miss my ride," Liz said apologetically. It was her turn to look at her watch.

"Sorry, sweetheart. Susan, I'll have to catch up with you after—"

"Sure. No problem." Susan stifled a yawn as she watched the two of them disappear through the doorway and down the hall. She could hear the clicking of Liz's palomino-colored suede boots on the firm's hardwood floors, the melodic sound of her carefree laugh. Liz and Susan were about the same age, and Susan was surprised to find herself feeling envious. Having a profession had been so critical to Susan, so essential. She had sacrificed her marriage for it; she had sacrificed her twenties. But suddenly, sitting here too dead tired to move, considering the life of her contemporary, she had to wonder about who had chosen the smarter path, whose life was richer and more fulfilling. At the moment, Susan believed there was no contest.

What was so wonderful and satisfying about working her ass off as an attorney, falling asleep over dull and lengthy documents? As usual, Paige was right. How clever to let someone else do all the work and just get to enjoy life, to play, and to be supported. Kreegle's wife could hardly be accused of being dull or a parasite. She was active in the contemporary art museum, bringing into the fore budding artists. She was a talented potter herself. She always looked perfect, was able to fly off to Europe to buy the latest designer collections, had time to master the various languages of the countries to which she traveled. She had *time* to read newspapers cover to cover, *The Los Angeles Times, The New York Times,* to be informed and well read. She had time to maintain an impressive seventeen handicap on the golf course, ski, play tennis. Participate in worthwhile causes. And raise her two adorable little kids.

So Susan had her career. That was clearly all she had. That and a case of bloodshot eyes from straining over small print all night long.

* * *

In the short time it had taken Susan to drive home, shower, get dressed, and wolf down breakfast, the sun had vanished behind thick, fast-moving clouds the color of coal, which looked ready to burst with a downpour at any second.

Flying out the door, she bumped into Mark just arriving on his motorcycle, a beat-up helmet on his wonderful head, golden curls still visible beneath it. He kissed her a quick hello as she hurried past him, seemingly oblivious of the fact that he had broken her heart.

"You look fantastic," he said, grabbing her hand and detaining her a moment longer, breaking down the defenses she kept thinking she had constructed so immutably in his absence.

Then why are you mooning over my roommate instead of me, she wanted to snap. Instead, she smiled and produced a breezy thank you, inwardly thanking God for the invention of makeup that had blessedly concealed last night's all-nighter. She was wearing a lightweight winter-white suit, a knockoff of this year's Chanel, or so the woman who had sold it to her had claimed. Her briefcase added just the right touch. It made her feel secure.

"Paige and I are catching a movie tonight. Want to join us?" he asked, following her to her car and opening the door for her.

"Thanks. But I may have to work late tonight," she answered, scooting inside.

"Never going to snare that eligible multimillionaire if you keep working these hours," he was quick to tease her, his blue eyes connecting with hers, both from behind pairs of glasses, making her think of the beautifully blue-eyed but farsighted kids they could have together.

"I may just be on my way to *snare* one now," she replied too sharply, regretting the remark immediately after she had said it.

As sweet as ever, Mark closed her door for her, tucking her skirt inside so that it wouldn't get caught. All day long she knew she would be remembering the feel of his hand passing along her thigh, touching her knee.

And yet he was probably going upstairs right now to screw his brains out with Paige. Damn it all. Mostly damn Paige.

Only an hour later, driving toward the City of Commerce in

her rented Toyota, with her windshield wipers swiping at the torrent of rain, having been briefed by Kreegle on her assignment, Susan found herself part nervous, part excited, part amused. As it turned out, she *was* on her way to meet with one of those eligible multimillionaires Mark had been ribbing her about, though *snaring* him appeared unlikely.

Her destination was a factory that manufactured fiberglass hot tubs, catamarans, Windsurfers, surfboards, and dinghies. The *client,* and owner of the company, it turned out, was none other than Kit and George's friend, Susan's dinner partner of the other night, the "Rat" who had never bothered to ask her for her phone number or call. She wondered what his response would be when he saw her. God, L.A. was turning out to be as small a town as small-town Stockton.

According to Kreegle, Jack Wells' factory was in a state of severe upheaval. Only a couple of months ago Jack's workers had voted to bring in the Teamsters' union, claiming unsafe working conditions, inequitable treatment, no health insurance, low pay: and now management was in the throes of heated union negotiations, with the workers out on strike because of management and union's inability to come to terms.

The unruliness was increasing daily as the truckloads of replacements continued crossing the picket lines, inciting a mounting rage and uproar among the strikers that was apparently getting out of control.

No wonder Jack's stance on unions had been so adamant. Probably *that* was why he had neglected to pursue her, she tried to rationalize, though weakly. He had sensed where her real sympathies lay . . .

All personal thoughts of Jack Wells and Mark flew out of Susan's head the moment she actually drove up to the plant. She found she had entered a near war zone. There was virtual pandemonium, with yelling and screaming and egg throwing. A truck was being torn apart as a horde of enraged strikers broke a shipload of surfboards in half, while others smashed bottles in the driveway that was already ankle-deep in the sharp debris so that the armored trucks bringing in the replacements would be obstructed from driving through.

Susan was just considering turning around and getting the hell out of there, thinking she would never get through this bedlam and into the building in one piece, when suddenly one of the big armored trucks full of replacements came barreling up from behind her, going maybe forty miles an hour and causing her to have to swerve out of the way, nearly running down a throng of picketers and finally crashing into one of the garbage cans that had the traditional strike fire blazing within it.

The fire had her terrified, and she tried to get out of the car but could not. First of all, the door was locked and she couldn't figure out how to unlock it. Where was the button or the latch on this damn rental? There were people pounding at her windows; someone had smashed open the one on the passenger's side; there was a hose spraying water; and, for the life of her, she couldn't work the contraption that released the seat-belt harness. The noise was almost as upsetting as the flames beginning to lap at the front of her car, and she was having trouble breathing, although she couldn't tell if it was because of the smoke or her own suffocating panic, the thought of the car blowing up, premonitions of further disaster reeling in her head.

She remembered thinking she needed a white flag in order to emerge safely. She remembered worrying about the papers in her briefcase, the letter in there from her mother that she had not yet gotten to read, which she had only just picked up this morning from the house. And then she remembered nothing.

"Feel any better?"

Susan was sitting in a plain, industrial-looking office, not much bigger than her own, that looked carelessly thrown together with an old, commercial-type desk and drab walls that had pictures and ad campaigns of the various products Jack Wells' company manufactured. The windows looked down into the plant itself instead of outside, with the noise, she presumed to be deafening because of the workers' protective ear coverings, sealed out.

Jack Wells himself was sitting close to Susan, administering a towel with ice to her forehead, which felt more frozen than bruised. She kept trying to keep her hands from shaking as she held unsteadily onto a Styrofoam cup filled with water.

She nodded, and then smiled self-consciously. "I'm fine. Embarrassed, but fine."

He removed the improvised ice pack and set it onto the desk. "Embarrassed? Why should you be embarrassed? Those guys are maniacs out there. I can't believe your firm even sent you over here, with what's been going on this week—"

Susan was about to argue. This was, after all, her job and the incident had nothing to do with her being female, which was what he was getting at; it had to do with her driving a dinky Toyota instead of a monstrous armored machine. The same thing would have happened to Joe Dickson, her colleague who had been in on the bulk of the union negotiations, but Jack cut her off, reapplying the ice and smiling as he read her thoughts.

"Okay, Dickson probably wouldn't have fared any better. He just wouldn't have looked as pretty or as vulnerable, and so we wouldn't have made such a fuss over him. I'd have let him hold his own damn ice pack." Jack grinned again. He was dressed like one of the workers in a plaid lumberjack-type shirt, grubby jeans, and a Budweiser cap crooked on his head, the look definitely more his style than the put-together dinner clothes she had seen him in at Kit's. With his shirt sleeves rolled up she was able to get a good look at the tattoo on his forearm, though she still couldn't decipher what the design was intended to be, other than that it was clearly Oriental and strangely exotic.

"It looks like you're going to be stuck with me for a while anyway, female or not," she informed him. "Joe will be here tomorrow and the rest of the week to smooth the transition of my replacing him, but he's taking off a month for maternity leave starting next week."

"Maternity leave? What is this?" he asked, as though she were joking, unconsciously rubbing at the persistent growth along his jaw, which she remembered as being heavy from last time.

"It's a new world," she reminded him, taking a sip of her water, feeling herself beginning to relax. "His wife is a gynecologist, and it's tougher for her to take time off than it is for him. She had only two hours of labor, no episiotomy, feels fine, and is ready to go back to work. The law firm gives *two* months maternity leave to all its female lawyers, so this morning Joe requested half of the same privilege."

"What about all those fancy nurses or nannies?"

"Joe thinks the first month or two is critical for bonding. He doesn't want the baby bonded with a stranger. Actually, we're all having a lot of fun with it." Susan winced because the ice pack was getting too cold again and she took it from his hands, setting it back onto the desk.

"You're going to have a nice bump," he diagnosed, examining her forehead with his fingers.

She helped herself to a metal letter opener from his desk and by angling the blade was able to assess the damage through the reflection. Unsurprisingly, her forehead was swollen and gaining in color, but with a quick adjustment of her bangs she had it nearly hidden. "What bump?" she asked with a cavalier shrug, and they both smiled.

"So here we are talking babies again," he said.

The reference to the night when he had neglected to ask her for her phone number caught her up short, but she laughed in spite of her bruised ego.

"Honestly, Susan, with all this violence and uproar, I still don't get why your firm didn't replace Dickson with a man," Jack said as diplomatically as possible. "I'm serious. It's really gotten rough. You saw what's going on here."

Susan glanced evasively over at a framed newspaper clipping of Jack sitting on a stretch of untamed beach in the midst of a bunch of eager Chinese, all wearing straw hats and broad grins, a couple of surfboards wedged into the sand, accenting the photo. The caption read Surfing Diplomacy Goes to China.

He followed her gaze, waiting for her to respond.

"Believe it or not, I'm an ace labor lawyer," she said smiling to soften the cockiness of her reply. But the fact was she wanted this assignment. She didn't want to remain in the law firm, pencil pushing; she wanted an opportunity to prove herself. "Why don't you wait a few days before you start complaining," she suggested in a firm but friendly challenge.

"I wasn't complaining, and I'm sure you *are* an ace labor lawyer. I'd just hate to see you a mauled labor lawyer. One egg on your head ought to be enough," he added, touching the throbbing memento she already sported.

"Just think of me as one of those five seven, wiry, and supremely courageous Tunnel Rats," she joked, watching carefully for his reaction.

He threw up his hands and slouched back in his chair, resigned but not displeased. "Tunnel Rat, eh? I guess that means I'll have to lend you my TR badge and bush hat."

"Sounds good to me. What color is the hat?" she wondered, glad because she could see by the amused curve of his thin lips that she was finally winning him over.

"It'll look great on you. And I must say, counselor, I like your spunk."

Susan only wished she were as spunky as she sounded now. This was going to be a tough act to keep up. She was just plain, shy Susan, wired now because of all that had happened. "What's this—Surfing Diplomacy Goes to China?" she asked, curious about the clipping on his wall, his fixation with the Far East.

"A little over a year ago I organized an expedition to introduce surfing to China, the first surfin' safari to hit the People's Republic—" Jack glanced over at the photo, readjusting his Budweiser cap. "This was shot on Hainan Island."

"Where's that?"

"Off the coast of North Vietnam. Between the Gulf of Tonkin and the South China Sea. They've got a lot of great virgin coastline."

"A slump in American sales?" Susan teased.

"Not funny," Jack joked back, pointing a finger at her.

A loud beep coming from the telephone interrupted them, and they both turned toward it. "Jack, Malcolm Lear just called from his car phone. He's been stuck in traffic, but he said they're only about twenty minutes away." It was the husky, smoker's voice of his secretary.

"Union agents," Jack explained to Susan.

She nodded, already having been briefed on the cast of players to expect at the negotiating meeting. There would be the Teamsters' agents, Malcolm Lear, a beefy guy with a bad temper, and his shadow, Buddy Clayton, a beefy guy with no temper, who had the soul of a social worker trapped inside the body of a thug. Also present would be a committee of four employees who Joe Dickson had said weren't long for their jobs anyway, because they were the ones who were holding up the works, voting everything down, imposing the stalemate. Jack was apparently champing at the bit to get them all canned, which was tricky to do legally. And of course there was the company committee, Jack himself, his general manager, Carlos Urizer, and his attorney, formerly Joe Dickson, now, at least for the time being, Susan.

"The meeting won't start for another thirty minutes or so. You up for a quick tour before we get started?" Jack asked, rising up from his chair.

Susan checked her watch. One of the things Kreegle had stressed was that she be sure to get statements from the witnesses about the violence of the strikers on the picket lines, some additional statements from the replacements inside, and from the union officials too. They were trying to get as many strikers fired as possible to finally tip the voting ratio, since they all knew the Teamsters could exercise some muscle over the replacements' vote. The incriminating statements were crucial since, legally, a worker couldn't be fired for striking, but he *could* be fired for causing violence on the picket line, and Jack made no bones about it: he wanted the worst of the troublemakers caught in the act and axed. The negotiations had been going on so long that, at this point, all union and management both wanted was to get a contract agreed upon and signed.

Guessing what she was thinking, Jack told her she could get the statements tomorrow. Nothing was going to change, he assured her. "You've seen the strikers in action. Come see what it is they're *supposed* to be doing."

Susan had to smile as she followed him out of his office because she could see how eager he was to show off the huge and clearly productive plant that he had built entirely on his own.

In the forty-five minutes it took to tour the factory, with Jack carrying around a cordless phone and accepting dozens of brief, to-the-point phone calls along the way, Susan felt as if she were learning everything there was to know about the production of hot tubs, catamarans, dinghies, Windsurfers and surfboards, viewing the procedure through glass-lined corridors. The plant was noisy, colorful, and exciting, with everyone working at a pace that seemed almost frantic.

For the hot tubs, the process began with ceramic-and-metal molds of varying shapes. The molds were sprayed with hot liquid fiberglass, which shot out of thick, unwieldy-looking hoses. In that division, everyone wore masks. The smell was apparently awful and the fumes dangerous. The procedure demanded working quickly because the fiberglass would harden almost immediately, leaving a lot of chance for error, something the workers were up in arms about because they were held personally accountable, getting docked in pay for any imperfections, though *they* blamed the cause of the imperfections on imperfect materials, cheap resin, and flawed molds. The tubs, after being sprayed, were moved into either heated rooms or ovens to dry. Then to separate the fiberglass from the molds, workers would force air through heavy hoses between the mold and the tub, causing the dried fiberglass to pop free.

The procedure for manufacturing Windsurfers and surfboards Susan found to be equally fascinating to watch. They would begin with huge old blocks of Styrofoam, which would be skillfully sanded with an electrical sander into the appropriate and familiar shapes. Thin sheets of fiberglass were then stretched onto the shaped foam and, after that, the fiberglass was painted with vibrant colors. The workers' grievances in this area were that the Styrofoam used in making the Windsurfers and surfboards was a by-product of gasoline, and the dust created by the electric sanders was dangerous since the body is incapable of breaking down any form of gasoline. Another dispute was that production people on the Windsurfers and surfboards were sometimes given bad gloves, or no gloves at all when they ran out, and ended up with glass particles embedded in their skin from stretching the fiberglass sheets over the forms.

Watching the buzz of activity and the staggering output, it was difficult to even remember that there was a strike going on outside. Jack Wells was hardly being put out of business.

The factory was substantially larger than it appeared to be from the outside, and Susan presumed that Jack had to be making an extraordinary living from the water sports industry of America, hot tubs included as sport. She couldn't help but feel the spirit of Paige trailing behind her, performing an extensive mental inventory, calculating copious profits. Worse still, Susan had already spent so much time with Paige that she could even hear her brazen roommate's words, clear as day, as though she were watching from some invisible post, her advice reverberating plainly in Susan's head. *Think of the easy life your boss's wife has, Kreegle's well-rested, gorgeously outfitted, well-traveled wife . . . shouldering none of the financial responsibility. Free to do what she wants. Free from the monotony and pressure of work. Think of Kreegle's well-rested, gorgeously outfitted, well-traveled wife . . .*" Paige's telepathic message came through unrelenting, unambiguous.

"Here, have a sailboat," Jack said when they were all through with their tour. Susan couldn't believe the size of the souvenir he was thrusting on her. "Do you know how to sail?"

"Yes. But, I can't accept this," she objected, as he hollered instructions to one of his men to crate up the sabot-type sailboat for her and have it sent.

"You do?" he asked, looking surprised, and continuing to ignore her protests. "Where'd you learn how to sail, hailing from inland and coming from a trailer park? I was hoping to toss in private lessons as part of the package."

Susan felt a tingle of pleasure at his recall, and was definitely flattered by his offer. "San Francisco Bay," she answered. "It was my weekend escape during law school. But honestly, Jack, I really can't accept this kind of gift."

"Why not?"

"I don't know. It's unprofessional—" she tried, but they both started to laugh.

"No, unprofessional is being late to our meeting," he argued, pointing to the clock on the wall that indicated they were already fifteen minutes late. "Oh, and tell the firm that as far as I'm concerned they ought to give the new father *two* months maternity leave," he added. "As long as we're all keeping the kinds of hours we're keeping—these meetings can go on until midnight—

I'd sure as hell rather be working around the clock with you. . . . No offense to Joe," he joked.

Susan laughed, finding his smile hard to resist, *unable* to resist a quick glance back at her new sailboat.

Chapter 19

From the moment Nicky Loomis had seen her on the dance floor, he had known not only that they would meet but that it would be more than just an ordinary encounter. She reminded him of himself twenty years ago, when he had been known as "lightning legs Loomis," the great wide receiver of the Green Bay Packers, out to conquer, out to play, to win and to love, so that it was always one for the records.

That thick mane of russet-colored hair that she would unconsciously sweep up off of her face, her sassy smile, those wild green eyes, the color of new money, continued to haunt him with ever-increasing clarity.

He couldn't get the feel of her out of his mind, the smooth, sensual quality of her skin, her shapely curves and the way she knew how to use them, sweeping against him, making him aware of every square inch of his body, of her body, so that only kissing, with which he ordinarily tried to dispense, had taken him back to the days when he had to worry about his passion exploding in his pants.

He hadn't been long in the bathroom, fussing over his hair, swishing some of the hotel's complimentary mouthwash in his mouth, taking a leak, then manipulating his cock back into an erection so that he could put on the rubber. With his penis erect and shielded, breath freshened, and ready to fuck her brains out, he had emerged from the bathroom in sweet anticipation of finding her already nude in bed waiting for him, hot, wet, and wanting.

When he found the bed undisturbed, vacant, flowers intact across the pillows, he had simply presumed she was in the bathroom off the living room, that she would be joining him momentarily.

He remembered lying there alone beneath the cool sheets, stroking himself as he waited for her, envisioning her rapturous bare form, thinking about her on top, riding him, his hands overflowing with those ripe breasts. Then he had imagined her there, *along with* the Bobbsey Twins, their three sumptuous bodies entangled all around him, devoted to pleasing him, the redhead's mouth on his cock, the blonde's mouth on his thighs, Paige's mouth on his mouth, creating a great panoply of legs, breasts, and taut rear ends—an enviable collection of perfect but varied female forms.

Beyond paradise.

Still stirred, he recalled how his thoughts had then jumped to business, to their upcoming hockey-season blackboard, where they were in the midst of making some final decisions, to the storm reportedly moving up from Mexico, threatening death at the box office for the following night's tennis matches.

Rain and peak news events pouring in all in one day insured instant indigestion.

After awhile, growing curious at Paige's failure to materialize, Nicky had finally gotten out of bed and gone into the living room to look for her.

He remembered thinking it would be just like her to have something wild and wanton planned for him in there, to keep him on his toes. Another game, another surprise.

He had pictured her nude on a fur spread in front of a lit fireplace, or even lying below the great span of window, illuminated by moonlight, drinking champagne straight from the bottle, ready to pour it all over him and lick it off. He expected to discover her with an impish look on her ravishing face, primed to play and tease him into blissful exhaustion.

What a shock he had had when he found her gone, himself stranded, without his tuxedo, his underwear, without anything except his lipstick-graffitied tux shirt bearing a message obviously meant to put him in his place.

And that it had. With a towel wrapped around his waist, he had relaxed down onto the couch to polish off the rest of the champagne and enjoy a good laugh. He had always been a good sport, and he took in Paige's ploy with surprise and hearty appreciation, wanting her even more than before.

This broad was going to be a real challenge, for a change, he had noted, eyeing the comical outfit she had sent up for him. This had been her show and he had mistakenly tried to take over. He had treated her like all the other little groupies he was accustomed to having just lie back on the bed with their legs spread, and she was letting him know that she was not one of them.

He was the kind of man that even if he were robbed, if the crook did it well, he'd have to be impressed. He was impressed by Paige, by her style and ingenuity, by her guts.

Nothing near to this had ever happened to him before. The way in which she had orchestrated this whole thing in the first place, getting herself invited to his home, cutting off her dress and sending it to him the way she had, exchanging their respective dates, and then succeeding in luring him up here to a scene that had been admirably set.

On *her* terms she had taken him to *her* room to lay *him*.

Which was where he was sure he had gone wrong. He had tried to commandeer the controls. He had moved into automatic pilot once on top of her on the couch, dispensing with the requisite foreplay too abruptly, making a premature dive for one of his trusty rubbers, and then hitting her with those smug, admittedly insensitive remarks, especially the one about the Bobbsey Twins.

However, while he was a man who enjoyed being taught a lesson, he hadn't banked on not being able to track her down afterward.

He had tried everything. First, the desk clerk at the Château

Marmont, only to learn with a mix of frustration and fascination that her suite had been registered under the name of *Joe Smith*.

There was no phone number, no address, no credit card by which to trace her, something he found surprising since he was sure she would *want* to be found.

The Aston-Martin Lagonda she had been said to be driving, the parking lot attendant claimed had no plates. Nicky couldn't help but wonder about the two-hundred-thousand-dollar English car. Who was this gal?

Amused and intrigued, he had plodded on, trying the telephone book, where there was no listing, pulling strings with contacts at the Department of Motor Vehicles, which had no record of a California driver's license ever being issued to any Paige Williams. He even had his secretary locate this Stan Parker, with whom Paige had supposedly gone to his party. But when they had gotten him on the phone in Philadelphia, where he lived, he claimed to know nobody by the name Paige Williams.

Later, Nicky learned that Stan Parker was married and attributed his plea of ignorance to the fact that his wife's family owned the company of which he was president.

It did occur to him that Paige Williams might not be her real name, but his instinct told him that it was. She responded too naturally when addressed. The name suited her.

He found it curious to realize that they had talked only about him; they hadn't talked about her at all. He had no idea where or if she worked. Where she lived. Or who her friends were.

"Your Cinderella obsession again? I can't wait to meet her," exclaimed Nicky Loomis's attractive daughter, Marni.

They were in his office at the StarDome, where she had dropped in to visit him, and she snatched the photograph of her father's mysterious obsession from out of his hands, softening her gesture with a kiss on the cheek.

The StarDome, built by Nicky Loomis only ten years ago, was located in the San Fernando Valley, near the Burbank Studios. His office, housed within the large domed sports arena complex, was cluttered and buzzing with commotion. There were people wandering in and out to consult the blackboard of events slated for the StarDome, a separate blackboard of events slated for other stadiums, plus a network- and cable-ratings readout featured on a large-screen terminal. Leaning up against a dated-looking hunter green plaid couch was the final mock-up for the hockey billboard about to go up on the Strip, to be seen as well riding along the sides of nearly twenty-five hundred buses across the Los Angeles metropolitan area.

Familiar faces dominated the room; large color photographs of sporting events in dark wood frames eclipsed the walls, paying homage to Nicky's illustrious career and his unique life-style. There were photographs featuring McEnroe playing tennis, Nicky surrounded by Olympic gold medalists from the U.S. team, Nicky with his L.A. Stars hockey team, the Harlem Globetrotters, a shot of him with Pete Rose from the Cincinnati Reds. And there were a couple more weathered photographs of Nicky in his youth—one with him in a semihuddle formation with his teammates from the Green Bay Packers, another showing him with his arm around the man who had been like a father to him, the General Patton of sports, coach Vince Lombardi. Even idols had idols, and Vince Lombardi had been his.

Attesting to Nicky Loomis's obsession about staying fit was a framed spread from *Los Angeles Magazine,* with a glossy photo of Nicky in only a pair of gym shorts, flexing with a set of weights, featured in a special issue on celebrities and their private trainers.

Nicky leaned back in his chair, swiveling toward his daughter, who was curiously examining the photograph of Paige. He had found it in the pile of proofs that had been taken on Carnival Night at his house.

The two females, while close in age, both beautiful, bright, and savvy, weren't anything alike. While he sensed that Paige had street smarts, was as tough and unconventional as he was, a risk-taker, highly competitive, and choosing to live on the edge, his daughter, Marni, was the protected, soft, and extremely conventional product of all his money, her speech and carriage marking her privileged, moneyed, Ivy League background.

Father and daughter were mutually fascinated with each other. Marni put up with her father's often embarrassing antics, his endless stream of women half his age, his abandonment of her mother; and Nicky put up with his daughter's straitlaced snobbishness. Though different, the two were the best of friends. He had told her all about Paige and, while untrusting, his sleek, auburn-haired daughter was as caught up in the suspense of it all as he was.

"Maybe she simply didn't like you, Daddy," Marni teased him now, fiddling with the waistband of the leather pantsuit they had recently bought together in Italy. It was the color of Paige's almost iridescent green eyes. "Maybe you didn't work out to be the stud you're reputed to be—" she chided with a cruel wink.

Nicky gave his daughter a swat on the behind and laughed. "No. *That* was the problem. My being such a stud—"

"Yeah, you keep saying that, but y'know, you're getting up there. Pushing sixty . . . Or maybe she didn't like the way you kissed—"

"She loved the way I kissed, you little smartass," he teased back, patting his thinning head of hair into place.

"I think she's moved on to bigger and better—"

"You're such a little bitch. How'd I raise such a bitch?"

"Really, I'm just jealous, Daddy. Usually you don't give them even a passing thought. Now you've got a picture of her on your desk. There aren't even any pictures of *me* around here—"

"Bring one in for me. I'll put it on my desk."

Marni regarded the clutter. "Yeah, where?"

Nicky smiled, and slid some of the mess over to one side, freeing up a spot on his desk and patting it with his hand.

"Maybe it was just a joke—" Marni considered, back on the subject of Paige Williams again. "Played by one of the millions of teenyboppers you never called back. Like the one whose mother kept calling and pleading with you to see her precious Mary Jane again—"

"Her name was Mary Jane? I thought it was Sue Ellen—"

"Mary Jane. Sue Ellen—" Marni tossed Paige's picture back down onto Nicky's desk.

He picked it up, smiling because he loved looking at Paige. "A *joke,* huh? If it was all a joke, what's the punchline?"

Marni thought for a moment, looking away. Then curiously she seemed to change her mind.

Nicky, following her gaze, turned toward the door to his office, where his secretary was carrying in his shanghaied tuxedo, draped neatly with a plastic cleaners' bag. Stapled to it was a sack, presumably containing everything else he had on that night.

"This girl has nice timing. She probably has your office bugged—" Marni remarked drolly, catching his eye.

"And a messenger stationed at reception—" Nicky added, noting the royal blue writing printed across the clear plastic sheath. There was a receipt stapled onto it, and he tore it off, disappointed but not surprised to find that it bore his own name and address, not Paige's.

"Well, now we know she wasn't just out to steal your tux, Dad," Marni said, taking the dry-cleaned tux from his hand and moving primly over to hang it up in the closet.

Intrigued and relishing the game, Nicky balled up the receipt and tossed it into the trash, slouching back down thoughtfully into his chair, doodling on an unfinished crossword puzzle from his desk.

"Hold on a minute. Let me give this a try," Marni said, returning to retrieve the crumpled receipt, then picking up the phone from the opposite side of his desk and punching out the number.

"No way," Nicky said to her, more amused than frustrated, as she smiled at him. "There won't be any record . . . they won't have a clue who she is."

Marni put her finger to her lips. "Shhh," she ordered, but with her pretty face displaying a waning confidence.

Nicky leaned back in his chair and watched her, only half listening to his daughter's interrogation of the cleaners, who as he had guessed, knew nothing. It only confirmed how well he had this one pegged. Paige Williams remained, for now anyway, untraceable.

She was playing with him, and it would have been too simple if he could have tracked her down this way. She was going for more punch. The returning of his tux was probably simply so he wouldn't forget about her. She may not have even figured out yet how she was going to engineer their next meeting, but he had no doubt that when she did, it would be more dramatic than the cleaners.

"Whatever woman catches him will have to be a cheerleader, a prostitute, and a hell of a cook," Paige had determined, after three weeks' worth of extensive research on Nicky Loomis.

Following along with a Julia Childs videotape on the compact TV in the kitchen, whipping egg whites for the "no-fail" soufflé she was learning to master and, at the same time, trying to memorize football basics from one of the sports books she had checked out from the library, Paige let out an exasperated sigh.

Not only were the egg whites failing to form light, fluffy peaks and amass volume, but in one month's time, which was the timeframe she had allotted herself for research, she wondered if she would ever be able to absorb enough sports material to have anything worthwhile stick.

The day after her encounter with Nicky, Paige had headed straight for the library, culling a stack of sports-related titles, thinking that if she wanted to snare "Mr. Sports King" then she had better at least learn the vernacular.

She had already been through a series on basketball and hockey, undertaking them first because they were the two kinds of teams Nicky owned.

Current information, sports industry gossip, such as who was being traded to whom and why, salaries, drug problems, personality problems, Paige had been garnering from television broadcasts, magazines, and newspaper articles.

The book on football she was reading now, about Vince Lombardi, she had been especially interested in since she knew that Nicky not only used to play for the late, great coach, but that Vince Lombardi had helped shape his life. There hadn't been a single interview in which Nicky hadn't deified his old coach, crediting him with the success he had gone on to achieve in his later years, away from the football field.

But unfortunately the book was a whole lot drier than the man.

Chapter One: "Defensive Line Play . . . Linebackers and Defensive Backs. . . ."

A long, boring definition caused Paige to go on to Chapter Two, then Chapter Three, then back to Chapter One again, where she was intent on absorbing the fundamentals and techniques of the sport, the responsibilities of each player, the subtleties that were purported to make champions.

Tackles, defensive ends, linebackers, receivers. Passing, pass receiving, pass blocking, the kicking game, special teams.

She pored over a couple of the illustrations, trying to make sense of the diagrams, reading the same captions over and over again until something penetrated.

Good God, couldn't she have found Mr. Fashion King or Mr. Music Industry King or Mr. Movie King, or anything other than Mr. Sports King?

"And now . . ." Julia Childs' grating voice in the background, recaptured Paige's attention. "When your egg whites are all nice and white and frothy . . . *like this* . . ." she instructed.

Paige looked apprehensively away from Julia Childs' snowy concoction to regard the white slush in her own copper bowl and frowned. Disheartened, she switched off the electric beaters and pushed the bowl aside, attentive to the next series of directions. She and Julia both had a chocolate mixture cooling on their respective countertops, and she went to get hers, waiting for the next step, wondering why her sauce had gotten grainy-looking, when Julia's was as smooth as pudding, wondering why she was bothering with soufflés altogether.

Just because she had read how much Nicky liked to eat? Maybe he was a meat-and-potatoes man. Maybe he hated the sweet, airy stuff, preferring something into which he could sink his teeth. The man was a jock, not a gay gourmand. He probably liked plain old chocolate cake, cheesecake, and pie à la mode.

Besides, her arm was getting sore from having to hold it in that position over the bowl for so long, elbow up, wrist suspended over the bowl and moving in a circular motion.

It had been almost two weeks since Paige had returned Nicky's tuxedo to him, and she was beginning to grow uneasy about not having figured out what her next move should be. Daily, she racked her brain, devising different schemes, then discarding them.

She wanted to come up with something original, something that would make him laugh, perhaps something connected to sports.

If only she knew how to play hockey and could show up on his team, she mused, dumping the chocolate sauce and the gross-looking egg whites into the sink, also giving up on Vince Lombardi's football tips.

"So much for your unsinkable soufflé, Julia," she sneered aloud, snapping off the video, the oven, and then retreating into the den to watch the news. "Now all I'm left with is a mess on the maid's day off."

Allowing herself a handful of nuts, she rested back against the soft down pillows, watching Jerry Dunphy but not really listening. Once she got caught in the groove of trying to figure this thing out with Nicky, she could stay on it for hours, appearing to function on the outside but actually in a trance on the inside, fixated on her dilemma.

Nicky. When, where, and how. She had considered applying for a job at his office, imagined letting him discover her working there—his vanished Cinderella reappearing miraculously behind a Selectric or behind the wheel of one of his collection of limos as his chauffeur, her mass of hair swept up into the cap. But then she decided she didn't want to be one of a series of gold-digging female employees trying to lay her boss.

Thoroughly obsessed, she had even driven by his house numerous times, seen his daughter and son, both of whom she recognized from an article on his family, hoping through osmosis to gain a clue, any clue. Laughingly, she had pictured them having to address her as "Mom." *Hardly.*

She had also gone to some of the restaurants which she had read he frequented, The Palm, Morton's, and Jimmy's, hoping to see him there, though not yet ready to let him see her.

The doorbell rang and Paige, startled, looked at her watch, surprised to see how late it had gotten. Jerry Dunphy was long gone, replaced by Lucy, Ricky, Ethel, and Fred all shouting at one another on a rerun of *I Love Lucy.*

The doorbell chimed a second time and she sprang up from the couch to get it. It would be Mark arriving for dinner, and she decided it was a good thing he had offered to bring in a pizza. The way things were going in the kitchen she would have probably burned a frozen Celeste.

Knowing Mark, he had also had the foresight to stop by Robin Rose's Ice Cream and pick up a pint of their fabulous chocolate-raspberry chambord for dessert. Just in case . . .

"Well, did it *rise*?" he teased, when she opened the door for him, an impish grin on his face, the predicted Robin Rose ice cream bag balanced on top of the pizza box.

"Not as well as this," she teased back, as he rubbed playfully against her, hoisting dinner up over her head and out of the way. The wonderful aroma of the pizza clung temptingly in the air.

"No? That's too bad. I was kind of looking forward to being your test case."

Paige grinned, framing his great baby face with her hands. "I'm sure you were."

"It's probably significant—" he murmured, pausing to kiss the tip of her nose, then moving over to her neck. "You know, one thing rising and one thing . . . not."

"Yeah?"

"Seriously." His blue eyes sparkled at her from behind his glasses.

She ran her pinkie finger along the crease of his dimple, deciding to shift the subject away from Nicky. "How were your classes today?" she asked.

"You ought to sit in sometime. Learn what to do with all that *money* you want to have one day—"

"Well, we both know I don't need an economics class for that—" Paige touched her tennis shoe to his, trying to get the bow of his shoelaces to flip the other way, not missing his sarcasm, but not acknowledging it either. "I'll know exactly what to do with it," she promised.

"My courses focus on making it multiply, not disappear."

"So, why don't you do it then. Instead of just *professing*—"

"Why? Would you marry me if I did?" he challenged, maneuvering the toes of his shoes to pin down hers while kissing her on the lips. Then, turning away from her, he headed toward the kitchen.

"It depends on how long you thought making it would take—" she answered lightly, catching up with him. "I haven't got all the time in the world, you know."

"God, you're a superficial bitch," he replied, careful to match his tone to hers.

"Why? Because of the money? Or the time?"

"Maybe both."

"I'm honest," she rallied in her own defense, scooting around him to open the kitchen door and let him in.

"To a fault," he pointed out, glancing at a Johnny Cat cat litter commercial playing on the TV set, then sticking the ice cream sack into the freezer. She watched, feeling more guilty than she thought she should feel, as he pried the pizza from the cardboard carton, dropped it onto a cookie sheet, and then rammed it noisily into one of the ovens, squinting through his glasses to set the dial. It was a gesture that she knew had more to do with anger than poor sight.

"Would you rather I lie?" she asked, frustrated.

"I'd rather you *lie down,*" he snarled, shoving her roughly against the granite island, then tenderly fondling her breasts.

She looked at him leerily, then running her hands along the taut muscles of his back, she sighed. This was getting to be more and more difficult. They weren't supposed to get involved. And yet they were.

Mark was becoming increasingly possessive, though he kept insisting he was not, that their relationship was just as Paige had set it up, for fun, for friendship, great sex, and lots of laughs.

The truth was, it wasn't easy for her, either. If she didn't keep a careful guard on her emotions she could easily let herself get too deeply involved with him as well. She was crazy about his looks, his brains, the way he made love, everything, *except* his financial status and his patent lack of drive. There wasn't anyone else with whom she could talk the way she could to Mark. She could be herself around him. He was nonjudgmental.

It took all her willpower, all her collective years of lousy, hurtful, go-nowhere romances and the cynical outlook she had cultivated through them, to keep herself from letting down and falling for him.

She kept asking herself—was that the way she wanted to live the rest of her life? Scrimping on a professor's salary, in a tiny rented apartment, a life like Kit's down the tubes.

No. Emphatically no.

The romance would wear off. The fantastic sex would wear off. He'd probably be off fooling around with his cute little co-eds. At least if Nicky fooled around on her, she would be taken care of; there would be some compensation; there would be *great* compensation.

"Paige, listen, I'm sorry," Mark apologized, his hands gently caressing her breasts again, arousing her. "I'm glad you're honest to a fault," he said, taking off his glasses and rubbing his eyes as if they ached. "Maybe it's what I like best about you."

"No, it's me who should apologize," Paige whispered. "I don't know, Mark, maybe this is unrealistic. Maybe I'm not being fair." She shivered, tingling all over from his touch. "Maybe we shouldn't see each other anymore," she forced herself to say, hoping that he would counter, not sure that she could handle it if he didn't.

She didn't know what to think when he didn't answer, pressing his lips against hers again, harder this time, their tongues colliding, their kiss gaining momentum, lips grazing, brushing, then driving against each other's until the world seemed to swerve upside down. She felt a thrill of relief when he began tearing her shirt out of her jeans, seemingly possessed, unhooking her bra almost in the same motion, until his hands closed on the silky fullness of her breasts.

With equal longing she was tugging his shirt up and out of his jeans, languishing in the feel of his skin, the heat behind it, his scent.

Her nipples rose like hard little rocks beneath his fingertips while his cock pressed urgently against the front of her jeans.

Supporting her by the waist he lifted her up and onto the countertop, undoing her jeans and wrestling them, along with her panties, down below her knees. The granite was like ice against her bare behind, but it felt tantalizingly sexy, with his hands eagerly massaging her thighs and then between her thighs, while she unfastened *his* jeans and then struggled from her awkward position to get them and his Jockey shorts down. When she had succeeded, his penis sprang free, released from the stretchy white cotton, and she caught it lovingly between her palms, growing more and more excited from his excitement.

The expression on his face jarred her, evoking the still-vivid memory of Nicky standing in the buff like that at the Château Marmont, having stripped down to nothing in a moment's time, so proud of himself, so sure of himself, strutting his swollen cock like a medal, a prize he was going to share with her. Here was Mark, worlds apart from Nicky in every way imaginable, and yet here he was with that exact same look in his eye.

Mark's *prize,* she noticed with a touch of irony, was bigger than Nicky's prize—as though to balance out the purse.

"This is so fucking cold," Mark cried out, when he heaved himself up onto the slippery countertop, on top of her, sliding them both backward so that there was enough room.

"But it feels so fucking fantastic!" they both bellowed at the same time, laughing and enjoying the shock of it as he entered her with a delicious moan and wild-man's thrust, moving deep inside her.

Paige was responding to the awkwardness of their clothes half on, half off, their bawdy, frenzied reflections mirrored in the stainless-steel fixture above her, the brazen, off-color image of the two of them screwing frantically on top of the freezing island in the kitchen.

There were some reprehensible thoughts rushing through her head, fueling her approaching orgasm, arousing her still further. Bad, teasing thoughts pledging Mark as just a playtoy, *her* toy, a silent pact with herself that they were fucking just for the fun of it. No entanglements. Just great sordid screwing. Mark couldn't possess her; nobody could possess her. His moaning heightened her pleasure until she could barely stand it anymore.

Then on the brink of a climax, she happened to glance over at the TV set where she noticed a news teaser highlighting the World Championship boxing match slated for next week at the StarDome, promoting the station's preshow interviews.

Nicky Loomis's StarDome.

The idea struck Paige with luscious force, a force that nearly put her over the edge. *The World Championship Boxing Match at the StarDome.* It was a stroke of genius. It was a stroke of luck.

Of course Nicky would be there, in the private box she had been reading about.

She would flash him their private password across the big advertising message board. *Less Is More.* He would understand immediately.

Less Is More. It was *their* phrase. *Go to concession stand at aisle number . . . whatever.*

Nothing could be more perfect. She would meet him there.

He would want to screw her on the spot.

But she would make him wait, insist that he had to understand. After their last episode, if he wanted her he was going to have to get to know her first, of course with the unsaid promise that she would make it well worth the wait when he did.

She could see it clear as day. They would embark upon a relationship that would be totally novel for Mr. Fast-Fuck Sports King. He would bring her up to his box, introducing her to his daughter, son, groupies, and assorted friends.

Probably none of them would trust her. Probably none of them should.

Paige imagined herself making love with Nicky now.

She conjured up the look of him, the feel of him, drawing on sensations still intact from the Château. But the image wasn't as satisfying as the reality, as opening her eyes and seeing her gorgeous lover going out of his mind on top of her, listening to him moan and cry out.

His lovely eyes opened, as though he had sensed that she was watching him. His mouth formed an exalted O.

And like that they came together, in unison, holding each other tightly, letting the glorious release take over.

Paige felt like crying afterward, pleasure producing guilt, producing tears.

Maybe it was guilt. Maybe it was nerves. Maybe she was just premenstrual.

* * *

She drove up to the StarDome a nervous wreck, having changed clothes thirteen times, trying to decide on the image she wanted to portray.

Miniskirt—yes or no? Jeans? Maybe better. Leather pants? Suede skirt? The long flowing one or the short, tight Alaïa knock-off? Innocent or sexy, or both?

She had to remember that his kids would probably be there with him, his friends. Some of them might remember her from her last stunt at his party. They would be watching her carefully. Judging her.

Still torn, she had finally put back on her stone-washed jeans, faded blue work shirt with big shoulder pads, a tan snakeskin belt, which matched her cowboy boots, and a bold tan Stetson hat.

Stealing a last glance in the rearview mirror and adjusting the angle on her Stetson, she took a deep breath and got out of her car, heading toward the modern-looking structure of the StarDome. The parking lot was jam-packed with every imaginable mix of car and fight fan. There was a potent, aggressive, very male-type anticipation in the air, the sense of rowdy aggression about to be vented, lots of lusty whooping and drinking and big bets.

Paige's first hurdle was going to be getting in without a ticket. She had made every effort to buy one, calling scalpers, offering to pay far more than she would have ever dreamed of paying, but for the first World Championship boxing match ever to have been fought in L.A., there simply were no seats to be had. Or bought, anyway.

The sell-out event was yet another major coup for sports entrepreneur Nicky Loomis, another bold feather in his cap.

Paige pressed anxiously through the crowd.

Usually there were people hawking tickets at the door. But now all she saw were people trying to buy. The tickets, if there were any to be had, would be up to about nine hundred dollars now, she figured.

She was getting closer to the entrance, fretting over still not having come up with a solution. She was barely even moving at this point, finding it unnecessary, thrust forward by the movement of the crowd.

She noticed a number of tickets held precariously in unsuspecting hands. If only she could snatch one of them away, one lone ticket that would surely mean more to her. She saw a woman in very dark chic-looking sunglasses who appeared bored to tears, the type who would hate fights, would find them barbaric, was only there to appease her husband. Paige was longing to grab *her* ticket. The woman would undoubtedly be relieved to be spared having to go inside and endure all that sweat, blood, and brutality. The woman would be grateful.

"Ticket please." Paige looked up, startled. The man accepting the tickets at the admission gate shot her a dirty look. He waved his hand impatiently at her, annoyed. The crowd was growing annoyed behind her. They were all in a hurry to get inside. Pushing. Crowding up behind her.

"Here," Paige said, winging it, handing him air.

"Very funny, lady. Try again." His yellowed teeth were bared in a snarl.

Paige glanced innocently down at her empty hand, then cried out, pretending confusion, her heart pounding for real. "It was just here. I had it a second ago," she stammered. "Somebody must have taken it!" Acting for all she was worth, she broke into a panic, an easy emotion to summon up at this point, with the chance of not getting in looming closer, not to mention all these angry people shouting and shoving behind her, the line swelling out of proportion. Producing an appropriate welling up of tears in her eyes, she continued her performance. "Honestly. I . . . I just had it. I don't know what happened . . ." She let her voice trail off as she bent down onto the ground, searching desperately, not sure where to go from there.

"Yeah. Sure, lady." When she spied the ticket taker cocking his head at Security, her pulse sped up even faster. She had to hold to her story. Maybe somebody would feel sorry for her and let her in.

The crowd behind her was demonstrating split sympathies. Some of them were yelling at Paige. Some of them were yelling at the ticket taker to just let her in. Paige played it on the brink of tears, exclaiming how important this fight was to her. *They had no idea. She had to see it. They had to let her in.*

Then in the midst of the commotion, a white stretch limousine pulled up to the curb directly outside the entrance. Nicky Loomis, bulky and bursting with energy, along with a raucous entourage came barreling toward them, with Nicky asserting his position as owner of the sports arena, wanting to know what all the ruckus was about. When he discovered Paige in the center of it, he broke out laughing.

Paige, ready to shrivel up and die of embarrassment, recognized his daughter standing coolly behind him, regarding her with an unreadable smirk.

"We meet again, Miss Williams," Nicky said expansively, running his large hands along the thighs of his jeans, beginning to get the picture from all the shouting in the background. "Or *is* it Miss Williams?" he questioned, the look in his small, lively eyes charging her with hope, making her believe that he had been doing his homework as well.

Encouraged but ever-vigilant, she held her breath as he guided her artfully away and out of the path of his paying customers, astonished by the crowd's rowdy support. They were rooting for her now, cheering, shouting, "Oh, c'mon, let her in, *Nicky*. The gal's a looker." It amused Paige that he was so recognizable, that these people were fans of *his*. A few of them asked for his autograph.

She felt herself loosening up as she waited, watching him distribute signatures. Her plan was now definitely down the tubes, but thankfully a *new* plan had been born out of luck.

When he was finished signing his last autograph and had doled out his last public smile, he turned expectantly back to her, warning her in a look that she was playing with fire.

Undeterred, conscious of the attention they were continuing to draw, the various looks his family and friends were communicating, she slyly met his gaze. Many men she knew had the kind of presence that filled a room. But Nicky Loomis, she noticed with a flush of pleasure, had the kind of presence that filled a stadium. *His* stadium.

"You're a hard gal to find," the still powerfully built sports mogul observed.

She felt a flood of relief at the confirmation that he had tried.

She smiled, saying nothing, not missing the signal he gave his daughter, who then ushered their group away and into the building.

"So where do we go from here?" he asked shrewdly after they had all left, his thin lips drawn thoughtfully together as he appraised her. "To bed, I hope—"

"Still not pulling any punches, are you?" she replied, continuing to be winded by his style, or lack of it, watching him grin as if he had her at last. "Didn't you get the picture last time? I'm dying to go to bed with you, Nicky Loomis," she pronounced carefully, with a green-eyed glare and a smile that could always turn heads. "But first I'm going to get to know you. And you're going to get to know me." While she felt herself blush at the tight delivery of the words, she had rehearsed a variation of it and rationalized that it had to be said.

Saying nothing, giving nothing, feeling like she was playing poker with big stakes and an only so-so hand, she watched as he broke up laughing again, that great belly laugh that she remembered, his penetrating eyes reading her with amusement. "You didn't strike me as being that traditional," he charged.

There was a brief contest of wills as they stood, each waiting for the other to give ground.

Then he laughed again, a what-the-hell kind of laugh. "Are you really that good?" he dared her.

"Are *you* really that curious?" she shot back, feigning absolute confidence.

"Yeah, I guess I am," he acquiesced, raising a smoky gray eyebrow as he took her hand.

Paige felt herself glowing as he escorted her into the StarDome, past the agitated ticket taker, through the crowd that was *his* crowd, up a special elevator, and into the famous private box.

A burst of applause shook the stands, and even though it was for defending champion Tommy Sykes, Paige felt like it was all for her.

Chapter 20 ~

Paige and Susan were sitting out by the pool drinking coffee and eating breakfast as Paige read aloud from the letter Tori had sent to them.

"Dear Paige and Susan," she began. "I'm so full of the native drink they invented here called *batida de cocos* that I hope I'm coherent enough to write you this letter. (Note: This marvelous and *very* potent brew prepared by the children on the island warrants a quick description. The adorable native kids climb up the coco trees like monkeys, bringing down bunches of green coco nuts, which they chill in ice chests. Once the coconuts are cold, the kids use machetes to whack off the tips, then spill out enough of the coco water to make room for a sugar cane brandy called *pinga.* Slip in a straw and, *voilà,* the sweetest concoction I've ever sampled. Hmmm . . .)

"Even if I'm *not* coherent enough to write you this letter, I'm going to proceed anyway, so bear with me because I have stupendous news.

"On top of being smashed from *batida de cocos* on the private totally deserted beach here, I'm also madly in love.

"At long last, we can nail down the lid on Travis Walton's

coffin. Dead and buried, girls. No regrets. Richard Bennetton, it turns out, was the perfect antidote to my former Georgia love.

"I'm not only in love, but I'm also *engaged.*

"Paige, you'll just love this one—my engagement ring is an eight-carat Colombian emerald, which we bought in Buenos Aires. It's absolutely the most dazzling, mesmerizing thing I've ever laid eyes on.

"Richard said that when I present him with a son, I'll receive earrings to match. When I present him with a daughter—a necklace. Optimistic and crazy as he is, he already has the jeweler looking for three similar stones for us, which, thank goodness, are not easy to find, or he would be finding himself in even greater debt than I'm sure he's already gone into so far on this trip.

"Truly, the kind of money he's been spending makes my head spin. You should see the polo ponies he bought from Alejandro. These horses are magnificent—*riding* them was magnificent. Susan, you would go out of your mind; I can't wait for you to come out to Santa Barbara with us when we get back (the horses will probably beat us there), so we can all go riding together. Paige, you'll come too; we'll 'un-urbanize' you a little.

"I feel like I'm living this dream fantasy—traveling in a stratosphere that's totally foreign to me. Richard has friends everywhere, each of them more interesting than the last. We've been switching back and forth from English to Spanish to French, with a little Italian sprinkled in—*so* cosmopolitan.

"Everywhere we go, we're extended a brand of hospitality that makes even my own homegrown southern-style hospitality look inadequate.

"It's as though there's a global clique, the super-rich from every continent, all of them connected in one way or another, relating on the same level, sharing the same elevated culture, the same elevated tastes, the same elevated obsession with fun.

"Like Dustin Brent being there at the Carballos' *estancia.* Wasn't that too much? (I trust you did get my postcard from Alejandro and Elena's *estancia.*) I still can't get over it. Whoever might happen to still be unattached when he returns to the States has cause to remain optimistic. Just in case you've forgotten,

Dustin Brent is Michael Douglas, Mikhail Baryshnikov, Armand Assante, and William Hurt all rolled up into one. And speaking of machetes, you should have seen our handsome benefactor splitting open his cast with a machete, mounting a big strong spirited horse directly afterward and galloping off to his next adventure—our hero!

"Anyway, it's a new dizzying world for me. And yet every now and then, when I feel the effects of it wearing off—like the tail end of a champagne buzz—I feel guilty. We could feed nations, as they say, on the extravagant whims of our country's rich. The poverty we've seen all over South America is so acute and so upsetting that you either need to block it out entirely or roll up your shirt sleeves and do something about it.

"That's the kind of mood I was in when we happened to stop for gas in this one particular town. Seemingly from out of no-where, we were suddenly surrounded by all these pathetic-looking children, with those big hungry eyes staring out of gaunt faces, their bellies distended from want of food, their hands extended to beg for pesos. It wasn't an unusual sight, but at that moment it struck me as such an unjust contrast to life at home, their listlessness and their utter lack of hope. We've all had the privilege of growing up with a sense of control over our destinies, the sense that we could dream and work hard to achieve those dreams, but these kids—it's hard to even imagine what kinds of dreams they've got.

"On an impulse, Richard had money wired from the States and presented the obscure little town with a hundred thousand dollars to improve their hospital. He *seems* spoiled and even callous at times but, underneath it all, he has the biggest heart.

"He's terrifically thoughtful. Romantic. Everywhere we go, he writes me these wonderful little notes on napkins or matchbooks or whatever, numbering them, telling me to save them for my scrapbook, which of course I have.

"I just wish I could fly you all out here to be with us—it's been so interesting, and so much fun.

"From Rio we met up with another friend of Richard's who sailed us on his yacht down to a group of islands known as Angra dos Reis and we've been island-hopping ever since. It's a rare experience because there are no hotels on the islands, only sprawling private homes, nestled away in this unforgettable landscape, surrounded by wild palm and coco trees.

"Today we had lunch in the small village of Buzios, on the coast—supposedly Brigitte Bardot's favorite spot. There was one main street with shops where the most popular item to buy was their daring 'string bikinis.'

"Of course I bought us each a couple. The Brazilian girls *known* for their perfect bodies wear them well, but we will too . . .

"The island we're staying on now is privately owned by a world-renowned plastic surgeon (Paige, you may have heard of him), Ivo Pitanguy, and we've been invited here as his guests. It's paradise, with nothing else on the island *except* Pitanguy's house, and nothing to do except laze around, water-ski and scuba dive in water that is nearly transparent as it washes up onto a spectacular stretch of crystallike white sand.

"I'm so tan and healthy-looking that, I swear, y'all wouldn't even recognize me. Richard says that my body looks like perfectly molded milk chocolate, so what do y'all think of that? From Caspar the Ghost to molded milk chocolate! I'm also getting rounder and rounder with all the wonderful food they have here. Bowls full of rich black beans. Lobsters either grilled or steamed, caught fresh right off the island for dinner every night. *Farofa,* a typical Brazilian dish referred to as 'slave food,' which they make by melting butter in a pan, stirring in eggs, then stirring in *mandioca,* a coarse native flour, and a dash of salt. It comes out all warm and crusty and loaded with butter. Mmmm. Am I making you hungry? I'll be sure to try to re-create it when I get back.

"The weather is sublime—warm, with the barest whisper of a breeze. I'm not sure how I'll ever come back down to earth.

"Anyway, I gotta run. One of the kids on the island is going to teach us how to boogie board. It's the big thing here. Like string bikinis. As a gal who can barely swim, I sure hope I don't drown and miss the heavenly life Richard's been promising me. I'd hate to hit heaven quite so literally right now.

"Can't wait to see y'all. I miss you lots. Love, Tori."

"Well. That's one down," Susan said, grinning and toasting her coffee cup to her absentee roommate. Paige raised her cup as well, incredulous.

Chapter 21 ↶

A ray of light danced vividly in Tori's emerald engagement ring as Richard held on tightly to her hand, causing the two of them to smile as they glanced down at it.

"It's really exquisite," Richard shouted over the wind. *"You're really exquisite."* They were racing along the freeway in his jet-black Ferrari, the gentle evening air rushing through their hair as they sped away from LAX, having just returned home from South America, on their way to Richard's parents' house to announce their engagement.

It seemed like an appropriate forum; Richard's father and stepmother were having a big black-tie bash there now, celebrating their ten-year wedding anniversary.

Tori and Richard were already dressed for the party, having showered and changed into their formal evening wear on board Richard's plane. The dress Tori was wearing was emerald green to match her ring. It was a very simple, short silk strapless—the color and contoured fit of the design making just the right statement; a matching green silk cape was worn over it as a wrap. Richard had bought it for her in Buenos Aires expressly to wear to the party, just before catching their flight home. With her Brazilian-born tan and the happy sparkle in her eyes, she looked as dazzling as the gem on her finger. Richard was in a smartly tailored tux.

He squeezed her hand even more tightly, knowing she was a bundle of nerves at the prospect of meeting his parents. "Relax," he said, winking at her.

"Maybe we shouldn't tell them tonight. Maybe we should wait until tomorrow—" she began again.

"Tori, they're going to love you. How could anyone not love you?"

But she was already smarting from the reception she expected to receive. She knew what they would think. She knew what *she* would think if she were in their position. "That's not the point. The point is that we hardly know each other—"

"Oh, but I can prove how well we *do* know each other . . ."

Tori looked into his eyes and melted.

"What's my favorite color?" he demanded, making her laugh.

"The color of your eyes, blue."

"And . . . what's my favorite song?"

"Richard!"

"C'mon—"

" 'Satisfaction'—"

Scrunching up his face in formidable Mick Jagger fashion, he belted out the rock refrain, abandoning the steering wheel in favor of a mock guitar. "Do I like *ice* in my diet Coke?"

"No—"

"What kind of *underwear* do I prefer?"

Tori felt her cheeks color and a happy laugh bubbling up in her throat. "Plain white boxers for you," she replied, "the short ones. Pink lace panties for me, cut high on the thigh."

"Sounds like you know me pretty well," he warranted, as he maneuvered his hand beneath her dress, beginning at her knee, then working his way up to get at the pink lace panties she was wearing for his benefit now. "Okay, here's a tougher one." His perfect teeth flashed at her. "If I were to order a cheeseburger and the waitress gave me a choice of three cheeses, Jack, Swiss, and Cheddar, which one would I choose?"

She looked at him, caught, trying to think back to the omelets or cheeseburgers she had seen him order, debating. He smiled a good strong smile that sparked her memory: *the first day in Bue-nos Aires, at the hotel, at breakfast.* "First you'd ask for Muen-ster, and then if they didn't have it you'd choose Cheddar."

Richard began flashing the lights of his car, like a game-show signal for *win,* cheering along with the display.

Tori turned to look nervously behind her. If there were any cops, they would have gotten stopped for sure. "You're crazy," she hissed.

"Crazy about you, Georgia Peach. Say 'panties' again, sounds so sexy with your li'l ol' *drawl*—" he drawled himself, his long, stick-straight saffron-colored hair whipped back by the wind.

The senior Bennetton's condominium was in one of the loftier high rises on Wilshire Boulevard. Tori and Richard rode up the all-brass and mirrored elevator in silence, each of them preparing in his or her own way, gearing up.

Richard had insisted that he wasn't in the least bit nervous, but Tori could tell that he was. There was a tenseness in his face she had never seen before. His eyes seemed more complicated, dis-tracted. His jaw was tight, almost clenched. When she reached for his hand it was clammy.

A butler opened the door for them before they even had a chance to ring the bell. He greeted Richard formally, taking Tori's wrap, and escorting them in. "Hello, Mr. Bennetton. It's nice to see you."

"Nice to see you, Raymond. Meet Tori Mitchell . . ." Tori felt her heartbeat speed up and her face flood with color again as Richard smiled in charming hesitation, his words hovering pre-cariously. "My . . . uh—"

"Hi. It's nice to meet you," she jumped in nervously, pumping the butler's hand, slipping Richard a look at the same time. They had deliberated about her wearing her engagement ring, with Tori uncomfortable that everyone would notice it. Now touching her vacant wedding-ring finger with her thumb she felt relieved that she had finally convinced Richard to carry it in his pocket until the correct moment.

A waiter passed by with a tray of empty champagne glasses

and a bottle of Taittinger's Compte de Champagne, pausing obsequiously to pour out a glass for each of them.

Tori's glass teetered as she brought it up to her lips, her taste buds totally nonfunctioning at this point, but her brain in acute need of its medicinal effects. She was in a dumb state of oblivion as Richard introduced her to a whirl of guests, smiling, accepting handshakes and compliments, beginning to feel nauseated.

Nobody's name registered. Nobody's face registered.

She was stealing glances around the starkly furnished penthouse, awed by the panorama of galvanizing views, the glow of city lights rippling in the mirrored walls, producing an almost dizzying effect, she thought.

Or maybe she was just overwhelmed, her nerves and energy shot from the seventeen-hour flight. Her body felt taut, on alert as she waited for the *key* introduction, trying to be ready for it.

Pretend you're Paige, she urged herself in response to a mounting panic. *Be cool and collected. Sassy and lighthearted like Paige. In charge. Pretend it's a game. Snow them with your southern charm.*

Tori, they're going to love you. How could they not love you? Richard's reassuring words, already repeated to her dozens of times, floated back into her head, helping to steady her some, as her reflection bounced out at her from one of the mirrors across the room. Her image appeared superimposed onto the sparkle of city lights as though to buoy her confidence, proof of how dazzling she looked, with her deep, glowing tan setting off the fiery green of her dress, creating an aura that was both exotic and radiant at once.

She tried to convince herself that it didn't matter if his parents liked her or not. Their son did. Their son wanted to marry her.

"Richard! You made it." Tori turned to see an older version of Richard striding purposefully over to embrace the younger version, a small but befitting proportion of extra bulk to his tall frame, his hair a steely gray next to Richard's ash blond and his keen blue eyes aglow with fatherly affection as he held his son close for an extra moment.

Tori held her breath as the debonair senior turned politely toward her, his hand outstretched in greeting. "And *you* must be the illustrious Tori Mitchell I've been hearing so much about," Elliot Bennetton said with friendly caution. *"Not* from my son, he never tells me anything, but through the grapevine at the office. Though I understand they haven't had the opportunity to see too much of you, my dear."

Tori smiled woodenly at the not-unwarranted dig. It was true —she had been hired by Bennetton Enterprises, at a significant salary, but she had been absent more than she had been present, getting paid while gallivanting across the globe with his jet-set, playboy son. "Hello, Mr. Bennetton. I'm so glad to finally meet you," she responded, measuring each syllable. "And I'm afraid that's true, about my being off the job more than on it," she apologized guiltily, venturing her best smile. "But hopefully you'll approve of my contribution to your company in the months to come."

She felt her confidence returning as he smiled approvingly back at her, enveloping her hand warmly between both of his, those keen Bennetton eyes taking her in. "I'm sure I will," he remarked generously. "Your résumé was impressive. And I happen to know your former employer quite well. We did a project together once in Kentucky."

Tori felt him measuring her surprise as he touched his index finger to his temple, rubbing it there for a moment, seeming to grow lost in the calculation, or maybe the memory, as though sent back in time for an instant.

"Really? Jake Shavelson—?"

"Years ago," he acknowledged. "Around 1952, I think. Long before you were born. When I saw his name and telephone number on your résumé right there in front of me, I couldn't resist giving him a call."

Elliot Bennetton smiled, responding to her look. His smile was so remarkably like Richard's that it disarmed her. She had expected suspicion, but not a private-eye routine, requisitioning her résumé, checking her out. His son was hardly that vulnerable.

She made an effort to contain her surprise. Not that the call could have possibly hurt her. She knew Jake would only have had flattering things to say on her behalf. Then she wondered if Elliot Bennetton had mentioned that she was off in South America with his son. She wondered if news of that had leaked back to Travis. Hopeful that it had, she felt a more genuine smile taking form on her lips. "Well, did I pass muster?"

"Jake couldn't have praised you more highly. Sounds like I'm lucky to have you. Every which way," he added meaningfully, his expression growing more complex as he turned to appraise his son. The senior Bennetton looked suddenly at a loss for words, circumspect. Yet he didn't appear the sort of man who would be at a loss very often.

"Isn't she a find?" Richard exclaimed, attempting to cut through the cloud of tension that had abruptly moved in, putting his arm around Tori and drawing her in close to his side.

"She's gorgeous," Elliot Bennetton concurred, smiling kindly, yet that tense, complicated look on his face, remained. "According to Jake, she's gorgeous inside and out." He seemed to have something to say, but no comfortable way of saying it. It made Tori wonder about the relationship between father and son. It was difficult to ascertain who was afraid of whom. She suspected it was mutual. Richard had said so little about his father. Tori thought it was a sad fact of so many parental relationships, parent and child *wanting* to communicate, but neither party really knowing how.

"So, how was that part of the world? Did you have a nice time?" Elliot Bennetton finally broke the silence.

Tori replied with guarded enthusiasm, looking to Richard.

He smiled as one would for a photograph, responding to his father's mood. It was as though there were some sort of contest beginning, as the two men resumed their quiet study of one another. Maybe an old contest that had never ended. Tori wanted to find a way to excuse herself. She was just about to ask where the powder room was, when she lost her chance.

"So, I heard about your six-figure horse acquisition," the senior Bennetton announced thinly in a controlled voice. It became less controlled as he went on. "I see you're really going through with that sponsorship business—"

Richard's younger blue eyes narrowed combatively. "That was the purpose of my trip—"

"Two hundred thousand dollars on polo ponies?" Elliot Bennetton forced a laugh, then glanced uneasily at Tori, clearly wishing he had his son alone, but unable to stop himself.

"*Jones* reporting to you now?" Richard asked tersely.

"He *is* my accountant."

"It was a good investment."

"Don't bullshit me, Richard."

Tori was so taken aback by the confrontation that she didn't know what to think.

Elliot Bennetton smiled again—so much emotion contained beneath that smile. Tori felt a compounding urgency to disappear, a sense of foreboding, without understanding anything. Their smiles had *all* borne so many different meanings. This particular smile revealed a man of immense power—losing it.

Richard snorted. "Never bullshit a bullshitter?"

"I think we should talk about this later," his father said, getting a grip on himself at last, his eyes losing their anger, looking old.

Richard's eyes were still blazing. "Suit yourself," he yielded. Then, rather childishly, after a pregnant pause, he held up his glass in the gesture of a toast. "Happy anniversary, Dad," he declared levelly.

"Richard!" A statuesque woman in a glistening amber gown, which matched her very chic, bronze-schemed apartment, rustled toward them.

"Here we go again," Richard projected under his breath, taking a deep swallow of his champagne before she got there.

"Richard, I'm so glad," his stepmother effused, breathless from crossing the room. "With your flying in today, we didn't expect you here until late, if at all." Smiling warmly at them both, she looped her arm through her husband's.

"I never break a promise, Phyllis. And I promised to be here. Happy anniversary." He kissed her dutifully on the cheek, eyeing his father, who took a deep breath, then looked down at his shoes.

They were all waiting for Richard to introduce Tori, who held her breath, wishing for a way to preempt Richard from saying anything about their engagement just yet. The timing was clearly all wrong, and she was embarrassed at the size of the ring he would be sliding defiantly onto her finger.

But the look on his face told her that it was too late.

"Phyllis, I'd like you to meet my fiancée, Tori Mitchell," Richard announced indelicately, undisguisedly relishing the impact of the jolt as he dealt it.

Phyllis, plainly caught off guard, turned to face Tori, who was so tense she didn't know what to say. The older woman's umber-pencil-lined orange lips were parted in surprise, her intelligent-looking gray eyes blinked as she managed a polite congratulations.

"Thank you," Tori replied dully, shattered by the whole turn of events. Her mood had come plummeting down from cloud nine; the little bit of paradise she had glimpsed evaporated like a mirage. She felt used and was tempted to storm off. If her ring hadn't been in Richard's pocket she thought she might have thrown it at him.

Instead, she avoided looking at him altogether, afraid that if she did she would dissolve into tears. She felt Elliot Bennetton watching her, taking in her response.

"Well, this is a surprise! Is it official?" Phyllis Bennetton wondered, directing an uneasy glance over at her husband.

Richard dropped his hand ceremoniously down into his pocket, withdrawing Tori's engagement ring and then placing it onto her finger.

It had looked so magnificent only a little while ago in the car. Now it looked ostentatious. Blanching, she realized it was actually larger than the diamond belonging to her prospective step-mother-in-law.

What she didn't know was that Phyllis Bennetton could have bought *herself* that kind of ring without the help of Richard's father, that she was a very wealthy woman in her own right, having founded a chain of contemporary young women's clothing stores long before she met him. She was a brilliant merchandiser, enormously successful, and far too low-key to engage in the kind of flash Richard favored. It was no secret that she disapproved of his excesses.

"I guess it is," Phyllis acknowledged, an undecipherable expression on her face as she eyed the ring.

This time Richard's father spoke up, unrestrained. "All right, Richard. We have to talk."

"I thought you said we should talk later," Richard remarked, looking him squarely in the eye.

"I changed my mind—"

Phyllis put her hand on her husband's shoulder to calm him. "Elliot. Please, darling. Later—"

"Phyllis, I'm sorry. I just can't—"

"*No*, Phyllis," Richard interrupted. "I'm a big boy. I can take whatever it is he wants to say."

Tori felt like the incredible shrinking woman, growing smaller and smaller, the world around her looming more and more out of proportion. Nobody seemed to give a damn what she thought or felt, and yet she was being thrust into the vortex of this family feud.

"Darling, please," Phyllis reiterated, indicating the festivities going on just beyond where they were standing in the entry, the party they had only joined peripherally.

"What are you all doing hiding out here!" demanded a big-gutted man with a loud laugh and a pungent cigar. "Having a little family meeting? Richard, who's the pretty girl? He always finds the prettiest girls," he confided to Tori, by way of a back-handed compliment, folding his hands onto his belly. "Did you import her from South America?"

"Only her tan. Lawrence Keeler, meet Tori Mitchell, my fiancée," Richard reported cheerfully, shaking hands with his father's old friend.

"*Congratulations*, you sly dog, you. That's some news," Lawrence Keeler replied heartily, signaling for his wife, who was standing with a group of friends across the room. Tori noticed Richard and his father exchanging a look.

"Betty, Richard here is engaged. And this is his lovely young fiancée—what's your name, dear?"

Tori spied his wife and the three friends she had brought along with her, all gaping at her ring. In a kind of fluttery chorus they exclaimed their congratulations.

In no time, the party had converged around them, forcing the four of them toward the center of the room, with all of the Bennettons' guests rushing up to extend their best wishes, to dispense congratulatory hugs, to take Tori's hand and gawk at the eight-carat emerald Richard had bought for her.

It was as terrible a moment for Tori as when Travis had stood her up at Tiffany's, maybe worse, if that were possible. She was obviously jinxed when it came to rings and engagements. Instead of bringing her joy, as she had always imagined, all the occasion ever brought her was humiliation. And she had a sense that the worst was yet to come.

For the remainder of the party, she, Phyllis, and Elliot Bennetton all stood around smiling hollowly, enduring the gush of congratulations. Only Richard remained animated—looking like the cat who had swallowed the canary.

After all the guests had left, he looked more like a cat who had swallowed rat poisoning.

"All right. The party's over. *Literally over,*" Elliot Bennetton issued quietly, walking wearily over to pour himself a shot of whiskey before retiring onto the couch. Phyllis Bennetton sat down supportively beside him, saying nothing as he loosened the bow tie at his throat, releasing the neck of his shirt after that, and dropping the Cartier studs into a crystal ashtray.

Tori didn't know what to do with herself. With a stab of reluctance at staying altogether, she settled tentatively into a suede tub chair, facing an Andy Warhol portrait of Mao printed on Chinese silk. Richard, who had been holding her hand, crossed over to the travertine fireplace, leaning smugly up against it, ready to do battle. He had hardly spoken two words to Tori since they had arrived, although he had squeezed her hand, and delivered an occasional it'll-be-okay kind of wink, and she found she was more confused than angry with him.

"Tori, I'm sorry to be having this out with my son in front of you, but if you're planning on marrying him, this concerns you as well," Elliot Bennetton said, catching her by surprise, going on to surprise her further. "Richard, I don't know how to say this except to say it flat out. I'm cutting you off."

Richard's cocky, controlled expression vanished. Tori

watched, stunned, as he stood rooted in shock, unable to reply, his expression registering astonishment, fear, and then rage as he digested his father's curt decision. He never once looked over at her or at his stepmother. "What do you mean you're cutting me off," he demanded finally, his voice tight. "You can't just cut me off at will. I have a trust, from Mom. You can't touch that—"

"I can't touch it, Richard. But wait until you see what you have left after all this. You'll find it's all been frittered away."

"No fucking way."

"Give the bank a call in the morning."

"I thought you didn't believe in strings," Richard mocked bitterly.

"This has nothing to do with strings. It has to do with *abuse*. *That's* what I don't believe in—*abuse*. Talk to Ted Jones tomorrow. He'll lay out your financial situation for you. You'll be receiving your exact same salary, provided you don't go off on any more four-week jaunts for a while. You'll be treated like all of Bennetton's other employees. Three weeks' vacation time—and you've already had more than your share. Medical insurance. Plus the perks specified in your contract."

"Contract? What *contract?*"

"Jones will go over it with you."

"Well, just maybe I won't sign along the dotted line—"

"Then don't."

Richard glared hard at his father, making Tori wonder at the depth of bitterness, the malice that had sprung up in him tonight. She was torn, conscious of the obvious degree of truth in his father's accusation, having been a recipient of that excess herself. But the undercurrent of hurt she sensed in Richard, hidden directly beneath that malice, that bitterness, made her want to protect him, to rush over and hold him, to soothe him and tell him that it was all going to be all right.

"Richard, this is long overdue, and you know it," Elliot Bennetton said, with a surprising calm, sipping resignedly at his whiskey, looking down into the unlit fireplace beside his son, then looking him straight in the eye. "You can't go around pissing away money the way you do. Excuse my language, Tori, but that's the way it is. Your multi-carat emerald engagement ring probably didn't even seem all that extravagant as you listened to the numbers being tallied up on my son's other commitments there, the polo ponies, the sponsorship commitments, the *hospital* in that little village. I'm surprised he didn't buy himself an island. Richard, you've gone through two separate trusts already. Four million on your house. God only knows how many hundreds of thousands you have in cars, in your *subterranean parking lot* there.

"You appear to be competing with Norton Simon on your art collection. Your traveling gets more and more extravagant. Your lousy movie investments. And now this polo business—I've had it. You make it on your own and, fine, you can blow it any way you like—"

"*She* put you up to this, didn't she?" Richard raged, turning on his stepmother, whose lily-white complexion flushed with red.

"*She* has nothing to do with this—"

"My ass!"

Beginning to lose his temper now, Elliot Bennetton pointed a shaky finger at his son. "You just watch yourself—"

"She did, didn't she? What's the matter, Phyllis? Trying to steal a little more for yourself and your daughters?"

"I *told* you, she had nothing to do with this," Elliot Bennetton shouted.

But he was intercepted by his wife who left her place beside him and stormed over to slap Richard hard across the face. "Your father has given you *everything*," she hissed. "*Everything!* And you've given him nothing in return. You're self-centered, spoiled rotten, and this just might teach you some humility. This was unequivocally my idea, and I'm *happy* to take credit for it. I've been pleading with your father to do this for years. But he wouldn't listen to me. He felt too guilty over your mother dying. Over his being happy, and your *inability* to be happy. It's high time for him to stop taking the blame and for *you* to begin to bear some responsibility for your own life."

Richard's hand was still holding his cheek where his stepmother had slapped him. The two of them looked at one another, a store of old resentment bursting to the surface.

"If you want my opinion, which I'm sure you don't," Phyllis

went on more calmly, smoothing her already perfect bubble of hair, a stately expression on her face, "I think you should go to work somewhere other than at Bennetton. I think you should learn what it's like to really earn a living on your own, to feel the sense of pride and accomplishment that goes with that. I don't think you'll ever be happy, Richard, until you've learned that you're smart enough and capable enough to do that. I know what you think of me, and I really don't care because I feel so sorry for you."

Tori was astonished when Phyllis Bennetton's eyes welled up with tears, and she went from staunch and in control to awkward and self-conscious.

"I happen to love you, Richard. I know you'll probably never believe that. But I do. And I honestly believe, in my heart of hearts, that this is the right thing to do. I'll be pulling for you more than anyone you know. And so will my daughters, who incidentally, don't need one red cent of your money or your father's. I made it on my own, and they're making it on their own, and that's the way I believe it should be."

Everyone was silent after Phyllis's speech. Tori felt as though she had come into the middle of a movie, without the benefit of really knowing the players or their backgrounds, but was moved to tears anyway, rooting for a conclusion that would give everyone what he or she wanted.

Blinking, and forcing back the stirred emotion, she looked at Richard, finding him clearly more enraged than moved.

With a hard-boiled look on his face, he broke into a kind of mock applause. "Bravo, Phyllis—you and your great puritan work ethic. Except that I don't need to *work* to feel worth something. Going into an office eight hours a day every day doesn't make me feel any more of a man than having fun and doing whatever the fuck I want to do. I'm more interesting *because* I travel, *because* I meet interesting people and do interesting things. You're just jealous, and your values are hopelessly middle class."

Tori was mortified when he stalked over to grab her up by the wrist onto her feet, shoving her bejeweled hand in Phyllis's face. "Is this too *ostentatious* for you, Phyllis? Is it *too* breathtaking?

Too bedazzling? You work your butt off—but what's it all for if it's not to have a good time?

"You know, Phyllis, you really take life much too seriously. And, Dad, you're letting her take you down with her. Fuck you both. I'll do fine on my own. I won't gain any sick pleasure out of slaving away to get the bucks, but once I'm there, and I have no doubt that I'll get there, contrary to your dime-store psychoanalysis, I'm certain that I'll do just fine. So just fuck you both. And, Phyllis, I suggest you pass up the psychology bit and stick to young women's apparel—at least you're in the ballpark there."

The look of anguish on Elliot Bennetton's face made Tori turn around, hoping impossibly for a reconciliation as Richard stormed out of the room, still holding on to her hand, tugging her along with him.

The short stretch from the Bennettons' penthouse to Dustin Brent's home felt like an eternity, the stormy speed with which Richard attacked the distance only intensifying the interminability of the ride. Tori was afraid to utter even a single word.

When at last they approached the electronic iron gates sealing off the large Mediterranean-style house that reminded her now of a mini *estancia,* gingerly she handed Richard the key that would gain them admission.

As the gates hummed open, he impatiently threw his gears into a rough first and then sped up the grand palm-lined circular drive, only barely missing the fish pond as he killed the engine with a loud sigh. It was the first sound Tori had heard from him since they had left.

They sat there like that for as long as ten minutes, until she finally mustered up the courage to speak.

Slipping her engagement ring off her finger, she held it out to him. "Richard, I think you should get your money back for this," she began tentatively, trying to read what was behind his eyes, wishing some of the tension would break so that they could talk. "I don't need it—" she shrugged, taking his hand to place the ring in his palm. *I need you* was what she was about to say when he cut her off.

"Oh, that's very good. Fast work, Tori. I lose my inheritance, and you're gone with the wind—"

"I'm not *breaking off* our engagement," Tori argued, stung. "I'm just giving you back the ring. It's ridiculous, Richard. You're going to need the money; *we're* going to need the money. And I certainly don't need an eight-carat rock on my finger. If it's so important to you, you can buy me another one when you've gotten back on your feet."

Full of hostility, Richard shoved the emerald right back at her. "That's not the way I do things. You don't want it; then the engagement is off."

Tori looked at him, uncomprehending. "But Richard, I don't want it."

"Do you *not* want to marry me?" he insisted sullenly.

"Why are you doing this?" she asked.

"A test of faith."

"I don't like these *games* anymore, Richard."

"No games. A simple test of faith. Do you trust me? I need to know whether or not you trust me."

Trust him? He looked completely crazed, the object of a betrayal, plotting his revenge, his eyes dark with that brooding intensity that puts normal people over the edge. Tori felt backed up against the wall. "Yes. Of course I do," she said warily, not sure at all if she did.

He leaned across the car to kiss her coldly on the mouth. "Why would you want to marry me now, anyway?" he speculated edgily, toying with the delicate silk rose at her waist, then suddenly, as though asserting his wounded masculinity, ripping it off, arcing it up and out of the open top of the car. *"Now that I'm in hock up to my ears?"* he emphasized, watching the wisp of silk land in the gutter and then looking at her hard for a reaction.

"Because I love you," she answered trembling. "Because your money was not the reason I was marrying you."

Dustin's sprawling estate, lit up against the blackness of the night, rose up in silent contradiction, a symbol for the real purpose of the move out to Beverly Hills. Who was she kidding? That *was* why she had gone out with him; that *was* why she had fallen for him. She and her friends had moved out to California to meet and marry rich men, to obtain for themselves a life like Kit's.

"Would you have married me if I were a struggling artist?" Richard persisted huskily, "A ditch digger or a telephone repairman—" Then interrupting his own interrogation, blocking her protests, he began kissing her so roughly that he was actually hurting her.

"Richard, stop it," she cried, wrestling away from him, unable to shift her position even a fraction of an inch. The car was small and cramped, and she couldn't move.

"Why? Do I turn you off now?"

"You're hurting me—"

"So hurt me back," he dared, his breathing heavy and erratic as he cut her off, forcing his mouth over hers so that she could barely catch her breath.

He had her pinned against the seat, and he climbed completely over to her side, attacking the silk bodice of her dress, attempting to rip it right off her, growing more and more frenzied at his own violence. She couldn't hold back the tears any longer, and she finally began to cry and fight back in earnest.

Who was this person who was trying to hurt her, who had gone stark raving mad and was taking out all of his fury on her? "Richard, dammit, get a hold of yourself. Stop it!" she cried, wincing as the silk made a terrible ripping noise and a fresh spill of tears washed down her cheeks.

"Why should I! I'll buy you another one. It's just a dress. I'll fucking buy you another one! I'll fucking buy you anything you want," he shouted hotly, unzipping his pants and pulling out the swollen proof of his manhood, of his authority.

"I'll fucking buy *you* . . ." he ranted repeatedly.

"And I'm fucking getting out of this car," Tori shouted back at him, shaking as she tried to wrench away from him.

She felt the tears on his cheeks as well, hot, wet, mingling with her own, all that pent-up anger and hurt as his hard-on fizzled and he began to hold her close, apologizing and pleading with her not to leave him.

She gave up any further struggle and, maintaining a low whisper in his ear, insisted that it was okay, that it would all be all right, that she would help him, that she loved him for *him* and not for his damn money.

She wasn't that kind of person.

But even as she said it and she listened to her own words, she wasn't sure.

This had all shaken her to her roots, and she realized she wasn't sure of anything.

The Richard who swept her off her feet was lost to her. There was a different man in his place, who was icy, deeply troubled, shutting her out, but at the same time sending signals for help.

Or maybe before, she had been seeing only what she wanted to see.

The familiar sense of despair that she felt inside, of dreams cruelly shattered, the crushing ache of her heart, caused her to slip into thoughts of Travis again, a habit she had hoped she had finally kicked.

In doing so, she found herself hating him more than ever. And for a change she was blaming Travis more than ever.

Otherwise she had to blame herself.

Chapter 22

Tori and Richard were sound asleep in his bed when the telephone woke them up. Through a fog of sleep, Tori watched him reach over to fumble with the receiver, then grab it anxiously up to his ear, the trim clock radio beside the phone registering the predawn hour. Careful to keep her eyes closed, feigning a continued slumber, she found herself hanging on to every word of his end of the conversation, tensely conscious of him watching her.

It was the same tense state that had pervaded every aspect of their lives for the last two weeks, since their return home from Argentina and the freezing of Richard's trust.

In the beginning, after the initial shock, he had been fairly certain that he could get a bank loan, that he could sell enough stock and liquidate enough assets to insure that his life-style remain relatively unaffected.

But when he discovered that he had already sold most of his stock, except for a few certificates still registered in his father's name, that all the real estate he owned, he owned in family partnerships, with his share being nontransferable, *and* that his financial situation was dire enough so that even his closest banking relationships had stopped returning his calls, he panicked.

And yet stubbornly he refused to give up anything, refused to back down on any of his South American commitments, such as the polo ponies or Tori's emerald or even the polo matches themselves. The horses had already cost thousands of dollars each, just to fly them over to this country and transport them up to Santa Barbara, where they were being stabled, for God only knew how much a month.

Tori was immensely frustrated because she couldn't talk to him. He was distancing himself from everything and everybody, becoming impossible to connect with, possessed with finding a solution to his out-of-hand debts. Tori knew she would have had to be blind not to see that he was in way out of his depth, as she watched him stoically pursuing alternative resources, and blind not to guess that the bulk of the most recent ones fell on the wrong side of the law.

From his end of the conversation, Richard's terse responses gave away nothing, and Tori opened her eyes to find him still watching her. She gave him a small, sleepy smile, her eyes beginning to adjust to the dark, able to make out the purplish circles that were becoming more pronounced beneath his eyes.

"What time tomorrow night?" he asked into the phone, not happy at her sparked attention. After a couple more blandly delivered responses, he hung up the receiver and bounded out of bed, offering no explanation, looking unapproachable as he rushed around the room beginning to pack.

His bedroom, on the second floor of his architecturally celebrated home built on one of the better-view lots of Bennetton Hills Estates, was designed with a rectangular glass panel framed into the wall, positioned to look down into the living room and out through the room's sweeping expanse of windows, making a veritable theater of the city. His lacquered bedroom walls were painted the same color as the night, with voluptuous sand-colored ottomans, gently curved sofas and chairs all grouped around a modern stainless-steel fireplace. Through the panoply of gleaming surfaces, the beveled mirrors, the welded steel sculpture in the corner, Tori was able to observe Richard's reflection as he threw his belongings together with swift economy.

Dressed in a pair of jeans, an old Columbia sweatshirt, and

Reeboks, he slung his packed duffel bag over his shoulder and started toward the door.

Tori, feeling completely rejected, looked at him for an explanation.

"I have to go to Santa Barbara for a couple of days. I'll call you," he said, softening and retreating back toward the bed where she sat on her knees, the sheet wrapped around her body, feeling miserably vulnerable.

She wanted to ask him why he had to go, what was so urgent at three o'clock in the morning. She wanted to ask if she could go with him. She wanted to talk.

But after a distant kiss, he drew away, his mind occupied with something else, leaving her alone and worried, wishing she could turn back the clock.

Weary but awake, she watched him through the window-lined wall of his bedroom, his long-legged stride minimizing the distance as he passed through the living room snatching up his briefcase and then turning to look tensely back at her.

She hadn't been able to sleep all night after that and drove to the office when the streetlights were still sending off a diffused yellow light.

It reminded her of her early ambitious days at Jake Shavelson's company, when she had often been the first to arrive and the last to leave. The empty hallways and vacant offices always gave her a special kind of feeling. She cherished the absolute quiet those hours insured, the rare chance to operate in peace, with the phones at rest, offering stolen time to catch up, to work twice as fast and be twice as productive, with the sheer luxury of no distractions.

After depositing her purse, jacket, and briefcase in her own office, and then making herself a quick cup of coffee in the coffee room, Tori slipped self-consciously into the private sanctuary of Richard's office. She didn't believe in spying, but her curiosity and a sense of heightened foreboding had led her there anyway.

Leaning back in his glove leather chair behind his sweeping black granite desk, she sat there for a while, drinking her coffee and thinking.

Why was Richard running off to Santa Barbara in the middle of the night? Receiving disturbing phone calls at that hour? If only she knew what the conversation had been about. If only she knew what was going on.

Her relationship with him was rapidly deteriorating, and she felt absolutely powerless to do anything about it. She was in a helpless state of limbo, not breaking up with him because she felt too guilty.

She didn't want to desert him; she didn't want to confirm his assertion that the only attraction had been the money. Besides, in between shutting her out, there were those other times when he broke down and needed her.

Richard's father had shifted critical job responsibilities away from Richard and had assigned Pete Sharbut, one of Bennetton's experienced vice presidents, overlapping responsibilities to cover when Richard was not present, as though his son's disappearances were not unusual. Tori was assigned to answer to Pete and she found it almost a relief to be back in the swing of things, working normal hours, back under the gun, feeling productive.

Tori was also enjoying the opportunity of getting to know Richard's father. She could see that this was all just as hard on him. It had cost him nothing to let Richard run through money the way he had in the past because he had plenty of it. What had cost him was having to withhold it, having to endure his son's anger and the estrangement. Richard was his only son and he clearly wanted to give him every advantage. But by the same token, he also didn't want to ruin him.

Tori surmised that without Phyllis's influence, Elliot Bennetton would never have had the strength to go through with this. Though she would never have admitted it to Richard, Tori was inclined to believe that Richard would be better off for having made it through the impending ordeal—*if* he could make it through.

He was always running fast in too many directions, lacking some basic fulfillment inside. He was insecure and resentful. She just hoped it wasn't too late. No doubt Elliot Bennetton hoped the same thing.

Tori looked up at the photograph of Richard with his father.

They were so alike physically and so unalike in every other way. Or maybe it was only their backgrounds; maybe it was an interesting study in growing up hungry versus growing up "fat," their perspectives of the world, of themselves, and their needs being entirely different.

Needs. What were Richard's needs? Why did he seem to need so much? What was he trying to prove? Tori was growing increasingly worried about how mercurial he was. How could she ever hope to make a man like that happy? She wondered if he was capable of being married for the long haul, kids, station wagon, enduring the inevitable marital problems and crises, growing old together and not minding so much.

He had accused Phyllis of having middle-class values. Well, Tori had them as well. Middle-class values were solid values. What was Richard talking about, anyway?

Leaning forward in his chair, beginning to scan the various papers and files across his desk, looking for something, but having no clue as to what, she passed over big color brochures and materials on their various projects—Bennetton Estates, Bel Air Highlands, Sienna Heights, files on property just acquired downtown, a project in Irvine. Another in Seattle.

There were stacks of bills and they had been left all askew, as though Richard had been in the middle of paying them, or trying to pay them anyway, when he had left work the day before. His MasterCard bill was among the ones left open, and Tori uncurled the sheet of paper, glancing down at it.

The forty-five-thousand-dollar total she saw reflected in the little box at the bottom of the statement didn't seem possible and she picked the bill up off the desk, sure she had misread it. When she saw she had not, she was flabbergasted, finding it hard to imagine that MasterCard would even run such a limit.

Growing concerned about the time, she began to rush, looking through his other bills, rationalizing that if she were going to marry him, his debts and his problems were hers as well.

MasterCard.

American Express.

Visa.

Tiffany.

Neiman-Marcus.

Claude Montana.

Neon.

Jimmy's Restaurant.

There were additional overdue statements from his landscape architect, his pool engineer, the company that had put in his tennis court. The total picture was beyond her comprehension and, when she picked up his checkbook, which had also been left out, opening the register portion and leafing through the first month, it became too clear not to acknowledge that Richard's father was probably justified in cutting off his son, after all. The monthly payments on his four-million-dollar house alone were a sobering twenty-two thousand dollars.

Tori threw the statement she was holding back down onto the desk, amazed that, with his life collapsing down around him, he refused to back down, refused to sell anything or give up anything, refused to even talk about it.

It was beyond her understanding why he wouldn't just take his medicine and adjust his life-style until he could afford it on his own. Why he didn't at least have the sense to return the horses he bought from Alejandro in Argentina, or arrange a resale, and call off his polo sponsorship. The Chubb Insurance binder covering the horses, which she had seen on his desk, made it apparent that he had no intention of giving ground there.

He was too damn proud. That was his problem. He was spoiled and proud and hurt, and his ego had him fired up to do battle at any cost. Which was precisely what had her so concerned.

She jumped when the phone rang, feeling caught, alarmed because of last night's unsettling call *and* because it was Richard's private line. Tempted to pick it up, she listened to it ring over and over again. What if it were Richard trying to find her?

But why would he call her there? she realized. He wouldn't.

After the ringing had stopped, the metallic black phone began to seem ominous, as though it contained a secret, a missing piece of the puzzle. When it began ringing again, as though in direct response to her anxiety, she made a deal with herself. Seven rings and she would pick it up.

One. Two. Three . . . At the seventh ring, she snatched up the receiver, waiting for the party on the other end to say hello first.

"Hi, handsome. I miss you *desperately . . .*"

Tori was caught up short by the breathy female voice on the other end of the line. It was the kind of voice that went with a *Vogue* face.

"Richard—?" the voice sulked.

Tori debated. "No. This is his *secretary,*" she lied, strained. "I happened to be walking by and heard his phone ringing. May I take a message?"

The voice lost its seductive tone. "Is he in town?"

"Yes. I mean, no . . . not today. Who's calling?" she stammered, wanting to hang up.

"Jo-Jo. Listen, honey, tell him that I heard that he's engaged, that I send my congratulations. And that . . ." Jo-Jo laughed breezily. "And that I'll *miss* him."

Doing her best to sound secretarial, Tori assured Jo-Jo that she would pass on her message and then hung up. Served her right for answering his private line, she told herself, chagrined.

When the line rang again, she picked it up without thinking, only remembering after she had already said hello that it was his private line again.

"Richard Bennetton, please."

She thought about hanging up, but then, instead, curious about the thick Spanish accent, asked, "Who's calling?"

"Rio Grande Trucking Company."

"May I tell him what it's in regard to?" Tori found herself asking.

"I have the bid for him on transporting his horses from Santa Barbara to Nogales."

The Rio Grande Trucking Company? Transporting horses across the border . . . Tori felt her heart stop and she hesitated over the long-distance crackle. "Oh, good," she managed, stalling, the implications beginning to connect in her head. "Uh . . . I can take that information down for him." Her eyes shot warily over to the Chubb Insurance binder as she reached for a pencil and unsteadily wrote down the information he was giving her, trying to think, write, and understand his heavy accent all at once.

After she hung up the phone she sat dazed for a while, staring down at what she had written, trying to guess the full picture. She had come into Richard's office convinced she would find something, and now that she actually had she was shaking.

Frustrated, she began opening his drawers, rummaging through his benign-looking belongings, finding only pencils, pens, loose rubber bands, business cards, matchbooks, gum.

In another drawer she noticed an unlabeled file folder and brought it out, scanning the loose slips of paper it contained, then the top several sheets of a legal pad. When she saw Lloyds of London and then Chubb Insurance written down, along with fees and policy notations, she arranged the material in front of her on the desk and began examining it more carefully. His notes were messy and abbreviated, but clearly what she was looking for.

On another sheet of paper she found a list of border towns, specifying Tijuana, Mexicali, Calexico, and Nogales, with Nogales underlined. Beneath that he had compiled a series of trucking companies, both here in the States and in Mexico, all listed with phone numbers. There was Ace Trucking Company, Allied Trucking Company, Rio Grande Trucking Company, Pronto Trucking Company, plus a couple additional Mexican-sounding names, one of which was starred.

Carlos Aguilar's Camiones de Servicios.

Deliberating, Tori picked up the phone, about to dial their number, then hung up again, debating about calling Paige or Susan instead, but then not doing that either, since she hadn't even told them yet that Richard had been cut off. He had insisted that she not.

Beginning to feel sick to her stomach, she dumped the now cold remains of her coffee into his wastebasket, then picked up the phone and forced herself to dial *Carlos Aguilar's Camiones de Servicios,* having no idea what she was going to say.

After a series of rings, someone answered in rapid-fire Spanish.

"Habla Ingles?" she tried, afraid that she would get nowhere with her pidgin Spanish.

"Yes, but not too much," came the heavily accented reply.

Tori took a deep breath, then plunged blindly in. "My husband spoke to someone at your company about transporting some horses for us. He asked me to call to confirm the arrangements. Only I've forgotten exactly to whom it was I was supposed to speak," she said stumbling. It was a shot in the dark, but she had to go for it.

"*Sí, señora,*" the voice answered, not indicating the slightest bit of confusion. "Your horses are being transported from where?"

"Santa Barbara," Tori replied cautiously. Then, reading from Richard's list, she added, "To Nogales, I think."

Something seemed to register on the other end of the line. "*Sí, señora,*" he said again, this time with recognition. "I believe our driver should be on his way there now. If you want, I could find out for you—"

"No, never mind," she interrupted hurriedly, wondering why she had even called, dreading the possibility that Richard might find out she had.

As she hung up and glanced anxiously back over at the notes in front of her, she knew Richard's scheme could mean only one thing.

Richard was planning on defrauding his insurance company, on having his horses transported across the border so he could claim theft and collect on his policy. She wondered if he had already arranged a resale on the other side.

When his private line began to ring again, Tori nearly flew out of his chair. As it continued ringing, she restored his file to the condition in which she had found it and replaced it in his drawer.

Then she looked around for any other signs of her having been there, retrieving her coffee cup from his wastebasket, the file folder she had initially brought in with her from his desk, and slipping out just as the main line joined in the chorus of sound, marking that the day had begun.

Fortunately, nobody had seen her at Bennetton and she crept out, calling in sick from a pay phone in the parking lot.

"Yeah, there's a lot of flu going around," the receptionist sympathized in response, then asked her to hold as another line began to ring.

Tori held impatiently, feeling nervous, trying to collect her thoughts. She was staring down gloomily at her engagement ring, turning it to catch the light, all the complicated ramifications of the ring weighing on her, when she was suddenly hit with what she needed to do.

Sell the damn ring . . .

"Sorry Tori, but that was for you. A Travis Walton from Atlanta," the receptionist said, imitating Travis's drawl. "He said it was personal."

Travis. Tori was too taken aback to even respond as she took down the number, which was *their* number, and in a stupor hung up the phone.

Damn him for still having this effect on her, she thought, wanting nothing more than to be over him, to stop caring. She was engaged. Their relationship was history. And yet her heart was soaring at the mere mention of his name, rising with reckless velocity, paying no heed to the fall that was never very far behind.

The worst of it was that she needed to be sharp right now, and she couldn't begin to think straight, wondering and trying to anticipate what he wanted.

She guessed he had heard about her engagement, but *why* was he calling? To congratulate her? To plead with her not to marry Richard—to marry him instead?

Unquestionably, to throw her all off again.

Resolved not to let him, she reached for the bulky telephone directory, which was chained to the shelf beneath the pay phone. The pawnbroker listings were numerous, occupying nearly a full page, and she scanned the small text, barely able to concentrate, but trying.

Distrustful but desperate, she finally settled on one of the more established-looking boxed-in ads and dialed.

The first few calls got her nowhere; then she was referred to a jeweler in the 607 building downtown by the name of John Logan, whose primary business was dealing in colored stones.

In a nervous monotone, Tori repeated her inquiry to him.

"I can't tell you anything over the phone, if that's what you're looking for," John Logan interrupted her straight off the bat. "I'd need to see the stone—"

"If you could just give me an idea," Tori pleaded with him, trying to keep her voice even. "I don't have a lot of time, and I'm only asking for a ballpark figure. I also wanted to know if you have that kind of cash on hand—"

"The cash is not a problem, dear, but I'd still need to see the stone," he reiterated. Then, after a thoughtful pause he added, "I don't suppose you'd like to tell me how much you paid for the ring."

Tori frowned and decided, why not? "I don't mind," she replied. "We paid three hundred thousand. I don't have the receipt, but you can check with Ricardi Jewelers in the Plaza Hotel in Buenos Aires to verify the origin if you want—"

"That's a lot of money," he remarked, implying that she had been ripped off.

"It's an unusual stone," Tori argued. "My husband's not new to buying jewelry—"

"Well, you have to understand, dear, you paid retail and I buy wholesale—"

"How soon would you be able to get the money if you were to buy it from me?" Tori cut him off, getting the picture loud and clear.

"Right away," he answered coolly. "Do you have any other jewelry to sell, or is that it?"

She had to restrain herself from hanging up on him; his greed and pomposity were insulting. "No, that's it," she stated curtly. Then after asking for directions and how late he'd be open she wound up the call, bearing no false hope that this man would even begin to be fair with her.

When she saw a couple of people from the office walk by on their way to the elevator, she ducked dispiritedly around and out of sight.

Now what? Sell her three-hundred-thousand-dollar ring for ten cents on the dollar to bail out Richard, who might or might not even want to be bailed out, who might just throw the money at her and tell her she was a fool—which is exactly what she would be for making such an exchange. He had made it clear enough that he didn't want her help. But she couldn't just sit back and do nothing.

Trying to stay inconspicuous in the little alcove, she continued
to fight back tears. She couldn't think straight. She needed to talk
to someone. Damn it, why didn't Travis call when she was feeling
great, up. She wasn't even close to capable of carrying on a coherent conversation with him now. And she was so miserably
vulnerable.

Damn Richard, He didn't want her to tell anyone about this;
well, that was just too bad. She was going to find Paige. Paige
would know what to do.

Tori arrived at Sports Club/LA just as Paige was winding up
an exercise class, and she stood at the back of the room observing, as her sexy roommate, clad in a scintillating leopard-pat-
terned bodysuit led her frazzled group in a final round of
stretches.

As usual, Paige looked like a million bucks. Svelte and radiating energy. No wonder she had Nicky Loomis eating out of the
palm of her hand, waiting with boyish exuberance for her to
finally decide to gift him with her body, unaware of Mark, who
was getting it all the while for free—but not for keeps.

"Reach! Higher, *higher,*" Paige called out as though climbing
an imaginary ladder. "Now let it go!" she ordered, folding her
upper torso forward so that her honey-colored ponytail swept
against the carpet. "Let all the tension drain out of your body—
because all it does is make wrinkles and ulcers, anyway. And
what's a good body with wrinkles and ulcers, huh, kids? Now let
it *go* . . .

"Think about rejuvenating, making that deal you've been dying to make or the project you've been dying to start or get into
. . . Or that man or woman you've been dying to . . ." she let
her voice trail off insinuatingly. "Think energy! Think productiv-
ity! Think sex!" she teased.

The class laughed, used to Paige's playful repartee, pitching in
with their own comments.

Then they all shook out their toilworn limbs, blew twenty-five
times up toward the ceiling along with Paige, and applauded
their instructor for a class well led.

Tori didn't think Paige had noticed her, but she realized she was wrong when Paige made a beeline across the room in her direction.

"Hey, what's wrong? You okay?" she asked, wiping the sweat off her face with a towel from around her neck, her green eyes full of concern.

Tori, conscious of the attention they had drawn, afraid that she couldn't even respond without breaking down crying again, could only shake her head. *No. She was not okay.*

Paige, reading her wish for privacy, took her arm and directed her out of the exercise room, giving another instructor a signal that she was taking off, then veering off down a series of hallways.

"Do you want some carrot juice or something? We can spike it with vodka," Paige kidded, pushing open the white lacquer door of the club's snack shop and holding it open for Tori. "Actually the celery-apple juice tastes better with vodka . . ."

Tori made a face, looking distractedly around the all-white-and-chrome snack shop while Paige selected a quiet table off in the corner, mouthing to the busboy for coffee for each of them. "You hungry? Want anything to eat? Toast?"

Tori shook her head no, inhaling the aroma of the rich blend as the busboy slid a pastel-colored mug in front of each of them.

Unsure where to begin, she looked at the soft recessed lighting above her head and took a deep breath. "Richard's been cut off," she said after a moment, turning to watch Paige's intense green eyes narrow with the news, gauging her reaction.

"When? What happened?"

"The night we got back from South America," she confessed, relieved to finally be talking about it. "At his folks' anniversary party."

Paige looked surprised but said nothing, so Tori went on, getting it all off her chest, backtracking to the unfathomable high of their trip, which she had felt awkward talking about before, in light of how it had ended, catching Paige up to the present.

Her attention kept tearing back down to the ring sparkling on her finger, the vibrant green gem that could have been cut glass. It was a souvenir of a fantasy that had died.

Paige, slouched down in her chair, was digesting the information with a tough expression on her face, interrupting every now and then to cut through to what she considered the hard-line essentials, wanting to know exactly what kind of shape he was in. Did he have anything of his own? Was he bust? When she heard about the insurance fraud and Tori's decision to pawn her ring, she frowned and threw up her hands. "You don't want this guy. *No way,*" she asserted, worried. "Even if his father has a change of heart and reinstates him. Forget about him—"

"Oh? You're the one who's so into money," Tori argued with a weak attempt at lightheartedness, nervously rotating her mug again, taking a sip.

"Not like that, I'm not."

"I can't just run out on him—"

"He's bad news," Paige insisted.

Tori sat back in her chair and smiled ironically. "Speaking of bad news, guess who called this morning?"

She didn't take her eyes off Paige, who looked at her blankly, then buried her face in her hands. "Oh, God, don't tell me! You've had a helluva morning," she observed with a groan as Tori nodded. "He heard from your old boss?"

Tori shrugged uncertainly. "I didn't talk to him. He called just as I was calling in sick."

"You want my advice?"

"Probably not. But that's why I'm here."

"Forget them both."

Tori laughed futilely and rolled her eyes. *Easy to say,* she thought dryly, as Paige went on with advice she knew she could never follow.

"Don't call Travis back. Let this play out naturally with Richard. Don't even let him know that you know. In the meantime we'll think of what you should do, and *I'll* think of who we should replace Richard with. Honestly, Tori, he's bad news."

"It's been nothing *but* bad news since I got back from South America," Tori reflected. When she noticed a very built-looking guy in Sports Club/LA sweats giving her the eye, she leaned in across the table toward Paige. "I just hate this scene," she charged under her breath. "Getting *checked* out. The kinds of inane conversations you have to have meeting someone. I've always hated it—"

"Well it's not the smartest solution in the world to get yourself tied up in the wrong relationship to the first guy that comes around to avoid it—"

"Look, *you* have fun dating. You can take it lightly, not care. And men go nuts over you. I'm too serious. I don't think it's fun at all. I'm too old for this—"

"You were probably too old for it when you were sixteen. Why can't you just look at it like you're meeting a new friend? Having a good time? Going someplace fun? Meeting other people through them?"

"Because I can't. It's not me." Tori drank the rest of her coffee in silence, dreading the muscled menace still gawking at her, dreading her life.

"So what do you want to do?" Paige prodded gently, her clear green eyes moving down to her watch.

"I don't know. I'm sorry. Go back to work," Tori told her with a wave of guilt and indecision.

"You want to hock the ring, huh?"

They both looked grimly down at it as Tori nodded her head yes.

"You would," Paige mocked. Then with a resigned sigh she pushed up from her chair. "Okay. C'mon with me," she directed, taking charge. "But we're sure as hell not going to get picked off by some shark, or you might as well not bother. This is going to take some astute finessing."

Paige's specialty, Tori thought, relieved and grateful as she allowed herself to be tugged up to her feet and steered out the door, Paige's leopard-simulated spandex-covered form drawing envy and attention as they hustled toward the ladies' locker room.

She should have known to come to Paige in the beginning.

Execution of Paige's plan began at Van Cleef and Arpels on Rodeo Drive, where they were to do some groundwork and establish price.

Inside of the swank jewelry shop, she let Paige take over,

watching her attractive friend with keen admiration. Book smart, no, but Paige still had it all over anyone she knew.

She was unquestionably in her element now, wearing Tori's emerald, letting it flash as she canvassed the glass display cases, admiring pieces, turning to Tori to ask her what she thought of this and that.

"Would you like to see something?" one of the salesmen asked.

Paige turned breezily around to respond, replying that she was looking for a necklace to match her ring. She told him she was interested in getting a stone of a similar size and quality, and that she wanted to know about how much something like that would run.

Tori watched tensely as Paige wriggled the ring off her finger, handing it to the gentleman to appraise. The two women had decided that a realistic price for the ring would fall somewhere between Van Cleef's inflated price tag and what John Logan would think he could steal it for.

He took out a loupe and meticulously studied the stone, prolonging Tori's anxiety. "It's a nice stone," he commented, looking up to regard Paige curiously for a moment, then glancing at Tori. "A very nice stone. Good color. Clear. Very few inclusions. How long have you had it?"

Paige smiled professionally. "Only a few weeks. My husband bought it for me in Argentina."

"Hmmm." The man took a final inspection of the ring, clearly impressed, then handed it back to Paige. "We don't have anything in as large as yours; generally nobody does, but we can check around and get back to you. Or we do have several loose stones in the back, from about four to four and a half carats. One that's almost five—"

"What are you asking for the five carat?" Paige asked, giving Tori a sidelong glance.

"A hundred and seventy-five thousand. It's a spectacular stone. One of the best I've seen in a long time—"

"So for an eight carat of that quality—?" Paige probed.

Tori held her breath while she waited for him to respond. *Please let it be enough to make hocking it pay off.*

He toyed with the loupe, figuring. "It's hard to say. Between four and five hundred thousand. The price doesn't go up proportionately; it jumps because of the rarity of a good stone that size."

Exchanging an encouraged look with Paige, Tori masked her relief while Paige gracefully wrapped up their encounter, saying that she would talk to her husband and, hopefully, return with him.

"*Now* we go and see your Mr. Logan," she told Tori once outside, taking her hand and ushering her toward the car, ready to do business.

The jewelry mart was located in a bustling section of downtown and Tori stood outside of the large, congested complex waiting for Paige, who had gone in to see John Logan on her own.

Paige's scheme was to make Logan think she was interested in buying a stone of the same basic size and quality as Tori's, to set him up so that when Tori went in to see him afterward, she would be in a position to negotiate a fair price. A proponent of props, Paige had torn a Bulgari necklace ad from out of an issue of *Town & Country* and brought it in along with her, planning on saying that she had just recently been in the South of France and had seen a woman in a restaurant wearing one like it, that she wanted to know if he could make one up for her, and for how much.

She had rehearsed a series of little finishing touches to make it all look more credible, how she wanted to make sure the stone fit into the hollow of her neck, how maybe he could design the piece to double as a necklace *and* a pin. She would confess she had just been to Van Cleef, where the largest stone there was a five carat, which would do, but she would rather have a bigger one. She would add that she didn't have a lot of time to look around, that her husband had just closed a big deal and was in the buying mood *now*.

Leaning against the old art deco building while waiting for Paige, her stomach a vat of butterflies, Tori tried to busy herself people-watching. There was an energy and a pace to downtown Los Angeles that made her think of New York. The urban resurgence was exhilarating, and the new crop of buildings sprouting high into the skyline glistened beneath the strong afternoon sun.

Tori was just wondering which modern glass and steel tower housed Susan's law firm, when Paige sidled up beside her, her tight topaz T-shirt suggestively outlining her bust, her long linen skirt blowing in the breeze. "He's all yours, dearie," she announced grinning.

Tori closed her eyes in relief, wishing Paige could perform the next step for her as well.

Allowing a couple of hours for Logan to sweat over whether or not Tori was even coming in, and to keep it all from appearing too suspicious, the two of them headed up the street, attempting to kill time, looking disinterestedly into the windows of the various wholesale shops, on the lookout for someplace to eat.

Tori was in a fog throughout it all, going over with Paige what she should say, for what price she should settle, as well as what to say to Richard.

As for Travis, Paige made her promise not to call him back.

When it was time, they returned to the mart and Tori went inside alone, her ring back on her finger, sparkling above her clenched fist, feeling as though she were participating in some bizarre and terrible charade.

As Paige had predicted, Logan was ready to deal when Tori walked through the door. There were thick beads of perspiration clinging to his brow and over his lip, which he kept mopping away with the back of his hand as they addressed her precious green gem.

She hadn't expected to get so emotional, but as she worked the ring off of her finger, and watched him appraising it, she began to feel as though her heart were breaking all over again.

She was back in time at Tiffany's waiting for Travis to show up, the significant black velvet trays arranged across the countertop, her mother waiting without any faith in a chair just a few feet away.

Then it was a different stone with a different man, emeralds instead of diamonds, but the same cut of disappointment. She remembered the sheer intoxication she had felt shopping with Richard, the unreal thrill as he had slid ring after ring onto her finger, insisting that emeralds, unlike both their experiences with diamonds, would be forever.

Wrong. Wrong. Wrong.

Tori found herself also beginning to sweat, something a well-bred southern belle never did, as she haggled with the unctuous jeweler, neither of them budging. They went at it for well over an hour, John Logan growing more and more agitated, a sore loser and apparently unaccustomed to such stony resistance.

"Don't back down! The stone is magnificent, great quality, and exactly what he knows I want to buy." Clinging fiercely to Paige's words, replaying them over and over again in her mind, Tori held her ground, intent on not settling for a penny less than Richard had paid for the ring in Argentina.

But she wondered if it were not a Pyrrhic victory when she emerged at last from the bank on the first floor of the building, the cashier's check in hand. Looking down at it and then down at her now vacant wedding-ring finger she found herself missing the dazzling shock of green that had lit up her hand for the last couple of weeks.

She found herself having doubts over what she had done—or rather *undone.*

Chapter 23

It was just after eight o'clock when Tori arrived in Santa Barbara, still in her work clothes from that morning, a lightweight teal suit that was crumpled by now. Richard owned a condominium within the Polo Club complex, and she parked her car, hoping she was not too late.

It seemed that she and Paige had gone over virtually every scenario, *except* the "too late" scenario.

Projecting a courage she didn't feel, she climbed down from Dustin Brent's Bronco, keeping her eyes alert for any sign of Richard, his car, or a truck or trailer emblazoned with *Carlos Aguilar's Camiones de Servicios,* as she descended into the brisk night.

Ordinarily the faint scent spiking the air would have calmed her, the odor of horses, the ocean nearby, under the brilliant black sky above looking like an open treasure chest of stars pitched for wishing. But in this instance she knew nothing could calm her.

Nothing short of Richard rushing toward her, promising that the nightmare was over, that it was all okay now.

But Tori was beyond fantasizing at this point and she reached gloomily over for her purse, uncomfortable as hell about walking around with a three-hundred-thousand-dollar cashier's check. It was as though the soft pouch-fashioned leather bag contained something lethal. Maybe it did, she considered, as she slipped it over her shoulder and began walking toward the brightly lit condominium complex, feeling the crunch of gravel beneath her heels.

Richard's condo was up on the first level, overlooking the sprawling stretch of polo field, and Tori knocked tentatively on his door, unsure what to expect, if he would even be there.

When she heard his voice, she felt more nervous than relieved, even thought about turning and running off. But then the door was suddenly opened and he was standing facing her, surprised, but not unfriendly.

"Tori. What are you doing here? Something wrong?" he asked guardedly.

She swallowed hard, trying to find her voice. "I need to talk to you," she murmured uncertainly, feeling like an intruder as she peered beyond him and into the room he seemed to be screening off from her, wondering if there was somebody inside.

His jaw tightened, and he ran his hand over his unshaven face. "I guess I should have called," he apologized quickly, mistaking the reason for her being there. "But I had something up here that I had to take care of, right away, and I just didn't get a chance to get back to you. It's been kind of crazy. I'm sorry." He looked awful and Tori felt sorry for him. His eyes were bloodshot and the circles beneath them more pronounced.

"It's okay," she said, slipping her unadorned wedding-ring finger out of sight and into the back pocket of her skirt, undergoing a rash of second thoughts. What if this were all innocent? she considered guiltily. What if she were completely off base? This had all happened in such a compressed timeframe that she began to wonder if she hadn't jumped to false conclusions.

"You cold?" he asked, surprised because it was a warm night and, even though she was wearing a jacket, she was shivering.

"No, just nervous," she answered truthfully, trembling from a prickly, anxiety-induced chill that had nothing to do with the climate. She was wound up so tightly inside that she could barely respond, could barely think. Her conversation with the Mexican trucking company hovered like a black cloud.

He eyed her curiously, as though sensing something. "Nervous? That's not like you. Why?"

She felt as if she were being *Gaslight*ed. He had to know why. Unable to hold it in any longer, and lacking the presence of mind for tact, Tori blurted it all out, everything, how she had gone into his office in the morning, the phone calls, the file she had found, weakly justifying her actions, but shrinking under his mood.

He dropped all pretense of friendliness and went stone-cold as he listened, turning darkly away from her and stalking off into his condo.

She followed timidly, closing the door for privacy, relieved to see that there wasn't anyone else there.

"What kind of fucking game do you think you're playing?" he shouted, as she told him about selling the ring. His face had gone beet-red with rage and when she reached into her purse for the cashier's check she had gotten from John Logan, Richard seized her purse from her grasp and sent it flying across the room.

"This is just fucking great," he ranted, looking betrayed, violated. "First my father, then my *fiancée*—"

"Richard, I was *concerned*—"

"Concerned?"

"Yes—"

"That doesn't give you license to—"

"I knew you were in trouble and I was only trying to help—" Tori argued, stunned at the depth of his anger, his bitterness.

"I don't need your help. I don't need anyone's fucking help—"

"Everybody needs help. Why can't you just admit that you're human. Okay, so you have to change some things in your life for a while, until you get back on your feet and get everything squared away—"

"You don't get the picture. I *am* changing things. And this is none of your fucking business. Don't you *ever* fucking *spy* on me—"

He had his finger pointed in her face and she recoiled, pushing it angrily out of the way. "It *is* my business. I'm you're fiancée. Or have we called all that off?"

"Hey, *you* called it off when you sold your ring," he sneered vindictively. "I told you how I felt about that ring. About your trusting me. Now *I* don't trust *you*—"

"Richard, you can't go around defrauding insurance companies—"

"So instead of the insurance companies getting to fuck me, this time I'm getting to fuck them," he scoffed. "After a lifetime's worth of paying their damn premiums, I assure you they'll still come out on top."

"That's not the point—"

"No? What is the point?"

"That you can't go around making dirty deals and getting away with it. This is stupid. It's shortsighted. I just got three hundred thousand dollars for you. Take it and call this damn thing off, if it's not already too late."

"It's not too late," he replied treacherously. His contemptuous look shot right through her. "But I have no intention of calling it off. *God,* are you naive! While it's none of your fucking business, Tori, just to set the record straight—do you want to know about all the *dirty deals* my pious father made in order to get to where he is today, in order to earn his pillar-of-the-community status? The payoffs? The agreements he reneged on? The guys he picked off or cheated along the way? All so sanctimoniously in the name of *business* . . .

"Don't delude yourself, princess. There isn't anybody who's made a lot of money who hasn't stepped outside the law, worn blinders. Look at all the robber barons, like Joe Kennedy or John D. Rockefeller. You think they didn't bend the rules to suit their purposes? You think they didn't walk all over people, engage in *questionable* business practices, joint ventures with guys they knew were on the take? Only their descendants had the *luxury* to go straight. After the family had made it. Now *I* need to make it."

Richard was so overwrought that Tori thought it pointless to even go any further. While she wanted to help him, this was all so far over her head she didn't know what to do or say. He was obviously messed up, cracking under all the pressure. And she half wondered, Who wouldn't? There were partially consumed bottles of Scotch and cognac out, grass and coke paraphernalia, greasy pizza cartons, Chinese take-out. Quite a binge for only one day.

She had no idea if it were true or not, what he was saying about his father, and she didn't even know if it mattered. What mattered was that this was a different time, and Richard was a different person, with different opportunities—opportunities that he was about to blow. She didn't want to see him doing something foolish, something for which he would find himself paying for the rest of his life, just because he was hurt and angry. Tori knew it had to be difficult growing up in the shadow of a man like Elliot Bennetton. She could see after working there these last couple of weeks that while Richard's father was a generous man, fun, with a keen intellect, and deeply loved his son, his ego could easily be emasculating. He would want Richard right up there beside him, but then, unable to control himself, he would *compete* with him. The powerful elder sparring with his younger, greener seedling, out to prove to himself that his excessive virility was still intact, that he was still on top.

Hoping to break the ice, to turn things around, Tori crossed over to Richard, standing very close.

He drew her left hand up quietly, fondling where the large emerald rock had occupied her finger, looking wounded by its absence.

"I'm sorry," she whispered, wishing she had listened to Paige. Even if Richard were wrong for her, even with what she had learned about him after his disinheritance, she hadn't been prepared for what she had provoked. She ran her hand gently across his beard, grazing the blond-hued stubble. "It was *only* a ring, Richard," she ventured timorously.

"No. It was *more* than only a ring," he countered with acerbic regret, his voice so low that it was unnerving. "It was my *engagement* ring to you. *Remember?*"

Releasing her hand he walked across the room, bending down to retrieve her purse, and then flinging it over to her to catch. "Like I said once before, no ring, no engagement. You can do whatever the fuck you want with the three hundred grand, little Georgia Peach," he remarked stingingly. "I don't give a damn about it, and I don't give a damn about you. The fact is, now it *is* only *money.*"

"Don't kid yourself. It was always only money—and you happen to need the cash from it right now more than I need the ring. Break off our engagement because you're not in love with me. That I can accept. But this is bullshit," Tori exploded shrilly, struggling to get the check out of her purse and throw it right back at him. "Keep your bullshit *and* your money. I don't want any part of either."

But Richard was already on his way out the door, his back to her, one of the half-empty bottles of Scotch dangling from his hand. Sneeringly he turned around, refusing to acknowledge the money falling at his heel.

Wishing she could think of something that would finally penetrate his thick skull, but unable to, she walked out without saying anything, stepping around the check, chasing out past him, through the doorway, and then moving swiftly to where the Bronco was parked.

"You got too much fuckin' pride, Georgia Peach," he shouted after her, a mocking grin on his fatigued but handsome face, taking a swig from the whiskey bottle. "You oughta at least keep the money. *You earned it!*"

Tears stung her cheeks as she sped up her pace, working hard to ignore him as he continued calling after her.

"Oh, *I* know. You want *love.* Not money. Payment in *kisses* and *reverence. Love* and *virtue.* You want to be *loved to distraction.*"

"So do you, you bastard!" she couldn't help hollering back at him, whipping around just long enough to get the words out.

"No, I'm far more practical than that. You should be too," he urged loudly, his words dripping with sarcasm. "I want *money,* first and foremost. See where love gets you? You should have learned that li'l ol' lesson from your hunk *boyfriend* in Atlanta. Love begets pain whilst money begets *more* money—begetting power and then all the love you can handle."

"Well, it all kind of loses something in a jail cell, don't you think!" she shot fiercely back over her shoulder without turning

around. "You better hurry up or you'll miss your Mexican truckers."

"Ooooh! Very good! You're so *cute* when you're mad, Tori."
She could hear him beginning to run only a few feet behind her
now and she tried to wrench free as he caught up with her,
grabbing her by the waist. "C'mon, let me buy a little fuck in the
bushes. Take the three hundred grand and let me fuck your little
pussy in the moonlight," he growled, pleading, overpowering her,
dragging her behind the hedge and then tackling her onto a
stretch of damp grass.

"Goddamn you! Get away from me!" she screamed, fighting
him off with every ounce of strength she possessed. *"Not for all
the money in the world."*

"Okay. Have it your way then, *for free.*"

"Not on your life," she shrieked even more fiercely, swinging
at him as he grabbed her hair and yanked her head back. She
tried to catch her breath as he thrust the whiskey bottle into her
mouth, pouring, so that it went sloshing all over her and him and
onto the ground, causing her to gag. It was impossible not to
swallow, and the rush of Scotch traumatized her throat as it went
down. The fumes reeked heavily on his breath as he eclipsed her
mouth with his, his tongue probing hard, running along her
teeth.

If she had known how to gauge the blow so that it would only
knock him out but not kill him, she would have torn the bottle
away from him and cracked him over the head with it.

"Oh, don't even think about it," he taunted, seeing where her
eyes were fixed, reading her mind.

Laughing lustily and pinning her down on the grass with one
hand, he pulled up her skirt, then began pouring a stream of
whiskey over her panties, spilling it generously, then soaking it
up with his mouth.

"This is a cock*tease,* not a cock*tail,*" he crooned lewdly, his
breath hot, moist, making her squirm. Intent on arousing her, he
continued to pour, pulling down her panty hose and then her
panties, so that the Scotch washed over her directly, stinging and
yet feeling unexpectedly sensuous at the same time.

Alarmed but past struggling, confused, she lay absolutely still,

every muscle taut. She was intent on making him think she felt
nothing as she lay frigid, that she had given up on fighting and
was merely enduring. She was too angry, too upset, to give in to
the oddly erotic sensations she was beginning to feel.

He was crazy; this was lunacy. Who knew who could walk by?
And she was still smarting from all the verbal assaults.

She had no idea what to think. She had never felt so mixed up
in her life. Was their engagement genuinely off? *And what did she
even want?* Was Richard just venting his frustration before giving
in, his pride fractured, behaving like a kid at the windup of a
tantrum? Maybe she had gotten through to him and he was going
to call off the horse theft.

"Let go of me, you son of a bitch," she screamed, trying to
wrestle free from him again, a fight he seemed to enjoy because
he smiled meanly, climbing over to straddle her. "This is too
much. I don't care what you're going through . . ."

"You love it," he shouted back through gritted teeth.

"You arrogant bastard! I hate it! I hate you!" she screamed,
infuriated at the inequity of physical power.

Breathing heavily, he unzipped his jeans and pulled them
down, his erection bold and exposed as he drained what was left
from the bottle of Scotch then leaned over and in the pretense of
a kiss released it into her mouth, instructing her to hold it there,
then hastily moving up to crouch braced over her face.

"Take me in your mouth," he ordered coarsely, his blue eyes
narrowing.

Demoralized, she shook her head, still sustaining the mouthful
of Scotch, tempted to spit it in his face instead.

Without waiting for her consent or compliance, he thrust his
cock into her mouth, in doing so releasing another cascade of the
alcohol. *"Oh, God! Yes, darling, darling . . ."* he bellowed,
moaning with what seemed like a culmination of pleasure and
pain, calling out her name, continuing to deify the experience,
thrusting into her mouth until she began to gag and he had to
pull out.

Before she could even react, he had lowered himself and was
screwing her in an almost cruel pursuit, his hips slapping hard

against hers, thrashing into her with an emotional vengeance, his pace harsh and demanding.

As he drew her legs up and around his waist, he began telling her how much he loved her, breathing heavily into her ear. She didn't know where to concentrate first, with all the mixed messages, receiving sensations from all directions, still conscious of the damp grass beneath them and the faint breeze stirring the air as he began kissing her passionately on the lips.

And then in the distant background of this ghastly experience, she heard him crying out as he climaxed.

They lay together quietly for a moment. She was afraid to even breathe, feeling used, mortified, and at the same time torn because she could see the kind of pain Richard was in. She was wondering if this were some kind of bizarre reconciliation, wondering if that's what she wanted it to be. She was half expecting Richard to break down and apologize, to reveal to her all the things he was feeling inside, the turmoil, the conflict, the crushing emotional anguish.

But then instead, his abruptness seeming intentionally ruthless, he sprung off her, zipping his jeans closed with a curt motion, and then, taking a moment to glance at his watch, he strode off.

"Time for the *big* score," he clarified mockingly over his shoulder, heading into the darkness, presumably toward the stables to meet with the Mexican truckers.

Feeling like a hole had been blown into her heart, Tori couldn't do anything other than lie there and watch, pledging, never, as long as she lived, to allow herself to be so humiliated again.

She cried the whole way home from Santa Barbara. One of those long, deep-in-the-chest cries that begins triggered by one thing and then, by the time you're really into it, snowballs so that finally you're crying about everything, feeling as though your world is completely collapsing, with no way out, nothing salvageable, no solution.

She kept envisioning driving into the center divider of the freeway and just getting it over with simply, the coward's way. She could barely see where she was going anyway, needing a windshield wiper for her tears.

She thought about driving into the ocean, submerging her misery beneath its great mysterious depths, or walking along the beach, unresistant and perverse prey for a prowling derelict, who unsuspectingly would be doing her a favor by adding her to the murdered-while-walking-along-the-beach-alone-at-night mortality statistics. But, God, what if *he* raped her too?

She needed to be cleansed. Purged.

It was a case of melancholy unleashing melodrama—the Pandora's box sprung. Dominoes.

Richard. Travis. Her mother. God! even work. Bravo, Tori. She had even managed to screw up her career, formerly the only safe and secure area of her life.

Was this all her fault? she wondered miserably. Was she so self-destructive that she made these things happen?

Bleakly, she went on with self-recriminations, hearing her mother's voice, adopting her tone, expanding perfectly, poignantly, so aptly and so realistically that it was as if she had her mother sitting in the car beside her or plugged into her thoughts. She thought if she called her at home in Atlanta right this very moment, she wouldn't even wake her because she was already up, busy sending extrasensory communications to her daughter anyway. She thought that her mother would be relieved to know that her communications were being received.

When Tori drove back home through the electronic wrought-iron gates of Dustin Brent's home and up the driveway, it wasn't her *own* voice in her head caustically and, yes, enviously, noting Mark Arent's motorcycle in the driveway.

Nor was it her own voice that predicted that Paige and her prize-sap boyfriend were upstairs screwing in Paige's bedroom, when Tori let herself into the big old Spanish house.

Nor was it her own voice snidely commenting after each message left on the answering machine as she played them all back, listening through two from Nicky calling from New York, where he was away for a couple days on business, a couple more for Paige from other men, one for Susan from an associate at her law firm, calling to fix her up again *but warning* that she was about to give up since Susan refused to ever come up from work for air.

It was indubitably her *mother's* voice, continuing to point out, again and again, what a failure Tori was and would always be.

The cutting edge of her voice faded only after it tore apart the last two messages, which were both from *Travis,* and after a last nasty commentary on how Paige and Mark were *definitely* upstairs screwing, must have been for quite some time, since there was such a pile-up of messages left on the machine.

As Tori wrote down the last one, trying to eradicate her mother's domineering presence from her mind, the phone rang and she picked it up, thinking *Travis, Richard,* praying *not Mother,* then deciding it was *probably just another call for Paige.*

The familiar, honeyed drawl of Travis's voice coming in uncertainly over the line permeated every aspect of her being. If she had been a high-risk heart patient, she would have gone into cardiac arrest and died, but *ah, so contentedly.*

Was it Travis to the rescue, just when she needed him more than ever? Had he come through for her this time?

She couldn't concentrate on a single word he was saying or decide how to respond, knowing only that, after a seeming eternity, she was hearing his voice again.

He rambled on about how much he had missed her, telling her everything she wanted to hear, wreaking havoc on all her stored-up resolve. It was a dot-to-dot conversation composed of so many only previously fantasized ones, connecting smoothly and in all the right places, spelling out sentiments that were so sweet and dear to hear that they seemed fresh and almost as though she hadn't heard them all a million times before.

Travis had learned about her engagement through Jake Shavelson and then through her mother who had seen his mother at the market. He told her how he had been going crazy these last couple of months, pining away, unable to believe that she had really meant business this time.

He said he found it impossible living in their place without her, every inch of space reminding him of her. The art on the walls that they had collected together. The all-knowing living room couch on which they had made love and war, and sometimes a little of each within the course of the same battle. The selection of Laura Ashley wallpaper in the bedroom, for which she had spent weeks lobbying. The colored tissue in the bathrooms. The stereo that was always on when she was around, that was now never on. All the empty spots where their photographs used to be.

It was a better speech than usual because their separation had been longer than ever before and because the stakes had soared, with her now living in L.A. and having become engaged.

Thank God, she was composed enough to not let him know that her engagement was off, she thought, feeling otherwise out of control.

"Tori. Would you at least say something?" Travis insisted. "Go ahead and let me have it. Tell me to drop dead, to go to hell if you want, but at least *say* something."

He was telling her exactly what she wanted to hear, what she had been waiting a lifetime to hear, and yet she was powerless to react.

She had worked so hard all these weeks at *not* caring, applied all that self-hypnosis on how to get over her lover, spent so much precious energy trying to quell the fire that had burned her repeatedly, that now she was caught between relieved, giddy excitement and, on another level, feeling nothing.

It was so tough to discern if the emotional block producing the "nothing" was for real or not.

Trying to cut through the emotional thicket to read her heart accurately, she glanced out through the large, arched window of the den where she was sitting at the bar, out through to the softly lit garden where he was supposedly laid to rest, pronounced "dead, buried, and forgotten" beneath a patch of purple and yellow petunias now in full bloom, a profusion of macabre celebration.

"Tori?" Travis repeated, exasperated, very much alive.

What was he asking her to say, she wondered in a trance. *All's forgiven? I'm coming home?* His voice felt farther away than Atlanta. More like an echo from a dream, and she was so tired that she had to wonder for a moment if it weren't.

She felt herself melting as she pictured him as clearly as if she had seen him yesterday, wanting to throw her arms around the image and yield.

If they were on the "all-knowing" couch now, they would simply be making love, and she wouldn't have to answer him with words, only with her soul, which said *yes* always to anything he asked.

But her words were governed, at least partially, by another force. Not only her heart, but her brain, her mind, logic, and some small grain of self-preservation, which told her emphatically that she was *not* out to self-destruct, in spite of what had happened only a couple hours ago with Richard.

The message *resist* unfurled from the same part of her brain that issued pride, dignity, and reason, by way of past experience and memory.

And it was this part of her brain that generated the words that reminded Travis how she had heard so many versions of all this before, that made her stop and ask if he had gotten any farther on in obtaining his divorce, and that sorted through the bullshit of his response to see that, for all practical purposes, he had not.

In the middle of a slightly updated alibi she hung up the phone, resisting only a weak, dull urge this time to pick up the phone and call him back.

Her temptation was equally great to call Richard in Santa Barbara. And yet she knew that would only result in a downward spiral.

She kept thinking about all the abusive things Richard had said to her, feeling dirty, used, and even ashamed.

A door closed upstairs and Tori tensed, wondering if Paige had heard her. The last thing she wanted to have to do right now was talk to anyone, even to Paige. She didn't want to have to talk or explain.

When nobody appeared, Tori, relieved, looked over in the direction of the bottle of Armagnac, whose contents were steadily disappearing. Longing for a drink, longing to drink herself into oblivion, she stepped to the bar to pour herself a glass then lifted it up to toast her reflection in the mirror.

What a sobering sight she was, with makeup smeared all around her bloodshot eyes from crying, streaked down her cheeks.

A grim view of a young woman's sorrowful state—a young woman who kept messing up when it came to men.

Tori raised her glass up higher, following the angle with her chin. "To the new life I moved out here to find. To putting old things behind me and going forward. To staying on track," she proposed sincerely.

As she brought the glass to her lips, tasting a residue of salt from so many spilled tears, a picture of Dustin Brent that she hadn't noticed before caught her eye.

Wryly she redirected her glass up toward him instead, drawn by his smile that was so genuine and so comforting she found it hard not to smile back at him.

The truth was she had *him* to thank, to toast, for her new life, for the possibilities and opportunities opened up to her, waiting to be experienced if she only possessed the nerve. Looking at him now she felt inspired to try.

His kind of nerve, she thought, tipping her glass to him, thinking about the kind of fortitude that drove and sustained him in building a multimillion-dollar company from scratch. Then the kind of grit and spirit to sell it as he had, turning to meet new challenges.

Maybe it was that his ego seemed so healthy and buoyant, freeing him to be honest, straightforward, and unshrinkingly sure of himself in a way that Travis or Richard could never be. She thought of the postcard she had received from him when she had returned to L.A., congratulating her on her engagement to Richard and telling her that if she changed her mind he'd catch a flight right back to the States to claim his rightful place, if only he'd had his eyes open at Kit and George's wedding when he'd met her. The tone of his note had obviously been joking, but she considered the irony, thinking of him clear across the world, where he said he'd now be keeping tabs on her.

It was the sense of Dustin watching her from afar, like a wise and caring old friend that kept her from picking up the phone now and calling either Travis or Richard.

She could handle Dustin Brent watching her drink herself silly, as she sat there consuming shot after shot of Armagnac, growing woozy but failing to feel its full numbing effect. But she couldn't handle him watching her swallow her pride and play the fool.

Dustin's presence, growing as real as her mother's earlier, fused with the Armagnac, finally lulled Tori to sleep, right there at the bar, feeling distantly surprised that she could still smell the fresh scent of her soap from this morning's shower as her nose nestled into the crook of her arm, which was the best she could do for a pillow right now.

Just before she lost consciousness she thought fleetingly of Paige and what her reaction to all this would be—Paige who was upstairs gamely enjoying the best of both worlds.

Chapter 24

Seated at his corner booth in the steak house near his plant, Jack Wells had his ear to the phone and was speaking dogmatically to the party on the other end of the line. His brow was furrowed. His wide, hooded eyes appeared even moodier than usual. The small, white-clothed table in front of them was littered with paperwork, files, and newspaper clippings about the strike, all crammed around his unfinished plate of plain broiled sole and rice without butter. It looked as cluttered as his desk in his office, Susan thought.

As usual, it was a working lunch. Just as dinners with Jack Wells were always working dinners. As far as Susan could see, her client did little else.

Of course he would probably say the same of her. They were a perfect pair. All work and no play. Except that as a pair they had never yet gotten beyond work.

It was a very strange relationship. Jack Wells was a very strange man.

Susan vacillated in her feelings for him, finding him appealing but tough, difficult to connect with for any length of time. Just as they would start to relax and have fun, talk about themselves, laugh a little, he would tighten and retreat, giving her mixed signals, making it so that she never knew where she stood.

The strike negotiations at his plant had escalated to such a degree that they were all working around the clock, with Susan now working exclusively on Jack's case, breaking her neck to work out a resolution between her thick-headed client and his equally unyielding workers, in what had become an unbridgeable stalemate. Every session, their arguments went round and round in the same vicious circles, the union leaders ready to give way, and the rank and file members refusing to compromise.

"Goddamn," Jack said, hanging up the telephone.

"What's happened?" Susan asked, dragging a French fry though a mound of catsup on her plate, then eating it.

Her client was stewing. "Some joker got that incident this morning on video, and ran it for the police and the networks. It'll make more great copy," he remarked, slapping a pile of newspaper clippings with the back of his hand. "A Mercedes hauls ass through the picket line and winds up with a Teamster decorating its polished German hood. As it lurches to a stop, the striker reels off and onto his feet, cocks his arm, and discharges his fist through the driver's window, redefining the glass into a spiderweblike mass and wrecking his hand. The driver of the Mercedes is unimpaired. But he gets the message: 'The poor angry strikers.' I'm so tired of all this publicity crap. Why doesn't everybody just go back to work and do their job?"

Susan smiled over her glass of Pepsi, the top of her glass knocking into her eyeglass frames as she polished off the balance.

"Hey, Kendell Brown, you represent *me*, counselor, not *them*, this time. So knock off the smirk and keep your sympathies in line with the source of your paycheck."

"They are," Susan insisted, even though they were not. "You have a problem with my representation?" she teased.

"Your representation is perfect. But I can read your mind, and I don't necessarily like what I read all the time," Jack frowned and stabbed at his fish with his fork. "Hey, so go represent the workers again. You know how it goes: you represent management, you eat steak; you represent the workers, you eat prewrapped sandwiches and tacos."

Susan smiled again, and he allowed himself a brief laugh, running his finger absently over the slashlike scar across his face.

"I know, you *like* tacos," he said.

Going for her last French fry, she shrugged in accord. Then conscious of maintaining the appropriate level of professionalism because she knew that was important to him, she shifted gears, launching into a strategy that had occurred to her this morning on her way over to the plant.

He interrupted her midstream, looking down at his watch, and beginning to grab up his files. "We'd better start back, huh?"

"I take it you're not too keen on my strategy," Susan observed, dabbing at her mouth with the cloth napkin from her lap, then discarding it onto the table.

"Actually, I am," he said, leading the way out, looking down at his watch again. "We'll just be more comfortable discussing it in my office. Your lunch all right?"

"Fine—"

"Listen, what are you doing tonight? How about a nonworking night together, for a change," he asked, surprising her by putting his free hand around her waist. "No business discussions permitted." It was the first clear-cut romantic overture Jack had made to Susan and, caught off guard, she looked at him.

"What did you have in mind?" she asked, skeptical but pleased. They'd gone this long maintaining perfect professionalism, she couldn't help wonder how this might affect their working relationship.

He smiled mischievously, continuing to lead the way out. "Have you ever had a shiatsu massage?"

Surprised and still dubious, Susan laughed. "No."

"Hmmm. You can't imagine what you're missing . . ."

"Oh, really?"

"Trust me."

She eyed him again and then they both laughed.

"I thought I'd take you to my Korean hideaway in Koreatown."

"What's that?"

"It's built over a natural hot springs, very therapeutic, and very exotic. They have spectacular private baths, all done in marble and sparkling clean. Private hot and cold mineral baths, steam, sauna, massage, where they really do walk on your back, and a wonderful Korean dinner."

"Your average first-date kind of place," Susan joked. "Let me guess the attire . . ."

He grinned, looking her up and down in a way he never had before and making her blush.

"Can't we work our way into something like this? I hate to sound like a prude, but—"

". . . you're a small-town girl from Stockton, I know," he finished for her. "Listen, you and I have had more dates and spent more time together than I've spent with any woman in a long time."

Susan looked at him curiously, wondering if that was true. Given the amount of time he seemed to spend away from work, she believed him.

"They have towels and kimonos. The Koreans are very modest. I'll close my eyes and behave like a perfect gentleman," he promised, deadpan.

Susan wanted to ask him why the sudden change? What had caused him to want to shift gears? Then she decided she was taking this all too seriously. Why not just let everything play out? Wasn't this the kind of overture she had been waiting for? Why was she thinking so much? Why couldn't she just go with it?

"Mr. Wells," the maître d' called after him, just as they were about to step outside. "Telephone for you, sir. Would you like to pick it up at the front desk?"

When Jack asked the waiter to forward the call to his office, stuffing a fiver in his hand without slowing down his pace, Susan looked at him surprised. It was completely uncharacteristic of Jack Wells to not take a phone call, any place, any time, to not even ask who it was. He missed her perplexity because he was already preoccupied, looking down at his watch.

They returned to the plant to find the truckloads of plant replacements just leaving, lined up and waiting to exit behind the gate, which was routinely opened at this hour by a guard.

It was a typical scene, unruly but usual, with strikers hurling eggs at the trucks, both sides shouting at each other, actively venting their anger and frustration. Susan, in her heels, had to step over the broken shards of glass, alert and ducking eggs. She nearly bumped into a dummy, which had a placard strung down around its neck, forewarning Death of a Scab.

Here was *exactly* the kind of tension that put fists through car windows, she thought, recalling this morning's incident and taking in the chaos around her, watching the picketers taunt and curse the truckloads of temporary workers, accusing them of stealing their jobs.

The substitute workers replied by waving their paychecks in the air.

And this strike was tame compared to some of the strike lockouts involving the bigger chain operations, like the big chain markets or meat packers unions where trucks were being towed to the warehouses, with radiators and tires shot out, having been ambushed with gunfire, substitute drivers wounded.

Susan remembered the time a driver was treated for burns after a large firecracker had alighted in his lap and exploded. Then another time when four substitute workers driving out of one of the big chain supermarket warehouses were rammed from behind by a pickup truck, reeled around, and rammed twice more. One person had been only slightly injured, but the supermarket chain, distraught over all the bad publicity, had offered a ten-thousand-dollar reward for the arrest of the driver of the pickup. After that, they had felt compelled to hire a horde of additional security guards, many with permits to carry guns, to follow the trucks.

Thankfully, the strike at Jack Wells' plant hadn't risen to that degree of warfare.

It was a more common-looking strike zone, full of aggression but no flying bullets. On one side of the front there was the Teamsters' bivouac, where portable toilets were lined up. Nearby, lazy flames were lapping from inside a rusty fifty-five-gallon drum (they had cut back on the fires since Susan's accident), and across the way was an old camper belonging to a retired trucker and his wife who were there daily, sustaining the strikers with homemade chili, chicken soup, hot coffee, and moral support. Susan couldn't help her deep-rooted feelings of sympathy as she passed through troops of picketers, thinking of her father and his friends, trying not to look anyone in the eye.

With the aggression mounting, it suddenly occurred to her that there was no guard on duty to open the gate for the departing trucks. Instead, a burly-looking replacement had finally taken it upon himself to jump down off his truck and open it himself, muscling his way through the throng of jeering strikers.

As he approached the gate, amidst the usual shouting and commotion, he passed close by the group of workers Susan knew from the strike negotiations; then, for no apparent reason, he shoved the pregnant wife of one of the men down to the ground. She was also a worker in the plant, and as she hit the pavement, falling back spread-eagle, her picket sign went reeling through the air.

Without thinking, Susan started to run off to see if she was all right, then was surprised to feel Jack's grip on her arms holding her back, insisting under his breath what a pain in the ass the woman and her clan were, that they had been asking for this.

Restrained from interceding, Susan was forced to watch, baffled and helpless, as the husband, in response to the incident, went berserk and threw himself onto the replacement, pummeling him until four more scabs climbed down out of the truck and jumped *him,* setting off a full-fledged riot as packs of strikers rushed to the aid of their coworkers, bloodying the replacements who, by now outnumbered, were wisely retreating, fighting their way back into the truck for safety.

What struck Susan was that just as the violence had begun to grow out of hand, at least two dozen security guards had appeared, as though on cue, some armed with billy clubs, others armed with cameras. Since photographs were not permitted in peaceful picket lines, Susan was dubious of the seemingly induced outbreak that had conveniently legitimized their admissibility. She wasn't buying the sudden timely appearance of all these cameras, produced just at the right moment by suddenly double the ratio of security guards than had previously been in Jack Wells's employ, all ready to converge at this instant to document the uproar.

It seemed staged to her.

Jack's anxiousness to rush back to the plant. The camera-armed guards exchanging silent communications with Jack, as though they were carrying out his orders.

And the key subjects whose pictures had been taken, by no coincidence, Susan feared, just happened to be the workers who were refusing to go along with the union leaders and yield in the strike settlement. They were the one group holding up the works.

She could already guess Jack's scheme; the set-up seemed so blatant. Everyone in the pictures would get fired, creating an unscrupulous but efficient way for management and union to finally come to terms, maneuvering a legitimate axing of those impeding the process. Susan couldn't help but wonder if she wasn't one of the pawns in his plan as well—if his sudden romantic interest wasn't a calculated maneuver meant to manipulate her or distract her from the unjust method he was using to settle his strike.

Susan felt a renewal of pressure on her arm, as Jack, apparently having seen enough, began to direct her away from the commotion and over toward the building.

He looked almost satisfied, she thought, turning back around to see if the pregnant woman was all right, expecting to find her collapsed in a friend's protective embrace, crying.

Instead, she found herself looking at a woman who knew how to hold her own against bullies of her employer's sort. The pregnant female striker stood glaring, unintimidated, in Jack's direction, punctuating her rage with a proudly arced spit toward his back, looking as if she could have just as easily have aimed it squarely in his face, if proximity had permitted her to do so.

Unsurprisingly, Susan and Jack's Korean adventure had been postponed at the last moment, with Jack getting called off to an urgent meeting, one in which Susan had not been included.

The part Susan *had* found surprising, as well as extremely confusing, was that Jack had seemed genuinely disappointed. If he had planned all this anarchy at the plant he would have known that he wouldn't be free to *play* that night. Unless that was part of the strategy.

Maintaining the new personal dimension he had added to their relationship, he had made her promise him a rain check. And not knowing what to believe or think, Susan had kept her thoughts and suspicions to herself and accepted. If he was using her and trying to throw her off, he was a convincing actor and for the most part succeeding.

It was past midnight when Susan returned home from another one of her late-night work marathons at the office, tired, still puzzling over the day's turn of events.

As much as she wanted to believe otherwise, Susan couldn't help but feel that something unethical was going on, and as Jack's lawyer, she especially didn't like being kept in the dark.

Like it or not, she smelled a rat, a decorated sort of Viet Nam Tunnel Rat, with special training to move swiftly and devastatingly through to any specific end, viewing himself as above the law and duty-bound to eradicate interferences when they got out of hand.

Clearly he would see the dissenting workers as an interference.

Tentatively, she had suggested her suspicions to Kreegle when she returned to the firm, but he had only made light of them. "It's the union's job to look after the workers," he had reminded her.

Jack had called her at the office later to check on a legal matter involving something else, completely ignoring what had happened earlier. He had such an intimidating way about him that she found she was unable to bring it up herself, either.

Their relationship was so unsettling. They hovered on romantic involvement without ever crossing the line, working intense hours, on the verge of being physical and then not. Not that Susan knew whether or not she wanted to be; his moods seemed to conduct her feelings, making them rise and then deflate on a moment-to-moment basis. She thought her vulnerability was a function of not having anyone else.

The fact that Jack had never made a pass at her, other than his perplexing invitation for tonight, hadn't helped to buoy her confidence. She had kept wondering, was it *her,* or was it *him*?

The question had plagued her for weeks.

Was she so undesirable that her former boyfriend in Stockton had felt compelled to cheat on her? That made her invisible to

Mark—so that he had eyes only for Paige? That had enabled Jack to maintain perfect professionalism—even though they had been working halfway through the night together, often fortified by brandy or a bottle of fine red wine from his cellar?

Or was Jack gay? Or asexual? Or did he have a sexual problem and not want to put himself in an uncomfortable position? Maybe his work was enough for him, she had speculated. Maybe he was one of those men who didn't need a woman. He was certainly self-sufficient.

Feeling half asleep, and only more baffled than ever by Jack's curious and long overdue proposition, she punched the house alarm code into the security box outside the front door and then let herself inside, nearly tripping over a pile of UPS boxes addressed to Paige, which tempted her to kick them across the gleaming terra cotta floor.

Paige somehow always ended up with it all. Clever, sex kitten Paige, who underneath that soft facade was just a wily barracuda.

First, all the gifts arriving from Philadelphia. Now, a steady flow from Nicky Loomis.

Susan felt strangled with envy and resentment. *She* hadn't even received as much as flowers—nothing—from anybody. Except the painting from Mark, which she refused to count since in nearly the same breath he had offered *himself* to Paige.

It drove Susan nuts to see her provocative roommate with her hands all over Mark all the time. Prompting the kind of public displays of affection that should be reserved for behind closed doors.

Susan would be having a conversation with the two of them and then, midsentence, Paige would give Mark that doe-eyed God-I-can't-keep-my-hands-off-you look and start making out with him right on the spot, so that Susan would be left standing there, feeling like a jerk, as if she were a videotape on pause.

It was obscene and highly inconsiderate.

It made Mark look like the first-rate jerk that he was, putting up with Paige's craziness. She was using him. Just as she used everybody. Mark had been an interim plaything for her. And with her relationship growing more serious now with Nicky Loomis, she was treating Mark worse and worse, canceling on him at the last moment because *Nicky* wanted to see her, or meet her somewhere, *anywhere.*

God, didn't he have any pride? Was Paige really that good in the sack that he could justify putting up with her!

Susan's own relationship with both of them had become so strained that she avoided being around them.

Happily, nobody was here at the house now. She had it all to herself. Relishing the silence and the privacy for a change, Susan dropped her briefcase in the hallway by the stairs, then hiked up yawning toward her bedroom, thinking how even Maria, Dustin's housekeeper, was out for the evening, her boyfriend having bought tickets to a Miami Sound Machine concert.

Tori and Paige were out with Nicky Loomis and some friend of Nicky's with whom they were fixing Tori up.

God, how Susan dreaded all these blind dates. She couldn't bear thinking of how many she had endured since she had been in L.A., well-meaning fix-ups arranged by Kit and George, by her law firm colleagues who generously included her in their plans for football games or dinners or the symphony, or urged her to meet available clients, if *only for a drink.*

Susan called it "lottery dating" and wasn't particularly optimistic about coming up lucky. The truth was, she found dating in Beverly Hills not much different from dating anywhere else. The men here were just richer and more spoiled, with eccentricities that appeared more pronounced. Like Jack, or even Richard Bennetton. Like Nicky Loomis. They seemed to feel they could buy anything, do anything, that their money made them omnipotent, providing them with the passkey for any obstacle.

Susan preferred to stay sequestered behind the safe shelter of her work, content with a quiet night of writing, researching, thinking, analyzing, or even working with Jack. It saved her from having to be "on" with people who didn't make her *feel* "on" naturally. It was such an effort to have to rush home after work and get all showered and dressed to kill, then have to smile and be entertaining for the duration of the date.

Movies were the best dates because they afforded two hours of not having to manufacture conversation—a time-out period. It was a way of being with someone without having to be with him.

Then after the movie they had a guaranteed common ground to tide them over through the quick cup of coffee that was the obligatory follow-up on that kind of date.

Longing to soak in the tub and say nothing, think of nothing, Susan, in the mood to treat herself, ran an extremely hot bath, pouring a blend of fragrant oils and powders beneath the faucet and watching as the foamy turquoise-tinted water rose to the desired height, in the mood to treat herself.

Ordinarily, she was meticulous about hanging up her clothes, but she was so tired and so anxious to get into the bath that she simply dropped her linen suit into a pile on the floor, jacket, blouse, skirt, panty hose, bra, and panties, expending effort instead on picking out a mellow Steve Wyndham compact disc from her collection and switching on the player. She didn't even bother to tie up her hair; she just let it fan out in the water, drenched in bubbles and oils, smelling and feeling wonderful. As she had hoped, the steamy temperature of the water penetrated her tension, drawing it out, melting it away. Therapy.

Funny how the relief of tension dulled grudges, lifting them, she thought guiltily, removing her steamed-up glasses and parking them on the side of the bath, filled with forgiveness toward Paige, Mark, Jack, even Kreegle. Even Billy Donahue. Even her father.

They were all just being themselves. People couldn't be more than they were.

Susan's head was resting against an inflated plastic pillow and she felt herself pleasantly drifting off, little nerve endings untying, leaving her loose and free.

She made a mental note to remember to call her parents tomorrow and see how they were.

To call Lisa too, to do a little fishing to find out what *was* going on with Billy Donahue.

She made a pledge to herself to try to be more patient with Paige.

Then she thought of Mark, and her thoughts held there, filling her up with a multitude of emotions and sensations, soothing and so deliciously real as she let herself fantasize about him. She imagined that he had a change of heart. That he wanted *her* now instead of Paige.

She imagined him telling her that he couldn't hold it inside any longer. Paige was only a fling. But with Susan he envisioned a serious relationship. Susan was everything he had always dreamed of. *And more.* Smart. Beautiful. Sensitive. She imagined his big blue eyes full of frustration and longing, *longing for her now, not for Paige.*

She imagined herself resisting, then caving in.

She saw herself sailing with him, the two of them alone and working in concert with the wind, riding the crystal-white crests of the Pacific on her boat.

Or hiking, camping out near Santa Barbara, listening to the quiet, roasting marshmallows by campfire, making love by the glowing embers.

All these magical things that she would love to do with him that didn't cost a dime.

Paige and Tori could have their extravagant gala parties, expensive trips and restaurants, all the costly clothes that lost something anyway the second and third time you put them on. Susan wanted a man with whom she could be happy doing the more mundane things—who made the mundane things *feel* extravagant. She was tired of pretending just to be polite that the hundred-dollar bottle of wine tasted any different from the seven-dollar bottle of wine.

Instead, she conjured up the lazy, vivid sensation of Mark there in the bathtub with her, climbing into the big tub and luxuriating in the silky texture of her richly oiled skin, massaging her breasts with the precious oil, her stomach, her thighs, kissing her, making love to her.

She felt her nipples taut beneath her fingertips as she imagined Mark's fingertips, his hands enveloping the slippery fullness of her breasts, the slinky sensation of the path that led down toward her hips and beyond.

If only she could have reached out to him through her mind, made him want her as she wanted him now, this instant, made him want to possess her as she wanted to be possessed.

She set her body and soul to the task, *focusing,* trying to mas-

ter the air waves to his mind, to the essence of his being, wishing
herself into his psyche, wanting to control it. Anything to have
him there with her, touching her, loving her as she felt she could
only love him.

Climbing toward an orgasm, she heard a knock at the door
and Mark's voice, calling out her name. Mortified, she sank
down into the water.

"Susan? Are you there?"

She thought about not answering, pretending she was not.
Good God, had he read her thoughts?

It was about time!

"Yes . . . yes." She had to clear her throat and shout over the
music.

"What?"

"I said, *yes. I'm here.*"

"I can't hear you. Can I come in?"

"*No.* I'm in the bathtub. Can you wait a min—"

"What? I can't hear you."

"I said, *not yet,*" Susan hollered, flushed, sighing and deciding
she had better get up and answer the door. She wondered what
he was doing here? How had he gotten in?

"Yes?" he verified uncertainly.

"*No.* One sec."

But as she stood up to reach for a towel, the fragrant, airy
white bubbles of her bath clinging to her skin and glistening from
all the air, he walked in, their eyes meeting head on before she
could grab a towel.

It was like an amusing addendum to her fantasy, only it was
real.

Laughing, embarrassed beyond words, Susan lunged for a
towel and wrapped it modestly around herself, dripping wet as
she stepped out of the bath, automatically reaching for her
glasses. "Hi," she said, still laughing, warmed by the blush that
went clear down to her toes.

"Hi," Mark replied, equally awkward, putting his hands to his
eyes, then looking at her. "Sorry. I couldn't hear you over all
the—"

"S'okay," she assured him, the fantasy he had interrupted still stirring her thoughts. "What are you doing here?" She was smiling the kind of smile that started deep inside of her soul and radiated out. She wondered what Paige would think if she were to come home now and find the two of them here like this in her bathroom.

Undeterred by any feelings of guilt, the thought amused her. Mark belonged to her first. It would be a case of stealing back what was rightfully hers to begin with.

He smiled. Still embarrassed. Looking additionally embarrassed by the reply he was about to give. "I was supposed to meet your roommate here, but it looks like I've been stood up. Maria let me in before she left, and then I fell asleep rereading *War and Peace* on the couch. When I woke up and saw your briefcase and shoes by the stairs . . . I just wanted to say hi—" he trailed off self-consciously.

Susan couldn't help the impulse to let him squirm a little longer before replying. She was enjoying the moment and wanted it to last. She imagined she was Paige, taking full advantage of her soapy, wet state of undress. She let her eyes roam over his pale, angelic face, then travel down to his work shirt and jeans, thinking how he looked so right in them. Nicky had picked Paige up here numerous times in his work shirt and jeans, but it hadn't been the same. Nicky looked like a middle-aged man trying to dress cool. Mark looked genuinely cool.

And now Susan needed to *act cool.* "You want a cup of coffee or something?" she asked, enjoying how uneasy he appeared watching her as she tucked the top right corner of her towel into place to secure it around her torso before reaching for another towel for her hair.

"Sure. Thanks," he answered agreeably. "Why don't you let me make it," he offered, recovering with a smile that made her heart lurch forward.

"That'd be great. Thanks."

"God, we're polite," he laughed, not yet moving to leave.

"All things considered," she observed, resecuring her towel, then smiling ironically as she went to sit in front of the dressing table to blow-dry her hair. She had to raise her voice over the noise of the dryer as she switched it on. "How's your art going?"

"Painting or selling?" he asked, picking up a perfume bottle from the table in front of her, smelling it briefly, then smiling as he returned it to the table. "Hmmm. That's nice."

"Thanks. I like it."

"It reminds me of you. Fresh, innocent, but not too sweet. Straightforward—"

"A straightforward scent?" Susan mused skeptically, aiming the dryer at her roots as she ran her fingers rapidly though her hair, sifting through layers for fullness and then scrunching it for curl.

"Nothing contrived or *trying* to be complicated about it," he explained thoughtfully, "more like the wild outdoors on a clear spring day just after a good torrent of rain."

"Hmmm. Sounds heavenly," Susan replied, easily conjuring up the picture, watching him through the mirror watching *her*. She was surprised when he took the blow-dryer from her hand and began blowing her hair himself, stirring his fingers through her hair as he directed the dryer.

"An artist, an economics professor, *and* a good blow-dryer, all in one package. You could be too much to resist," she chided, nervously responding to the feel of his hands in her hair, amazed at how sensual the ordinary task had become, performed by him.

She held on to her towel as he motioned for her to bend and flip her hair upside down. She was overly conscious of being naked beneath it so close beside him, the feel of his hands massaging her scalp. She felt her glasses slip down her nose and pushed them back up, trying to think of something witty to say.

"I love the feel of your hair; it's baby-fine, like silk."

"I hate to tell you this, but that's considered lousy hair."

"Not in my book," he countered suggestively, his fingers working at the nape of her neck, confusing her more than relaxing her, making her wonder what was going on.

What was this new-found intimacy? Why was he flirting with her, playing with her this way? Was he mad at Paige and trying to get back at her through Susan? Or was he just lonely? Or was this a belated revelation?

Not sure what to think, she sat subdued, saying nothing as he shut off the blow-dryer and then picked up a brush from the dressing table, brushing her hair with smooth, competent strokes, sending a trail of goose bumps all down her spine and down her legs.

"What are you trying to do? Seduce me?" she asked with a lightness she didn't feel, leaning her head back and succumbing to *whatever* it was that was going on.

When he didn't reply their eyes met in the mirror, where he continued to study her, looking torn, still playing with her hair, which fell soft and blond around her shoulders, full and radiating out. She looked pretty and surprisingly relaxed, her blue eyes clear and connecting with his. She felt a restrained, anxious surge of pleasure as he continued brushing her hair, his movements slow and leisurely, then becoming tentative. The moment seemed to link them back to square one, pre-Paige.

"I was asking you about your art," she reminded him distractedly, jumping back to the presumed safety of her initial, unanswered inquiry.

"I'll have to show you what I'm doing. I've started a new technique. I'm still working with plastic and acrylics, but this has a smoother, glassy look. It's more—"

"I'd like that . . ."

There was a hesitant pause by both of them. Susan surmised that they were both thinking about Paige.

"I've really enjoyed my 'Mark Arent.' I get comments on it all the time," she said truthfully.

"Do you?" He looked so pleased with the compliment that she had to laugh. It was the first time they had referred to the painting since he had hung it for her. She hadn't been able to before. In fact, she had been tempted over and over again to take it down. Its presence had been like a pressed corsage delivered in advance of a date who had stood her up.

The phone rang before she got a chance to say anything else, startling them both, and she reached for it, wondering who would be calling at a quarter past one in the morning, then wondering if it was Jack. "Hello?" she said, still looking at Mark.

"Susan Kendell Brown, please."

"Yes. Hello. This is Susan."

"Hi. Sorry to bother you at this hour, but you've got several urgent messages from a Juan Jimenez—" It was the law firm's answering service, and Susan realized that, with her upset over Jack and the pregnant striker, she had neglected to check her messages when she left the office. After seven, calls went directly to the service. "We just received another call from him and he said it was an emergency—"

"Juan Jimenez?" Susan repeated, interrupting, trying to place the name, then remembering him as one of the rabble rousers. She took down his phone number from the answering service and then, hesitating, called him back.

The anxious-sounding Mexican answered immediately, his tone clandestine, expecting Susan's call.

He explained briefly and without ceremony how he had sought her out in the belief that he had found a sympathetic ear. His situation and that of his peers was dire and they needed her counsel. Somehow he had discovered that prior to her present job, she had represented unions and not management, and he was sure that she would want to know the truth of what was going on. He implored her to meet with him right away, insisting that it couldn't wait until tomorrow, nor could it be done over the telephone.

"I'm not letting you go out there on your own in the middle of the night. Are you crazy?" Mark said.

"Mark, I'm used to this kind of thing," Susan assured him, though she wasn't really. The intensity of the strike was escalating and she was leery of going on her own, worried that she was merely being used.

"I'm going with you," he maintained.

"No, it's okay. I'll be fine," she countered, leaving him an out if he wanted one, but hoping he would argue as she rushed over to find a pair of jeans and a sweater.

"I know you're brave and self-sufficient. But I also know you have better judgment than to go out there on your own at this hour."

"What is it you think they're going to do to me?" Susan laughed. "And what do you think *you're* going to be able to do to protect me?"

Mark was sitting on one of the twin beds, juggling three small pillows up into the air, watching her. *"Run,"* he teased, trying to capture her off guard and tossing one of the pillows at her.

As she dove to catch it, her towel came unfastened and dropped to the ground, embarrassing them both again.

"God, would you get dressed already," Mark pleaded as she tried to cover herself with the jeans and sweater she was holding, retreating, bare-assed and blushing again, backward into the bathroom to change. "Before I wind up unfaithful to your already unfaithful roommate."

"Spare me," Susan stressed, refusing to feel even an iota of guilt or sympathy for Paige, kicking the door closed this time to insure some privacy, smiling at him as she did so, and, for the first time in a long time, feeling alluring.

Chapter 25

The factory was dark and silent as Susan and Mark rode up to the entrance gate on Mark's motorcycle. Susan's car didn't have enough gas, and they didn't know where to go for a refill at this hour, so they had taken his bike. They were both wearing heavy leather jackets, oversized goggles covering their glasses, and around her head Susan had tied a scarf, which she undid now, shaking her hair free.

"Well?" Mark asked, turning around to her, producing a flash light and shining it just under her chin. "You nervous?" he asked, squeezing her arm before releasing it.

The excitement of her arms still clinging tightly around his waist, his leather jacket scrunched up just beneath her nose, the wind-whipping ride on his bike, and the dangerous sensation of being here with him now like this in the middle of the night to meet surreptitiously with the *other* side, the sympathetic side, had Susan barely thinking straight. "A little," she admitted, snatching the flashlight from him and swinging her right leg around and off the bike. "I'm only *L.A. Law,* you know, not Nancy Drew."

"What does that make me?" he asked, getting down also to catch up with her.

"I don't know—*Lassie*?" She chuckled, feeling giddy and nervous at once. If she had been alone it would have been a straight case of nerves.

"Make me a hero, but not a canine one, okay? How about Superman?" he suggested, joining his arm through hers.

"I don't know—can you fly?"

"Effortlessly."

"You *want* to be Superman?"

"Only if you're . . . what's her name?"

"Lois Lane."

"Yeah."

"Shhh. There they are," Susan whispered, sobered by the sight of the three figures walking toward them. The plant itself was surrounded with barbed wire. There were very few lights. She switched the flashlight back on and aimed it at them. They waved in acknowledgment and began to step up their pace.

Their introductions were awkward. Susan was acquainted with both men from the strike meetings, but she hadn't met Carmen Jimenez, Juan's pregnant wife, whom Susan suspected to be at the vortex of the crisis, given the incident that had erupted earlier on the strike line.

As bold as the pregnant woman had seemed then, that's how shy she seemed now, looking down at her flowered maternity dress, her hands stuffed into the pockets of the parka she had over it, every minute or so removing them from the pockets to rub them protectively over the new life she carried in her belly. She was wearing heavy dark hose and pumps the same pink as the background of her dress.

"This is my friend, Mark Arent," Susan said, continuing with the pleasantries as they all shook hands.

Juan Jimenez and his small group were proud but still deferential as they exchanged cautious hellos. Then without any pretense of small talk, Juan took up his lead as spokesman for his peers and began an explanation for having called her, not bothering with an apology this time.

"Today on the strike line, with Carmen getting pushed down and everything, man, we *know* it was a set-up," he reported hostilely, grabbing one thick finger, then the next, as he ticked off his suspicions. "Like, when I took a swing and four scabs got out of the truck and got all four of us. The guard just *happened* not to be there at the gate. The security guards just *happened* to be there taking pictures for documentation. And those scabs, we hear, all just *happened* to get jobs somewhere else in union shops."

Susan stood absolutely still, thinking that it was a mistake to have come out here. But what had she expected? To be confronted with something that *wouldn't* put her in a position of conflict? What the worker was saying mirrored her own feelings, and she was torn, wanting to right the situation, but on the other hand conscious of her professional obligation to her client, not to mention her *own* position at the firm.

It wasn't her duty to save the world, or these people, she thought, looking away as they looked at her for answers. If there were an easy way, perhaps she might have been swayed. But there were dirty dealings on both sides of the fence. And as Kreegle had said, it was the union's job to look after the workers. Not hers. Not the firm's.

The squat swarthy striker construed Susan's silence as sympathetic interest and went on, nervously rubbing his hands along the sides of his jeans, insisting that the union leaders were trying to cut a deal with management and, in the process, were selling out their workers.

"Everyone knows that the union brass are only interested in getting their dues," he asserted bitterly. "They got us to go out on strike to get rid of us because they know management'll never go for what we're asking. Man, they had this planned all along, as soon as they realized they weren't gonna get us to go along with their bullshit contract. All of us out on strike, we're all gonna lose our jobs."

Again, Susan couldn't argue. The strikers probably *would* all end up losing their jobs. She felt Mark watching her, waiting for a response. But there was nothing safe to say. She was trying to keep a professional distance, something she recognized she had already sacrificed by being there in the first place.

"Man, what we're asking for is fair," he contended, his face tight. "Your client, he's got serious health violations. You know that. *Enseñele sus manos, Carmen,*" he ordered his wife, prying her hands from her stomach to hold them out for Susan and Mark to see. They were chalky and rough, with dozens of tiny little scars. "You see these marks? They come from fiberglass splinters because your son-of-a-bitch client is too cheap to get enough gloves for everybody. Look at my hands. Look at Carlos' hands. Happens to all of us.

"And we're sick and tired of paying for the rejects that come from *his* using cheap materials. Man, he's buying cheap resin, cheap materials and using molds that should be junked and *we're* getting blamed; we're paying for it outa our paychecks—"

Carmen Jimenez placed her hand lightly on her husband's back as though to get him to settle down. He took a deep obliging breath before going on. His cohort continued standing very still, saying nothing.

Susan took the moment to glance at Mark, who seemed intrigued by the whole encounter, feeling grateful he was there with her.

"Can't you get us our jobs back?" Jimenez began again, upset but controlling himself. *"They're* the ones in violation. We're just out there trying to earn an honest living. Sure, we got a lot of anger and frustration. But *you* know there hasn't been any real violence in this strike. Guys just getting their frustration out, that's all.

"They want people to think we're the bad guys. We're not the bad guys. *They're* the bad guys," he charged, gently cupping his wife's engorged belly with the palm of his hand, his face toughening again. "But let 'em start *firing* us like this. Then they're gonna see some real violence."

Carmen Jimenez enclosed both of her smaller hands over her husband's larger one, finally getting the nerve to speak up. "Ees true, Miz Susan, it get . . . *muy malo,* very bad, *rough,"* she interjected, reticent about her English, which was not as practiced as her husband's but still desperate to appeal to Susan. *"Pero* violence, *no!* No ees true. We make some tires go flat, throw some eggs," she shrugged. "Ees not such big thing. No? *'No big deal,'* like you say. *Pero,* lose jobs over this—this no ees right. These strikers, they ees good people, they ees all good people. Nobody want hurt nobody."

Juan Jimenez looked emotionally from his wife to Susan. "Can't you do something for us?" he pleaded. "Maybe negotiate for us with them? Tell them we know we were set up. All we want is our jobs back and a fair deal."

As he shook his head and directed his eyes down at the ground, Susan found it hard not to be affected by the frustration he was trying to contain, the kind of injustice she had spent all her years as a lawyer working against. She turned to Mark, needing some sign from him, some grounded confirmation that what she was about to do was the right thing.

Juan Jimenez, Carmen Jimenez, Carlos, all of them. These people had been sold out, set up, as they said. Her client had most likely initiated the double cross; he had supported it anyway.

Without committing herself, she told them that she needed some time to think about it, that she would get in touch with them the following day, dully aware that she had *already* committed herself when she had driven out there.

Her head was throbbing, pounding, as she held on to Mark's waist afterward, riding behind him on his bike through the streets of cast L.A. There was a crushing pressure at her temples, behind her eyes, at the back of her head, and continuing down her neck. Mark was sensitive enough to know not to talk. To let her ingest what had just gone on, what she was involving herself in, to mull it over without distraction.

God, what a day! What a long day. It was three in the morning. The city for the most part seemed asleep.

They ripped through the seedier portion of downtown, taking in the run-down tenements, the street people who made the pavement their home arranging bags of trash to lean against and use as pillows, cardboard cartons set up as tables, wearing worn wool hats, torn gloves, and heavy jackets, even though the last days of summer hadn't yet passed.

She felt someone looking down at her, and she met his gaze uncomfortably. Hanging out of a double-hung window over a liquor store in an old brick tenement building was a man in a white tank-style undershirt drinking from a bottle of beer. He had it better than the poor bundled-up bums on the street, she thought, her thoughts shifting to Juan Jimenez, Carlos, the others, wondering what their living conditions were like.

There were so very many levels in this country. All of them cognizant of the top level, bombarded by the subliminal tease of affluence in advertisements, seeing it on TV or in the movies, reading about it in books and magazines, and striving toward it in one way or another, if not for themselves then for their children.

Except the street people, who she could see now sporadically lining the sidewalks. Somewhere along the way they had abandoned the race, given up, were existing on food stamps and charity, *barely* existing, from the looks of it.

And then there was the blue-collar working class, the Juan Jimenezes of the world, trying to better their lot, to make the world a decent place for their children, putting in an honest effort, an honest day's work—and getting shafted.

Susan was surprised when Mark veered over into a parking place and cut his engine. Looking around, she realized they were in the flower-market district.

"What are we doing here?" she asked as he turned around to her. "It's the middle of the night."

"Aha, to you and me, yes. But to them it's not," he corrected her, indicating the bustle of another world that surrounded them. Operating in full swing, accustomed to working by moonlight instead of sunlight, the flower market's world didn't begin until midnight and didn't end until most others began, around seven or eight in the morning.

The area was so well lit that it didn't feel like the middle of the night at all. There were trucks all over, people carting dollies loaded with newsprint-wrapped bunches of flowers contained in plastic buckets of water. There were people walking around eating fast food snacks from wax paper wrappers that they had most likely bought from the catering food truck just a couple of yards away. It was all action. Action and breathtaking masses of flowers, as the wholesale trade loaded up to service the retail trade.

"I wanted to buy you some flowers to cheer you up, but I wanted to be sure you had a good selection," Mark said, lifting off his helmet as he got off the motorcycle, then taking her hand to help her off the bike as well.

He removed her scarf, untying it from under her chin, then stuffing it into her pocket while she looked around, thinking it would be impossible *not* to be cheered up with all this, enchanted by the riot of colors and floral varieties that overwhelmed the district.

Why did my roommate get you, instead of me getting you? she thought, her head still pounding, feeling burnt out from the range of emotion. She wished she could say it aloud. It was blunt, true, direct, with a little bit of humor and irony splashed in. It was the *self* she rarely displayed. The self she wanted him to know.

His framed blue eyes studied her for an extra beat, looking confused, uncertain, as he removed his goggles. Maybe even uncertain as to what he wanted now, as though he were reading her mind and didn't know or understand the answer. Susan sensed the pull. At last she felt the attraction that had been waylaid, shortstopped by her sex-goddess roommate. Susan knew exactly why. And it was tough to compete.

Paige was *Penthouse.* Susan was . . . Lois Lane.

Superman or, perhaps more aptly, her curly blond-haired Clark Kent, took her hand and led her inside the flower market, where she was hit with the intoxicating blend of fragrances from all the hundreds of varieties of flowers. Distilled, it would have been a miracle scent. It was surely a miracle moment.

Mark appeared to be known and liked by many of the vendors, who said hello to him by name and shared best-buy leads, cutting prices for him out of earshot of other workers or customers, so that before Susan and Mark knew it they were weighted down with more cone-shaped wrapped bundles of flowers than they could carry.

He said he loved being surrounded by flowers, and since they were so expensive in the retail shops and not nearly as fresh, he liked to come down here a couple of times a month and load up.

"Feel any better?" he asked, catching her eye as they rounded a corner down another aisle, accepting a cart from a sympathetic bystander and releasing their bountiful score into it.

She did feel better. Her headache wasn't gone, but it was lifting. She was thinking about French tulips, French roses, lilac branches, lilies of multitudinous varieties, the showy, white bell-shaped version blooming from a thick green stalk, the more delicate-looking tiger lilies, the exquisite and yet still hearty Journey's End, which were a vivid white with speckles of hot pink. They had gathered bunches of peacock-blue hybrid delphiniums, iris, baby roses, new breeds of daisies, and, from another area, tall tropically bred stalks of ginger and birds of paradise imported from Hawaii. Their more exotic finds ranged from garlic strands to Brussels sprout stems to reindeer moss to horsetail. The world had grown small enough to be able to enjoy flowers grown and picked fresh from all over the globe—Jamaica, Africa, Australia, New Zealand, Israel, Mexico, Holland, France, the Orient, exchanging blossoms otherwise never glimpsed and enjoying flowers off-season.

Across the street from where the American vendors were set up were the Japanese vendors, the street dividing the two factions tagged the "Suez Canal."

The Japanese side, Mark explained, was especially interesting because it still embodies so much tradition. Many of the Japanese had relocated during the war, and most of them were growers selling their own product.

It was fascinating to see the way their stalls were run, with the elderly Japanese grandfathers remaining behind the scenes, still preferring to do their accounting calculations sliding beads back and forth on their archaic abacuses, while their sons and grandsons manned the front wearing Walkmen and blitzing through tallies on their micro-sized calculators.

Amazingly, Mark was able to cram their multiple flower purchases into soft leather saddle packs he kept fastened onto both sides of his bike, so that there was even enough room left over to add a sack of produce they picked up afterward at the equally bustling produce market on their way to the legendary Vickman's for a predawn breakfast.

The old cafeteria-style restaurant, located in the hub of the produce market, was always packed at any hour. It was filled with regulars from the area, the produce moguls seated beside lower-level workers or truckers at the long strips of Formica-topped tables, all of them minding their own business—which was, while they were there, most frequently a small glass beaker of coffee, a danish, and one of any of the array of newspapers sold up in front.

Walking very close to each other, charged with something different in the air, Susan and Mark took one of the booths that lined the length of the wall, waiting for the short-order portion of their breakfast to be brought to them by the waitress. Mark had their coffee and blueberry muffins on a tray, which they had already picked up cafeteria-style.

"Thanks, Mark, for everything," Susan said, feeling calm and grateful, her headache finally gone. This was a moment she never in her wildest dreams really expected to realize and she found herself nearly shaking as she tried to let the nearness of him register, flooded with relief, with gratitude and with all sorts of feelings she couldn't even fathom.

He was sitting across the table from her, watching her trying to slow her pace as she wolfed down her blueberry muffin, both of them hungry from their all-nighter.

"The only thing you and Paige seem to have in common is your appetite," he observed, breaking off a chunk of his muffin and depositing it thoughtfully into his mouth as he regarded her.

The mention of Paige's name acted like a short circuit in Susan's brain.

Maybe it was the lack of sleep. Maybe it was all the wild emotion of the day. Maybe it was the gut feeling that Jack didn't really give a damn about her either, that he was just using her because of the strike situation and the slippery, dishonest dealings he was hoping to get away with. But she felt herself losing her grasp.

Was Paige Williams all Mark could think about? Was that why he was here with her now? To pour out his heart to her? Had she only imagined everything else? "What about *you*? I guess you could say we have *you* in common," she snapped brashly, wanting to stun him, wanting to force a reaction. Susan rarely lost her temper, but when she did there were no holds barred. The cen-

soring mechanism that kept such a tight lid on just about everything she ever thought or said would go haywire.

Mark seemed surprised, confused by her outburst, by the flash
of anger. He picked up his coffee cup and took a long contempla-
tive swallow, clearly at a loss as to how to respond.

She was too keyed up to let him off the hook and she sat very
still watching him. Inside she was quivering, wanting to run out
of the restaurant, wanting to run fast and hard away from the
confrontation she couldn't stop herself from bringing to a head.

"You have *me* in common?" he repeated uncomfortably.

"Don't pretend to be surprised. Please. I'm not an idiot. You
know damn well how I've felt about you. Admit it. It was a shitty
thing to do, coming over to see me and then falling all over
yourself with my roommate the way you did."

Mark sat back against the scruffy orange-painted booth, hesitating, looking guilty. "I know," he said finally, his voice low,
confessional. But she was going for the jugular. "I'm sorry," he
apologized, groping, picking up his coffee cup again, then returning it to its saucer without taking a sip. The rattle of dishes
being carted off by busboys seemed amplified.

What did *sorry* really mean? That he felt sorry for her? That he
was sorry that he was still in love with Paige? That he couldn't
force feelings for Susan he didn't have?

When she didn't reply, he went on. "I've never done anything
like that in my life, coming over to see you and then leaving with
her like that. But you all had dates. And she was there. I don't
know, I realize that's not much of an excuse.

"But then, when she told me why you'd all moved out here, I
figured it didn't make any difference. It put everything on another level. Or that was how I justified it anyway. I don't know
what got into me. I couldn't help myself."

Susan knew exactly what had gotten into him. It wasn't only
sex. It was Paige being persuasive, wanting Mark, and manipulating the situation. As she manipulated everything.

"What's the difference, anyway? You all moved out here to
meet and marry rich men," Mark summarized bitterly. "And I'm
sure you will. Paige has her prince all lined up. Tori's Bennetton

prince turned into a frog, but I'm sure she'll find another royal prospect without too much ado. And you have yours—"

"*Mine?*" There was an edge to Mark's voice that Susan matched in her own as she cut him off. "I have mine? Who's *my* prince?" she came back dryly, knowing full well he meant Jack Wells, that he was presuming more than there was to their relationship because of all the long hours they spent together at work. His dig seemed to reach deeper, considering what he had learned about Jack tonight.

The waitress delivered their scrambled eggs to the table, rearranging cups and plates to make room for them, providing a tense lull. "The rich, but not necessarily ethical client " Mark reminded her darkly, after the waitress had left.

"I don't *have* a prince to turn into a frog," Susan replied angrily.

"No?"

"No. And I don't believe in fairy tales," she added with a tough glare across the table. "Who do you think you are, anyway? Do you think you're better than these other guys because you *don't* have money? That your lack of wealth makes you the genuine article, the prince without the facade?"

Mark took a couple of bites of his eggs, looking as if he weren't tasting them. The directness of Susan's response seemed to throw him and he answered curtly, looking as upset as she was. "So why did you move out here with them, then?"

"The same reason that they all moved out here. Because we were all stuck in our own kinds of ruts. Because we needed to make changes in our lives. Not that it's any of your damn business. Who the hell do you think you are anyway, sitting in judgment? You don't know anything about me, really. Or Tori. And Paige is so damn complicated you probably don't even really know anything about her, either, other than how to satisfy her in bed." In a burst of anger and frustration Susan stood up, reaching into her purse for some money to throw onto the table, wanting to get out of there as fast as possible. She didn't have to sit there and justify herself to him.

"Now that's a low blow," Mark shot back, standing up also.

"I can't help it. You deserved it," she exclaimed angrily.

"What are you doing? Sit down," he argued, blocking her way.

"Just leave me alone, Mark. I'm tired. I'm leaving. I've got a lot on my mind."

"What, you're going to catch a cab at this hour?"

"Just get out of my way." She wished she had never started this. Paige could have him, for all she cared. She couldn't believe she had said as much as she had said. She had made a complete fool of herself. "Now would you just get out of my way?"

"Not until we finish this—"

"I am finished—"

"Well I'm not."

The two of them stood there staring at each other until Susan finally averted her glance down to the cheap linoleum floor, close to tears.

Gently, Mark directed her back down into her seat and then slid in beside her, backing her all the way into the corner. Her heart was pounding and she couldn't stop herself from trembling.

She was thinking about Juan Jimenez. His pregnant wife. Jack. Kreegle. The blow-up she could anticipate with them all tomorrow. How she had jeopardized her job. And then she was thinking about Mark walking in on her as she was getting out of the bathtub. The way his hands had felt in her hair. The feel of her arms around him and the wind whipping back at them as they tore through the streets on his motorcycle.

"I'm sorry," Mark began softly. "I really am—"

"For what?" she interrupted defensively, feeling dizzy from the nearness of him. She felt an electric-like current from his hand only a fraction of an inch away from hers, from his lips practically touching hers.

"For a lot of things," he murmured, not letting her look away this time. "For that first night with Paige. For hurting you. And you're right. I didn't know you at all . . . And I want to know you . . ."

She felt him about to kiss her and she was scared to death. She knew she should push her way around him and out of the booth. That she should leave. That she should not be accepting Paige's sloppy seconds so easily. That she shouldn't be so sane and forgiving. But she couldn't help herself. She had never felt anything so powerful in her life. She couldn't believe they were really talking about all this. She felt weak and vulnerable.

Before she could even come close to summoning up the willpower to resist, he had pulled her into a tight embrace and was kissing her as though nobody else in the world existed. They both took off their glasses at the exact same moment, laughed about it for half a second, and then resumed kissing, as though making up for all those months of lost time.

Without even thinking, Susan had slipped her hands inside his shirt and was feeling the chest she had only envisioned feeling before. It was warmer than the chest in her fantasy, and the curly blond hair growing wild and dense there felt silky and exciting.

She was reeling from all the sensations of him, the intense heat, the caress of his lips, which were soft and sensual, that familiar face pressing against her own, the blond stubble of his beard rough from the long night's growth. All the sensations previously only imagined, now being realized and explored.

"God, let's get out of here before I end up making love to you in the restaurant," Mark said, breaking reluctantly away for a moment and jarring them both into a hazy state of cognizance.

All at once aware of where she was, Susan looked up embarrassed and then relieved because nobody seemed to be paying any attention to them. The restaurant's diverse clientele were all minding their own business, buoying themselves with their newspapers, their coffee and sweet rolls, looking half asleep themselves.

Susan and Mark's eyes met again like magnets. Susan figured they were probably both wondering the same thing. Where did they go from here?

She smiled self-consciously, about to put on her jacket as Mark touched her hair and then her cheek and then began kissing her again. "I want to start seeing you," he whispered, only barely coming up for air as he went on emphatically but almost nonsensically, unable to keep his hands off her. "I'm sorry for everything. I'm sorry for being so blind. For being such an idiot. And I know I really screwed up. And I know this is going to be unbelievably awkward. But just say yes. You can change your mind later if you have to, but say yes now. God, I had to be out of my fucking mind."

Moving her lips away from his for only an instant, Susan cautioned him as to how *awkward* could just be the understatement of the day.

Chapter 26 ~

"What is this, Tori? You hock your engagement ring to bail out your rich fiancé—who breaks up with you over it—and then give him all the money, anyway. And, *Susan,* you're going to get us all killed, exposing some union conspiracy in order to get health insurance for a bunch of poor workers you don't even know. What kind of rich-husband manhunt is this?" Paige admonished, intent on getting on with her own.

It was like the good old days when they had first moved out here, all of them together at the house gathered around in the den and sharing crises.

Paige thought all they did was bump into one another now in passing, on their way out the door. But this morning it felt collective again, collective problems, collective help. Tori and Susan were the sisters she never had and she looked at them, unable to smile through the tight, egg-white face mask itching and restricting, but, hopefully, beautifying her face, trying to convey what she felt for them through her eyes.

She hadn't wanted to analyze a whole other aspect of this just this moment, about what appeared to be blossoming with Susan and Mark.

It was eight A.M. and her small-town Stockton roommate had

only recently come in, looking like sunshine dropped down to earth in the guise of a woman, disheveled but radiant, loaded down with enough flowers to overwhelm a shop. She was keyed up over the union situation, but clearly distracted and glowing on account of her escort.

Paige, on the other hand, looked like hell in her Bloomie's nightshirt and facial mask, her hair full of shark-oil conditioner, drawn back into a ponytail, and a trail of Kleenex separating her toes from the pedicure she had just given herself. She had gotten up early to squeeze all this beautifying in, since she had a couple of private sessions to teach at clients' homes before her first class at Matrix.

At least Mark wasn't mad at her for having stood him up the night before, she had been forced to rationalize, swallowing any jealousy she may have felt, unquestionably taken aback at the sight of her roommate and her boyfriend sailing in together after having been out all night.

Their good-bye to one another was awkward but unmistakably intimate, Paige had thought, wondering about it, reminding herself that she had basically dropped Mark like a hot potato when she had started seeing Nicky. Reminding herself that Mark was a poor, starving—by her standards—professor who was great in bed, but not cut out for the boardroom.

Wide awake for someone who hadn't slept in twenty-four hours, Susan plopped down on the couch, gratefully accepting coffee from Maria and telling them all about her dilemma with the strikers, the set-up revolving around Carmen Jimenez, their suspicions about a conspiracy, and the precarious position it put her in with her law firm, with Jack Wells. Not to mention the union thugs, who wouldn't be too pleased with any investigative efforts.

Tori, Paige thought, resembled a sleepy Persian cat, cuddled up in one of the big overstuffed chairs, wrapped in the mink-colored silk bathrobe Kit had given her for being one of her bridesmaids, also drinking from a mug of coffee and listening intently to Susan's story.

Her blind date from the night before, Nicky's friend, had flipped over her, but even Paige had to admit what a geek the man was, even *with* his millions. Not only was he so short he needed a special booster seat for his Rolls-Royce in order to see over the steering wheel, but he wore one of those foppish wigs that had you tempted all evening to yank it off.

The encouraging aspect of the evening was that Tori had finally shown a sense of humor about enduring a blind date, which they both took as a good sign, laughing their heads off about him during ladies' room runs, and afterward. Maybe the dreamy-looking brunette was getting over the rotten men in her life after all.

"We're counting on *you,* Paige, to save the day," Tori chimed in, accentuating her southern drawl. "You marry your rich husband and then take care of all of us."

"Tori, I think you personally will be able to support us, the way you're doing at Bennetton these days," Paige said, duly impressed with the accolades Tori was receiving at Bennetton. Now that she was working there without the distraction of Richard, who had disappeared off on another of his extended vacations to God only knew where. "I'm waiting for the old man to appoint you as his successor. To take you under his wing to supersede him when he retires, since we can certainly write off his son. And Susan will be *dead.* So that's no problem. We all know how the union handles their opposition. Why do you think all their presidents wind up dead themselves or in jail?"

"Not the present one," Susan corrected her. "The FBI is too entrenched with this one, so he's only been under investigation." Her blue eyes sparkled beneath her glasses, the same sky-blue tint as her jeans.

"Great. And you want to start investigating their *conspiracy?* I thought you were supposed to be the brainy one here."

"C'mon. I'd just be like a fly to them, a small irritant, buzzing around on a small deal."

"Wonderful. And what do you do to flies? Do you let them *buzz* around, or do you run for the fly swatter?"

"Spray Raid," Susan joked.

"What does Mark think about all this?" Tori interceded, curiously meeting Paige's glance for only a moment.

"Mark!" Paige answered for Susan. "Mark and Susan are a

great pair. He'll be all for this kind of escapade. He'll think he's Zorro or something."

Susan laughed, tempted to correct Paige and call him Superman.

She had been waiting for some remark from Paige. She hadn't missed the look in her eyes when she and Mark came into the house together. If Paige's face hadn't been concealed behind a mask, it would have turned colors.

"Mark doesn't have a shred of common sense. Or business sense. He lives in a romantic bubble," Paige continued, her warning not exactly unbiased as she rose to go wash off her mask, complaining that it felt like hardened fiberglass; if she didn't remove it now it would be sealed onto her skin for good. Also complaining that it was making her nauseated; it was so tight and so restrictive it made her feel claustrophobic.

"You're using so much junk, how can you tell what's working and what's not?" Tori asked, giving Susan a significant smile as they followed Paige upstairs and into her cluttered, topsy-turvy bedroom. If Dustin were to return home and find his guest room turned upside down like this, he would probably kick them all out, Susan thought, aghast at the mess as she realized how long it had been since she had been in there. She wondered what Mark thought about Paige being such a slob.

"I can't," Paige admitted freely, going into the bathroom and turning on the sink faucet, then leaning against it for a moment as though she really didn't feel well. "I'm covering all my bases using *everything,*" she remarked, as though deciding not to give in to her discomfort, instead to get the mask off as soon as possible.

"I'm impressed that you can remember what to put where, when to put it there, and why," Tori commented, as Paige went about melting down her mask with a hot washcloth, removing it carefully.

Susan, leaning against the door, surveyed the confusing array of creams, oils, vials, scrubs, and masks scattered across the white marble countertop, and laughed at Tori's question.

"I *can't,*" Paige quipped again, pausing to roll up the sleeves of her nightshirt, before they became soaking wet. "The ones that

really get me are the preventatives. Sixty dollars for some mysterious anti-aging serum that offers no visible results but promises
to speed up cellular renewal, the effects of which you can only
take the manufacturer's word for, and wait. They sucker you into
these because of the what-if-they-do-work? syndrome. Who can
afford to take the chance?"

Paige leaned in critically toward the mirror, frowning at hair-
line flaws still visible beneath her eyes and around her mouth,
imperfections that were supposed to have been corrected by the
expensive chemist's concoction she had just washed off. It was a
mask made from dried egg whites and other rejuvenating elements, which were supposed to completely correct the skin, clean
it, lift it, nourish it, smooth out lines and *also* help slow down the
aging process, at forty dollars a crack.

They're all such liars, she thought, looking into the mirror,
opening a tube of botanical eye gel and smearing it around her
eyes for a temporary plumping affect, still stubbornly hoping for
magic, *needing* magic in order to keep up with the demands of a
man like Nicky.

Gifts aside, they didn't cover her overhead.

It wasn't like dating Mark, where, no matter what she did to
herself or wore, he always thought she looked terrific.

Terrific to Nicky meant hair and makeup done just right,
dressed to kill, dressed to wow his friends and turn heads. The
look that appealed to him was high heels, a lot of leg, and clothes
that showed off her figure.

Paige called it "the kept-mistress look," only she was still
keeping herself at this point, and it was a struggle. She always
worried that if she appeared in the same outfit twice it would
signal the beginning of the end, reminding Nicky of just how long
and how frequently he had been seeing her, and that he would
run for the hills.

She already knew from his friends and kids that she was a
living, breathing record for him. And that was some record, considering that she and Nicky weren't screwing yet, that there was
the added pressure to their relationship of having to talk and get
to know each other.

"Why couldn't I be dating a man who didn't have such perfect

vision?" she went on. "Can you believe he was giving me a hard
time about these wrinkles? Saying that most of the girls he dates
aren't old enough to have developed 'expression' lines. One of
those only *half-kidding* remarks that sends you straight to a
plastic surgeon for comfort."

"Did you tell him that most of the girls he dates aren't old
enough to have any expression, period?" Tori asked.

"Don't make me laugh. It'll just make them worse." Paige
steadied her expression, waiting for the eye gel to set.

Tori took the tube out of her hand and began reading the
directions and claims of wonder aloud. "Here, Susan—after staying up all night, you could probably use some of this," she said,
handing it over to her.

"Why? Do my eyes look that bad?" Susan asked, squeezing in
to look in the mirror, thinking she looked pretty terrific for someone who had gone without any sleep and attributing her glow to
Mark. *Nothing a little Visine and Moon Drops won't cure,* she
decided, unconcerned, tossing the tube of eye gel back to Paige.

"Suit yourself," Paige said, thinking *lucky Susan;* Mark
wouldn't mind soft, natural aging. He would find it becoming.
But let's see how Susan looked next to Paige when they were
both forty, and what Mark thought then.

She maneuvered around Tori and Susan, out of the bathroom
and over to her closet to get her work-out clothes. Feeling a
sudden rush of impatience at seeing the two of them not any
farther along with their personal lives when her *own* mind was
made up as to exactly what she wanted, she decided tonight was
the night for her big move.

Sure, Tori and Susan had changed cities, but they were back in
their old patterns, still channeling all their brain power and energy into their careers, feeling thwarted because the rewards were
not the rewards for which they were looking right now.

Paige believed in taking little steps, but all in one direction,
and all of them exceedingly well thought out. She believed in
linear focus. So she would put her career aside for now. Later, if
she felt the urge, she could pick it up again or go for a new one.
She knew she could go only for one thing at a time, if she wanted
to reach.

And swinging a marriage proposal from Nicky Loomis was unquestionably reaching.

Tonight she was going to sleep with him, using all of her resources to drive their relationship up to the final level, the level that would have him hooked on her for good. She hoped.

Nicky's world was an exciting one, and so far she had managed to jump right into the swing of things, fitting in with an ease that continued to catch him by surprise, proving that she was sharp, funny, gutsy, not at all intimidated by his celebrity friends or life-style, showing him that he might have met his match in this younger female counterpart.

What made it easy for her was that she wasn't in love with him, so she wasn't worrying about getting hurt. She didn't feel vulnerable.

Or did she? she asked herself, still feeling queasy and beginning to have doubts. Maybe her system was upset from having seen Mark and Susan together, looking at each other the way they did. Paige had been able to feel her hold over Mark evaporating, like a sorceress's fading power. It was like a sappy ending to an old tale, with the sweet, innocent heroine stepping in during the final act to reclaim what was rightfully hers, power to the benevolent restored.

Maybe the queasiness had to do with taking the simple step she had inadvertently turned into a quantum leap, making love with Nicky. Why did she keep putting it off, if she were so sure of herself?

The answer suddenly appeared obvious; because making love *would* make her vulnerable, vulnerable to rejection. Vulnerable to the heightened possibility of a collapsed goal that would put her back at square one again, if he were to lose interest immediately afterward, the challenge she had posed suddenly met, his conquest complete.

She reminded herself that she had felt ready to sleep with him the last few times they had been together, ready, even eager for the consummation, but there was a small part of her that wouldn't yield, that was reluctant, even afraid.

After this big build-up, she wondered what it would take to not have it all feel like a lot of hot air. It was a pressure she

hadn't anticipated and she was surprisingly shy now about initiating the next step. *He* had finally stopped trying, once she had
started taking care of him. He was playing it her way now, waiting for her.

And so it was up to her.

And it was time.

Holding on to a lavender bodysuit and a pair of leg warmers,
she turned reticently to her friends, who were both stretched out
and talking to each other on the bed.

She wanted to tell them about her concerns, to air them and
ask for support. She wanted to let them know just how momentous this evening might be for her and how nervous about it she
was. She wanted to tell them how she felt it in the pit of her
stomach, about the weakness in her limbs.

But she found she simply wasn't able to.

That wasn't the Paige Williams they knew and loved.

Susan arrived at her law firm by ten o'clock, showered, dressed
in a new fall suit that was a lightweight linen but bronze and
beige to accommodate the nearing shift in seasons, feeling surprisingly refreshed for having missed a full night's sleep.

She walked down the corridor to her office, busy volleying
options in her head as to how to handle her suspicions about
union and management's off-the-record cooperation, anticipating
calls from Jimenez, from Jack, from Hank Piedmont, one of the
union lawyers, reports of workers being fired, of retaliation, hoping there was a call from Mark.

"Hi."

"Good morning."

"Yo, Susan."

"How ya doin'?"

"Hey, sexy."

"Have to talk to you later."

Susan responded to the various greetings as she rounded a
corner near her office.

The final greeting came from her secretary, followed by an
offer of coffee.

Promising to cut back soon on so much caffeine, she accepted.

"Thanks, Linda. God, who didn't call?" she remarked to her secretary, hanging her jacket on the hook behind her door, then riffling through the small stack of messages.

Linda chuckled. "Been one of those mornings. Nice suit."

Susan smiled. "Thanks."

"Is Mark Arent the artist who did your painting?" Linda asked, pointing to the colorful collage of chicken wire overwhelming the wall behind Susan.

"Yep," she answered, happily coming upon his message and thinking that no matter what happened with this incident with the strikers, even if she got fired today, nothing could burst her bubble. The message gave his number and read "Dinner tonight at eight, chez Superman. Regrets only."

"Cute," Linda noted, chuckling. "He paints. He cooks. What else can he do?"

"Hair," Susan answered, more to herself.

"What?"

"Economics. He's an economics professor. Where's my coffee?"

"Coming right up."

"Good."

Susan sat down at her desk, her brain humming with thoughts. She stole a last glance down at the message from Mark, rereading it with a wave of pleasure, tucking it into her top drawer to save, then looking up at the painting he had given her.

Jimenez, she reminded herself, *think Jimenez, think strike, think of all these calls you have to return, think of how you're going to handle your unenviable position of possessing evidence that your client may be in violation of the law.*

A mug of steamy black coffee was placed in front of Susan. "Who do you want me to get on the phone for you first?"

"What time is my first appointment?"

"You've got a ten-thirty here with a prospective client. And I have you blocked out from noon on to be over at the surfboard plant. Maybe you should return Jack Wells' call first. He said it was important."

"Get Kreegle for me first. I need to talk to him. Never mind, I'll just walk down there," Susan decided on second thought, getting out of her chair again and heading down the hall toward the senior partner's large corner office at the end of the corridor.

She knew what Kreegle was going to say. The same thing he had said yesterday—to turn her head, that it was the union's job to look after the workers, not hers. But she simply couldn't look the other way. She might attempt to do so, but it was an ability she knew she didn't possess. One pathetic pleading call from Jimenez or his wife and she would be right back where she was now, feeling compelled to investigate the situation, to right what she knew in her gut was clearly wrong. Her background and all her true sympathies, were with the workers. They weighed too heavily on her conscience for her to turn the other cheek.

"Susan, I don't understand you." Kreegle responded as predicted. "You've been working around the clock for us since you started. You're certain to set a record for speed on associates made partners. We think your work is outstanding. Don't let yourself get distracted." Kreegle gave her a fatherly smile. But she could see he thought she was being a pain in the ass.

"Distracted?" What kind of response was that?

"You've got a lot of promise. You're smart. You're pretty. You're a hard worker. You've got the potential to be working on some of the biggest labor cases in this country. Don't blow it over trivialities. Over small-potato inequities."

"You misunderstand my ambition, sir," Susan replied hotly, sick of this.

"How's that?" Kreegle made an unsuccessful stab at masking his surprise.

"Not all ambition is aimed at money and prominence," she replied bitingly, looking around at his expensive wood paneling, the antique furniture, the blue-chip art on the walls, the massive photo-on-canvas portrait of his family in a field of grass, leaning against Kreegle's Bentley. "Some ambition is still aimed at integrity and excellence first."

"Don't give me this holier-than-thou crap, Susan," Kreegle charged, rising, whipping off his glasses and tossing them angrily down onto his desk. "I marched in peace lines, did my share of drugs, and swore off materialism too. If you want to get stuck in the time warp of the sixties, enmeshed in causes that only take you around in circles, be my guest. Go ahead and blow your whole career on health insurance for a bunch of poor workers you don't even know. But don't plan on doing it here."

Susan couldn't believe he had hit upon the same remark as Paige. *Getting health insurance for a bunch of poor workers who she didn't even know.* Maybe she was wrong. Maybe she was being incredibly naive. For all she knew, *she* was set up. These were the rabble rousers who had been causing trouble all along. Why was she just accepting their suspicions at face value?

Because they went along with her own, that's why.

"What kind of evidence do you have, Susan? Huh? Some pissed-off striker's assumptions? Grow up!" Kreegle snapped, sitting back down in his chair, his anger fading. Susan continued to stand rooted, but wilting. "Listen, I like you. Otherwise I'd have sent you packing for this kind of indiscretion. You don't owe those strikers anything. The union owes them. Let them carry their own responsibilities. Be smart about this and don't return Jimenez's phone calls. Just go on with your work as though nothing ever happened."

"They're going to retaliate if they're fired," Susan pointed out softly.

Kreegle threw up his arms. "If they retaliate, they retaliate. Jack Wells is a big boy. If he made some kind of deal axing these guys out of their jobs, he didn't expect to get off scot-free. Just do your job and mind your own business."

Susan took in the better part of downtown Los Angeles through Kreegle's expanse of window, weighing her position, sizing up her chances if she were to go against the firm and go to the mat for Jimenez and his group.

Her prospects for battle were depressing. The obvious alternative was for her to go to the National Labor Relations Board, but she would have to have enough of a case to prove that this was a conspiracy to violate the workers' rights, that the union did not represent the workers fairly, and that part of the conspiracy was the employer. All the laws were against her and she knew it would be almost impossible to prove. Not to mention that she could wind up disbarred. She didn't know anyone who had ever prevailed in any similar case. Another route would be going to the Teamsters for a Democratic Union, which was an organization within the Teamsters attempting to right what they saw as wrong. But from all she had heard, they were just as rough a group as the Teamsters' leaders themselves.

Even if Jack were to admit the truth to her, he would be protected by attorney-client privilege, so she was powerless there as well.

"I'm taking a group of people to L'Orangerie tonight for dinner. Would you like to come? One of Liz's friends is recently divorced and a real terrific guy." Susan knew it was Kreegle's way of bridging and burying this whole episode. He knew he had her. Or at least he thought he had her, anyway.

Susan wasn't sure where she stood. "Thanks. That's really nice, but I've got a date," she replied pleasantly. As she said it she couldn't help but smile in spite of everything else. The date was with *Mark*. A real, honest-to-goodness date and she couldn't wait.

Kreegle mistook the smile as a surrender, but she didn't think it mattered one way or the other. "Yeah? Who's the lucky guy?" He swept his hand unconsciously over his head, smoothing what little hair was left to smooth. His grin was cute and warm.

She smiled again, relaxing a little. "A friend," she replied shyly.

"A rain check then?" He wagged his finger at her waiting to elicit a yes. "Soon?"

"Sure," she replied, frustrated, wishing they could discuss the strike situation as colleagues, not as employer-employee, where his only concern was simply not to alienate their client. "Listen, uh, I've got an appointment in my office with a prospective client," she said, awkwardly dismissing herself, looking down at her watch.

"Raymond West?" Kreegle asked.

"Yes," Susan replied, incredulous that Kreegle managed to know everything that was going on at the firm. It meant always watching her step.

Jack called just as she returned to her office, before her client got there.

She picked up the receiver nervously, wondering if he knew

that she knew about the set-up, if he had heard, somehow, that she had met with the strikers last night, unsure what to say to him if he confronted her.

"There's been a bomb threat. We've all been evacuated," he stated.

This was the last thing she expected to hear. She was too stunned to even reply.

"We had to shut down the plant and get everyone out of there."

"My God! When? What happened? Where are you calling from?" Susan reached for her coffee cup, but it was empty. Then, worried, she searched through her messages looking for the ones from Jimenez to read them more carefully. Obviously he had interpreted her not returning his phone calls to mean that she wasn't going to help. She couldn't really blame him. He had reason to be wary.

"We're at my apartment. I've got a bunch of guys over here discussing how we're going to handle this. We're sure it was the group of picketers we axed yesterday."

Susan swallowed deeply. "What's the union's reaction?"

"They're trying to find them, talk some sense into them. They think the bomb threat is bogus. But we don't want this going any further—"

"How many people did you let go?"

"Ten, I think—"

"All of Jimenez's group?"

"Damn right."

"Why don't you just give them their jobs back?" Susan asked flatly, sorry as soon as she had said it.

"I'm not going to give those bastards their jobs back. Are you crazy? We're finally going to reach a resolution without them there holding up the works, and you know it."

She was shaking but she couldn't stop herself from going on. She kept seeing Carmen Jimenez's face, her swollen belly, those hands. It was a stupid thing for them to have done, but her heart bled for them. Her father would have never agreed to those tactics, but her father was meek. She could imagine plenty of the guys she had known growing up doing exactly this. "Then give them some settlement so they won't be flat broke while they're looking for new jobs. Give them something. Jack, these guys have been backed up against a wall. You haven't given them any choice."

"Choice?"

"Yes, choice."

"What are you talking about? If I'm not happy with someone's work, all of a sudden I can't *can* 'em?"

"This had nothing to do with their work, and you know it."

"Watch it, Susan."

"I represent *you* . . . I *know*. But dammit, why can't I be honest with anyone? What if *you* had a whole house full of little kids and couldn't support them, and you were being shafted at work?"

"C'mon Susan. Give me a break here—"

"What if *your* wife were carrying your baby and your baby's life was being threatened by unhealthful working conditions?"

"That's all environmental bullshit. They haven't proven anything. Those statistics are incomplete, they're—"

"Yeah, but what if those studies do bear out? The kid gets cancer and you say, Oops, sorry. The statistics didn't really *sound* so bad—"

"They've got too many damn kids, anyway," Jack joked.

Susan tried to contain her temper. "What if *you* were being fired unfairly and didn't have a dime to put food in your family's mouths?"

"Why don't they save their damn money? Why don't they stop having so many kids if they can't afford them?"

"That's none of your business—"

"And *this* is none of your business. You're out of line, counselor—"

"We're all out of line at this point. But I'm telling you, as your lawyer, that you're better off settling with them. If you don't, you're going to have a war on your hands and it'll only cost you *more* time and money."

Susan could hear some commotion coming from Jack's end of the line, a few guys talking to him at once.

He lowered his voice when he came back on the line. It was his more personal voice. The voice he used every time she thought they were getting close to breaking the barrier of their strictly-business relationship.

"Susan, knock it off," he said quietly, like one would to a good friend. "I know how you feel personally about all this, but stick it in the back somewhere. We can argue philosophy later. But right now I, *me,* your client, have a crisis on my hands. Are you going to help me or aren't you? I need a lawyer. I already have a conscience."

Susan wondered if he really did. "Just tell me this, Jack, and then I'll lay off. If you were Jimenez, what would you do? Would you just stand by and take it? Credible grievances and all?"

"I guess I really do need a new lawyer," Jack replied, sighing. "I didn't want to have to do this but *you're* pushing *me* against the wall."

"Thanks, Wells. You just answered my question. You *wouldn't* sit back and take it. Go right ahead and can me, too. Why not, you're on a roll."

They both slammed down the phone at the same time. Susan's hand flew up to her mouth. She couldn't believe what she had just done, what she had just said. What had gotten into her? How could she speak to her client that way? she chastised herself, wondering if she should grab up the phone and call Jack back to apologize, trying to imagine what he would even say to her.

She guessed she was trying to appeal to a different side of him, the compassionate side that she was sure existed buried somewhere deep inside the armor he wore on the outside. Perpetual jerk that she was, she still believed that to be true. In the midst of her anxiety she was half expecting the telephone to ring and for it to be Jack calling back, apologizing. She couldn't comprehend that she couldn't—if she really applied herself or pressed the right buttons—get through to him.

Kreegle was passing by Susan's office and he paused to stand in the door. "You all right?" he asked, sounding concerned.

She looked up at him, certain that she didn't look all right at all, sure that most of the blood had drained from her face and that she had turned a ghastly white. "Fine. Thanks," she said, also sure that he was going to receive a scathing telephone call from Jack any minute and that when he did all hell would break loose.

"Sure you're okay?"

"Mmmm. Thanks."

He put his hands in the pockets of his trousers and rocked back and forth on his heels. "Raymond West still not here? I thought I'd stop by and say hello."

"No. Uh—"

Susan's secretary, Linda, appeared in the doorway. Kreegle let her pass. "Mr. West called. He said he'll be another fifteen minutes. He got held up."

"Thanks," Susan said, turning back to Kreegle, glad for the answer so that she didn't appear uninterested.

The phone rang again and, since her secretary was standing there and it was easier for Susan to catch it herself, she picked up the receiver.

"Should we add you to the list of fired casualties yet?" Mark's voice came in soothingly over the line. Her eyes must have lit up because Kreegle gave her a look, then mouthed: "the date?"

She smiled mysteriously as he turned to leave, then she looked at Linda as though for commiseration, since she knew Linda would have heard at least a portion of her conversation with Jack. The door was open and she hadn't been speaking softly.

"I'm in the about-to-be-fired category. And inching precariously close," she said to Mark.

"With your Wells character? Or the firm?"

"I really got into it. With both."

"Don't worry about it. If you get the ax, I'll take care of you," Mark joked sweetly. "I offered my services in the beginning and I have every intention of seeing it all the way through to the end with you."

"Promise?"

"I'm not sure I can take care of you in the manner to which you've become accustomed," he continued joking. "But you won't go hungry and I'll make you laugh a lot."

"Sounds wonderful. Now I'm really going to be aggressive about this thing, in the hopes of getting fired as soon as possible."

"Dinner at eight?"

"Unless they fire me earlier."

"Do you miss me?"

She had to laugh. She had been missing him for months.

Paige's day had been manic.

First the blow of seeing Susan and Mark together, looking at one another in that ridiculous moon-glow way, as though they were on the brink of discovering something that every idiot falling in love hadn't already discovered a thousand times over.

Didn't they know the condition is called "*falling* in love" for a reason?

The verb preceding the noun is a dead give away, an obvious reference to the casualty. When you *fall* you get hurt.

Fall.

Drop.

Ouch.

That rude awakening at the end of the fall, to which people still in motion believe themselves impervious.

The high, heady sensation merely comes from being off-balance.

Paige wasn't off-balance. She was just nervous. Nervous about beating out all the fantasies she had planted in Nicky's head about how memorable she was going to be in bed.

And she was run ragged from rushing from one place to the next.

This morning she had taught two back-to-back private sessions at clients' homes, pulling in some extra cash to pay for the present she was going to buy for Nicky.

Then one of the instructors had called in sick at Sports Club/ LA, so she had had to teach a double shift there, pushing well past her endurance, having to keep up with her bionic students. She had been so fatigued after the last class that during the cooldown, she had thought she was going to faint. Then overcome with nausea she had finally had to run into the ladies' room to throw up.

After that, she had squeezed in two more privates, then gone driving around the city collecting extravagant foodstuffs for the surprise picnic she was planning on setting up in Nicky's bed this evening, all of which had her back at home considerably later than planned.

Fortunately, she had gotten bathing and getting ready for him down to a forty-five-minute science.

Nicky's daughter, Marni, was pulling out of the driveway as Paige pulled in and they waved to one another. She had gotten her hair cut kind of punk, and Paige was surprised to see her looking so hip. She figured the change had come about on account of the rock promoter Nicky kept complaining about. Marni had met him at an after-concert party in the StarDome's green room and Paige knew Nicky was having the guy checked out, looking for skeletons in the closet, maybe even hoping for them. His persistence made her wonder if he weren't the type of father who found something critically wrong with all his daughter's suitors. The old Freudian complex squashing his perspective.

Although it was only twilight, the lights of the twenty-two room mansion were already glowing as Paige got out of her car and approached the entrance. She drew a quick breath before ringing the bell this time, her mind busy planning. What if he was already downstairs and ready to leave? What then? What was she going to say when he asked what was in her shopping bags?

Inside one was the present she had bought for him, a gorgeous Bijan robe, which she had really bought for herself to wear because the color of his was all wrong for her and she didn't like the cut. Inside the other shopping bag was the dinner that was going to replace their dinner at Chasens.

The door was answered by Sammy, Nicky's Filipino houseman. "Hi, Miss Williams. You look great!"

She had on a clingy white knit dinner dress, which she had thought was appropriate for the occasion, sexy but sophisticated, perfect for the girl he would want to whisk off to bed, still in good taste for a wife.

"Thanks. He upstairs?" she asked, hoping he were to simplify the logistics of her seduction.

"Yes. I'll let him know you're here," Sammy said, about to move to do so when Paige put her hand on his arm.

"It's okay," she said, stopping him, then heading toward the stairs on her own and giving him a little wink.

Nicky was just putting on his tie in front of a mirror over his dresser when she tapped lightly on his open door and walked into his room, slyly leaning back against the door to close it behind her. Naturally there was a sporting event on TV.

"Hi. Don't you look ravishing!" he exclaimed, turning to appraise her with a wicked leer. He looked exceptionally dapper in a dark suit and tie. If they had kids together, Paige thought they would be great-looking, tall, nicely built. If they had a girl, and she had his nose instead of Paige's she might need a little plastic surgery, but the glint in his eyes, if she got that, would make her a winner.

She walked over to help him with his tie, even though she had no intention of letting him leave to go anywhere. Their dinner date at Chasens with his friends was about to be intercepted.

While she measured and looped the dotted Italian silk at his throat, he circled his fingertips around her nipples, making them grow hard so that they stood out through her dress.

Leaving one hand on her breast, he dropped his other hand down around to her behind, murmuring over the perfection of the shape. She wasn't wearing any panties and when he realized that, he lifted up the skirt of her dress and cupped the bareness of her ass with a look of eager surprise.

"God, how am I ever going to concentrate at dinner," he complained, running his hands down the sides of her thighs, pressing his swollen excitement against her. "You're such a tease. One of these days I'm going to just jump you, you little bitch," he threatened huskily.

Paige perfected the knot on his tie, then moved in closer to trace her tongue along his large athlete's neck, inhaling the familiar scent of the soap from his shower, tasting the freshness. "Promises, promises."

"Oh, yeah?"

"Yeah."

"How are *you* going to concentrate?" he asked bringing his hands around to where her panties would ordinarily have been, reacting to the wetness there.

She enveloped his hard-on with both of her hands and massaged lightly, moving down to encompass his balls and then up slowly again along his shaft, applying more pressure while biting gently at the tip of his earlobe.

"You make me so crazy. I can't even talk to you on the phone without getting a stiff prick."

Her thighs drew in tight around his hands as they played there, inducing a pleasurable weakness that she hadn't let herself feel with him before. At last she felt free to let go, released, because tonight there would be no need for restraint.

"Oh, shit. I can't go like this, Paige," he groaned, starting to unbuckle his pants and tug at the zipper. "I want to feel your sassy little mouth around me. C'mon baby, suck me off before we go."

Paige stepped back and laughed, enjoying the anguish on his face, unzipping the back of her dress and letting it drop to the floor. "I'll do better than that," she offered, with a wily smirk, standing in only a pair of high-heeled lizard pumps, her long legs accentuated as she stepped out of the puddle of fabric and sauntered over toward his ornate bed. She took her time while undoing the bed covers, then climbed up and stretched out on her side to bid him to come closer. The mirror over his bed demonstrated that the effect was a good one.

But so did the expression on his face, which she thought was priceless, along with the massive bulge distorting the line of his custom-tailored pants.

"We're supposed to be meeting everyone at Chasens in fifteen minutes—" he began, torn, having to clear his throat.

She laughed and rolled over onto her back, sensuously cupping one of her breasts, stroking the ripe mound of flesh there, then looking up into the mirror as she continued drawing her fingers luxuriously down her belly. "Where would you *really* rather be in fifteen minutes? Eating chili at Chasens, or here in bed with me."

An executive decision. While shedding his clothes, Nicky picked up the phone by the side of the bed and began dialing.

By the time he finished getting his party on the line and giving them the message that he wouldn't be able to make it, she had his pants down and her tongue maneuvering up the inside of his thighs, moving stealthily up toward the engorged target of his private parts. As he was about to say good-bye she laughed again, savoring her power, *relieved* because she felt confident again. Looking up playfully into his adoring eyes, she snatched the phone out of his hands and dropped it down onto its cradle.

"I'm going to fuck your brains out, Nicky Loomis," she warned, boldly snapping off the damn remote control of his TV set as they slid together to the center of the bed, the rest of his clothes discarded in all directions. "Mr. Sports King," she chided lovingly, nibbling at his love handles, then kissing his cock. "I'm going to make you *lose consciousness.*"

"You little bitch. You still trying to rope me down the aisle?" he asked, closing his eyes and exclaiming in pleasure as she enveloped his enormous erection entirely in her mouth, drawing in cool breath to react against the heat, and sucking at the same time.

"Did you think I was kidding?" she asked, pausing for a moment to read his eyes, which were glazed with longing.

He laughed and shook his head. "No—" But before he could comment further he lost his train of thought and let out a loud, long moan instead that seemed to travel all the way up his barrel of a chest and then out his mouth.

Paige had never been very musical, but when she was making love, she felt musical. He was the musical instrument she had never before played, and her natural rhythm from dance took over until they were both carried away in a song in their minds.

She was playing him her way, making him lose consciousness, as she had said. She was feeling close to losing it right along with him, seduced by the silkiness of his skin, his body hair which she found even softer than silk so that she couldn't stop running her fingers through its dense growth.

Intent on maintaining control, she drew herself up over him so that she was on top, kicking away the sheets and straddling him. His thick arms she pinned back behind his head so that she could watch the intensity of expression on his face.

His eyes were squeezed closed, tense, his mouth open, almost wincing, wanting, reaching, his thin lips nearly disappearing in the grimace as she rode him, instinctively attuned to his pace.

As she arched back and felt him thrusting still deeper inside of her, she caught his face again in the mirror overhead. It was filled with something primeval, something so raw and passionate that a massive thrill shimmied down her spine. She could see that he was about to explode, that he was riding the crest of his nearing climax as long as he could, while she continued taking him higher and higher, wanting to shatter all known limits. They were both drenched in hot sweat, hers mingling with his. She could see that he was going to come any second and she couldn't take her eyes off him. She was on an odyssey of total control, feeling riveted by the sense of power.

His face had gone from completely relaxed to this amazing, almost savage ruthlessness giving way to a total abandon, a take-over of the senses.

It all felt so incredibly private and intimate, a rare, otherwise forbidden, glance into his very being.

She felt as though she were glimpsing a secret part of him that you had to screw him in order to know, only she wanted to stay linked into that view for a longer fragment of time, to draw it out, maybe forever.

When he started to come, she was actually disappointed because their moment was going to be over. She found herself actually fighting back tears, when she *never* cried. *Never!* She believed fiercely that crying only made people more vulnerable. Paige hadn't cried since the day her mother died.

But then the power of his orgasm ripped through her, sweeping her into a climax of like force toward the last wave of his, creating an overlapping of private sounds and feelings so intense it made her head spin.

"Oh, God, Paige! I can't even believe what you do to me!" he cried, holding her close afterward, maintaining himself inside her as he turned them both over so that now he was on top, his cheek pressed against hers, until his spent erection slipped out anyway, followed by a warm sensation that felt sweetly significant.

It was the quiet after the storm and Paige was taken aback because he didn't roll impatiently off her immediately afterward, as she had anticipated. Instead he arranged one of the soft, down-filled pillows beneath her head.

His unexpected tenderness had her overwhelmed. *God, could I really have it all?* she wondered, scared to hope, fighting tears again because there was this broken but pasted-back-together part of her that didn't believe she could.

Money, great sex, *and* tenderness, she thought to herself with her usual edge, knowing that her anxiety would be crushing while she waited for the fall.

The inevitable drop.

The ouch.

Chapter 27

Fans were already pouring into the StarDome, keyed up in anticipation of this evening's game that had all basketball aficionados in suspense. A rookie from Arizona State with "can't miss" written all over him was playing with the L.A. Stars and everyone was abuzz with his pro debut.

Nicky and Paige climbed out of the backseat of his white stretch limousine and hustled toward the entrance, besieged by autograph hounds. She felt a sense of importance, being ushered through the boisterous crowd by the tall, bawdy sports mogul, his arm wrapped proprietarily around her waist, both of them pausing every few seconds so he could dash off a signature while making their way toward the awesome round structure he had erected.

When they reached the entrance they were met by guards who then shielded them the rest of the way, seeing to it that they were able to get into the elevator alone.

After a quick interview spot for a local television station, where he delivered the obligatory two-sentence answer to the question he had been asked twenty times in the last two weeks. "What do you think the prospects for your team are now, with the addition of the rookie, Roberts?" Nicky and Paige then joined Nicky's guests in the private dining room of his StarDome Club, where he routinely hosted a large horseshoe-shaped table filled with friends and acquaintances, many of them celebrities.

Tonight she knew Joe Namath was going to be there with his little boy. Jimmy Connors and his son. O.J. Simpson. Astronaut Scott Carpenter was supposed to be there. Mayor Tom Bradley. Kirk Douglas. His son Michael Douglas. And crazy-as-a-loon Jack Nicholson.

The established protocol of Nicky's pre-show entertaining was for the guests to order and eat whenever they got there. Usually steak and lobsters. It was all very casual. Nicky was generally one of the last to arrive.

Threading their way through the narrow aisle, Paige followed Nicky to the place always reserved for him at the head table, where she could see tonight she would also be sitting next to his son, Tip Loomis.

On their way to their seats she noticed Nicky nodding to an attractive redhead at the other side of the table, who was laughing with a group of friends. "She's going to be the new Revlon girl," he explained quietly to Paige, who had followed his glance. "Her fiancé, the guy with the leather jacket, claims to be Jimi Hendrix's illegitimate son or something. And that young lady with them is about to be the hottest new sex symbol since Raquel Welch. I used to date her."

Date being synonymous with *screw,* Paige thought, giving him a frosty smile as she sat down in the chair he had pulled out for her, taking in the dozens of young pretty women with whom she knew she would always have to contend if she did manage to permanently snare Nicky.

"Who, *her,* or Raquel?" she remarked.

He smiled so that she could have killed him. "Both."

It served her right for asking. She had been set up for that one. *Of course both.*

A waiter appeared, ready to take their order.

"I know, you're *starving,*" he kidded Paige, because it was her usual greeting to him. She was perpetually starved.

She shook her head no and ordered only a bowl of soup instead of her usual lobster. The word alone triggered a fishy odor in her brain that made her feel instantly sick to her stomach, a feeling she had been experiencing all too often lately.

"*Not* starving? You feeling okay?" The waiter looked at her askance, his pencil still poised over his small pad of paper.

"I feel fine. Just not *ravenous* tonight," she replied, glad that Nicky had turned the other way and had all his attention focused on a joke one of Hollywood's old-time comedians was telling.

She was beginning to have this low, gnawing anxiety about the queasiness that never seemed to go away, about the aching fullness in her breasts. It wasn't so much that she had missed a period and was now late for this one that had her wary, since her menstrual cycle had rarely been reliable. But it was the constant nausea.

"What about you, Mr. Loomis? New York rare—?"

The comedian had just finished delivering the punch line of his joke and had everyone seated around him laughing loudly. Nicky, naturally laughing the most raucously of them all, turned around briefly to confirm his dinner order, then turned back to the guys to deliver his own joke.

When a four-letter word appeared in the first sentence of the joke, one of Nicky's guests kiddingly protected his son's ears with his hands, as though shielding him from his host's profanities.

"I've heard the word *fuck* before," his kid argued, loudly draining the balance of his Shirley Temple drink while pushing away his father's hands.

"Yeah?" someone asked him. "What does it mean?"

"I forgot," he said, his small cheeks filling with color.

"But you *did* know?"

He shrugged shyly and went back to draining his already empty glass.

Everyone laughed as his father also shrugged and Nicky went on with his joke.

"So how's business?" Paige asked, turning toward Nicky's thirty-two-year-old son. He was extremely good-looking, with his long hair drawn back into a ponytail, but moody as hell. "Doing well. Thanks," he replied vaguely.

The *business* she was referring to was a small computer business, which his father had happily funded after Tip had returned to Los Angeles, lost, floundering, and stripped of his inheritance.

Tip Loomis had been one of the thousands of lost souls seduced and brainwashed by the Rajneesh up in Oregon where, in order to be members of the secret cult, they had to surrender all their earthly belongings to him.

It was a great racket the leader had going for himself, inculcating his wishes into the heads of these groping kids. They all wound up penniless and trusting, supposedly happier for their lack of material baggage, while the great and pure Rajneesh greedily stockpiled his own.

Until one day, out of the blue, the infamous leader suddenly ceased talking.

His sea of followers, lost without their voice—*his* voice, would come out daily and just sit, waiting for him to begin to speak again or do something. Finally, to the great relief of the parents who had lost their kids to the cult, there was nothing left to do but give up and return home.

The great charismatic Rajneesh had apparently done his last bit of prophecy. Maybe he had screwed too many women in too short a timespan and his brain had short-circuited.

Nicky had been so grateful to have his son back and doing something halfway normal that he had completely backed Tip's computer venture and updated all the StarDome's systems through his new company. Nicky said Tip was bright, just weird.

Paige half wondered if he weren't dealing drugs as well as dealing Apples. She had never seen him when he didn't look like he was on something.

God, how hard it had to be, raising kids, she thought, pressing the palm of her hand to her own flat belly.

Whose kid would it even be if she *were* pregnant, she worried, growing even more squeamish at the thought. Would it have curly blond hair, dimples, and intense blue eyes? Or would it be big and burly, with small, impish brown eyes like Nicky?

She might have wanted to *pretend* it was Nicky's, but the timing, she knew, had to be off by at least a month.

Nauseated by the potential glut of complications and tired of calculating, she directed her attention back to Tip, who hadn't noticed that he'd lost her attention in the first place.

"Do you do much advertising for your company?" she asked him, hoping to draw him out.

She caught Nicky looking over at her as though he were pleased that she and Tip were talking to each other. She slipped Nicky a quick private look, thinking no wonder he was such a magnet for his friends and the press. It wasn't just his money and his position because even in this power-stacked group he managed to stand out. He had a special aura about him. The way he looked so relaxed, so in control, so powerful, and yet still so exuberant.

But could she put up with his stadium-sized ego or the grabby groupies always lurking around?

"We do some advertising," Tip answered.

"Like where?"

He took several stabs at his salad, collecting as many leaves of lettuce onto his fork as possible, while appearing to consider her question. "Oh, the usual."

He wasn't the easiest dinner partner she had ever had. "Newspapers? TV?"

He looked at her as if she were an idiot. "TV's way too expensive. You don't advertise for a store like ours on TV."

So she'd asked a dumb question. "You should have your dad flash it on the electronic board out in the stadium. Mass exposure for free."

Giving her no reaction whatsoever, Tip went back to his salad and Paige felt relieved when the waiter finally brought her soup to the table.

Not that she could manage to eat it. She couldn't even stand the smell of it.

She felt as if she were going to throw up, between the mingling of food odors wafting her way and her futile attempt at connecting with Nicky's moody son.

She had had much better luck with Marni. Marni at least was from this planet.

* * *

After a triumphant basketball game a group of them went out to celebrate at one of the new underground clubs downtown, pumped up from the exciting finale of the game where, with only two minutes left to go, the L.A. Stars had retrieved the lead and snatched victory from the jaws of defeat.

The club was smoky and packed. Paige, barely able to stand still, with the music blasting inside, held on tightly to Nicky's hand as they were admitted in front of the mile-long line, their coterie in tow. Dancing never failed to recharge her battery. She couldn't wait to get out there onto the dance floor and lose herself in the beat. Her nausea had finally vanished, quelled by bread and later by popcorn, and she felt relieved, spirited even.

The music shocking the sound waves inside the tight, frenetic quarters was more New Wave than disco, and she worried Nicky would find it loud and grating. Be too old for it.

She was surprised when he instead seized her hand and swung her out onto the dance floor, moving so that he was a match for any of the twenty-year-olds.

Everyone was staring at them, excited by the celebrities who were in the mood to take the club by storm.

The sea of young, hip kids parted to make room for them on the dance floor.

Nicky must have known at least half a dozen of the girls there, or at least they knew him. They materialized in a dependable stream, coming up to kiss him hello—to flirt with the famous party laureate.

It was irritating, but Paige could take it. These blossoming females *looked* like women, until they opened their mouths and were revealed as the innocuous teenagers they were.

Dancing and drinking went on until about two in the morning, when they all piled back into Nicky's limousine and were driven home.

After the chauffeur had dropped off the last of their bunch and returned to Nicky's house, Paige started to climb out of the car in front of Nicky, but he held her back. There was something serious about the way he maintained his grip on her arm and kept looking at her.

"What?" she asked with a giddy, self-conscious chuckle.

"You're gorgeous. You take my breath away."

She leaned in and gave him a tender, lingering kiss on the lips. "Honestly. And you were great tonight."

She didn't really know what he meant, but she said thanks anyway.

"With my friends, my kid—" he trailed off, his long legs stretched out over the jump seat in front of him. He hadn't said more than a couple of words to her after they had dropped off the last of their group and she looked at him curiously, wondering what was on his mind.

She smiled, trying to look understanding, hoping to encourage him to go on. The driver was standing a few feet off from the car, smoking a cigarette and looking out at the bushes.

"He's a tough cookie, that kid of mine."

That kid was only a year or so older than Paige, and it felt odd to hear Nicky keep referring to him that way.

"He's all right," she replied, thinking it couldn't have been easy growing up as *Nicky Loomis's son.* Failure seemed inherent in the typical rich-kid syndrome. Tip, Richard Bennetton. There was too much expected of them.

And most likely too much competition while they plodded after their goals.

Perhaps it was easier for a daughter, she considered—unless the mother was the superstar.

Paige wondered how she would have turned out, raised in the shadow of a spotlight. Some kids were strong enough to jump into the spotlight themselves. Some kids were strong enough to not have it affect them, period.

Most kids, it seemed, got squashed.

Up in his bedroom, she waited stretched across his bed and drinking champagne, wearing only a skimpy jade satin bra and panties she had bought to bring out her eyes, and a pair of bronze high-heeled pumps. She was busy singing along with an old Frank Sinatra album she had put on the stereo, drinking in the rich sound of his voice while trying to mimic that unique Sinatra phrasing.

"Close your eyes, gorgeous," Nicky ordered her from outside of the room.

"What?" she asked, turning to look for him.

"I said close your eyes."

"Why?" she asked, though obliging without waiting for an answer.

"You're always playing games. This is *my* game. Now shut your gorgeous mouth . . ."

It felt weird, eerie, lying there in the darkness, just waiting and having to wonder what was going on.

The shade of darkness seemed to deepen, as though he had turned out the lights.

She kept thinking she felt him nearing the bed, but then nothing would happen. There were several seconds of silence between songs on the stereo, and the absence of sound felt amplified. She started to giggle out of nervousness, excitement, and anticipation, dubious as to what he had in store for her. She kept wanting to ask him questions, but she was afraid that he would get mad, that she would break the mood.

Finally she felt one side of the bed begin to sink beneath his weight, and she knew he was there beside her. She kept waiting for him to touch her or to say something. What kind of charade was this? Why all the mystery? She couldn't help but feel a tinge of apprehension, wondering if he were going to do something kinky or depraved.

Then, before she knew it, she was reacting to something light and ticklish being drawn up between her legs, over her panties, her belly, circling her breasts, trailing up the line of her neck, then passing over her lips to pause beneath her nose.

It was silky and fragrant. There were different sections to it.

It was a rose.

She smiled at the recognition, and it was suddenly whisked away, as though she had guessed right and he was moving on to part two of the quiz.

Next came something plump and cold. Heavier.

It was taken up the same path, only he rocked it back and forth.

It was a ball of some sort, only not completely round. Firm and *so* cool on her skin. When it reached her mouth she instinctively licked it but tasted nothing. The smell didn't get her the answer, either.

"Take a bite," he suggested, putting it over her mouth again.

"What is it?"

"Just bite it; bite into it."

She laughed, feeling nervous. "What if I don't like it?"

"Then spit it out."

Warily, she took a bite. The skin was tough. She had to really sink her teeth into it, and as she did the juices came streaming down her face.

It took a moment before she was able to identify it as a *tomato*. The delayed ability to recognize the taste mystified her, and she found herself eager for his next diversion, the next sensory illusion.

Clearly not food this time, she thought, as he dabbed at the mess trickling down her cheeks, down the side of her neck, and onto the pillow. He used something soft and fleecy-feeling.

As he dangled it over her arms, swinging it provocatively across her stomach and thighs, it felt like cashmere or a baby blanket or a diaper.

But what would he be doing with a baby blanket or a diaper?

A rush of queasiness came over her again as she began worrying about the real significance of his game. What if he somehow suspected she was pregnant?

But that was ridiculous.

She was just psyching herself out, and she vowed to go out and buy a home pregnancy test to resolve her anxiety once and for all. The moment the test results read negative she knew her nausea would vanish, and her belated menstrual flow would be released.

This wouldn't be the first time she had sweated over a late period.

"You give up on this one?" he asked.

"You know me better than that."

"Don't open your eyes!"

It was so hard keeping them closed. Letting her mind wander, she concentrated on the sensation, the texture of what she was sure was some kind of fabric, wanting to give it another shot. "A sweater or scarf. Cashmere—"

Whatever it was, it disappeared. The next sensation felt arctic-cold, slender, and fairly lightweight as it tickled her toes, then traveled all the way up from her ankle, around her calf, her thigh, stopping at her crotch where he began drawing small deliberate circles over and around her panties.

It felt like a tool or utensil of some sort.

The icy metal sensation was arousing. Arching up her hips, she decided it was definitely metal but nothing as crude as a tool; it was too sleek-feeling, the surface too smooth.

Maybe it was a watch, she guessed uncertainly, growing more and more relaxed, enjoying herself as he drew the mystery object up along her shoulder, her neck, and then stuck it in her mouth.

Her teeth clinked on the hard metal and, as he let her lick the form of it, its shape gave it away as a *spoon*. She was three for four. Not bad.

Now he's getting dirty, she thought smiling, wanting to open her eyes but not wanting to ruin his game. Down at her ankles again was a small bulbous form that was either his tongue or the tip of his penis. It was slippery and it felt great. And she tried to stop smiling as it slinked up along her hips, velvety and hard, curving in with her waist until she decided it was too large and spherical to be his tongue. "I would know that anywhere," she said, as he held his nasty little treat just beneath her lips.

"You would, huh?"

Reaching with her tongue, she began to lick the tip teasingly, demure flicks meant to alter the balance of power, but then as she went to take a tender, ladylike bite, her teeth sank into something elusive and bland, surprising her as it crumbled in her mouth.

It was a hard-boiled egg, that rat!

"That's what I love about you, Paige. You have such a dirty mind," he said, abandoning the egg to drag something of an entirely different composition across her stomach. "You'll like this one."

It was long and cordlike, with an almost sticky, rubbery texture. In fact, it felt like a utility cord or a whip of some sort, and Paige conjured up images of what he planned on doing with it.

"Just so there isn't any confusion, I don't like pain," she enlightened him, wishing she could open her eyes just a sliver to see.

"No pain, no gain," he teased in a sinister voice, starting to tie her wrists together. "I'll Never Smile Again" began to play nostalgically in the background.

"Help . . . help . . ." she called out in a small voice, the heroine tied to the tracks.

He cackled like the villain, then brought her bound wrists down toward her mouth. She decided it smelled too sweet to be a cord. The scent was more like clay, Play-Doh, or even a candle.

"Edible restraints," he told her, as she bit tentatively into the hard rubbery cord, thinking it didn't taste terribly edible. It tasted like cherry cough drops, but by the shape she realized it was a *licorice whip.*

Funny, she always thought she loved licorice whips! What a surprise to find out how awful they tasted with her eyes closed.

Securing her bound wrists above her head, and barking at her to keep her eyes closed, he brought out his next prop.

Smiling, she thought it felt like a slab of marble, but not quite cold enough. Maybe a candle or a brick of clay.

It was luxuriously smooth and probably additionally stirring because now she had lost not only the control of being able to see, but the command of her hands as well.

She was vulnerable and at his mercy.

The velvety slab of whatever it was had curves; it was oval she discovered, as he began moving it up over her stomach, which shrank involuntarily from the contact.

The fragrance hit her as soon as the object reached her chin. "Hmmm, smells so good," she murmured, sniffing at the fresh scent of *soap* that smelled like Nicky after a shower.

Sticking out her tongue to complete the experiment, she found the taste foreign, a little bitter, but she wanted a few extra moments to take in the pleasure of the clean, memorable herbal scent.

Next came something light and airy. It felt weightless like a silk scarf dancing over her skin and giving her goose bumps as he drew it over her crotch.

It had edges to it, she realized with surprise as he swept it up higher, making her think it could be paper of some sort. Or gauze.

When it reached her throat, she thought it could be a fan, a greeting card, or even a playing card. Except it seemed too flimsy, not stiff or thick enough.

Sniffing hard as he held it beneath her nose, recognizing the distinct odors of paper and ink, the answer came to her.

How could she miss the smell of crisp new *money!*

"Okay, now open your eyes because part of this is in the visuals," Nicky insisted.

It took Paige a moment to have her eyes readjust. Before she knew what was happening, she found herself being showered with bills.

Hundred-dollar bills.

A seemingly endless downpour of that same crisp, new money she had just been feeling all over her body, feeling, smelling, and trying to place.

Nicky was sitting beside her on the bed, wearing the new robe she had given him, his pile of props on the nightstand beside him while he continued to pour from a bucket that must have been overflowing.

He was right, the visuals made it unforgettable.

As sensuous as everything had been that had preceded the bills, this broke the bank on erotic.

They were languishing in the cool bills, which felt fresh off the press, crisp and vivid, throwing them up in the air and watching them float back down again.

It even beat the sacred pleasure of romping in the first fall of leaves, bountiful autumn piles that in her childhood had felt profoundly sensual.

"Hmmm. Do I get to keep all this?" Paige joked, biting into the licorice whips securing her wrists, literally eating her way to freedom, then laughing as she got up onto her knees to study the effect in the mirror above them, playfully stuffing her bra with the bills.

"Not for that," he said, releasing a cascade of cash as he unhooked her bra and tossed it across the room. "They're perfect without embellishment. Firm and softer than satin," he pronounced, closing his eyes as he continued caressing them, "round and just the right size. I know," he teased, as though playing his game again, only this time playing the subject's role. "They're tits —nice, big, American breasts!"

"You're good at this," Paige teased him, swiping the sash from his robe and then tying it over his eyes while she crawled on top of him inside the robe, enjoying the warm contact of their skin and letting her long mane of hair drag over him. He groped for her panties and pulled them off.

"Did I ever tell you that green makes me sexy?" she confessed, arranging herself on her knees just behind his straining erection, which she took possessively in her hands. She plucked a bill off the bed with her teeth and flicked it lightly across his chest. "Green makes me dangerously sexy. *Beware,*" she emphasized, with the cash gripped between her teeth.

"You didn't *need* to tell me. I saw it in your eyes," he assured her, arching up to maneuver his mouth around one of her breasts, doing pretty well for a guy wearing a blindfold. "There are *sea-green* eyes, *jade-green, apple-green.* You, my love, have *money-green eyes.*"

Smirking, she let the *money-green* bill drop out of her mouth and bent down to gnaw gently at his lower lip. "So after we make love, *inspired* by its glorious *money-green* value, how are we going to spend all this lovely loot?" she demanded, unhurried, as she mounted him, her hands grasping his thick, athletic thighs, her lips pressing against his.

He untied the sash from his eyes and looked up into the mirror, cupping her bottom with his hands and letting out a deep groan of pleasure as she continued riding him.

She rolled her head back and met his gaze in the mirror, feeling her hair dangling low near her waist.

"You sure you can handle it?" he asked, bringing in an element of suspense, flipping them both over so that he was on top riding her, thrusting harder and faster with a mounting speed, his weight heavy and pounding against her.

There were bills sprayed in every direction, beneath her, on top of her, and on both sides as she looked up in the mirror again. Nicky's ass was tight, the muscles constricting and growing more defined as he pushed for satisfaction. "Hmmm. I can handle it," she promised, moving her hips to meet his as he controlled the pace.

"I don't know why I'm doing this," he hedged.

"Because you can't help yourself," she suggested, growing intrigued, both of them growing more turned on by the second.

"God help me for this decision."

"What decision?"

Nicky looked as if he couldn't stand it anymore.

He was going to burst inside her any second. She felt herself climbing with him, being elevated higher and higher until she could barely concentrate, but she couldn't *not* concentrate.

What decision? She was waiting.

"Oh, God, Paige!" he bellowed so loud that she was sure he could be heard throughout the house.

"Tell me," she insisted, stopping to hold up his orgasm, to tease him past his limits. *"Tell me!"*

His face was filled with tension; she was sure he had been thinking about changing his mind, of backing out of what he had admitted he might regret, and she was pressing him.

"I want you to go out and buy yourself the most ostentatious diamond rock you can find," he managed in a choked voice that still held the appropriate tone of irony.

Then the second she started moving again, he started to come. "Marry me, you gorgeous little bitch, you," he finished, grasping her closer still.

Marry me.

Marry me.

Marry me.

Marry me.

It was an implausible echo. The words rolled off her like honey over oil; the sweetness of the message eluding her. She couldn't manage to get it to stick.

"Yes," she rejoiced, exalted, relieved, soaring straight toward heaven, higher than she had ever been before.

Chapter 28

Paige left Nicky's house the next morning in shock.

She had anticipated a prenuptial contract. A man in his position would be foolish, she realized, not to insist on one. But for him to stipulate no children, specifying if she got pregnant and had a baby while she was married to him, she would lose everything—that she found unconscionable.

She had never, by any stretch of the imagination, been obsessed with having babies. But it was an option she didn't like having revoked in writing, especially with the penalty for noncompliance so drastic, she thought, gunning the gas pedal of Dustin Brent's Aston-Martin as she wound down around the canyon, driving away from Nicky's pristine pink mansion, her hands clutching the steering wheel.

"There's just one detail we have to get out of the way" was how he had broached the prenuptial, walking nude across the room to his briefcase, putting on his reading glasses, and bringing the contract back to the bed.

Paige had presumed the very legal-looking document would spell out a series of details she would find less than pleasing. And the very concept of a prenuptial stung. But, on the contrary, as she began to read she had been pleasantly surprised.

"I think you'll find this all more than fair," he had insisted, scrutinizing her as she scanned the pages.

She had been relieved, even excited at first because the terms all seemed favorable; she was about to become a very wealthy woman. If something were to happen to Nicky, if he were to die, she was going to inherit a fortune. Even if they were to wind up divorced, she was going to find herself exceedingly wealthy.

But just as her excitement at the generous terms of the contract began to build inside her, it was dashed when she came to the fateful provision.

If she got pregnant and chose to have the baby, he had provided that she would receive only minimal support for the child, and nothing for herself.

"God! What have you got against kids?" she had asked him, flabbergasted and yet struggling for lightness, sliding over and wrapping her long legs around his waist.

The king-sized bed was still strewn with hundred-dollar bills and they appeared to mock her as she picked one up, reading uncomfortably into Benjamin Franklin's enigmatic expression, as though he were judging her, waiting to hear how she would resolve her dilemma. "What—you're going to abandon me if you knock me up by accident?"

It was hard for her to believe, but the look on Nicky's face had left her cold. Seeming uncomfortable, he replied, "Look, I'm selfish at this point in my life. I just want you. No kids. No job for me to have to compete with. Just *you.*"

His look had softened as he'd drawn her up close beside his chest, stroking her hair. "Look, Paige, I'm wild about you. I don't want to have to *share* you. I want to be able to travel with you. I want the freedom to be able to say *C'mon, let's go to Italy tomorrow.* I want to be able to pick up and do it with a free conscience. Without feeling guilty about having left a baby behind."

As he sat there struggling to make her understand, she wanted to argue, but there was nothing she could think of to say.

And it was so strange to find herself in the position of arguing for something she wasn't even sure she wanted herself. She would be resisting only to keep the option open, and the stipulation out of the contract.

Of course Paige had consented.

He had offered to let her have a lawyer look over the terms, Susan or someone at Susan's law firm. Whoever she wanted. But Paige had merely reached over, taken the pen from his hand, and then signed over her fate on the dotted line.

Waiting for the light to change at the corner of Sunset and Whittier Drive, Paige felt all at once so sick to her stomach she threw the car into Park, clambered out the door, and then rushed over to the curb to throw up.

She stayed there for what seemed like a long time, crouched on her knees on the grass and hugging herself, feeling scared and vulnerable. She couldn't understand her reaction at all.

Sure, *Tori* and *Susan* wouldn't be able to handle the idea of not having any kids, but not *Paige.*

Paige who had never cared that much one way or the other.

She hadn't been the kind of girly-female whose *lifeblood* was to have babies.

She hadn't even been that big on dolls. And when she *had* played with dolls, it was only to live out the fantasy of being a teenager, playing with Barbie or Barbie prototypes in the context of how they related to Ken, their wardrobes, and what kinds of exciting things they were going to do with their lives.

It certainly hadn't been to satisfy any overpowering mothering instincts. She hadn't ever been *into* mothering.

And yet, suddenly, she missed her own mother. She wished she could communicate with her, wherever she was, up in heaven, playing cards, probably, with her girlfriends. Mah-jongg or pan.

She wanted to ask her mother what she should do. She wanted to be *held* by her mother, comforted, reassured, and given strength.

But her mother would only have been baffled. She wouldn't have understood Paige any more than she had understood Paige's father. She had had no patience or compassion for dreamers, for people who felt compelled to reach beyond comfortable— *jeopardizing* comfortable in the wake of their reach.

She was convinced her mother would think she was a terrible person.

She certainly felt like a terrible person.

Marrying for money instead of for love. Not even believing in love anymore.

Why should she? Had her parents stayed in love? No, they had only stayed "in guilt," resenting each other.

Why couldn't she think of anyone who had truly stayed in love, who could give her something to aim for, a reason to go for something bigger or more real or more spiritual.

A reason to tear that prenuptial contract to shreds and throw it in Nicky's famous face.

If she had believed, even a little, in perfect packages, she would never have signed. In fact, she wasn't sure she could live with herself for having done so.

What a betrayal of the baby she suspected to be growing inside her. And what a betrayal of Mark.

Dissolving into tears and crying as she hadn't cried since she was a kid, that profound sobbing that results in breathless, stuttering gasps afterward, she returned to the car and, instead of driving to work, drove straight to Mark's apartment.

Scared, vulnerable, desperately in need of some tender loving care, she sat down in the hallway outside his door, praying he would return home from his classes early.

"Paige?"

She felt like hell, hung over, even, when she heard her name being called out. It was the soothing sound of Mark's familiar voice at last and she woke with a start, looking up to see him walking toward her, his key in one hand, his satchellike briefcase swinging from his other. He looked so refreshing, his curly blond hair forming a wild halo. Those wire-rimmed glasses and their cockeyed fit. As usual, he was in jeans and he was wearing a blue plaid cardigan sweater she had never seen on him before.

Her vision was muddled instantly, tears spilling over as she tried to talk.

Concerned, Mark helped her up from the floor, putting his

arm around her while leading her into his apartment and then sitting her down on the couch.

She'd had no idea that she had been sitting outside his door so long. She was surprised to see that the sky outside was a bright orange. Mark's window looked out onto another apartment complex similar to his, and the balcony directly across the way had laundry hanging from an improvised clothesline. With rent control, the landlords did little to maintain the buildings; they all looked sorely in need of paint.

It had been about a month since Paige had been there, and his apartment seemed smaller, more dingy than romantic, which it had seemed to her before. The fabrics on the antique furniture he had picked up here and there were worn and probably cheap to begin with. From where she was sitting on the couch she could see just about every inch of every room. Nicky was so much of a Goliath; picturing him there was like picturing him in a cabin of a ship, where he would practically fill the whole room, having to move sideways and duck a lot.

"It's okay," he assured her, while she tried to pull herself together to explain.

"Shhh.

"Don't talk yet.

"Just calm down.

"Nothing can be that awful; we'll fix it."

He had sat down beside her and was holding her close. She had her head on his shoulder, and his shirt was becoming soaking wet with her tears.

It felt so comforting to be in his arms again, relaxed, not having to work at being *on,* but feeling free to be herself. He kissed her head and made soft soothing sounds, encouraging her to just let it all out.

"You want something to drink?" he asked, pulling away for a second to look at her.

She nodded.

"Some juice? Milk? 7-Up? Something harder?"

She nodded for something harder. He disappeared and then returned a moment later carrying a bottle of red wine, an opener, and two glasses. She knew it was one of his more cherished bottles, a gift from another professor, and she was touched that he was opening it for her.

Under his arm, he braced a Kleenex box, which he let drop into her lap. "You want something to eat? You hungry?" he asked while removing the wine cork.

Though it was nearly dinnertime and she hadn't eaten since breakfast, she felt another swell of nausea and shook her head no, covering her mouth with a sheaf of Kleenex.

Then after a couple of calming sips of the wine she turned to him, afraid of what his reaction was going to be. Unsure what she *wanted* his reaction to be. Keeping her voice just above a whisper, she said, "Mark, I think I'm pregnant."

She flinched at the abrupt shift in his body language as he got up and walked across the small room, his hands thrust down so low in the pockets of his sweater it looked as if they would tear through. "So, is it mine? Is it *his*? How late are you?" he asked guardedly, without commitment.

"I've been sleeping with Nicky only a little over a month. If I'm pregnant, then I'm at least two months pregnant."

The realization registered quietly in Mark's face. But he seemed too hurt to give in to it.

Trying not to cry again, she took a deep swig of wine, hoping to swallow back the painful lump in her throat.

She watched him guzzling his wine as well, leaning uncomfortably against the bookshelf, at a loss as to what to say to her.

Dammit, she hadn't cried in years and now she couldn't stop herself. The attacks came in waves and her eyes burned as she fought against the determined flow. Mark's suppressed response was killing her and she kept wondering what Nicky's reaction would have been if she had told him the baby had been his, if he would have had second thoughts on the prenuptial and ripped it up.

"Last I heard, there are methods of finding out if you're pregnant or not," he snapped at last. "Why don't you go and take a damn test?"

Paige slammed her wineglass onto the table and glared at him, sorry she had come over in the first place.

He glared right back at her, his tone fierce. "What do you want from me, Paige? I'm just your *toy,* remember? What kind of reaction am I supposed to have? Dammit, you can't play with people the way you do—"

"I know. Forget it. I'm sorry," she interrupted, too conflicted to continue. "Mark, I'm sorry. I'm leaving—"

"The hell you are. I'm entitled to some answers! Like why are you even telling me this? Are you going to have the baby? Or are you going to have an abortion? What—?" he ranted.

"I don't know what I'm going to do. I'm just all mixed up and I don't know anything anymore. Okay! I probably shouldn't even have come over here in the first place. I just needed to—" She had to stop for a second, grappling with another rush of tears.

"You needed to *what*?" he pushed angrily.

"I needed to talk to you. I needed . . . I don't know what I needed." She put her hands over her face because she couldn't bear to look at him as she delivered the next blow, thinking she would give anything if she could only soften it. "Last night Nicky asked me to marry him."

She felt Mark's rage mounting to an even higher pitch. "Congratulations," he hissed, wrenching away her hands and forcing her to face the pain he was in. "What did you tell him? Did you tell him you were pregnant?"

Paige shook her head no.

There was another long pause while Mark tried to sort out his thoughts. She tried to read his expression, but this time it was blank.

"I can't imagine you said no when he asked you to marry him. That would be too much for you to pass up."

Paige's silence confirmed his charge.

"What are you going to do?" he asked, his voice tight, the verdict out of his hands, divided somewhere between her belly and her brain.

She shrugged uncertainly, wondering about her *heart,* feeling worn down. She was sitting on the couch again and she leaned over to fidget with a primitive art book he had on the coffee table. "Why did you have Susan get on the phone and talk to your mother?" she asked impulsively, suddenly crying again.

"What?"

"Susan told me about how she had this cozy conversation with your mother. You never had me talk to your mother—"

"Did you *want* to talk to my mother?"

"Maybe."

"Paige. You wanted us to be something that had nothing to do with real life. Remember?" He charged, exasperated. "Just fun. Play. Make-believe. How was I supposed to explain that to my mother? *Here, Mom, say hello to the girl I'm sleeping with, but who doesn't want to get involved with me because I'm not upwardly mobile enough for her, not rich enough to fit into the bigger scheme of her dreams.*"

Mark went on acting out the whole conversation, elevating the pitch of his voice when he spoke for his mother, which was, Paige realized, really speaking for himself, releasing an anger and resentment he'd had trouble containing toward the end, anyway.

HER: The bigger scheme of her dreams?

HIM: She wants to be rich. Filthy rich. She wants to be so rich she doesn't have to feel or think—just glide—on a kind of gilded automatic cruise control—insulated.

HER: No! What about love? What's the matter with this girl? What's she hiding from?

The truth smarted like a slap in the face.

"She's not hiding from anything," Paige defended herself. "She's tired. She wants to be taken care of." Then after a moment of neither of them saying anything, she asked, "Are you falling in love with Susan?"

"Why? Are you jealous?"

It was more of a revelation for her than a confession. "Yes, I am," she admitted tentatively.

"Paige . . . I don't know," he answered, his anger appearing to drain as he downed what was left of his wine and then sloshed out another full glass for each of them.

"Are you sleeping with her?" she pressed, knowing she shouldn't.

"It's none of your business."

"If I'm carrying your baby, then it is my business."

"You're *acting* like a baby. You don't even know if you *are* pregnant. So what's this all about? Huh? I think you're just jealous. And greedy. And scared about marrying a guy who's old enough to be your father, that's what I think. You're not sure if the money's worth it, after all. It's called buyer's remorse, Paige. Don't worry. It's kind of like a twenty-four-hour bug. It goes away. Does the old bastard even want to have any more kids?"

Paige started to lie and say she didn't really know, but she had always been completely honest with Mark about everything, and she found herself telling him the truth.

His reaction was thoughtful and sympathetic as he listened. "Do you really want to marry him? Can you live with that?"

"I don't know." Paige gulped back more tears, looking at Mark through the compelling veil that continued to obscure her vision. "I'm scared. I don't know what I want. I don't know what I'm doing with my life. *I miss you.* If I *am* pregnant, there's this part of me that wants never to see Nicky again, that wants to say the hell with the money; I'd rather have you and love." The insecurity she heard in her voice sounded so alien to her.

Mark returned to the couch and sat down beside her, enveloping her in his arms again. "You don't have a clue what you want really, do you?"

"I *do* know what I want," she heard herself insisting. "I want you. I *miss* you." And she really did. She missed being in his arms like this, being coddled and indulged. She wished she could just freeze time and let the moment be her eternity. She wished life were less complicated than it was. She wished her needs were less complicated.

"You know what I think?" he asked, holding up the Kleenex box for her to take a fresh one.

Reluctantly she shook her head. "No. What?"

"First of all, I think we should walk to the drugstore and pick up one of those home pregnancy tests and you should take it. And then I think you need to honestly sort out what it is you want from you life, what it is that's going to make you happy."

"Oh, that's a simple prescription," Paige said sarcastically, aware that the latter half could take her a lifetime to figure out.

"C'mon." He kissed her softly on the lips, then looked into her

eyes for a moment before tugging her up to her feet. She wanted
to keep kissing him, but it hadn't been that kind of kiss.

They held hands walking through the narrow streets of the
Venice neighborhood, looking out over the street-lit canal, having
to dodge bikers and roller skaters as they headed over toward
Main Street where the local pharmacy had been in business for
years, before the area had become chic again. There was an ice
cream shop on the way and he bought them each a double scoop
of peppermint.

The pharmacist gave them a knowing sort of look when they
purchased the home pregnancy test. "Good luck," he offered,
seeming to mean it which ever way good luck applied.

Doing this alone, Paige knew she would have been a wreck,
seeing only the bleakest side of everything, agonizing over the
outcome and what to do about it.

Instead, back at the apartment with Mark, opening up a second bottle of wine, none of it seemed so grave.

The alcoholic haze helped to diminish the reality.

While they waited for the results, they sat getting looped from
the wine and crying their hearts out over *An Affair to Remember*
with Cary Grant and Deborah Kerr. Mark had made up a batch
of popcorn the purists' way, in an old iron pot, and the old-
fashioned taste felt comforting.

"Are you a gambler? Do you believe in fate?" she dared him
during a commercial, feeling dizzy from all the wine as she
snaked over to the easy chair he was sitting on and popped a fat
white kernel into his mouth, her anxiety intensifying because in
ten more minutes the results of the pregnancy test would be
ready to read. She couldn't get rid of the image in her mind of a
rabbit lying dead on the bathroom countertop where they had
left the simple test-tube kit that should have seemed more humane.

"Why?" he replied, looking wary.

She knew he felt funny about being alone with her like this.
She had been sensing it all evening, whenever they seemed to get
too close. She wondered what he would have done if Susan
hadn't had a staff meeting that evening at the law firm. "Just *are
you* or *are you not* a gambler?"

"It depends—" he said, his eyes bloodshot from all the wine.

"If you have to think about it, then you're not—"

"Actually, I think I am, but I'm not a stupid gambler. I like to gamble from an informed perspective, and with a chance to analyze the odds—"

"Oh, don't be so intellectual about this. Are you a gambler? Yes or no? No qualifying allowed."

"Okay, yes," he yielded, tensing as she dumped a kernel of popcorn down his shirt and then slipped her hand down inside to retrieve it. One of his buttons came unfastened as she reached in and let her hand linger. "Really, I'm too drunk to follow any of this. Or to be held to any wager. You'd be taking advantage of me in one of my weaker moments."

Weaker moments, my ass. Men are just the weaker sex. Or that's how he would justify his being unfaithful to Susan, anyway. She felt him getting aroused, looking at her the way he used to look at her only a month ago, and yet still fighting it. His jaw was tight and his breathing heavier. It was obvious he was trying to make excuses in case he did get carried away, his libido overpowering his willpower, leading him astray.

So much for Susan's true blue love, she thought, recognizing how men are all alike, resenting his ready erection and that glazed look in his blue eyes.

How many times had she seen that look in Nicky's eyes? She could imagine him in this situation, with another woman endeavoring to put him under her spell as Paige was, and she couldn't picture him doing anything other than giving in.

Mark, misreading her tears, held her close again and as she started to kiss him, he began kissing her back.

She found herself clinging to him, aching to blot out all reality. There was so much riding on the results nearly ready to be read and she didn't want to think about it. She wanted to keep kissing him instead. She wanted to make love with him more than she had ever wanted to make love with anyone in her life.

"So, what's the wager?" he asked huskily, giving in to the sensuality of the moment.

"The wager is," she proposed, breathing into his mouth, keeping her lips lightly in place over his. "If I *am* pregnant, you and I run off and get married. If I'm not, I let you off the hook and I marry Nicky. We'll read the test like an order of fate."

"You're crazy."

"I am," she confessed, trying to keep the desperation out of her voice as she gnawed at his lip, kissing him with such force that she felt him submitting completely, roving his hands all up and down her, and cursing because he hadn't wanted to give in. It was the kind of recklessness that made Paige feel free and daring, mean, but invincible, reducing things to a state of insignificance so that she couldn't be hurt.

They both stripped off all their clothes and stood touching one another. Mark ran his hands over her belly as though trying to glean the truth through his fingertips. He bent down onto his knees and put his ear to her navel, listening for some suggestion of life inside her womb.

She waited, sharing the suspense, as though he possessed some kind of rare mystical power, thinking he was the most sensuous man she had ever known.

As he began kissing her waist and her stomach, scattering light, tender kisses, she found herself wondering for whom they were meant, for her or for the baby conceivably blooming within her. She sensed an attachment already forming, and it undid her.

As though thinking along the same lines, Mark suddenly straightened back up and took her hand. "I have to know," he said with such urgency that she was taken aback. "The damn results should be ready."

"Make love to me first," she said, scared.

"No. C'mon—"

She grabbed his arm as he started to turn away from her. "I want you to make love to me. *Now.*"

"I said no—"

"Why?"

As he looked at her she saw how confused he was. It was because of Susan. She knew it. His guilt had overtaken his libido at the critical moment. Redeeming him? Maybe. But not completely.

"Make love with me now, or I'm leaving and I never want to see you again," she challenged rashly, feeling monstrous but out of control. His mind was clearly telling him one thing, his hard-on, which was still intact, another.

Wouldn't anyone ever love her enough to take a risk for her? To do something he shouldn't do? Apparently not.

Instead of getting mad, Mark wrapped his arms around her again, the proof of his desire still hard against her thigh. "Paige, you're going to have to sort out your life first. I *can't* make love with you now. I obviously want to. But I just can't. *God, you're so selfish.* How do you think I feel? If you're pregnant, then that's my baby, too. *You* at least have control. Try and imagine how frustrated *I* am. *I* have no control. If I were carrying the baby, I would have it."

Paige had no doubt in her mind that he would. With or without her.

Like two children themselves, they walked hand in hand toward the bathroom, unselfconscious about their state of undress and Mark's still-prominent erection, bracing themselves.

They both seemed to know before they got there. Call it parental instinct—they simply knew.

The vivid red ring that had materialized on the test tube was irrefutable.

It read positive and was clear as could be.

Unfortunately the decision as to what to do about it couldn't have been more *unclear.*

Paige felt overwhelmed by what she had already known inside, as if she were standing alone atop a giant precipice, the drop so great she could not see what lay below or on either side. And yet she was going to have to jump one way or the other, make a choice. Only she was paralyzed by the gravity of either commitment.

"I really don't want to be by myself tonight," she said to Mark in a small voice, turning to him, wanting to put the decision off until morning.

His blond head bobbed as he nodded in understanding.

"I promise. No more seducing. I just want to sleep next to you in bed. I think I'll go crazy otherwise."

He nodded, looking as if he were fighting tears himself. "Okay. But don't let me seduce you, either."

"You're really losing your head over my roommate, aren't you?" she said, smiling but hurting inside.

The expression on his face confirmed her answer. Saying nothing further, he took her hand again and led her toward the bedroom where they climbed into his creaky but comfortable old bed, his grandmother's bed, which Paige would miss.

On the pretense of getting something to drink she disappeared into the kitchen for a moment and took the phone off the hook. It was her last night with him, and she didn't want to be disturbed. *Sorry Susan. He's all yours. But not until tomorrow.*

He fell asleep with his hands resting protectively on her belly.

She fell asleep with her cheek in a puddle of tears, in the midst of thinking she would never be able to fall asleep.

Torn about what to do.

What a marvelous day!

What a load off her mind.

Susan's thoughts were spinning so fast and she was so elated that she could hardly sit still at the staff meeting.

Concentrating on what her colleagues were saying was out of the question. Their legal jargon floated right over her head while she sat there at the long conference-room table doodling with her pencil and feigning quiet interest in what was being debated.

First of all, she was amazed that she hadn't been fired.

Ever since the incident with the strikers, she had been waiting in dread suspense for the moment when she would be called into Kreegle's office to receive his grand termination speech.

And though she had been on pins and needles waiting for the bomb to drop, it hadn't happened.

He had been pleasant to her in all their dealings.

He hadn't uttered a word about Jack Wells, other than to say he was putting Joe Dickson back on the case and taking her off it to work on some of the many entertainment contracts the firm handled.

She had been conspicuously shifted into an area where she would be less likely to get herself into trouble, negotiating contracts that would hardly incite her passions.

The stars' contracts were a little hard to take. For instance, negotiating into soap-star Zelda Cooper's contract a white limousine, and *white only,* or she would have grounds to not show up on the set. Her own dressing room trailer, which she refused to share with her costar (and it had to be *larger* than the one assigned to her costar). Plus her own private yoga instructor to keep her calm between takes.

It was definitely an area in which Susan was not going to get riled up. Or inspired.

With all this circumspect shifting around, she couldn't help but feel as though she were on probation, being scrutinized, with a chance for redemption before getting dropped.

Her worries were finally quelled this afternoon when, returning to her office after lunch, she spotted an envelope marked "Susan Kendell Brown" lying on top of her desk. Anxiously she had opened the envelope, half expecting a dismissal notice. What a relief when she found instead a pair of round-trip tickets to Europe along with a note from the law firm's senior partner informing her she had just become a partner in the firm. Moments later, Kreegle stepped into her office to tell her that while her actions with regard to Jack had not been well advised she was too damn good a lawyer for the firm to lose, and that making her a junior partner in the firm was their way of telling her she had a bright future and they expected big things from her.

She was jubilant at having preserved her integrity and her job at the same time. Notwithstanding the fact that she might never see Jack Wells again, she was satisfied that she'd had some impact on him, that the workers who had been fired had been reinstated, and that many of their terms had actually been met in a contract that, according to Joe Dickson, was close to being put to bed. She had asserted her opinion, made a stand for fairness, and, in her mind anyway, won.

God, she was so excited she couldn't wait to call her folks in Stockton and tell them of her new status as junior partner. To call Lisa and Buzz. Her brothers. They would all go out of their minds.

She considered calling her old law firm in Stockton and casually letting the news drop while in conversation with her old philandering boyfriend, Billy Donahue. What a thrill it would be to hear his reaction to the *new* Susan Kendell Brown. Assured. Happy. More sophisticated. Her name on the letterhead of one of L.A.'s most prestigious law firms. But then she thought, *who cares about Billy? Not me. Not anymore.*

The person she wanted to share her excitement with most of all was Mark. She couldn't wait to drive over and tell him the news tonight, the second this interminable meeting was adjourned. She also couldn't wait to see his reaction when she produced the pair of round-trip tickets to Europe. They could plan to take off and go together during his Christmas break.

The truth was, making her most happy was this growing sense of excitement inside that she could barely contain, the feeling that she just might have found her Mr. Right, after all.

Screw Paige for thinking she should "step up her goals" and the nerve of her for pointing out how much more money Susan made than Mark. As though Susan gave a damn. She was so tired of hearing that.

Mark was smart. And sincere. And talented. Good-hearted. *Not* twice her age, like Nicky Loomis. And not all screwed up like most of the rich jerks they had all endured. Mark had his feet on the ground. She could count on him.

The staff meeting had finally come to an end. Everyone was joking around, shuffling papers back and forth, closing up briefcases, closing up shop.

Congratulations were forthcoming from all parts of the room.

Kreegle regarded her from across the table, his smile hadn't lost its measured edge.

Smiling back at all of them, Susan rose up from her seat, briefcase in one hand, airline tickets in the other, anxious to get to Mark.

She hurried down the hallway into her office to give him a quick call. It was eleven o'clock. He had said he was going to spend the evening painting.

His number was in her automatic memory dial; all she had to do was push 4, which she did with sparked expectation.

Hi, Mark—

Hi, handsome—

Hey, sexy—you in the mood to celebrate?

I can't hold it in any longer. Even if this scares you away—I love you!

She blitzed through the greetings in her head, dismissing one for another when, in the end, all she would say would be hi.

Busy. Damn.

She pushed the code for redial.

Still busy.

She pushed it again.

Then she set it for automatic redial and sat down at her desk to go over some papers. Realizing that all she was doing was pushing papers back and forth, that she was so excited to see him she couldn't possibly concentrate on anything else, she decided to skip the phone call and just drive over there.

Her excitement shriveled at the sight of Dustin Brent's Aston-Martin parked out in front of his apartment, and she wasn't sure what to think.

Was her sexy roommate there as an ex-lover seducing Mark— or just there as a friend?

Trying to ward off panic, she told herself that maybe his motorcycle had gone on the fritz, so Paige had lent the car to him, that Paige wasn't there at all. But his motorcycle was parked right beside the car, and it appeared perfectly fine.

Glancing up, she found herself growing more and more agitated. The windows of his apartment were all dark. What she couldn't see seemed worse than what she could see. If he were asleep, why was his telephone busy?

Too uncomfortable to go inside and uneasy about what she might find if she were to do so, Susan drove around killing time and returning every twenty minutes or so.

Her worst suspicions were confirmed when she finally gave up and drove home, finding Paige not there, and a number of messages from Nicky looking for her.

Chapter 29

Susan couldn't get the scream of sirens out of her mind.

The rage of sound overpowered her own scream of warning and Paige's of powerless dread.

It replayed mercilessly in her head, the tense, shrill blare of alarm unaided by the tranquilizer they had insisted she take in the ambulance on the interminable drive to the hospital.

The little yellow pill muted the volume but failed to make the picture any less ominous. When she closed her eyes there was *red*. The color of alarm. The blood red lights of the ambulance. The blood-red of the water enveloping Paige. The blood-red deluge from her scalp . . . The blood-red sailboat. The blood-red screams that had filled the thick sea air.

And then the blood-red silence of her friend lying unconscious. Vacant. Looking like a different person, without that mind of hers flying a million miles an hour.

Still in her jeans and tennis shoes from sailing, Susan was roaming helplessly back and forth in the dreary emergency waiting room of the hospital in Santa Monica, going over in her mind for the thousandth time what had happened, trying to understand it, desperate to recapture the moment and turn back the clock.

The gloomy-looking room was mobbed. There were kids running around, some injured, some fine and only along for the ride. One kid had a deep gouge below his eyebrow and was waiting for the doctor to stitch him up. Another one had lost a tooth. There was a man stretched out on a bench and moaning from a kidney stone.

It had all happened so fast. That's what Susan couldn't get over.

A surge of murderous thoughts on her part, the kind of horrid ones only Paige could inspire, and then, suddenly, as though she had wished it so, this monstrous accident.

An accident she had helped set in motion, which she had inadvertently activated, provoked.

Susan felt shaken to her roots from all that had transpired in the last forty-eight hours.

Thursday night seemed like an eternity ago, when she had driven over to Mark's and found Paige's car parked out in front of his apartment.

After a sleepless night, remaining alert for any sound of Paige returning home, unable to think about anything else, Susan had fled Dustin's house before sunrise, intent on avoiding a premature confrontation with Paige, who would undoubtedly return to shower and change for work. Feeling too shattered to even run into Tori.

The plan that had evolved, as she'd sat there seething at the office, kidding herself into thinking she was working, was to go ahead and go sailing with Paige the following day, as previously planned, pretending nothing had happened, as though she knew nothing and then, once out alone in the water, just the two of them, with no distractions, nowhere for Paige to run and hide, she would have it out with her.

Mark, whose calls she had been dodging all day and whom she still couldn't face talking to, she decided to call back when she knew he'd be in class. She'd leave a message with the department secretary at UCLA, saying she had to break their dinner date on account of work, that she would be incommunicado all day, but would talk to him late Saturday.

That evening, Paige went to a game at the StarDome with

Nicky. Tori went to dinner with George and Kit and a man she had been out with a couple of times.

And Susan stayed sequestered in her office—hiding from everybody, refining her plan of attack, ready to pounce.

Then that morning, when the three women were all having breakfast together in the kitchen, Paige had attempted to back out of their sailing date, feigning fatigue and an upset stomach.

Guilt. She can't stand facing me, Susan remembered thinking, bristling, loathing her attractive roommate and how easily things always came for her.

She probably planned on marrying Nicky and keeping Mark on the side. It would be just like her to want *everything* and find a way to have it all.

She wondered how long Paige and Mark had been seeing each other on the sly. At the beginning, when Susan first started going out with him, she was sure he and Paige weren't seeing each other. But when had they started up again? Was Thursday night a first? A first and last? Or one of many?

God, how Susan hated Mark for leading her on. For making her feel like a first-rate fool.

What had ever possessed her to think she could compete with Paige, live up to her sex-goddess image, when Susan was so blatantly only mortal

Paige probably knew all these exotic, sensual maneuvers.

She was soft and feminine and flirtatious.

A man's woman. A rich man's toy —out on loan to her not-nearly-rich-enough but irresistible artist-professor boyfriend. *Susan's* boyfriend, *dammit.*

It wasn't fair. Susan embodied wholesomeness, while Paige embodied sex.

And what wholesome American male wouldn't prefer sex?

It was driving Susan mad, agonizing over all the comparisons Mark must have made.

Like all of Paige's scintillating lingerie, when Susan felt contrived in anything other than sensible cottons. Susan's big move in that direction had been to buy *sexy* sensible cottons but, honestly, how sexy can sensible cotton underwear really ever get? Compared to Paige's array of lacy little nothings.

Things like black lacy stockings with lacy built-in garters that held them up at the thigh. Scanty, sheer black lace teddies in lieu of a bra and underpants, which snapped at the crotch for convenient access.

Susan would feel like a French whore in the kind of underflash Paige wore. And ridiculous because she didn't approach suiting the part. While Paige would savor playing it to the hilt, getting *into* the role and driving him crazy.

How could he ever get over her?

Tori had checked Paige's pulse to see if she had a fever, swallowing her act about not feeling well. Sweet, guileless, Tori who would never suspect a thing. Susan knew Tori couldn't understand why she had kept pressing, when Paige clearly didn't want to go.

Well, now she would know. Now everyone would know everything.

Susan had called Mark and left a message for him indicating briefly what had happened and that they were at the hospital. She had also put a call in to Nicky, who she was told was unreachable, out flying in a small plane somewhere, scouting property for a real estate deal.

Tori was the only one she had succeeded in getting on the line, and she was on her way to the hospital now.

A kid threw a paper cup at Susan's head and she jumped, on edge anyway. "Noah, knock it off now. Just sit down next to your brother or I'm taking you home," his mother snapped at him.

There was some tittering as the two brothers sat down on the vinyl-cushioned bench next to one another, endeavoring to contain their restless energy.

Their father was the man on the bench with the kidney stone, and he glared at them between groans.

"Excuse me," Susan pleaded, barreling over to the woman at the admittance desk, feeling as though she were falling apart. "I've been here over an hour. Can't someone please give me some information on how my friend's doing?"

"Now, who's your friend again?"

Susan could have strangled her. She had only told the woman twenty times. "Paige Williams," she repeated painstakingly.

"Paige Williams . . ." It was taking her forever to locate Paige's name on her clipboard. Finally, Susan reached over and jabbed at where *Paige Williams* was clearly written. "Oh, yes. The boating accident."

"I just want to know if she's regained consciousness, or what's going on, how she's doing. Nobody's told me anything—" Susan was drumming her fingers impatiently on the desk.

"If you'll have a seat, I'll get back to you."

"What seat?" Susan demanded, indicating the overcrowded waiting room. "Look, you keep saying that and nobody is telling me anything—"

"I'm sorry, but it's a weekend and we're very busy."

"Can't I just go back there?" Susan pleaded.

"I'm sorry, but you'll just have to take a seat like . . ." Catching herself, she eyed Susan, then coolly completed her sentence. "You'll just have to wait in the waiting room like everyone else."

Telephone call for Susan Kendell Brown. Susan whirled around as the announcement blared over the loudspeaker.

"Where do I catch that?" she asked, turning back to the half-wit at admittance.

The woman pointed to a phone off to the side.

Taking a deep breath, Susan picked up the receiver, feeling guilty and nervous at once. It had to be either Mark or Nicky, and she didn't know what to say to either of them.

Hi. I pushed your girlfriend out of the boat and into the water, shouting at her that I hoped she drowned, and she almost did.

Susan had confronted Paige as planned.

They had both been especially quiet as they headed out the channel in Susan's sailboat, seeming to lose themselves in the rhythm of tacking and trying to catch the wind while Susan directed them just outside the breakwater, where there was not quite so much traffic.

Fuming, without any preamble, Susan had let her have it, launching into a full-blown inquisition.

She was there, Thursday night, at Mark's apartment, wasn't she? Susan had seen her car. Dustin's car—

"Yes," Paige had replied somberly, without resistance.

She was there alone with him. Trying to seduce him. Going after what was no longer hers. By her choice—

"Yes."

She had spent the night with him. Taken the phone off the hook so Susan couldn't get through—

"Yes."

She couldn't stand not having Mark at her beck and call anymore, could she? There whenever she wanted him.

She was all messed up. Not so sure she could go through with marrying a man nearly twice her age.

Just because he was rich and powerful.

The sacrifices were starting to get to her, weren't they—

"Yes."

Like the thinning hair he had to swirl way over from one side of his head to cover up the vacant patches.

The old skin that there was no disguising. No matter what kind of shape he was in.

Paige was forfeiting youth for money.

Selling herself.

Being Nicky Loomis's wife had nothing to do with sharing her life for love, building a future together, becoming a partnership greater than any other partnership.

Marrying Nicky was more like accepting a job.

Title—Mrs. Nicky Loomis.

Job description—hostess-slash-whore.

Salary—high.

"Yes."

Maybe she was panicking about all of his vintage friends?

The kids she would be inheriting. Who would never accept her. Who would always think of her as their father's whore.

Just another fortune hunter. And wasn't she?

"Yes."

She couldn't stand it that Susan and Mark were so happy, without money, starting to fall in love, with a shot at the kind of life with which Paige wished she could be satisfied, but could not. She had to go and prove to herself that she could still have Mark if she wanted him. She had been jealous since the morning Susan and

Mark had walked in together, hadn't she? Caring only about her-self. Not caring that she was screwing things up for Mark and for Susan. Supposedly her friends. Maybe her best friends. Was there anyone on this earth to whom Paige was capable of being loyal? Whom she cared enough about not to run roughshod over or use them?

"Stop just saying *yes!*" Susan had finally screamed at her. "Give me reasons. Make me understand. Make me understand how you could be so selfish. How you could do this to me. How you could do this to Mark. You're going to go off and marry Nicky anyway, so why do you have to go and screw up our lives? What kind of monster are you?"

The small sailboat had suddenly become so confining that Susan had felt as though she were crawling out of her skin. Paige wouldn't fight back. She wouldn't deny a thing. Susan could have been talking to a wall, except that the wall looked ready to crumble.

"Goddamn it, Paige, you owe me an explanation. Now give me one. What happened to your big mouth and all your famous courage? Say something, or I'm going to explode."

Finally, enraged, desperate for a response, Susan had broken into a flood of tears and shoved Paige out of the boat into the water, shouting at her that she hoped she drowned.

For a second, it had been a release of tension for both of them. They had connected. Something in Paige's immutable surface had broken, and she had begun to cry also. Susan had never thought she would see the day when Paige would cry.

But then before they knew what had happened, it had been sheer panic for both of them. A boat pulling a water-skier had seemed to appear from out of nowhere and was ripping across the water in their direction. The driver of the boat attempted to veer away but it was too late, and the quick motion of the detour had sent the skier flying across the wake, crashing into a terror-stricken Paige.

It was all one big blur after that. A patrolling coast guard was radioed onto the scene and Paige, unconscious and badly injured, was rushed to the hospital, accompanied by a shell-shocked Susan.

"Susan? It's Mark. What's going on?"

Susan's mind went blank at the sound of his voice, confused and urgent over the line.

"Are you okay? What's happened? Is Paige all right?" he asked.

She found herself gripping the telephone cord, twisting it, trying to get her brain to work. She was submerged in guilt. Yet his frank, vital concern over Paige smarted so; she found herself wanting to lash out at him.

She spoke rapidly, trying to conceal the hurt. "I was out in the boat with Paige. We got into an argument and I got so furious I shoved her out. She had on a life jacket. We both did. It shouldn't have been any big deal. But then all of a sudden there was this boat careening in our direction, pulling a water-skier. The boat tried to cut away but it was too late, and the skier came flying across the wake and into her."

There was an awful silence on Mark's end. Susan cradled the phone and wrapped her arms across her stomach. She felt weak and ill. Frightened beyond measure. But still, a small ravaged part of her remained angry. A small but deep pit of anger and resentment. Of jealousy. Mark didn't dare ask what the argument had been about.

"I'll be there in five minutes," he stressed, pushing some hidden button inside her heart that released another flood of tears.

Her poor brain felt waterlogged. She was too choked up to manage much more than a clipped "Okay. Thanks."

"And Susan—" he said as she was about to hang up.

"What?"

She felt him hesitating, torn. What did he want to say? To confess and get it off his conscience that he was sorry? That he loved Paige and couldn't help himself? That he would rather have part of her than all of Susan? The last thing Susan wanted was pity from him.

"I miss you," he whispered, sounding grief-stricken. "I don't know what your argument was about, but I have an idea. You shouldn't feel so guilty about this. It was an accident. I know you, and you wouldn't ever deliberately hurt anyone."

"You don't know me at all. I wanted to hurt her. I wanted to hurt her so badly it was killing me," Susan shouted, crying. "But I didn't see the boat, obviously. I would never—"

"Shhh. It's going to be okay. Paige is tough."

"She's *unconscious*. And she was hit in probably the only instant in her life when she wasn't tough. It was Paige like she must have been when she was young, *pre-hurt*, or whatever it was that made her this way, *pre-bravado*. She didn't even look like herself. If I'd seen her being wheeled down the aisle here on a stretcher, I'd have barely known her. *Mark, I'm so scared.* She was really cut up badly, too. I'm sure they had to take a ton of stitches."

"Anything broken?"

"I don't know. They won't tell me anything. I'm going crazy. Please hurry," she urged him in a small, unsteady voice, still crying.

"I can't stand it that I'm not there with you now," he replied, quietly hanging up the phone.

"Susan!" Tori walked through the doorway of the emergency room, eliciting stares as she hurried over to Susan. The stylishly cut skirt of her smart cherry-red suit hugged just above her knees, causing her to have to take twice as many steps to maintain her pace. "What's happening? Is Paige all right? Has she regained consciousness?" she asked all at once, throwing her arms around Susan. "Have they let you in to see her yet? Are *you* all right?"

"I can't get anyone to give me any information," Susan said, sniffling and wiping away tears with the back of her hand.

Tori took a packet of Kleenex from out of her purse and handed it to her.

"Thanks," Susan said, blowing her nose and then stopping to catch her breath before going on. "I tried to go back there, but a couple of nurses pounced on me and sent me back to the waiting room. I don't even have any idea where she is."

It was such a relief to have someone there with her, Susan thought as she watched Tori weighing what to do.

"God, what was the name of that surgeon I went out with? George's friend—" Tori said, trying to jog her memory. "Maybe I should call him. You know how it is with doctors. If *he* inquires, we'll at least get somewhere."

"I didn't even think to call Kit," Susan realized, feeling remiss.

"Ed Littner . . . wasn't that his name?"

"I'm not sure—"

"C'mon. Where's the phone? There it is," she said, heading over toward the hospital extension Susan had just used.

"There are pay phones near the rest rooms—"

"Pay phones? *Fuck 'em,"* Tori drawled defiantly. "This is Dr. Mitchell," she asserted into the line, taking Susan's hand. "We have an emergency here. Would you please get me Dr. Ed Littner."

"He's not with this hospital, Doctor—"

"Yes, I know that," Tori bluffed. Then within four minutes Dr. Littner was on the line, anyway. "This is a Paige maneuver," Tori said under her breath to Susan.

Of course she didn't realize that it was the wrong thing to say just then.

Susan stood by quietly while Tori very briefly explained the situation to the surgeon she had snubbed.

"He's actually very nice," she whispered to Susan at one point, covering the receiver with her hand. "Ed, thank you. I really appreciate this. We're all worried out of our minds."

Ed told Tori he would call her right back, to sit tight until he could get some information for her.

Susan looked over to the entrance just as Mark was walking through the doorway. He jogged over to them. There was an awkward moment as he and Susan looked at one another, but then it was broken by the white-clad nurse hurrying toward them.

"Excuse me, Miss Kendell . . ."

The nurse's face was a mask—a study in the withholding of expression, but her hesitation made Susan sure something had gone wrong.

"Uhmm . . . your friend has regained consciousness," the nurse began deliberately, as though there were a hitch. They all braced themselves as she went on. "She's alert. She'll have to be watched closely for the next twenty-four hours or so. She shouldn't be alone or get out of bed. The doctor had to take quite a few stitches, but there appears to be no internal injury and miraculously there are no broken bones. However—"

Nobody wanted to hear the however.

"However, I'm sorry, the accident caused quite a trauma, and I'm afraid she did lose her baby."

Her baby!

Susan was dumbfounded. Her complicated and overwrought emotions ran all the way from guilt over having caused the accident and the loss of the baby she knew nothing about to jealousy and reignited rage about Thursday night.

She wanted to wheel around and look at Mark, but she was afraid to. Whose baby was it? His or Nicky's?

Feeling all eyes on her, Susan wanted to run and hide. She couldn't look at anyone and instead kept her eyes focused down on the ugly, speckled, vinyl floor.

The nurse, misreading Susan's reaction, reached for her hand. "Your friend's okay about it—she really is. It was the first thing she asked when she came to, and of course we told her. Then she closed her eyes and got a kind of sad, funny smile on her face and said something about how it was just meant to be. *She* told all of *us* not to worry. That maybe life would work out perfectly and she would have one in a later passage of hers. She wanted to know how old the fetus was, and we told her. It was about nine weeks old. And then she asked me to explain this to all of you. And afterward to have Susan come in to see her."

Blinking away tears, still not looking at anyone, Susan followed the nurse back toward Paige's room.

Bewildered, shocked, guilty, and greatly despairing, Susan ventured inside the antiseptic-looking recovery room where Paige lay on a small white bed, her eyes closed, her head swathed in bandages that were soiled where some blood and yellow ointment had seeped through. She was in a white hospital gown and Susan could see where some of the stitches had been taken on her arms and chest. In spite of her condition, she still looked beautiful.

Feeling Susan's presence, she opened her eyes and looked at her, indicating for her to come closer, to come over to the bed.

Susan was surprised to see tears in Paige's eyes again; they seemed so incongruous with the cat-like glimmer ordinarily lighting them up. Now they were mesmerizing green pools, brimming over with what looked like genuine regret.

And yet there was an ease to her expression.

Probably she is doped up, Susan thought, trying to distance herself, wondering what Paige planned on saying to her.

"C'mere, dammit," Paige said, weakly reaching for Susan with her arm and then grabbing her in closer when Susan finally did approach. "You have a right to despise me," she admitted falteringly. The green pools overflowed and Paige didn't bother to block the tears or even to wipe them away. *"That's* why I was over at Mark's Thursday night," she said softly. "I had been worried about being pregnant for at least a month, but I kept not wanting to believe it, wanting to block it out. I don't know how I felt, really. It was complicated. But then Wednesday night, Nicky asked me to marry him," she announced, surprisingly coherent for someone who was only just recovering from being unconscious. But that was Paige, Susan thought, far too anxious to hear what Paige was leading up to, to comment or interrupt.

"I may not be in love with Nicky the way you think you're in love with Mark," Paige said, "but I'm crazy about him. I don't see him as old. I see him as fascinating and full of energy, younger in many ways even than Mark, younger than his kids, who have all kinds of things repressed inside them. Nicky's not repressed at all. The kid in him, the kid that's in everyone, is right there at the surface. Never been buried. He's full of life and fun. And challenge."

This time Susan did try to interrupt, but Paige blocked her attempt with her hand, indicating for her to let her finish.

"Sure, if he didn't have any money I wouldn't feel this way about him," Paige went on honestly and with the same surprising display of clarity. "But taking his money away from the picture is like taking my looks away from my picture. We fall for the package. Not isolated areas of someone. Nicky's exactly what I want. I know what I'm giving up. But it's a conscious choice.

"The reason I didn't shout the news or tell anyone except Mark was because right after he asked me to marry him, he handed me a prenuptial contract his lawyers had drawn up, stipulating no babies. If I were to get pregnant and have the child, I was on my own, and without a red cent from him. Minimal support for the kid, but basically bust. Maybe the impact of it wouldn't have been so dramatic if I hadn't thought I was pregnant. But the stipulation of no kids when there was life growing inside me right at that very moment was too much for me."

The tears had stopped and they started up again. "Susan, you should know that I did not sleep with Mark. I wanted to. And I tried. But he wouldn't sleep with me. As nuts as he's been over me, when he had to make a choice he chose you. He let me spend the night in his bed because I was scared to death to be alone. But he didn't touch me."

Susan closed her eyes, overcome with relief and, oddly, grateful.

"Dammit, now it's *you* who won't say anything. Only there's nowhere to push you. Do you forgive me or not?" Paige demanded in spite of having insisted on Susan's silence.

"If *you* forgive *me, I* forgive *you,"* Susan responded, looking at her lunatic roommate through a haze of tears as they embraced.

She was being careful holding her, worried about all the bandages. "Does that hurt a lot?"

"Shit, yes, it hurts. But if you forgive me, I can bear it."

"I do. I really do," Susan said, realizing how deeply relieved she was that Paige was all right. "As long as you promise to keep your goddamn hands off my boyfriend, I forgive you," she added, somehow trusting she would.

"Hey, he chose you."

"Yes, but he may not always."

"He will," Paige said with quiet confidence. Then tensing, growing visibly anxious, she asked if Nicky was there. Had he been there when the nurse came out and told them about her losing the baby?

"No. I left a message for him with his secretary. But he hadn't—"

"Oh, thank God," Paige moaned with relief, sinking lower in the bed and looking more like her old self again. "I don't know what got into me. Hormones, probably. I had decided to take a chance and leave it to fate. If he were there and heard about my losing the baby, which clearly, by the age of the fetus, wasn't his, then I figured that would be the way it was meant to be, and however he reacted, he reacted. But by the same token, if he *weren't* there and didn't know, it would mean he wasn't meant to know. I don't know what I'd have done if he'd been there."

Susan was about to smile at Paige's logic when Nicky burst into the room, all out of breath, his face tight with concern, Tori and Mark hurrying to keep pace just behind him.

"Babe, I've been worried sick. I got the message from Dee and I didn't know *what* to think." Susan stepped out of the way as Nicky bounded toward the bed to envelop Paige in his big strapping embrace. "Are you all right? What did they say? Is anything broken?" He couldn't get it all out fast enough.

Susan felt touched by his concern, and she glanced at Mark, remembering with some guilt how she had felt at *his* concern. She found him looking at *her,* not at Nicky and Paige.

He was probably wondering what Paige had told her. If he had been exonerated or not.

She bit her lip, and felt her eyes well up again as she went to stand close by his side, wondering what he was thinking about Paige having lost the baby. She wanted to never let go when he seized her hand and continued to hold on so tightly it hurt.

"Are you okay?" he asked in a low murmur.

She shook her head yes, then asked him the same question.

"Now I am," he whispered in her ear.

Tori slipped Susan a little half-smile and Susan smiled back at her, her smile broadening when holding hands didn't seem to be enough for Mark and he pulled her into his arms.

"I've been going out of my mind," Nicky was saying to Paige as though they were the only ones in the room. The thought of losing her had obviously thrown him into a frenzy. "I was imagining the worst and kicking myself for not having run off and eloped with you Thursday night. Then we'd have been off in France or Italy or Spain, or someplace, celebrating our honeymoon and this would never have happened. Look at you," he insisted, examining the bandages on her head, all the bruises and areas that had been stitched. And yet Susan thought Paige looked unjustly radiant for someone who had nearly lost her life that day.

"I'm okay," Paige assured him. "Really, Nicky, I am."

"I don't want to wait. We're getting married a week from Saturday night," he said, making it clear he would not take no for an answer. As though Paige actually might protest. "At my place, *our* place." He grinned. "I could barely afford to pay a minister the first time I got married. I want this wedding to be the event of the season. It's going to make my Carnival Night affair look like it never woke up in the morning. I want to celebrate!

"And we want all of you standing up there with us," he said, turning for the first time to Susan and Mark and Tori. "We're going to put on a wedding like nobody's ever seen before. Decadence like F. Scott Fitzgerald only wished he had dreamed up. What do I work my ass off for if it's not to have a hell of a good time?"

Nicky sprang up from the bed where he was sitting beside Paige, and started hollering at the nurses down the hall to bring him a grapefruit or an orange or any damn piece of fruit, as long as it was round. When a lanky male nurse returned shortly with a grapefruit, Nicky asked him for a marker.

Within moments the burly ex–wide receiver had turned the ordinary piece of fruit into a small yellow globe, drawing out all the continents and starring a couple of cities. "Here, gorgeous," he said, presenting it to Paige. "You pick out any damn place you want to go for our honeymoon. The sky is the limit. Hell, if we could go to space, I'd buy us a rocket ship."

Paige, glowing, closed her eyes tightly, rotating the small makeshift globe in her hands and then stopping. Holding it in one hand, her eyes still closed, she aimed her index finger and pointed. "Here. I want to go here."

They all hovered in to see where *here* was.

"Egypt it is," her fiancé confirmed, peeling the grapefruit and then distributing the sections to all of them.

Chapter 30

As promised, Paige and Nicky's wedding became the affair of the season, the event everyone in town was talking about. All the more so because of its two weeks' planning fuse.

But that was typical of Nicky and typical of Paige, too. The more splash and the more attention they could elicit, the better.

There was no time for invitations so he had sent out a bundle of bright white Casablanca lilies to everyone, accompanied by a note spelling out the specifics.

All the guests were requested to dress in white formal attire, and the effect it produced was as spectacular as Nicky had planned, with this mass of people, all in white, flowing inside the house and outside into the gardens, being seated for the ceremony.

It was all white and wondrous. The flowers. The candles. The linens. The people. Everything sparkled. Paige was probably the only person Tori had ever met who would be confident enough to know she would still stand out. And Tori had no doubt she would.

Everybody was there. Kit and George, with Kit now extremely pregnant. Susan and Mark. Nicky's son, Tip. His daughter,

Marni, and her rock promoter boyfriend. Nicky's StarDome circle, of whom Tori had now met many. Surgeon Ed Littner, whom they had called to thank for his efforts at the hospital. *Miami Vice* stockbroker Dan Sullivan, who was as dull as Susan had originally perceived him to be, but who, it turned out, was one of Nicky's stockbrokers. Evonne, Dustin Brent's secretary.

With a guest list of four hundred, Tori thought it would be easier to keep track of those *not* present.

There were so many high-profile celebrities and politicians that there were guards posted on the roof with guns. They were the only ones not in white.

Standing misty-eyed under the lavish umbrella of a magnolia tree reminiscent of home, in position for the processional, Tori watched the last of the guests being ushered into the rows of seats, feeling nostalgic.

She was thinking of Kit's wedding. How she had felt then, standing and waiting for her cue to walk down the aisle, feeling as if she were doomed to be the bridesmaid forever and never the bride.

And blaming it all on Travis at the time as if he were the only man in the world who could alter her fate.

What a fool she had been to bank all her hopes on him and be so afraid to venture beyond the false cloak of security he offered.

More than anything else, moving to California had accomplished that for Tori and she was grateful. She felt free for the first time in her adult life, free and whole on her own.

It took distance to realize she should have left Atlanta *and* Travis a long time ago. That she would never grow up under her mother's vast and dominant wing, which there seemed to be no escaping as long as she stayed within a thousand miles of Georgia. That Travis was only a temporary refuge for her and, regardless of how hard she tried, she could never convert him into the man who would be right for her.

The fact was, Travis was already living with someone again. Tori had been replaced in her own condominium.

Her first reaction when she had heard was to feel violated. This girl was sleeping in *her* bed, looking at *her* Laura Ashley wallpaper, sleeping and screwing on *her* sheets, using *her* bathtub, eating cereal from *her* bowls, reading the newspaper that was from *her* subscription, going to dinner with *her* friends. The woman's picture was probably now even in *her* frames, smiling beside *her* man.

But then she realized it would be the same story all over again, only with a different woman playing the dolt.

He wouldn't marry her, either, if that's what his new live-in had in mind. As his friends had said bluntly enough from the start, Travis didn't want to get married again. He didn't want to get a divorce. And he would not. Tori just hadn't listened.

And while she would have gone to the ends of the earth for him all those years, the truth was she didn't even miss him anymore. Nor did she miss Richard Bennetton. It was strictly the *concept* of them she missed. The boyfriend. And yet she was handling it fine.

For the first time in her life she was not *with* someone, and she was *okay*.

She had a history that went back to the sixth grade of always healing her heart by falling in love with someone else, soothing the wounds and pasting the heartbreak of her last affair back together with another affair patched over it.

Finally, for the first time ever, she was beginning to feel genuinely healed.

Sure, she wished *she* were walking down the aisle. But she no longer had that sense of panic or desperation about it. Instead she felt a kind of peaceful patience, a confidence that in time she would. And that waiting for her at the altar would be someone well worth the wait.

Tori felt someone's hands at her waist and she jumped, startled. She tried to turn around, but the hands were strong and wouldn't allow her to turn or maneuver.

"What? Who is that?" she asked, struggling to see. Each time she turned her head, the angle of her body was propelled in the other direction.

Kit and Susan, who were standing in front of her, both turned around, their sumptuous white gowns swishing behind them, looking surprised but guarded, not giving anything away.

"Who is that? George? Mark?" she asked the joker behind her. The ushers for the wedding party were out of view in another area of the garden. When she continued to receive no reply, she twisted around and found herself looking into the arrogant peacock-blue eyes of her former phantom fiancé, Richard Bennetton.

As far as she knew Richard hadn't been invited, and a million thoughts rushed through her head as she tried to regain her composure.

She wondered if Paige had arranged this.

Then thought not. Or if he had wangled an invitation from Nicky.

Or if he had just heard about the wedding and decided to crash it. She wouldn't put it past him. He had the nerve to do that.

"When did you get back into town?" she asked numbly, conscious of her friends' polite efforts to appear as though they weren't listening.

"Yesterday," he said, looking at her as though his look held some special significance. Of what, she had no idea and she tried to ignore it. She hadn't seen or heard from him since their blow-up in Santa Barbara. She had heard from the office that he had been on one of his extended European excursions, but that was all. There had been an updated photograph of his twin daughters, who lived in France with their mother, in Elliott Bennetton's office so she had presumed Richard had gone there for a while as well and mailed it to him.

"Welcome home," she said icily.

"Thanks. You look beautiful as always."

"Thanks."

"I hear you're taking Bennetton by storm. They say you could be promoted over me if I don't watch my step."

Tori didn't reply. She wished the wedding procession would start. She felt like she was talking to a stranger. But, really, wasn't she?

Whom had she been kidding to think she and Richard were anything other than strangers to each other? The man she had

fallen for seemed to have vanished the minute the wheels of the
Bennetton jet touched down in Los Angeles. He was an apparition left behind in Buenos Aires. A spirit lost to her.

"Tori, I have to talk to you," he said, looking suddenly vulnerable.

"Why?" She vowed not to be duped.

His voice was so low she could barely hear him. He had
steered her off, apart from the others. "I've made amends with
my father. I've been reinstated. *I miss you—*"

"Why?" she asked again.

"Look, I'm sorry about Santa Barbara. I don't know how to
make you understand, but I did what I had to do."

"Forget it. I've forgotten it."

"No, you haven't."

"Why don't you quit while you're ahead?"

"Because I'm not ahead."

"What do you want from me, Richard?"

"I was half expecting you to run back to Travis."

Tori smiled coldly, happy she'd had the strength not to.
"Maybe I did," she hissed, finding herself wanting to hurt him as
he had hurt her. "Maybe I'm moving back to Atlanta."

He smiled, relaxing. "I have my sources. You thought about it.
Didn't do it. And he's got a replacement living with him now."

"Sounds like your father's kind of tactics," Tori replied galled.
"How much did you have to pay for that kind of information? I
could have saved you some money if you'd only asked." Richard
was more like his father than he liked to think. She remembered
how she'd felt when *he* had gone around checking her out. She
wondered if they had used the same source.

"It's more fun to get the other way. It affords me a two-dimen-
sional perspective—"

"You hypocrite! I thought you didn't like that kind of snooping
around. That kind of lack of faith—"

"Hey, don't get so riled up. I'm here to make peace, not war."
Richard raised both of his palms up in the air, gesturing his
surrender. In accordance with the requested dress, he was all in
white. His razor-straight blond hair looked as though it had just

been cut. He was tan and looked as though Europe agreed with him.

"I don't want to make anything with you, Richard."

"Not even love?" he joked, with a smug glint in his eyes. "Sorry. I couldn't resist that one. Tori, this is going all wrong. Would you just relax? Don't you get the picture? I want to buy back your fucking ring and give it to you. I want to *marry* you."

"Why? You're not in love with me."

"How do you know what I am or am not," he asked, angry now.

"Because you don't talk to people the way you talk to me when you're in love with them."

"Oh, are you some kind of expert on love now? Where do you get these ideas?"

"God, why are they so late in starting weddings," Tori said, wanting to get away from him.

"Look, I said I was sorry. What do you want? Do I have to get on my hands and knees and grovel? I made a mistake. You want me to go use the minister's mike and shout it to the world. Hell, the whole world's here, isn't it? *Do you, Tori Mitchell, accept the apology of this man, Richard Bennetton? Will you be joined in fucking matrimony or not—"*

Tori felt as though she'd had the breath knocked out of her.

Richard was mean. And cunning. She wouldn't put it past him to be using her to get back in his father's good graces. Telling his father that he had been off in Europe, thinking seriously about his life. That he'd come to the conclusion he wanted to mend his ways.

Richard knew Elliot Bennetton would think Tori would be the ideal wife. She was smart. Strait-laced. He liked her and was under the impression that she had her head screwed on right.

If Richard returned to work at Bennetton, contrite, becoming engaged to Tori, heading in the direction of a more orthodox life —orthodox for Richard anyway—Elliot Bennetton would melt in three minutes and reinstate him.

Tori didn't even believe that he had already been reinstated. Maybe Richard was planning on going to his father *after* he had talked to her. On the other hand, Richard was cocky enough to have been certain she would say yes, so maybe he already had.

Sure she was right, or at least close to being right, and not feeling even tempted by Richard—on the contrary, feeling cold as ice, Tori told him he could take his proposal and shove it.

She had a vivid picture in her mind of their confrontation in Santa Barbara. She had tried to block it out but it had been rekindled, and all she felt was rage.

"You'll regret this," Richard promised her. But then the music started and the wedding coordinator signaled her back over to the line.

"No, I won't," she replied confidently, feeling as though her dignity had been preserved.

"Yeah? Well, don't forget whose signature's on your paycheck!"

"As long as it's your father's and not yours, I figure I'm safe," she shot back, feeling liberated as she returned to her place in line behind Susan and Kit, in front of Nicky's daughter, Marni, who looked intrigued.

There was a slow dissolve of commotion as the wedding music started up and the processional began.

Each of the bridesmaids' dresses was different. They had all been commissioned by a young designer Paige had flown in from Milan. For the couple of weeks the designer was there, she and her assistants worked day and night, turning out one creation after another, each one more sensational than the next. Huge silk balloon sleeves worn off the shoulder on one. Fortuny-type pleats on another. Paige's was the only gown nobody had seen.

Tori watched, feeling half in a dream, mesmerized by the tall white candles flickering brightly from lavish, flower-festooned candelabra, drinking in the potent perfume of the flowers, which hung heavy in the air.

Competing flashes of light popped sporadically from the half a dozen photographers strolling around, angling for shots.

The violin strings seemed to be tearing at Tori's heartstrings as she watched Kit proceeding down the aisle first, a vision of loveliness, the all-white wedding serenely effective. The music was soft and old-fashioned, the kind you would have to be made of steel to not become emotional over.

She thought of Travis. And then of Richard.

Dreams gone up in smoke. Like the smoke rising from the candles, fading eerily into the atmosphere.

Susan walked down the aisle next, looking as glorious as a bride herself as she was joined by Mark, who looped his arm through hers, both of them taking slow, cautious steps as though they were on a test run. Tori was filled with warmth seeing the two of them looking so radiant together.

Susan had on the seed-pearl choker her old boyfriend from Stockton, Billy Donahue, had given her last year for Christmas, and it gleamed under the lights. Part present, part peace offering was how she described it, given to her after she had caught him sleeping with her secretary. She had almost not worn it. Putting it on and then taking it off again. And then she had decided the hell with Billy Donahue. The necklace was *white*.

It was Tori's turn next, and she smiled self-consciously as she stepped gracefully into view, met by Nicky's closest friend. Familiar faces smiled at her and she smiled back, all the way to the altar, where she and her escort parted to anchor opposite posts.

Following her came Marni and Tip.

Then a knee-high pair, resembling a pint-size version of the bridesmaids and ushers, stepping shyly down the aisle, eliciting *ahhhs* and laughter as the little girl sprinkled rose petals from a basket while the little boy balanced a velvet pillow bearing the rings. They were Nicky's niece and nephew.

The tension in the music mounted, then came to a complete halt, commanding everyone's rapt attention in anticipation of the bride and groom.

Paige had been so secretive about the details of the wedding and what she was going to wear that Tori was half expecting something like Madonna's "Material Girl" instead of "Here Comes the Bride" to come blasting forth from the orchestra for her long-awaited march down the aisle.

When the familiar conventional bridal march pounded forth instead, it came as far more of a surprise than anything else possibly could have, seeming to reveal another dimension of Paige, whose intriguing beauty took everyone's breath away.

This nostalgic, traditional side of her was evident in her awesome white train that seemed to go on and on, the illusory white veil draped over her composed, porcelain-perfect face, the lacy Victorian high band collar of her gown, and her father, flown in from New York for the happy event, there by her side to give her away.

But then, as she continued her demure walk down the aisle, Tori soon realized the gasps drawn from the audience were not solely for this breathtaking vision in white but because the back of the irrepressible Paige's gown was designed open and cut all the way down to her ass.

Now *that* was the sassy, venturesome Paige they all knew and loved, Tori thought. The Paige who had managed to captivate and snare Nicky Loomis. No wonder she wouldn't let anyone see her dress.

Leave it to Paige to make an entrance.

Tori noticed the minister standing there, smiling and waiting for the bride. *Wait till he gets a load of the back of her,* Tori thought, suppressing a laugh as she exchanged tickled glances with Susan and Kit.

The minister had no idea what all the hushed snickering was about as he delivered the words of the ceremony. He was just pleased that everyone was so alert and interested.

Nicky seemed to be enjoying Paige's show most of all. He kept peeking around behind her, amused, fascinated, looking as though the dress were a complete surprise to him, and a surprise he found wildly arousing.

As soon as the pair had pronounced their I do's, a gleaming white helicopter circled low above the property and then landed on the lawn. Nicky swept Paige up in his arms, dipped her down for a long, unvirginal-looking kiss, and then leaned over to borrow the minister's mike. "The rest of this party is for you!" he bellowed lustily to all his guests. "Have a helluva good time because it's costing me a helluva lot of bucks!"

The ethereal bride, laughing and holding on to her veil so that it wouldn't slip off, blew a kiss to them all.

First pausing for a moment of drama, she flung her hand-wired bouquet of white roses and imported Dutch white lilies high into the air toward the girls. But then a gust of wind from the helicopter intercepted its course and carried it off the other way, landing it in the arms of an innocent male bystander who would have had a hard time trying to catch it if he had tried, since both his arms were out of commission, encased in cumbersome fiberglass casts and then further restrained in a double sling. Sitting next to him was his secretary, Evonne.

"My God, I don't believe it! Dustin Brent!" Paige, Susan, and Tori all realized at once, exclaiming in unison.

"Did you know about this?" Paige demanded of Nicky, astonished as he carried her through the crowd over to the noisy aircraft, waving jovially to all their guests.

He smiled at her wickedly. "I wasn't chancing you changing your mind. I figured if he came back you'd need someplace else to live," he hollered over the whirr of the chopper.

"I'm serious."

"So am I."

"You tracked him down and invited him?"

"I asked his secretary to wire him an invitation."

"What about those broken arms of his?"

"Made his return make even more sense. Besides, he said he had additional incentive," Nicky replied jocularly.

"What was that?"

Nicky's eyes gleamed suggestively as he ducked into the helicopter, depositing Paige and all the yards of fabric from her gown onto the seat.

She turned to look out the window and saw Dustin and Tori sending each other silent but momentous messages through the highly charged air. Awkwardly, Dustin maneuvered the bouquet up to his nose and took an exaggerated sniff, his gaze remaining fixed on Tori, his smile seeming to promise her a brighter future.

As the helicopter spun off into the air, the rest of the bridal party still in their places at the altar, Paige leaned in to kiss her husband. She didn't buy for a moment that Nicky had really been responsible for getting Dustin back to the States. More likely, Dustin had injured himself again, and Evonne had phoned to tell Nicky that he would be back in town and wished to attend the wedding. After all, if it hadn't have been for Dustin, none of this would ever have come to pass. Dustin Brent had been their sponsor, the man responsible for all this magic.

But Paige preferred to nurture and let her new husband enjoy his fantasy that she believed every word he told her.

He could retain his fantasies.

And she would retain hers.

From rags to riches—it was a modern-day Cinderella story. Only she didn't slave by the hearth, she slaved over . . . . , and her rags were not really rags, but knockoffs of designer labels. And, finally, her prince was not really a prince, but a very rich . . . . . . who fell madly in love with his lovely young female . . . . . . And the pair was to live happily ever after in Beverly Hills . . . .

. . . .

. . . .

. . . .

. . . .

. . .